'Perhaps  ch a hurry to nat I have a de like to talk to that would benefit your father as well as yourself,' Ludo asserted calmly.

Riveted, Natalie immediately pulled her hand away from the brass doorknob and turned to face him.

'What kind of a deal?'

Pacing a little to help arrange his thoughts, Ludo took his time in answering. He stopped pacing to settle his gaze on the beautiful inquisitive face in front of him.

'I will increase what I paid for your father's business by half the amount again if you agree to come with me to Greece and play the role of my fiancée.'

Natalie turned as still as a statue, her stunned expression suggesting she wasn't entirely sure she'd heard him right. She moved across the room to a burgundy-coloured wing-backed armchair and slowly sank down into it.

When she glanced up again to meet his eyes Ludo experienced a private moment of undeniable triumph, because he suddenly knew she was going to give in to his offer.

The day **Maggie Cox** saw the film version of *Wuthering Heights*, with a beautiful Merle Oberon and a very handsome Laurence Olivier, was the day she became hooked on romance. From that day onwards she spent a lot of time dreaming up her own romances, secretly hoping that one day she might become published and get paid for doing what she loved most! Now that her dream is being realised, she wakes up every morning and counts her blessings. She is married to a gorgeous man, and is the mother of two wonderful sons. Her two other great passions in life—besides her family and reading/writing—are music and films.

Recent titles by the same author:

WHAT HIS MONEY CAN'T HIDE
DISTRACTED BY HER VIRTUE
A DEVILISHLY DARK DEAL
THE LOST WIFE

IN PETRAKIS'S
POWER

BY
MAGGIE COX

First published in Great Britain 2013
by Mills & Boon, an imprint of Harlequin (UK) Limited.
Harlequin (UK) Limited, Eton House, 18-24 Paradise Road,
Richmond, Surrey TW9 1SR

© Maggie Cox 2013

ISBN: 978 0 263 90027 9

Harlequin (UK) policy is to use papers that are natural, renewable and recyclable products and made from wood grown in sustainable forests. The logging and manufacturing process conform to the legal environmental regulations of the country of origin.

Printed and bound in Spain
by Blackprint CPI, Barcelona

IN PETRAKIS'S POWER

CHAPTER ONE

Having just dropped down into her seat after a mad dash to catch the train, flustered and hot, Natalie Carr delved into her voluminous red leather bag and unzipped an inside compartment to retrieve her ticket. The discovery that it was nowhere to be seen was akin to the jolting shock of tumbling down an entire flight of stairs. With her heartbeat hammering in her chest, she raised her head to proffer an apologetic smile to the guard.

'Sorry…I know it's here somewhere…'

But it wasn't. Desperately trying to recall her last-minute trip to the ladies' before running onto the platform to catch the train, she had a horrible feeling that after checking her seat number she'd left the ticket, in its official first-class sleeve, on the glass shelf beneath the mirror, when she'd paused to retouch her lipstick.

Feeling slightly queasy as a further search through her bag failed to yield it, she exhaled a frustrated sigh. 'I'm afraid it looks like I've lost my ticket. I stopped off at the ladies' just before boarding the train and I think I might have accidentally left it in there. If the train weren't already moving I'd go back and look for it.'

'I'm sorry, miss, but I'm afraid that unless you pay for another ticket you'll have to get off at the next stop. You'll also have to pay for the fare there.'

The officious tone used by the florid and grey-haired train guard conveyed unequivocally that he wouldn't be open to any pleas for understanding. Natalie wished that she'd had the presence of mind to bring some extra cash with her, but she hadn't. Her father had sent her the ticket out of the blue, along with an unsettling note that had practically begged her not to 'desert him' in his 'hour of need', and it had sent her into a spin. Consequently, she'd absent-mindedly grabbed a purse that contained only some loose change instead of the wallet that housed her credit card.

'But I can't get off at the next stop. It's very important that I get to London today. Could you take my name and address and let me send you the money for the ticket when I get back home?'

'I'm afraid it's company policy that—'

'I'll pay for the lady's ticket. Was it a return?'

For the first time she noticed the only other passenger in the compartment. He was sitting in a seat at a table on the opposite side of the aisle. Even though she'd flown into a panic at losing her ticket, she couldn't believe she hadn't noticed him straight away. If the arresting scent of his expensive cologne didn't immediately distinguish him as a man of substantial means and impeccable good taste, the flawless dark grey pinstriped suit that looked as if it came straight out of an Armani showroom certainly did.

Even without those compelling assets, his appearance

was striking. Along with blond hair that had a fetching kink in it, skin that was sun-kissed and golden, and light sapphire eyes that could surely corner the market in sizzling intensity, a dimple in his chin set a provocative seal on the man's undoubted sex appeal. Staring back into that sculpted visage was like having a private viewing of the most sublime portrait by one of the great masters.

A wave of heat that felt shockingly and disturbingly intimate made Natalie clench every muscle in her body. If she hadn't already been on her guard, she certainly was now. She didn't know this man from Adam, *or* his motive for offering to pay for her ticket, and she quickly reminded herself that the newspapers were full of stomach-churning stories about gullible women being duped by supposedly 'respectable' men.

'That's a very kind offer but I couldn't possibly accept it…I don't even know you.'

In a cultured voice, with a trace of an accent she couldn't quite place, the stranger replied, 'Let me get the matter of a replacement ticket out of the way. Then I will introduce myself.'

'But I can't let you pay for my ticket…I really can't.'

'You have already stated that it is very important you get to London today. Is it wise to refuse help when it is offered?'

There was no doubt she was in a fix and the handsome stranger knew it. But Natalie still resisted. 'Yes, I do need to get to London. But you don't know me and I don't know you.'

'You are wary of trusting me, perhaps?'

His somewhat amused smile made her feel even more gauche than she felt already.

'Do you want a ticket or not, madam?' The guard was understandably exasperated with her procrastination.

'I don't think I—'

'The lady would most definitely like a ticket. Thank you,' the stranger immediately interjected.

Her protest had clearly landed on deaf ears. Not only did he have the chiselled good looks of a modern-day Adonis, the timbre of the man's voice was like burnished oak—smoky, compelling, and undeniably sexy. Natalie found her previous resolve to be careful dangerously weakening.

'Okay…if you're sure?'

Her need to get to London was paramount, and it overrode her reservations. Besides, her instinct told her the man was being utterly genuine and didn't pose any kind of threat. She prayed it was a good instinct. Meanwhile the train guard was staring at them in obvious bewilderment, as though wondering why this handsome, well-heeled male passenger would *insist* on paying for a complete stranger's ticket. After all, with her bohemian clothing, casually dried long brown hair with now fading blonde highlights, and not much make-up to speak of, she knew she wasn't the kind of 'high-maintenance' woman who would attract a man as well-groomed and wealthy as the golden-haired male sitting opposite her. But if the smoky-coloured pencil she'd used to underline her big grey eyes with helped create the illusion that she was more attractive than she was, then at that moment Natalie was grateful for the ruse. For she knew she had no choice but to accept the man's kindness. It was vital that she met up with her dad.

She could hardly shake the memory of his distressed tone when she'd rung him to confirm that she'd received the train ticket and once again he'd reiterated his urgent need to see her. It was so unlike him to admit to a human need, and it suggested he was just as fallible and fragile as anyone else—she had guessed all along that he was. Once, long ago, she had heard her mother angrily accuse him of being incapable of loving or needing anyone. His business and the drive to expand his bank account was the real love of his life, she'd cried, and Natalie didn't doubt his obsessive single-mindedness had been a huge factor in their break-up.

When, after their divorce, her mother made the decision to return to Hampshire, where she had spent much of her youth, Natalie, then sixteen, had elected to go with her. As much as she'd loved her dad, and known him to be charming and affable, Natalie had also known he was far too unreliable and unpredictable to share a home with. But in recent years, after visiting him as often as she could manage, she'd become convinced that in his heart he knew money was no substitute for not having someone he loved close by.

From time to time she'd seen loneliness and regret in his eyes at being separated from his family. His tendency to try to compensate for the pain it caused him by regularly entertaining the company of young attractive women was clearly not helping to make him any happier. Several of her visits over the past two years had confirmed that. He seemed disgruntled with everything…

even the phenomenally successful chain of small bijou hotels that had made him his fortune.

'I just need a single,' she told the arresting stranger, who didn't seem remotely perturbed that she'd taken so long to make up her mind about whether to accept his offer or not. 'And it doesn't have to be in first class. My dad sent me the ticket, but I'm quite happy to travel as I usually do in second.'

She couldn't disguise her awkwardness and embarrassment as she watched the man hand his credit card over to the guard. She felt even more awkward when he deliberately ignored her assertion and went ahead and requested a first-class ticket. Natalie hoped to God he believed her explanation about her dad sending her the ticket. After all, she was sure she didn't resemble a typical first-class passenger.

Trust her dad to unwittingly add to her discomfort by making such a needlessly overblown gesture. He always travelled first class himself, which was why he'd automatically paid for his daughter to do the same. Now she really wished he hadn't.

When the satisfied train guard had sorted out the necessary ticket, then wished them both an enjoyable journey, the impeccably dressed stranger handed it over to her and smiled. Natalie was very glad that the compartment was occupied by just the two of them right then, because if anyone else had witnessed the man's astonishing act of chivalry she would have wanted the floor to open up and swallow her.

Accepting the ticket as her face flooded with heat, she prayed her see-sawing emotions would very soon calm down. 'This is so kind of you…thank you…thank you so much.'

'It is my pleasure.'

'Will you write down your name and address for me so that I can send you what I owe you?' She was already rummaging in her voluminous red leather tote for a pen and notepad.

'We will have plenty of time for that. Why don't we sort it out when we get to London?'

Lost for words, and somewhat exhausted by her growing tension, Natalie lowered her bag onto the seat next to her by the window and exhaled a heavy sigh.

With a disarming smile, her companion suggested, 'Why don't we help ease any awkwardness between us by introducing ourselves?'

'All right, then. My name is Natalie.'

It was a mystery to her why she didn't give him her full name. The thought that it was because she was momentarily dazzled by his good looks hardly pleased her. What did she think she was playing at? How often had she groaned at a friend who seemed to lose every ounce of common sense whenever a fit, handsome man engaged her in conversation and became convinced he must think her the most beautiful girl in the world? Such embarrassing silliness was not for her. She'd rather stay single for the rest of her natural life than delude herself that she was something that she wasn't.…

'And I am Ludovic…but my family and friends call me Ludo.'

She frowned, 'Ludovic? How unusual.'

'It's a family name.' Beneath his immaculate tailoring the fair-haired Adonis's broad shoulders lifted and fell as if the matter was of little concern. 'And Natalie? Is that a name you inherited?'

'No. Actually, it was the name of my mum's best friend at school. She sadly died when she was a teenager and my mum called me Natalie as a tribute to her.'

'That was a nice gesture. If you don't mind my saying, there's something about you that suggests you are not wholly English...am I right?'

'I'm half-Greek. My mother was born and raised in Crete, although when she was seventeen she came to the UK to work.'

'What about your father?'

'He's English...from London.'

The enigmatic Ludo raised an amused sandy-coloured eyebrow. 'So you have the heat of the Mediterranean in your blood, along with the icy temperatures of the Thames? How intriguing.'

'That's certainly a novel way of putting it.' Struggling hard not to display her pique at the comment, and wondering at the same time how she could convey without offending him that she really craved some quiet time to herself before reaching London, Natalie frowned.

'I see I have offended you,' her enigmatic fellow passenger murmured, low-voiced. 'Forgive me. That was definitely not my intention.'

'Not at all. I just—I just have a lot of thinking to do before my meeting.'

'This meeting in London is work-related?'

Her lips briefly curved in a smile. 'I told you that my dad sent me the train ticket? Well, I'm going to meet him. I haven't seen him for about three months, and when we last spoke I sensed he was extremely worried about something… I just hope it's not his health. He's already suffered one heart attack as it is.' She shivered at the memory.

'I'm sorry. Does he live in the city?'

'Yes…he does.'

'But you live in Hampshire?'

'Yes…in a small village called Stillwater with my mum. Do you know it?'

'Indeed I do. I have a house that's about five miles from there in a place called Winter Lake.'

'Oh!' Winter Lake was known to be one of the most exclusive little enclaves in Hampshire. The locals referred to it as 'Billionaire's Row'. Natalie's initial assessment that Ludovic was a man of means had been spot-on, and she didn't know why but it made her feel strangely uneasy.

Leaning forward a little, he rested his hand on the arm of his seat and she briefly noticed the thick gold ring with an onyx setting he wore on his little finger. It might be some kind of family heirloom. But she was quickly distracted from the observation by his stunning sapphire gaze.

'I presume your parents must be divorced if you live with your mother?' he deduced.

'Yes, they are. In any case, tonight I'll be staying at my dad's place…we have a lot of catching up to do.'

'You are close…you and your father?'

The unexpected question took her aback. Staring into the fathomless, long-lashed blue eyes, for a long moment Natalie didn't know how to answer him. Or how much she might safely tell him.

'We definitely were when I was younger. After my parents divorced it was…well, it was very difficult for a while. It's got much better in the last couple of years, though. Anyway, he's the only dad I have, and I do care about him—which is why I'm anxious to get to London and find out what's been troubling him.'

'I can tell that you are a devoted and kind daughter. Your father is a very fortunate man indeed to have you worry about him.'

'I *endeavour* to be kind and devoted. Though, to be frank, there are times when it isn't easy. He can be rather unpredictable and not always easy to understand.' She couldn't help reddening at the confession. What on earth was she doing, admitting such a personal thing to a total stranger? To divert her anxiety she asked, 'Are you a father? I mean, do you have children?'

When she saw the wry quirk of his beautifully sculpted mouth she immediately regretted it, surmising that she'd transgressed some unspoken boundary.

'No. It is my view that children need a steady and stable environment, and right now my life is far too demanding and busy to provide that.'

'Presumably you'd have to be in a steady relationship too?'

Ludo's magnetically blue eyes flashed a little, as though he was amused, but Natalie guessed he was in no hurry to enlighten her as to his romantic status. Why should he be? After all, she was just some nondescript girl he had spontaneously assisted because she'd stupidly left her train ticket in the ladies' room before boarding the train.

'Indeed.'

His short reply was intriguingly enigmatic. Feeling suddenly awkward at the thought of engaging in further conversation, Natalie stifled a helpless yawn and immediately seized on it as the escape route she was subconsciously searching for.

'I think I'll close my eyes for a while, if you don't mind. I went out to dinner last night with a friend, to help celebrate her birthday, and didn't get in until late. The lack of sleep has suddenly caught up with me.'

'Go ahead. Try and get some rest. In any case I have some work to catch up on.' Ludo gestured towards the slim silver laptop that was open on the table in front of him. 'We will talk later.'

It sounded strangely like a promise.

With the memory of his smoky, arresting voice drifting tantalisingly through her mind like the most delicious warm breeze, Natalie leaned back in her luxurious seat, shut her eyes and promptly fell asleep…

In the generous landscaped garden of her childhood London home she squealed with excitement as her dad laughingly spun her round and round.

'Stop, Daddy, stop! You're making me dizzy!' she cried.

As she spun, she glimpsed tantalising snatches of blue summer sky, and the sun on her face filled her with such a sense of well-being that she could have hugged herself. In the background the air was suffused with the lilting chorus of enchanting birdsong. The idyll was

briefly interrupted by her mother calling out to them
that tea was ready.

The poignant dream ended as abruptly as it had
begun. Natalie felt distraught at not being able to sum-
mon it back immediately. When she was little, she'd
truly believed that life was wonderful. She'd felt safe
and secure and her parents had always seemed so happy
together.

A short while after the memory of her dream started
to fade, the muted sound of the doors opening stirred
her awake just in time to see a uniformed member of
staff enter the compartment with a refreshment trolley.
She was a young, slim woman, with neatly tied back
auburn hair and a cheery smile.

'Would you like something to eat or drink, sir?' She
addressed Ludo.

With a gently amused lift of his eyebrows, he turned
his head towards Natalie.

'I see that you have returned to the land of the living. Are you ready for some coffee and a sandwich?'
he asked. 'It's almost lunchtime.'

'Is it, really?' Feeling a little groggy, she straightened
in her seat and automatically checked her watch. She
was stunned to realise that she'd been asleep for almost
an hour. 'A cup of coffee would be great,' she said, digging into her purse for some change.

'Put your money away,' her companion ordered,
frowning. 'I will get this. How do you take your coffee? Black or white?'

'White with one sugar, please.'

'What about a sandwich?' He turned to the uni-formed assistant, 'May I see a menu?' he asked.

When the girl handed a copy of said menu over to him, he passed it straight to Natalie. About to tell him that she wasn't hungry, she felt her stomach betray her with an audible growl. Feeling her face flame red, she glanced down at the list displayed in slim gold letter-ing on the leaflet in front of her.

'I'll have a ham and Dijon mustard sandwich on wholemeal bread, please. Thank you.'

'Make that two of those, and a black coffee along with the white one.' He gave the assistant their order, then waited until she'd arranged their drinks and sand-wiches on the table and departed before speaking again. 'You sounded a little disturbed when you were dozing,' he commented.

Natalie froze. Remembering her dream, and thinking that she must have inadvertently cried out at the very real sensation of her dad spinning her round and round, she answered, 'Do you mean I was talking in my sleep?'

'No. You were, however, gently snoring,' he teased.

Now she really *did* wish the floor would open up and swallow her. As the train powered through the lush green countryside she hardly registered the sublime views because she was so incensed.

'I don't snore. I've never snored in my life,' she re-torted defensively. Seeing that Ludo was still smiling, she added uncertainly, 'At least…not that I know of.'

'Your boyfriend is probably too polite to tell you.' He grinned, taking a careful sip of his steaming black coffee.

Her heart thudded hard at the implication. Not remotely amused, she stared fixedly back at the perfectly sculpted profile on the other side of the aisle. 'I don't have a boyfriend. And even if I had you shouldn't assume that we would—' Her impassioned little speech tailed off beneath the disturbing beam of Ludo's electric blue eyes.

'Sleep together?' he drawled softly.

Anxious not to come across as hopelessly inexperienced and naive to someone who was clearly an accomplished and polished man of the world and about as far out of her reach socially as the earth was from the planet Jupiter, Natalie bit into her sandwich and quickly stirred some sugar into her coffee.

'This is good,' she murmured. 'I didn't realise how hungry I was. But then I suppose it's because I didn't have any breakfast this morning.'

'You should always endeavour to eat breakfast.'

'That's what my mum says.'

'You told me earlier that she was from Crete?'

The less tricky question alleviated her previous embarrassment a little. Even though she had only visited the country a couple of times, she'd grown up on her mother's enchanting tales of her childhood homeland, and she would happily talk about Greece until the cows came home. 'That's right. Have you been there?'

'I have. It is a very beautiful island.'

'I've only been there a couple of times but I'd love to go again.' Her grey eyes shone. 'But somehow or other, time passes and work and other commitments inevitably get in the way.'

'You must have a demanding career?'

Natalie smiled. 'It's hardly a career, but I'm ex-tremely glad that I chose it. My mum and I run a small but busy bed and breakfast together.'

'And what do you enjoy most about the enterprise? The day-to-day practicalities, such as greeting guests, making beds and cooking meals? Or do you perhaps like running the business side of things?'

Privately she confessed to being inspired to do what she did because her dad had run an extremely success-ful hotel business. As she'd grown older she'd picked up some useful tips from him along the way, in spite of the eventual dissolution of her parents' marriage.

'A bit of both, really,' she replied. 'But it's my mum that does most of the meeting and greeting. She's the most sublime hostess and cook, and the guests just adore her. Taking care of the business side of things and mak-ing sure that everything runs smoothly is my respon-sibility. I suppose it comes more naturally to me than to her.'

Ludo's compelling sapphire-coloured eyes crinkled at the corners. 'So…you like being in charge?'

The comment instigated an unsettling sensation of vague embarrassment. Did he perhaps think that she was boasting? 'Does that make me sound bossy and controlling?' she quizzed him.

Her handsome companion shook his head, 'Not at all. Why be defensive about an ability to take charge when a situation calls for it…especially in business? A going concern could hardly be successful if someone didn't take the reins. In my view it is a very admirable and desirable asset.'

'Thanks.' Even as she shyly acknowledged the unexpected compliment it suddenly dawned on Natalie that Ludo had revealed very little about himself. Yet he had somehow got her to divulge quite a lot about her own life.

Was he a psychologist, perhaps? Judging by his extremely confident manner and expensive clothing, whatever profession he was in it must earn him a fortune. She realised that she really *wanted* to know a bit more about him. What sentient woman wouldn't be interested in such a rivetingly attractive man? Maybe it was time she turned the tables and asked *him* some questions.

'Do you mind if I ask you what *you* do for a living?' she ventured.

Ludo blinked. Then he stared straight ahead of him for seemingly interminable seconds, before finally turning his head and gifting her with one of his magnetically compelling smiles. Her heart jumped as she found her glance irretrievably captured and taken hostage.

'My business is diverse. I have interests in many different things, Natalie.'

'So you run a business?'

He shrugged disconcertingly. Why was he being so cagey? Did he think she was hitting on him because he was wealthy? The very idea made her squirm—especially when he had displayed such rare kindness in paying for her train ticket. Not one in a thousand people would have been so generous towards a complete stranger, she was sure.

'I would rather not spoil this unexpectedly enjoyable train journey with you by discussing what I do,' he explained. 'Besides…I would much rather talk about you.'

'I've already told you what I do.'

'But what you do, Natalie, is not who you are. I would like to know a little bit more about your life…the things that interest you and why.'

She flushed. Such a bold and unexpected declaration briefly struck her dumb, and coupled with the admission that he was enjoying travelling with her, it made her feel strangely weak with pleasure. The last time she could recall feeling a similar pleasure was when she'd had her first kiss from a boy at school she'd had a massive crush on. Her interest in him hadn't lasted for more than a few months, but she'd never forgotten the tingle of fierce excitement the kiss had given her. It had been tender and innocently explorative, and she remembered it fondly.

Threading her fingers through her long, gently mussed hair, she lowered her gaze and immediately felt strangely bereft of Ludo's crystalline blue glance. What would a kiss from *his* lips feel like? It certainly wouldn't be like an inexperienced schoolboy's.

Disturbed by the thought, she drew in a steadying breath. 'If you mean my favourite pastimes or hobbies, I'm sure if I told you what they were you'd think them quite ordinary and boring.'

'Try me,' he invited with a smile.

Natalie almost said out loud, *When you look at me like that I can't think of a single thing I like except the dimples in your carved cheekbones when you smile.*

Shocked by the intensity of heat that washed through her at the private admission, she briefly glanced away to compose herself. 'I enjoy simple pleasures, like reading and going to the cinema. I just love watching a good film that takes me away from the worries and concerns of my own life and transports me into the story of someone else's…especially if it's uplifting. I also love listening to music and taking long walks in the countryside or on the beach.'

'I find none of those interests either boring or ordinary,' Ludo replied, the edges of his finely sculpted lips nudging the wryest of smiles. 'Besides, sometimes the most ordinary things in life—the things we may take for granted—can be the best. Don't you agree? I only wish I had more time to enjoy some of the pleasures that you mention myself.'

'Why can't you free up some time so that you can? Do you have to be so busy *all* of the time?'

Frowning deeply, he seemed to consider the question for an unsettlingly long time. His perusal of Natalie while he was mulling over her question bordered on intense. Flustered, she averted her gaze to check the time on her watch.

'We'll soon be arriving in London,' she announced, reaching over to the window seat for her bag and delving into it for a pen and something to write on. 'Do you think you could give me your full name and address now, so I can send you the money for my ticket?'

'We might as well wait until we disembark.'

He bit into his sandwich, as if certain she wouldn't give him an argument. She wanted to insist, but in the end decided not to. What difference could it possibly make to take his address now or later, as long as she got it? 'Never a borrower or a lender be,' her mother had always told her. 'And always pay your debts.'

Instead of adding any further comment, Natalie fell into a reflective silence. Observing that she wasn't eating her lunch, Ludo frowned, and the gesture brought two deep furrows to his otherwise silkily smooth brow.

'Finish your food,' he advised. 'If you haven't had any breakfast you'll need it. Especially if you face a difficult meeting with your father.'

'Difficult?'

'I mean emotional. If his health has deteriorated then your discussion will not be easy for either of you.'

The comment made a jolt of fear scissor through her heart. She was genuinely afraid that her dad's urgent need to see her was to tell her he'd received a serious diagnosis from the doctor. They'd had their ups and downs over the years but she still adored him, and would hate for him to be taken from her when he had only just turned sixty.

'You're right. No doubt it will be emotional.' She gave him a self-conscious smile and chewed thoughtfully on her sandwich.

'I'm sure that whatever happens the two of you will find great reassurance in each other's company.'

The sudden ring of Ludo's mobile instantly commanded his attention. After a brief acknowledgement to the caller, he covered the speaker with his hand and turned back to Natalie.

'I'm afraid I need to take this call. I'm going to step outside into the corridor for a few minutes.'

As he rose to his feet she was taken aback to see how tall he was…at least six foot two, she mused. The impressive physique beneath the flawless Italian tailoring hinted at an athletically lean and muscular build, and she couldn't help staring up at him in admiration. Concerned that she might resemble a besotted teenager, staring open-mouthed at a pop idol, she forced herself to relax and nod her head in acknowledgement.

'Please, go ahead.'

As the automatic twin doors of the compartment swished open Ludo turned to her for a moment and, with a disconcerting twinkle in his eye, said, 'Whatever you do, don't run away, Natalie…will you?'

CHAPTER TWO

'I ASSUME THAT all the papers are ready?'

Even as he asked the question Ludo rapidly assessed the detailed information he'd been given, turning it over in his mind with the usual rapier-like thoroughness that enabled him to dive into every corner and crevice of a situation all at once and miss nothing.

At the other end of the line, his personal assistant Nick confirmed that everything was as it should be. Rubbing a hand round his clean-shaven, chiselled jaw, Ludo enquired 'And you've scheduled the meeting for tomorrow, as I asked?'

'Yes, I have. I told the client that he and his lawyer should come to the office at ten forty-five, just as you instructed.'

'And you've obviously notified Godrich, my own man?'

'Of course.'

'Good. It sounds like you've taken care of everything. I'll see you back at the office some time this afternoon to give the papers a final once-over. Bye for now.'

When he'd concluded the call Ludo leant his back against the panelled wall of the train corridor, trying in vain to calm the uncharacteristic nerves that were fluttering like a swarm of intoxicated butterflies in the pit of his stomach. It wasn't the call or its contents that had perturbed him. Finalising deals and acquiring potentially lucrative businesses that had fallen on hard times was meat and drink to him, and he was famed for quickly turning his new acquisitions into veins of easily flowing gold. It was how he had made his fortune.

No, the reason for his current disquiet was his engaging fellow passenger. How could a mere slip of a girl, with the reed-slim figure of a prima ballerina, long brown hair and big grey eyes like twin sunlit pools, electrify him as if he'd been plugged into the National Grid?

He shook his head. She wasn't anything like the voluptuous blondes and redheads that he was usually attracted to, and yet there was something irresistibly engaging about her. In fact, from the moment Ludo had heard the sound of her soft voice she had all but seduced him... Even more surprising than that, what were the odds that she should turn out to be half-Greek? The synchronicity stunned him.

Distractedly staring down at several missed messages on his phone, he impatiently flicked off the screen and gazed out of the window at the scenery that was hurtling by instead. The mixture of old and new industrial buildings and the now familiar twenty-first-century constructions rising high into the skyline heralded the fact that they were fast approaching the city. It was time he made up his mind about whether or not he wanted to act on the intense attraction that had gripped him and decide what to do about it. It was clear that the lovely Natalie was in earnest about reimbursing him for her train ticket, but he was naturally wary of giving his home address to strangers…however charming and pretty.

Although she'd transfixed him from the moment she'd stepped breathlessly into the first-class compartment and he'd scented the subtle but arresting tones of her mandarin and rose perfume, it wasn't in his nature to make snap decisions. While he was a great believer in following strong impulses in his business life, he wasn't so quick to apply the same method to his romantic liaisons. Sexual desire could be dangerously misleading, he'd found. It might be tempting as far as satisfying his healthy libido, but not if it turned into a headache he could well do without.

Sadly, he'd had a few of those in his time. He didn't mind treating his dates to beautiful *haute couture* clothing or exquisite jewellery from time to time, but Ludo had discovered to his cost that the fairer sex always wanted so much more than he was willing to give. More often than not, top of the list of what they wanted was a proposal of marriage. Even his vast wealth couldn't cushion him from the disagreeable inevitability of another broken relationship because the woman concerned had developed certain expectations of him…expectations that he definitely wasn't ready to fulfil. No matter *how* much his beloved family reminded him that it was about time he settled down with someone.

His mother's greatest desire was to become a grandmother. At thirty-six, and her only son, Ludo seemed to be constantly disappointing her because he wasn't any closer to fulfilling her wish. She was desperate for him to meet a suitable girl—'suitable' meaning someone who she and his father approved of. But it wasn't easy to meet genuinely caring and loving women who desired a relationship and children more than wealth and position, he'd found. And when his wealth and reputation preceded him it was apt to attract the very kind of shallow, ambitious women he should avoid.

Frankly, Ludo was heartily tired of that particular unhappy merry-go-round. The truth was, in his heart he yearned to find a soulmate—if such a creature even existed—someone warm and intelligent, with a good sense of humour and a genuinely kind disposition. He returned his thoughts to Natalie. If he embarked on a relationship with her and she should learn that he was as rich as a modern-day Croesus and counted some of the most influential business people in Europe as his friends, then he would never be sure that she was dating him for himself and *not* his money. Already he'd inadvertently let slip that he lived in the affluent area of Winter Lake. But then she must surely guess he wasn't short of money if he was travelling first class and could spontaneously pay for her ticket?

Regarding the ticket she'd lost, she'd told him that her father had sent it to her. Was *he* a wealthy man? Surely he must be. If that was the case then the pretty Natalie must have been used to a certain level of comfort before her parents had divorced. Would she be holding out for someone equally wealthy—if not more so—in a relationship?

Frowning, Ludo quickly decided it would make sense

to ask for her phone number if he wanted to see her again, rather than give her his address. That way *he* would be the one in control of the situation, and if he should glean at any time that she was a gold-digger then he would drop her like a hot potato. Meanwhile, they could meet up for a drink while she was in London under the perfectly legitimate excuse of his allowing her to settle her debt. If after that things progressed satisfactorily between them, then Ludo would be only too happy to supply more personal information, such as his full address.

Feeling satisfied with his decision, he exhaled a sigh, briefly tunnelled his fingers through his floppily perfect hair, and slipped his mobile into the silk-lined pocket of his jacket. Before depressing the button that opened the automatic doors into the first-class compartment he stole a surreptitious glance through the glass at the slender, doe-eyed brunette who was gazing out of the window with her chin in her hand, as if daydreaming. His lips automatically curved into a smile. He couldn't help anticipating her willing agreement to meet up with him for a date. What reason could she possibly have *not* to?

'I don't understand. You're saying you want to meet me for a drink?'

Blinking in disbelief at the imposing Adonis who was surveying her with a wry twist of his carved lips as they stood together on the busy station platform, Natalie convinced herself she must have become hard of hearing. Ludo's surprising suggestion sounded very much as if he was inviting her out on a date. But why on earth would he do such a thing? It just didn't make sense. Perhaps she'd simply got the wrong end of the stick.

Practically every other woman who'd disembarked from the train was stealing covetous glances over her shoulder at the handsome and stylishly dressed man standing in front of her as she hurried by, she noticed. No doubt they were privately wondering why a girl as unremarkable as herself should capture his attention for so much as a second. Her heart skipped one or two anxious beats.

'Yes, I do,' he replied.

His jaw firmed and his blue eyes shimmered enigmatically. For Natalie, meeting such an arresting glance was like standing in the eye of a sultry tropical storm— it shook her as the wind shook a fragile sapling, threatening to uproot it. She held her voluminous red leather bag over her chest, as though it were some kind of protective shield, and couldn't help frowning. Instead of sending her self-esteem soaring, Ludo's suggestion that they meet up for a drink had had the opposite effect on her confidence. It hardly helped that in faded jeans and a floral print gypsy-style blouse she felt singularly dowdy next to him in his expensive Italian tailoring.

'Why?' she asked. 'I only asked for your address so that I can send you the money for my train fare. You've already indicated that you're a very busy man, so why would you go to all the trouble of meeting up with me instead of simply letting me post you a cheque?'

Her companion shook his head bemusedly, as if he couldn't fathom what must be, to him, a very untypical response. Natalie guessed he wasn't used to women turning him down for anything.

'Aside from allowing you to personally pay me back for the ticket, I'd like to see you again, Natalie,' he stated seriously. 'Did such a possibility not occur to you? After all, you indicated to me on the train that you were a free agent…remember?'

Unfortunately, she had. She'd confessed she didn't have a boyfriend when Ludo had assumed that if she had he must be too polite to tell her that she snored in her sleep. She blushed so hard at the memory that her delicate skin felt as if she stood bare inches from a roaring fire.

Adjusting her bag, she endeavoured to meet the steady, unwavering gaze that was so uncomfortably searing her. 'Are *you* a free agent?' she challenged. 'For all I know you could be married with six children.'

He tipped back his head and released a short, heartfelt laugh. Never before had the sound of a man's amusement brushed so sensually over her nerve-endings—as though he had stroked down her bare skin with the softest, most delicate feather. Out of the blue, a powerful ache to see him again infiltrated her blood and wouldn't be ignored…even if he *did* inhabit an entirely different stratosphere from her.

'I can assure you that I am neither married nor the father of six children. I told you before that I've been far too busy for that. Don't you believe me?'

Ludo's expression had become serious once more. Conscious of the now diminishing crowd leaving the train, and realising with relief that they were no longer the focus of unwanted interest, Natalie shrugged.

'All I'll say is that I hope you're telling me the truth. Honesty is really important to me. All right, then. When do you want us to meet?'

'How long do you think you'll be in London?'

'Probably a couple of days at most…that is unless my dad needs me around for longer.' Once again she was unable to control the tremor of fear in her voice at the thought that her father might be seriously ill. To stop from dwelling on the subject, and to prevent any uncomfortable quizzing from Ludo, she smiled and added quickly, 'I'll just have to wait and see, won't I?'

'If you are only going to be staying in town for a couple of days, that doesn't give us very much time. That being the case, I think we should meet up tomorrow evening, don't you?' There was an unexpected glint of satisfied expectation in his eyes. 'I can book us a table at Claridges. What time would suit you best?'

'The restaurant, you mean? I thought you said we were only meeting for a drink?'

'Don't you eat in the evenings?'

'Of course, but—'

'What time?'

'Eight o'clock?'

'Eight o'clock it is, then. Let me have your mobile number so I can ring you if I'm going to be delayed.'

Her brow puckering, Natalie was thoughtful. 'Okay, I'll give it to you. But don't forget it might be me who's delayed or can't make it if my dad isn't well…in which case you'd better let me have *your* number.'

With another one of his enigmatic smiles, Ludo acquiesced unhesitatingly.

She'd never got used to a doorman letting her into the rather grand Victorian building where her father's luxurious flat was situated. It made her feel like an audacious usurper pretending to be someone important.

The contrast between how her parents lived was like night and day. Her mother was a conscientious and devoted home-maker who enjoyed the simple and natural things in life, while her father was a real hedonist who loved material things perhaps a little *too* much. Although undoubtedly hard-working, he had a tendency to be quite reckless with his money.

Now, as she found herself travelling up to the topmost floor in the lift, Natalie refused to dwell on that. Instead she found herself growing more and more uneasy at what he might be going to tell her.

When Bill Carr opened the door to greet her, straight away his appearance seemed to confirm her worst suspicions. She was shocked at how much he'd aged since she'd last seen him. It had only been three months, but the change in him was so marked it might as well have been three years. He was a tall, handsome, distinguished-looking man, with a penchant for traditionally tailored Savile Row suits, and his still abundant silver-grey hair was always impeccably cut and styled...*but not today.* Today it was messy and in dire need of attention. His white shirt was crumpled and unironed and his pinstriped trousers looked as if he'd slept in them.

With alarm Natalie noticed that he carried a crystal

tumbler that appeared to have a generous amount of whisky in it. The reek of alcohol when he opened his mouth to greet her confirmed it.

'Natalie! Thank God you're here, sweetheart. I was going out of my mind, thinking that you weren't going to come.'

He flung an arm round her and pulled her head down onto his chest. Natalie dropped her bag to the ground and did her utmost to relax. Instinct told her that whatever had made her father seek solace in strong drink must be more serious than she'd thought.

Lifting her head she endeavoured to make her smile reassuring. 'I'd never have let you down, Dad.' Reaching up, she planted an affectionate kiss on his unshaven cheek as the faintest whiff of his favourite aftershave mingled with the incongruous and far less appealing smell of whisky.

'Did you have a good journey?' he asked, reaching over her shoulder to push the door shut behind her.

'I did, thanks. It was really nice to travel first class, but you shouldn't have gone to such unnecessary expense, Dad.'

Even as she spoke Natalie couldn't help but recall her meeting with Ludo, and the fact that he'd stumped up the money for her ticket when he'd heard her explain to the guard that she'd lost hers. His name was short for Ludovic, he'd told her. For a few seconds she lost herself in a helpless delicious reverie. The name was perfect. She really liked it…*she liked it a lot*. There was an air of mystery about the sound of it…a bit like its owner. They hadn't exchanged surnames but every second of their time together on the train was indelibly imprinted on her mind, never to be forgotten. Particularly his cultured, sexy voice and those extraordinarily beautiful sapphire-blue eyes of his. Her heart jumped when she nervously recalled her agreement to meet him for dinner tomorrow...

'I've always wanted to give you the best of everything, sweetheart...and that didn't change when your mother and I split up. Is she well, by the way?'

Her father's curiously intense expression catapulted her back to the present, and Natalie saw the pain that he still carried over the break-up with his wife. Her mouth dried uncomfortably as she privately empathised with the loss that clearly still haunted him.

'Yes, she's very well. She asked me to tell you that she hopes you're doing well too.'

He grimaced and shrugged. 'She's a good woman, your mother. The best woman I ever knew. It's a crying shame I didn't appreciate her more when we were together. As to your comment that she hopes I'm doing well... It near kills me to have to admit this, darling, but I'm afraid I'm not doing very well at all. Come into the kitchen and let me get you a cup of tea, then I'll explain what's been going on.'

The admission confirmed her increasingly anxious suspicions, but it still tore at Natalie's insides to hear him say it. Feeling suddenly drained, she followed his tall, rangy frame into his modern stainless-steel kitchen, watched him accidentally splash water over his crumpled sleeve as he filled the kettle at the tap—was she imagining it, or was his hand shaking a little?—and plugged it into the wall socket. He collected his whisky glass before dropping wearily down onto a nearby stool.

'What is it, Dad? Have you been having pains in your chest again? Is that why you wanted to see me so urgently? Please tell me.'

Her father imbibed a generous slug of whisky, then slammed his glass noisily back down on the counter, rubbing the back of his hand across his eyes. Communication was suspended for several disturbing moments as he looked to be struggling to gather his thoughts. 'For once it's not my health that's at stake, here, Nat. It's my livelihood.' His mouth shaped a rueful grimace.

Outside, from the busy street below, came the jarring sound of a car horn honking. Natalie flinched in shock. Drawing in a steadying breath, she saw that her dad was perfectly serious in his confession.

'Has something gone wrong with the business? Is it to do with a downturn in profits? I know the country's going through a tough time economically at the moment, but you can weather the storm, Dad…you always do.'

Bill Carr looked grim. 'The hotel chain hasn't made any profit for nearly two years, my love…largely because I haven't kept up with essential refurbishment and modernisation. And I can no longer afford to keep on staff of the calibre that helped make it such a success in the first place. It's so like you to blame it on the economy, but that just isn't the case.'

'Then if it's not that *why* can't you afford to modernise or keep good staff? You've always told me that the business has made you a fortune.'

'That's perfectly true. It *did* make a fortune. But

sadly I haven't been able to hold on to it. I've lost almost everything, Natalie…and I'm afraid I'm being forced to sell the business at a loss to try and recoup some money and pay off the vast amount of debt I've accrued.'

Natalie's insides lurched as though she'd just narrowly escaped plunging down a disused elevator shaft. 'It's really that bad?' she murmured, hardly knowing what to say.

Her father pushed to his feet, despondently shaking his head. 'I've made such a mess of my life,' he told her, 'and I suppose because I've been so reckless and irresponsible the chickens have come home to roost, as they say. I deserve it. I was blessed with everything a man could wish for—a beautiful wife, a lovely daughter and work that I loved… But I threw it all away because I became more interested in seeking pleasure than keeping a proper eye on the business.'

'You mean women and drink?'

'And the rest. It's not hard to understand why I had a heart attack.'

Needing to offer him some comfort and reassurance, even though she was shocked and slightly dazed at what 'the rest' might refer to, Natalie urgently caught hold of his hand and folded it between her own.

'That doesn't mean you're going to have another one, Dad. Things will get better, I promise you. First of all, you've got to stop blaming yourself for what you did in the past and forgive yourself. Then you have to vow that you won't hurt yourself in that way ever again— that you'll look after yourself, move on, and deal with what's going on right now. You said you're being forced to sell the business at a loss...to whom?'

'A man who's known in the world of mergers and acquisitions as "the Alchemist" because he can turn dirt into diamonds at the drop of a hat it seems. A Greek billionaire named Petrakis. It's a cliché, I know, but he really did make me an offer I couldn't refuse. At least I know he's got the money. That's something, I suppose. The thing is I need cash in the bank as soon as possible, Nat. The bank wants the money from the sale in my account tomorrow, after we complete, or else they'll make me bankrupt.'

'Don't you have any other assets? What about this flat? Presumably you own it outright?'

Again her father shook his head. 'Mortgaged up to the hilt, I'm afraid.' Noting the shock in her eyes, he freed his hand from hers, winced, and started to rub his chest.

Natalie's own heart started to race with concern. 'Are you all right, Dad? Should I call a doctor?'

'I'm fine. I probably just need to rest a bit and stop drinking so much whisky. Perhaps you'd make me a cup of tea instead?'

'Of course I will. Why don't you go and put your feet up on the couch in the living room and I'll bring it in to you?'

His answer to her suggestion was to impel her close into his chest and plant a fond kiss on the top of her head. When she glanced up to examine his suddenly pale features, his warm smile was unstintingly loving and proud.

'You're a good girl, Natalie…the best daughter in the world. I regret not telling you that more often.'

'You and Mum might have parted, but I always knew that you loved me.' Gently, she stepped out of the circle of his arms.

'It does my heart good to hear you say that. I don't want to take advantage, but perhaps you won't mind me asking another favour of you?'

Her throat thick with emotion, Natalie smiled back at him. 'Ask away. You know that I'll do anything I can to help.'

'I want you to come with me to this meeting I've got with Petrakis and his lawyers tomorrow. Just for a little moral support. Will you?'

Instinctively she knew it would probably be one of the hardest things she'd ever done, watching her father sign away the business he'd worked so hard to build all these years to some fat-cat Greek billionaire who didn't have a clue about how much it meant to him, or care that the sale might be breaking his heart…

'Of course I will.' She lightly touched her palm to his cheek. 'Now, go and put your feet up, like I said. I'll make that cup of tea and bring it in to you.'

Her father's once broad shoulders were stooped as he turned to exit the room. Natalie had never felt remotely violent towards anyone before, but she did now as she thought of the Greek billionaire known as 'the Alchemist' who was buying his business from him for a song when he could no doubt well afford to purchase it for far more and at least give her dad a fighting chance to get back on his feet again…

CHAPTER THREE

IF NATALIE HAD had a restless night, then her father had had a worse one. Several times she'd heard him get up to pace the hallway outside their bedrooms, and once when he'd omitted to close his door she'd heard the sound of violent retching coming from his bathroom. It had so frightened her that she'd raced straight into his room and banged urgently on the en-suite door. He had pleaded with her to let him sort himself out, telling her that it had happened before, that he knew how to deal with it, and Natalie had reluctantly returned to her room, heavy of heart and scared out of her wits in case he should have a seizure or a fit during the night.

After not much more than three hours' sleep she'd woken bleary-eyed and exhausted to find blinding sunshine beaming straight at her through the uncovered window, where she'd forgotten to roll down the blinds.

After checking that her dad was awake, she stumbled into the kitchen to make a large pot of strong black coffee. She rustled up some toast and marmalade and called out to him to come to the table.

The dazzlingly bright sunshine wasn't exactly a good friend to Bill Carr that morning, Natalie observed anxiously. The complexion that she'd judged as a little pasty yesterday looked ashen grey and sickly today. He made a feeble attempt at eating the toast she'd made, but didn't hesitate to down two large mugs of coffee.

Afterwards, he wiped the back of his trembling hand across his mouth, grimaced and said, 'I suppose you could say I'm ready for anything now.'

The weak smile he added to that statement all but broke Natalie's heart.

'You won't have to face this alone, Dad. I'll be with you every step of the way…I promise.'

'I know, darling. And, whilst I know I hardly deserve to have your support at all, I honestly appreciate it and one day soon I'll make it up to you…that's *my* promise to you.'

'You don't need to make it up to me. We're family, remember? All I want is for you to be well and happy. Now, remind me what time we have to be at this Petrakis's office?'

'Ten forty-five.'

'Okay. After I shower and dress I'll phone a cab to pick us up. Where is the office we're going to?'

'Westminster.'

'Not far away, then. Well, you'd better go and get ready, too. Do you need anything ironed?'

Getting to his feet and digging his hands deep into the capacious pockets of his dressing gown, her father seemed completely nonplussed by the question.

Taking in a consciously deep breath to calm her disquiet, Natalie asked, 'Do you want me to come with you and check?'

'No, darling, it's fine. I'm wearing my best Savile Row suit, and my one ironed shirt has been hanging in the wardrobe ready ever since I got the call that the meeting was today.'

'Good.' Giving him an approving smile, Natalie stole a brief glance at the fashionably utilitarian stainless-steel clock on the wall. 'We'd better get our skates on, then. We don't want to be late.'

'For the execution, you mean?' His grimace, clearly tinged with bitterness and regret, had never looked more pained. Yet the comment also contained a hint of ironic humour.

'I know it must be hard for you to contemplate letting go of the business that you put your heart and soul into to building,' she sympathised, 'but maybe this could be an exciting new start for you. An opportunity to put your energies into something else…something a little less taxing that you could manage more easily. Even the direst situations can have a silver lining.'

'And how am I going to start another business if I have barely a penny to my name?'

'Is running a business the only way you can earn a living?'

'That's all I know how to do.' Exhaling a leaden sigh, her father drove his fingers exasperatedly through his already mussed silver hair.

Struggling with her personal sense of frustration at not being able to find an instant solution that would cheer him and give him some hope, Natalie dropped her hands to hips clad in the pyjama bottoms and T-shirt she'd borrowed from him to wear to bed and thought hard.

'What if we ask this Petrakis if he could extend some humanitarian understanding and pay you a reasonable sum for the business? After all, if you say he has a reputation for being able to turn dirt into diamonds then surely he must know that he's bound to make another fortune from your hotel chain? What would it hurt for him to pay you a fairer price?'

'Sweetheart…I don't mean this unkindly, but you know very little about men like Petrakis. How do you think he acquired his considerable fortune? It wasn't from taking a humanitarian approach to making money! Whatever you say to him, however impassioned or eloquent your argument, it would be like water off a duck's back.'

Natalie's grey eyes flashed angrily. 'And that's how the business world measures success these days, is it? Someone is only thought of as successful if he's single-mindedly ruthless in his dealings and doesn't give a fig about the psychological damage he might cause to anyone—not even a fellow entrepreneur who's down on his luck—just as long as he can get what he wants?'

Breathing hard, she knew how much she already despised the Greek billionaire even though she hadn't even set eyes on him yet. But there was also something else on her mind. If this meeting with Petrakis was too devastating for her dad—and she'd certainly be able to tell if it was—then she couldn't abandon him later on tonight to go and have dinner with the enigmatic Ludo. Even though she'd barely been able to cease thinking about the man since meeting him on the train yesterday…

'Apparently that is the case. But don't distress yourself by being angry on my behalf, love. I know I asked you to come with me for moral support, but this isn't your battle. It's mine. Now, I think we'd better go and get ourselves ready.'

Giving a resigned shrug, her father turned on his heel. With a heavy tread he made his way down the varnished wood-panelled hall to his bedroom, as if carrying the weight of the world on his shoulders.

'Ludovic…how are you? Traffic's bloody awful out there today. Everything's moving at a snail's pace.'

Ludo had been staring out of the window of his plush Westminster office, hardly registering anything on the road outside because his mind was fixed on one thought and one thought only. Tonight he was meeting the exquisite Natalie for dinner. He closed his eyes. For just a few short seconds he could imagine himself becoming entranced by the still, crystal-clear lake of her gaze all over again, and could conjure up the alluring scent of her perfume as easily as if she were standing right next to him. It was impossible to recall the last time he'd had this sense of excited anticipation fluttering in the pit of his stomach at the prospect of seeing a woman again…if it had *ever* happened at all. So, when the booming voice of his public-school-educated lawyer Stephen Godrich unexpectedly rang out behind him he was so immersed in his daydream that he almost jumped out of his skin.

With a wry smile he pivoted, immediately steering

his mind back into work mode. There would be time for more fantasies about the lovely Natalie later, after they'd met for dinner, Ludo was sure.

Automatically stepping forward to shake the other man's hand, he privately noted that the buttons on the bespoke suit jacket he wore had about as much hope of meeting over his ever-expanding girth as Ludo had of winning the Men's Final at Wimbledon… An impossibility, of course, seeing as polo was his sport of choice, and not tennis.

'Hello, Stephen. You're looking well…in fact so well I fear I must be paying you too much,' he joked.

The other man's pebble-sized blue eyes, almost consumed by the generous flesh that surrounded them, flickered with momentary alarm. Quickly recovering, he drew out a large checked handkerchief from his trouser pocket and proceeded to mop the perspiration that glazed his brow.

'Being an inveterate lover of fine dining definitely has its price, my friend,' he remarked, smiling. 'I know I should be more self-disciplined, but we all have our little peccadillos, don't we? Anyway…do you mind if I ask if your client has arrived yet?'

Glancing down at the platinum Rolex that encircled his tanned wrist, Ludo frowned. 'I'm afraid not. It looks like he may well be late. While we're waiting for him I'll get Jane to make us some coffee.'

'Splendid idea. A few choice biscuits wouldn't go amiss either, if you have some,' the lawyer added hopefully.

Already at the door on his way out to Reception,

Ludo raised a hand in acknowledgement, thinking that if the man would only cut down on his sugar intake his handmade suits might fit him a whole lot better.

Ludo and his trusted representative Amelia Redmond—who had put the bid in for the once prestigious hotel chain on his behalf—sat at the polished table in the boardroom along with Stephen Godrich and Ludo's affable and highly professional assistant Nick. The younger man was re-reading some documentation in front of him and his olive-skinned brow was furrowed in concentration. Why it should suddenly occur to him at that precise moment that Nick's family came from Crete, he didn't know. Except that he'd been thinking about Natalie again, and he recalled her telling him that her mother had grown up there.

Suddenly impatient to have this meeting over and done with—even though the purchase of this particular hospitality business was a genuine coup—he had a strong urge to take some time out from work to go for a swim at his private health club. Not for the first time he recalled the surprising question Natalie had posed to him on the train. 'Do you have to be so busy *all* of the time?' she'd asked.

Ludo frowned. His family had raised him with a bulldog work ethic second to none, and he'd more than reaped the rewards of his tenacity and hard work. Yet there was still a perverse sense of not being deserving enough running through his veins that didn't always allow him to enjoy those rewards. Somewhere along the line he'd forgotten that a body needed rest and relaxation from time to time to recharge its batteries. Lord knew he could easily afford to take a year off or more if he wanted to. But to do what? And, more to the point, with *whom*?

Straightening the cuffs of his pristine cobalt shirt, he glanced up, intuiting the entrance of his diminutive middle-aged secretary Jane a moment before she appeared in the doorway.

'Mr Carr is here, along with his daughter and his solicitor Mr Nichols,' she announced gravely, as was her habit. 'Shall I show them in?'

'Please do. Have you asked them what refreshments they'd like?'

'I have.'

At the back of his mind Ludo was wondering why Bill Carr had brought his daughter along to the meeting. Neither Nick nor the ultra-efficient Amelia Redmond had informed him that she had any shares in the business, and the last thing he wanted to deal with today was some unforeseen complication that affected the deal. The look on Nick's face told him that he was equally puzzled by the daughter's attendance. As Jane held the door wide, so that the trio in reception could enter, Ludo was the first to rise to his feet to greet them.

When he registered that the pretty brunette who came in with the two men was Natalie he honestly thought his heart was going to jump clear out of his chest.

He stared. Natalie was the *daughter* of the hotel chain's owner, Bill Carr? Was fate playing some kind of outlandish joke on him? The wide-eyed liquid-silver glance that mirrored his own profound sense of shock instantly had him hypnotised, and he couldn't help but murmur her name beneath his breath. It was impossible to deny the instantaneous jolt of almost violent attraction that zigzagged through him at seeing her again.

The faded jeans that hugged her long slim legs and the cerise satin tunic she wore were in direct contrast to everyone else's ultra formal attire. Yet he couldn't help thinking that the ensemble was utterly charming and refreshing. But, as much as he was secretly delighted to see her, Ludo knew potentially that this was one of the worst situations he could have wished for. Already he could sense that she was on her guard, but not by so much as a flicker of an eyelid did she indicate that she'd met him before. Clearly it was going to be hard for her to trust him after realising that *he* was the man about to buy her father's business—and not at the best price either. She must know he was selling it at a substantial loss to Ludo.

Steering his glance deliberately over to the two men, in a bid to buy more time and think what to do, he asked, 'Which one of you is Bill Carr?'

He couldn't help his tone sounding on edge. In truth, Natalie's unexpected appearance, plus the astonishing fact that her father should turn out to be the businessman whose hotel chain he was purchasing, had seriously shaken him. As Ludo endeavoured to win back his equilibrium, the rangy, almost gaunt-looking man in a traditional grey pinstriped suit stepped forward to shake his hand.

'I am. This is my solicitor, Edward Nichols, and my daughter Natalie.'

Sadly, she *didn't* step forward to shake Ludo's hand.

Instead, her beautiful grey eyes flashed a warning, as if to tell him that under the circumstances it would be unwise to acknowledge her personally. At that moment, he couldn't help but agree.

'I presume you must be Mr Petrakis?' Bill Carr finished.

'That's right,' Ludo responded, adding quickly, 'Why don't we all sit down? I understand that my secretary is seeing to some refreshments, but in the meantime allow me to introduce you to my colleagues.'

The introductions over, he reached for the glass of water on the leather blotter in front of him and took a cooling sip. Somehow he had to endeavour to compose himself and not let anyone see that the sight of Natalie had almost robbed him of the power of speech—never mind his ability to present himself with his usually inimitable self-assurance. After Jane had brought coffee and biscuits, then shut the door behind her, Ludo seized the opportunity to hand over the formalities of the deal to Amelia and Nick. While they outlined the offer he had proposed, Bill Carr and his solicitor listened intently, every so often asking questions and jotting down notes.

Due to the uncharacteristic guilt that assailed him because he was buying her father's business, the back of Ludo's neck prickled uncomfortably every time he inadvertently caught Natalie's eye.

He tried hard to recall everything she'd told him about the man when they'd spoken on the train yesterday. *'He can be rather unpredictable and not always easy to understand,'* she'd confided. Ludo wondered if that had anything to do with what he chose to spend his money on. His assistant Nick had uncovered a story in the business community about the man having a reputation for being reckless with his money. The story went that he regularly indulged in various costly habits...not all of them entirely wholesome. No doubt that was why he found himself in the painful position he was in now, having to sell his business for less than half its value to meet the debt those expensive habits had incurred...

Ludo's two assistants brought their outlining of the deal to a concise and professional conclusion. Then his solicitor confirmed the conditions of the sum being offered, to make sure that Bill Carr was fully aware of every aspect of the deal. All that remained after that was for the deal to be signed and witnessed and the money transferred to his bank account.

As Ludo's solicitor Stephen Godrich pushed the necessary document across the table for the man's signature, Natalie stopped them all in their tracks with a stunning question. 'Mr Petrakis...do you think that the amount you're offering my father for his business is entirely fair?'

Mr Petrakis? Ludo almost smiled at her deliberate formality. But immediately after his initial amused reaction he registered the less than flattering implication behind the soft-voiced enquiry.

'Fair?' He frowned, turning the full force of his sapphire-blue gaze on her lightly flushed face.

'Yes—fair. You must know that you're getting what is one of the most innovative and successful hotel chains in the UK for practically peanuts! You're a very wealthy man, I hear. Surely you can afford to pay a less insulting amount to a man whose ingenuity and hard work created the business in the first place, so he might invest some of it in another entrepreneurial venture and make his living?'

As Natalie's little speech came to an end it was as though a bomb had exploded. As if in fear of igniting another, no one moved a muscle or so much as rustled a piece of paper. They were all in shock.

Going by her pink cheeks and over-bright eyes, so was Natalie. As for himself, for a heart-pounding few moments Ludo was genuinely at a loss as to know how to answer. But then his well-honed instinct for self-preservation thankfully kicked in, along with the first stirrings of genuine fury.

Leaning towards her across the table, he linked his hands together to anchor himself. 'You consider what I am paying your father for his business *insulting,* do you?'

'Yes, I do.'

'Have you asked him how many other people put in tenders for it? If not, why don't you do that now? Go on—ask him.'

The man sitting next to her slid a long, bony-fingered hand across his daughter's.

'I know you mean well, love, but the fact is no one other than Mr Petrakis is interested in buying the hotel chain. No doubt he is a realist about making money in business—as *I* am. The current market is in a slump, and I'm actually grateful that someone has made me an offer. The hotel chain isn't the roaring success it once was, Natalie. Whoever buys it is going to have to invest a substantial amount of money to bring it up to scratch again and make it profitable. Maybe that's the point you need to realise.'

Natalie bit her lip, and her answering glance up at him was verging on sorrowful. 'But this whole thing has so badly affected your health, Dad. You know it has. What are you going to do for a living if you can't get another business venture off the ground? That's the only reason I want more money for you.'

Hearing the devotion and concern in her voice, Ludo couldn't help admiring her—even though her unbelievable accusation had temporarily embarrassed him. It wasn't hard to see that Natalie Carr was a naturally caring woman who clearly adored her father and quickly forgave him for any poor decisions or mistakes he'd made—even if those poor decisions and mistakes hurt *her*. All in all, it made the idea of a liaison with her even more attractive, and Ludo wasn't above using whatever means he had at his disposal to persuade her that it was a good idea. But first he had a little more business to attend to.

'As indisputably tragic as your story is, Mr Carr, I now have to ask you… Do you wish to complete the deal and have this money paid into your account today? Or, after hearing of your charming daughter's admirable concern for your welfare, have you changed your mind?'

As he came to the end of his question Ludo deliberately raised a wry eyebrow at Natalie, as if to demonstrate that he hadn't become a very rich man by being soft-hearted and swayed by every sob story that came his way. As much as he wanted to bed her, he wouldn't go back on the principles that had made him his fortune. Not for *anyone*…

CHAPTER FOUR

THE DEAL WAS signed. And, although Natalie refused to meet Ludo's enigmatic glance as she, her father and his solicitor started to file out of the traditionally furnished office, with its leaded diamond-shaped windowpanes and lingering scent of beeswax, she couldn't help regretting that the much anticipated dinner date with him tonight wasn't going to happen after all.

How could it after he'd so coldly refused her heartfelt plea to help her father by increasing his offer for the hotel chain? It was evident that making money was far more important to him than helping his fellow man. *Good riddance*, she thought, deliberately averting her gaze as she swept past him. But just the same her heart hammered hard as the warmth from his body mingled with the alluring scent of his aftershave and disturbingly reached out to arouse her.

'Natalie?'

To her astonishment he lightly wrapped his hand round her slender-boned wrist.

'I'd like a word with you, if I may?'

Before she could register anything but the sensation of his warm grip against her flesh and the glittering cobalt blue of his eyes he removed his hand and turned to address his waiting colleagues.

'I need some time alone with Ms Carr.' There was a definite tone of command in his voice and immediately they all stood up and filed out behind Natalie's dad and his solicitor.

Before Ludo could shut the door behind them Bill Carr returned, to plant himself in the doorway, a perturbed expression on his long lean face.

'May I ask why you want to talk to my daughter alone? If you're angry that she was a little outspoken on my behalf, please don't take it personally. I'm sure she meant no offence, Mr Petrakis,' he apologised.

Natalie found it hard to quell her annoyance that her father was being so meek. For God's sake—he almost sounded subservient! One thing she was sure of: *she* wouldn't be following suit...

'Don't worry, Mr Carr. Although your daughter's outburst was somewhat ill-advised, you can rest assured that I did not take it personally. I simply want to have a quiet word with her in private—if she is in agreement?'

Beginning to feel like a piece of property being bartered, Natalie bristled. Folding her arms across the cerise blouse she'd thrown into her tote at the last minute, she made herself meet Ludo's wry glance head-on, without giving in to the urge to demonstrate her annoyance and deliberately look away.

'Whatever it is you want to say to me, Mr Petrakis, you had better make it quick. I want to get to the bank before it closes.'

'No doubt to check that your father's money has gone

into his account?' Ludo commented coolly, lifting a lightly mocking eyebrow.

How she refrained from slapping his smooth, sculpted cheek Natalie didn't know.

'My father's money is nothing to do with me. Believe it or not, I do have my own bank account.'

He grinned disconcertingly. 'I'm very glad to hear it. Why don't you come and sit down for a minute so we can talk?'

Turning towards her father, thinking he must be wondering what on earth was going on between the two of them, she just about managed a reassuring smile. 'I'm sure this won't take long, Dad. Will you wait for me outside?'

'I'll meet you in the coffee shop across the road. Goodbye, Mr Petrakis.'

'It has been a pleasure doing business with you, Mr Carr.'

As soon as Natalie's puzzled dad had closed the door behind him she could no longer stem her irritation at the handsome Greek. 'What on *earth* can you possibly have to say to me after what you've just done? Whatever it is, I'm not sure I want to hear it. Unless you want me to convey to my dad your sincere apologies for being so heartlessly mercenary, I'd rather not waste any more time today hoping that a man who is deaf, dumb and blind to pleas for understanding will change his mind and be more compassionate. I think I'd rather put the whole thing down to bitter experience and be on my way.'

The expression on Ludo's face suddenly reflected a

severe winter frost. 'Your indignant attitude beggars belief. What just went on between your father and me was a business transaction—pure and simple. If you can't see that then you are more naive than I thought. It is clear that you have *no* idea about the vagaries of buying and selling, not to mention the effect of current market forces. If perhaps not the most successful businessman in the world, your father is at least a pragmatist and he does understand these things. I am sure he realises how fortunate he is to have had me make an offer for his business at all. It is not as though he was exactly overrun with them… At least now he will be able to pay off some of his debts.'

Natalie was shocked. 'How do *you* know about his debts?'

'I make it a point to investigate the credentials of anyone who hopes to sell me anything, Natalie.' Emitting a weary-sounding sigh, Ludo rubbed his hand round his lean, cut-glass jaw. 'I am genuinely sorry that your father has got himself into such a mess financially, but that does not mean I should be responsible for helping to get him out of it. I too have business interests to maintain.'

'I'm sure you do.'

Even though his chastising reply had irked and irritated her, Natalie had to admit that she had no right to berate him when her father had brought this whole unfortunate situation down on himself. He was right. Ludo *wasn't* responsible for her father's inability to hold on to his once successful business because he'd become distracted by his propensity for acquiring more and more unhelpful bad habits. Should she really be angry at Ludo because he hadn't agreed to pay more for the hotel chain? After all, she knew for a fact that he wasn't a mean man. Hadn't he spontaneously paid for her rail ticket yesterday?

Curling some long strands of drifting hair agitatedly round her ear, she inhaled a steadying breath. No matter how much she tried to square it with herself, it was still hard to understand why a businessman as wealthy as Ludo couldn't extend a little more understanding and kindness towards a fellow entrepreneur when he was in trouble. Weren't the newspapers and the media always banging on about the need for businesses to be more ethical these days rather than solely profit-driven?

'Was that all you wanted to say to me?' she asked, perversely wishing that he would talk to her about far more interesting and perhaps *personal* things rather than business—just so that she could hear the sound of pleasure in his voice and store it in her memory.

Almost as if he'd read her mind, Ludo's deliberately slow, answering smile made her shiver. Inside Natalie's lace bra her nipples prickled hotly, just as if he had run his fingertips over them...

Gravel-voiced he replied, 'No. It isn't. Did you forget that you agreed to meet me for dinner tonight?'

'No...I didn't forget. But that was before I knew that you were the man buying my father's business.'

'What does that have to do with us meeting for dinner?'

Natalie's grey eyes widened in surprise that he should even have to ask. 'How do you think my dad would feel if he found out I'd gone out to dinner with you? He'd feel betrayed. He's already been through more than he can take without me adding to his problems.'

'It sounds like you don't believe that your own needs should be met, Natalie. Why is that, I wonder?'

'What needs are we talking about?'

Her face burned, because even as she posed the question she knew *exactly* what he meant. It was undeniable that Ludo Petrakis aroused her. He aroused her more than any other man she'd ever been attracted to before... And what took her breath away was that, going by the licentiously seductive look in his incredible blue eyes, he seemed to be having similar feelings. But it didn't make the situation any less awkward or uncomfortable.

Yes, her dad had made some very foolish errors concerning his business, and consequently lost everything he'd worked so hard for, but Natalie didn't want to appear as though she was deliberately punishing him by seeing Ludo. Somehow she had to find the strength to walk away from the man, no matter *how* much her senses clamoured for her to see him again.

She tossed her head in a bid to demonstrate that the particular needs he'd alluded to meant nothing in comparison to the more pressing one she still had on her mind. 'The only needs I have at the moment are for my father to recover from this crippling setback and return to full health so he can find the energy and the will to start over again. By the way—not that you'll care—did your investigations tell you that as well as losing his business he's about to lose his home, too? Anyway, the reason I have to get to the bank is not to check that your money's gone into his account but to get some money out to pay you back for the ticket you bought me on the train. Fortunately I have discovered that there's an emergency code I can use to get some cash from my account.'

'Forget about that. It's not important. As far as I'm concerned you don't owe me anything. Rather than have you pay me back for the ticket I'd much prefer to take you to dinner tonight and start to get to know you a little.'

Even though it was flattering that Ludo was being so persistent, Natalie couldn't help but frown.

'Didn't you hear what I said? I'm sorry, but I can't risk upsetting my dad by seeing you again. You might assume that he's taking it all rather well under the circumstances, but he's most definitely *not* coping.' She stroked a not quite steady hand down over her tunic. 'Look, I really do have to go now. But before I do there's one more thing I want to ask. Why didn't you tell me you were Greek when we met on the train? Especially after I told you that my mother came from Crete?'

In his mind, Ludo confronted a familiar wall that he was still reluctant to climb. He was proud of his heritage, but it had been three years since he'd last visited his homeland…three years since his beloved older brother Theo had perished in a boating accident off the coast of the private island that Ludo owned. It had been the darkest time of his life, and the aftermath of the tragic event had seen him spiralling into a pit of despair that he'd feared he might never get out of.

Instead of staying home to grieve with his family he'd left quite soon after the funeral, hoping to find relief from his despondency by increasing his international business interests, travelling everywhere round the globe *except* for his beloved Greece… His parents couldn't understand why he wouldn't come home. Whenever he spoke to his mother on the phone she'd plead and cry for him to return. But as far as Ludo was concerned he had disappointed her on two unforgivable counts, so he wouldn't. Not only had he been unable to provide her with evidence of a healthy romantic relationship and the prospect of a grandchild, worse— *much* worse than that—his brother had died holidaying on the beautiful island paradise that Ludo had bought himself, as a reward for attaining the success he'd so often dreamed of as a boy, ultimately so that his parents might see that he was as good and successful a man as Theo. Now they would never see that.

Momentarily glancing away from the beautiful clear grey eyes that were so avidly studying him, he endeavoured to keep his tone matter-of-fact. 'At the time I was more interested in finding out about you, Natalie. Don't women often make the complaint that men talk too much about themselves?'

'I don't know about that. I just thought you'd have been pleased to tell me where you came from.'

'Why *is* that? So we might have exchanged personal anecdotes and stories about our shared heritage?' Ludo heard a spike of irritation in his voice that he couldn't hide because he'd been inadvertently pushed into a corner. He hadn't spoken about his country of birth or what had happened to drive him away from it to anyone… not even trusted friends. If he wanted things to progress with Natalie he was probably going to have to talk about it now, whether he liked it or not. 'Sometimes a man in my position is apt to crave anonymity,' he continued. 'Whether that's about where he comes from or who he is. Besides, do you really think our only point of connection is the fact that each of us has a parent who is Greek?'

'Yesterday I might have thought so, if you'd admitted it.' Hugging her arms across her chest, Natalie frowned. 'But since then things have unfolded to connect us in a way I never could have imagined. When I walked into that room today and saw that it was you—the man I'd met on the train—I was lost for words. It was such a shock. Anyway, going back to yesterday, you helped me out by paying for my ticket and, whether you want me to or not, it matters to *me* that I pay you back.'

'If that's the case then perhaps you will start to see the sense in meeting me tonight after all?' Ludo interjected smoothly.

'I can't.'

'You mean you won't?'

'I mean I can't. Why won't you listen to what I'm saying?'

Pressing the pads of his fingertips against his brow, he lightly shook his head. 'I'm listening, Natalie, but perhaps I'm not giving you the response you're looking for because *you* are not giving me the one that *I* want.'

Her eyes flashed with irritation. 'And no doubt you always get what you want?'

She released an exasperated sigh and her lithe figure moved purposefully back towards the door. His heart thudding at the realisation that the opportunity to see her again might disappear from right under his nose unless he took action, Ludo thought fast. As an idea presented itself he mentally grabbed at it, as though it might vanish in the next instant unless he expressed it. The idea was perhaps a little preposterous, but it made a strange kind of sense. Ludo decided to take the plunge and go with it.

'Perhaps you won't be in such a hurry to leave if I tell you that I have a deal in mind that I'd like to talk to you about? A deal that would benefit your father as well as yourself,' he asserted calmly.

Riveted, she immediately pulled her hand away from the brass doorknob and turned to face him. 'What kind of a deal?'

Pacing a little, to help arrange his thoughts, Ludo took his time in answering. It had suddenly dawned on him that what he was about to propose would benefit *him* too. The concept didn't seem at all preposterous any more. In fact it might potentially be the solution he'd secretly longed for—a way out that might bring him some peace at last.

He stopped pacing to settle his gaze on the beautiful, inquisitive face in front of him. 'The deal I'm offering you is that I will increase what I paid for your father's business by half the amount again if you agree to come with me to Greece and play the role of my fiancée.'

Natalie turned as still as a statue, her stunned expression suggesting she wasn't entirely sure she'd heard him right. Her next words confirmed it. 'Would you mind repeating what you just said? I'm afraid I might have imagined it.'

'You didn't imagine it.' Willingly, he repeated his proposition.

'You really will increase the money you paid for the business if I travel to Greece with you and pretend to be your fiancée? Why would you want me to do such a bizarre thing?'

Shrugging a shoulder, Ludo sighed. 'It will perhaps not be as bizarre as you might think when I tell you my reasons,' he remarked.

'Go on, then.' Moistening her lips, she patiently waited for him to continue.

'My parents—in particular my mother—have long hoped that I will bring someone home that I am serious about. Someone who will help give them hope that they might one day have a grandchild.'

Noting the brief flash of alarm in Natalie's candid gaze, Ludo forced himself to press on regardless. He told himself she wouldn't still be standing there listening if the idea was absolutely abhorrent to her.

'Unfortunately I have not had a long-term relationship in a long time and, frankly, they are becoming despondent that I ever will. The situation has become sadly compounded by my only brother's death three years ago in a boating accident. Now I am their only son and heir. Unfortunately I have not been home since the funeral. I did not want to return until I could give them hope that the future was brighter than they had perhaps envisaged. I know it is a pretence, Natalie, but the intention behind it is a kind one. I promise you that if you can convincingly act the part of my fiancée while we are in Greece, when we return to the UK I will make sure you are richly rewarded.'

'But even if I should agree to the pretence, how hurt will your parents be when they find out that the whole thing was a lie? They must be broken-hearted as it is to have lost their son. Nothing you can do for me or give me would make up for how terrible I'd feel about deceiving them.'

'The fact that you care so much about that aspect of the deal assures me that you are the right woman to ask this favour of, Natalie. I will be forever in your debt if you do this for me.'

She looked to be thinking hard for a moment. 'And how do I explain to my father that I am going away with you to Greece for—for how long?'

'At least three to four weeks, *paidi mou*.'

The soft pink hue that tinted her cheeks at his use of the Greek endearment momentarily distracted him, because it brought a lustre to her eyes that was nothing less than magical and gave him an irresistible glimpse of how she might look if he were to try and seduce her... prettily flushed and aroused. A little buzz of pleasurable heat ricocheted through his insides. He suddenly became even more determined to have Natalie masquerade as his fiancée... Especially as—in the hope of convincing his parents—he fully intended to play the part of devoted fiancé to the hilt.

'You can tell him that I have offered you the chance to learn the ropes of good financial dealing with an expert,' he asserted with a teasing smile. 'I am sure he will see the benefits of such an opportunity. If you take it, and learn what I consider to be the essential skills for success in business, your father will need to have no worries about your financial future, because you will know exactly how to go about securing it.'

As he came to the end of this speech Natalie moved across the room to a burgundy-coloured wing-backed armchair and slowly sank down into it. When she glanced up again to meet his eyes, Ludo experienced a private moment of undeniable triumph and relief, because suddenly he knew she was giving the offer serious consideration.

CHAPTER FIVE

WAS SHE CRAZY to consider Ludo's incredible suggestion that she go with him to Greece and assume the identity of his fiancée? It would fulfil her longed-for desire to visit Greece again, but the most important aspect of the deal he was proposing was that he'd promised to increase what he had paid to her father for his business.

Half the amount again would allow her dad to keep his flat and not be forced to sell it. The fact that he could keep his home would go a long way, Natalie believed, to helping him make a new start. Not only that, it might give his health a real boost too. This deal Ludo was proposing was too important to dismiss, she realised. How could she live with herself if she didn't take it and her dad's health and self-esteem sank even lower because he'd lost all hope in making things better for himself?

But now, as she let her gaze roam over the strikingly handsome man silently observing her, with his chiselled good looks and piercing blue eyes, a nervous cartwheel flipped in the pit of her stomach. Could she really contemplate playing the part of his fiancée? Would she be strong enough to pull it off without letting her feelings get involved? Being in close proximity with Ludo in

Greece and pretending to be his fiancée would surely mean holding hands, kissing and touching, perhaps *intimately*…

Natalie didn't allow her thoughts to venture any further, because they had already induced a powerful wave of heat that made her body feel as if it were near to bursting into flames. Lifting the heavy swathe of long hair off the back of her neck in a bid to help cool her temperature, she noticed that Ludo's previously confident expression had altered. Now his glance was more contemplative, as if he wasn't entirely sure that her response would be the one he hoped for. If that were true, Natalie wondered how such an amazingly successful and attractive man could ever be plagued by doubt of any kind. It didn't make sense.

'Well?'

He was levelling his gaze upon her a little more intently, and she got the impression his patience was wearing thin.

'Are you going to give me an answer to what I have proposed? Is it to be yes or no, Natalie?'

Sucking in a breath, she pushed to her feet. 'You make it sound so simple…to just say yes or no.'

'Are you saying it's more complicated?'

'Where emotions are involved no situation is ever going to be straightforward.'

'Why should emotions be involved?' Frowning in puzzlement, Ludo dug his hand into his trouser pocket. 'Are you worrying about your father and his reaction when he learns you're going to come to Greece with me? I shouldn't imagine it will be a problem, considering I have offered to increase the amount I paid him.'

Her heartbeat accelerating, Natalie felt herself redden. 'Actually, it's not my father I was worrying about. I don't have any doubt he'll be more than pleased with your new offer for the business, and as for me going to Greece with you—he'll accept it if he knows it's what I want, too. I was just wondering how, if I should go with you, I'm going to cope with playing your fiancée when we've only just met and I hardly know you? Aren't engaged couples supposed to behave as though they're crazy about each other?'

Ludo's amused smile emphasised his even white teeth and sexy, sun-kissed tan. She caught her breath.

'Do you think you will find it difficult to pretend that you're crazy about me, *paidi mou*? Most women I know tell me I am quite a catch. Some have even called me "irresistible"… Shall we put the theory to the test?'

Before Natalie realised his intention he walked right up to her and encircled her waist. Being up close and personal with his body as he pulled her towards him, smelling the alluring musky aftershave he wore, made her knees come very close to folding even before he embraced her. A stunned gasp left her throat as he lowered his head and kissed her. As soon as his lips made contact she opened her mouth and he expertly inserted his smooth, silken tongue inside to make the kiss even more intimate.

Every thought in her head vanished except the one that registered the fierce addictive pleasure of his taste and the sexy heated brand of his skin against hers. It felt as though a torch had ignited an unforgettable flame in her blood that no other man before or after him could ever hope to compete with… In the silence of her mind a renegade response came. *Okay…I'll cope. It can't be that difficult.*

She enjoyed the kiss so much she was genuinely disappointed when Ludo eased the delightful pressure on her lips. Lifting his head to gaze down at her, he moved his hands from her waist to rest them lightly on her hips. Up close, his stunning sapphire eyes were matchlessly blue, like a sunlit Mediterranean sea in midafternoon. Even his dark blond lashes were impossibly lavish. It didn't matter if he were rich or poor, Natalie decided. The man's physical assets were simply amazing.

'Hmm…' He smiled. 'That was nice.'

She hoped he wouldn't want a more detailed assessment from her on how *she* felt about the kiss. She might just have to tell him she'd like to try another one, just to make sure she hadn't imagined the spine-tingling pleasure it had given her.

'Can I take it that the idea of playing my fiancée is not as repellent as you might have thought initially?' he teased softly.

Natalie couldn't help but be honest. 'I'm sure you know that you're far from repellent. But it still doesn't make it easy for me to pretend I'm something that I'm not. I feel very uneasy about deceiving anyone, even in a good cause. Especially your parents.'

Reaching towards her, Ludo moved some silken strands of hair away from her face and gently stroked his hand down over her cheekbone. 'Because you are naturally such a thoughtful person I know they won't have a problem accepting you as my girlfriend,' he asserted confidently.

'A girlfriend is one thing…I could cope with that. But introducing me as your fiancée is much more serious, don't you think?'

Removing his hand from her cheek, he expelled a heavy sigh. The quirk at the corner of his exquisitely carved mouth suggested some exasperation. 'Think of it as a harmless game of "Let's Pretend". Believe me when I say that you are not hurting anybody. After all, you will be getting what you want for your father, remember? That and an opportunity to visit your mother's country…something you told me you'd love to do again.'

Stepping away from him so that she might think straight, Natalie knew she had to make a decision. She sent up a silent prayer that it was the right one.

'All right, then. I'll do as you ask and go to Greece with you. But if when I'm there it becomes in any way difficult or untenable for me to keep up the charade of being your fiancée then do you agree I can go home, no questions asked?'

Somewhat reluctantly Ludo nodded his head. 'I will not be happy about it, but I will agree so long as you remember I am paying your father a great deal of money for his business. You at least owe me the courtesy of staying with me until I tell you I am satisfied.'

'Satisfied?' The hot colour started at the tips of Natalie's toes and travelled in an all-consuming heatwave right up to her scalp. The word *satisfied* had many connotations, so why did she have to focus on the sexual one first? Transfixed by Ludo's shimmering blue gaze, she didn't have to search very hard for the answer.

'Yes—satisfied that you have acted the part of my fiancée to the very best of your ability and played it as convincingly as possible.'

'I'm no actress. I can only do the best I can. All right, then.' Briefly withdrawing her gaze, she glanced down at the polished wooden floor to help regain her equilibrium, because her heart was thudding alarmingly at the daunting prospect of what she was agreeing to do. 'You'd better tell me when you're intending to travel.'

'As far as I'm concerned, the sooner the better. Could you be ready to go in a week's time?'

'That *is* soon. I'll need to arrange help at the B&B for my mum while I'm away. I hope a week will be enough time for me to organise things.'

'You have already intimated to me that you are a good organiser, Natalie. I'm sure a week will give you plenty of time. You should be ready to leave next Monday, when I intend us to travel on an early-morning flight. As we will be departing from Heathrow you should probably arrange to stay with your father the night before.'

'I'm sure that won't be a problem.'

'I'm sure it won't.' With a mocking glint in his eye, Ludo drolly echoed her comment. 'Especially when he learns that I am not as uncharitable and hard-hearted as you both first suspected.'

'I never meant to deliberately insult you by what I said. I was just upset, as any loving daughter would be, at the prospect of my dad struggling to get by after paying all his debts. It seemed so unfair that after being forced to sell his business after so many dedicated years of hard work the proceeds wouldn't even leave him enough to live on.'

Even though she had felt entirely justified, Natalie was still embarrassed at being reminded of her accusatory outburst at the meeting.

Flushing, she glanced briefly down at her watch and declared, 'I really do have to go now—but there's just one more thing I need to say before I leave.' Her teeth nibbled anxiously at her lip. 'I'm really sorry to hear about your brother. Such a dreadful loss must have been devastating for you and your family...I really feel for you all.'

A shadow seemed to move across Ludo's bright blue irises, momentarily darkening them. 'Devastating is not a big enough word,' he murmured, awkwardly dragging his fingers through his thick fair hair. 'But I appreciate your sympathy.'

'Well, I think it's time I left. Presumably you'll ring me when you have the flight times?'

'You can count on it.' Moving with her towards the door, Ludo lightly touched her arm. 'But I won't just be contacting you then. I'm going to ring you during the week—preferably in the evenings, when I'm not working. I think it's quite important that we get to know each other a little before our trip, don't you?'

'Talking to each other on the phone is hardly the best way to get to know someone, but I suppose it will have to do if we can't see each other.'

'As much as I would like to, it's impossible for me

to free up any time to see you this week, Natalie. For now, phone calls will have to suffice.'

Meeting his enigmatic gaze, she could do no more than shrug in agreement, even though in truth she was disappointed. It was a mystery to her how Ludo had got under her skin so quickly. She'd never experienced such a tangible sense of connection with a man before, and everything that she believed about herself had been turned on its head.

'Okay. I'll expect your calls later on in the week, then,' she murmured.

'Good. By the way, when we arrive in Rhodes the weather should be seasonally hot. Bring plenty of suitable clothing and sun-cream,' he suggested.

The sociable smile that accompanied his words was far warmer than she'd expected after the sorrow he'd just expressed about the loss of his brother, and Natalie was already nursing a secret hope that he might talk about his sibling more fully during their time together in Greece. There was so much about this complex, surprising man that she longed to discover.

'I will.'

She couldn't help feeling shy all of a sudden, and curled her palm round the brass doorknob, then swept out of the office into the reception area—only to be confronted by the curious glances of Ludo's colleagues.

After giving her father the good news that Ludo had increased the sum he had paid for the business, and hearing that he was much more optimistic about his future because of it, the following day Natalie returned home to Hampshire. Trepidation, hope and great doubt accompanied her.

First and foremost, she could hardly believe that she'd agreed to go to Greece with Ludo in just a week's time and endeavour to convince his parents that they were engaged. Surely they would know immediately that an unremarkable girl like her was the least likely woman he would choose as a fiancée? For a start, she was a million miles away from the perfect-looking women who adorned the arms of rich and powerful men like their son in the glossy magazines.

But the following evening when Ludo phoned, trepidation and doubt instantly fled to be replaced by a totally unexpected wild optimism and hope. All it took was hearing the sound of his rich baritone voice.

Without preamble he announced, 'It's me—Ludo.'

About to take a bath, Natalie grasped the white bathsheet she'd wrapped round her torso to make it more secure, just as if he'd suddenly appeared in the room and his arresting cobalt gaze was resting on her semi-naked form. Dropping down onto the bed, she sent up a fervent prayer that her voice wouldn't betray how strongly his call had affected her. Despite agreeing to go to Greece with him, it felt somehow surreal that the handsome businessman should call her personally.

'Hi,' she answered, the nerves she'd hoped she'd banished already alarmingly evident. 'How are you?'

'Tired and very much in need of a holiday.'

The surprisingly unguarded reply took Natalie aback and filled her with concern. 'Well, thankfully you don't have too long to wait before you get away…just a few more days.'

'Presumably I don't need to check you *are* still coming with me?'

With thudding heart, Natalie said quickly, 'No, you don't need to check. When I give my word I keep it.'

'Good. Do you have a pen and paper at hand? I want to give you some flight details.'

When she'd written them down she asked, 'Is that all?'

'No.' She heard a disconcerting smile in his voice.

'I'd like to talk to you some more. What have you been doing with yourself today?'

Sighing, Natalie smoothed her hand down over the soft towelling nap of the bathsheet. Not that it remotely mattered, but if Ludo intended talking for much longer then her bathwater would be turning unpleasantly cold.

'What have I been doing? Helping to organise some help in the B&B while I'm away, and also seeing to some rather tedious administration, I'm afraid. But thankfully it was alleviated by my mum's baking. Just after three she brought me in some homemade scones and jam with a cup of tea. No one in the world makes scones as melt-in-the-mouth and tasty as she does!'

'You have an extremely sexy voice, Natalie. I can't be the only man who's ever told you that.'

Dumbfounded, Natalie automatically shook her head, as if Ludo was indeed in the room. The only thing she could conjure up right then wasn't an answer but a mental picture of him smiling at her. The sculpted planes of his tanned cheekbones, chiselled jaw and intense sapphire-coloured eyes were more than enough to drive away any intelligible reply.

'Natalie? Are you still there?'

'Yes, I'm still here. But I ran a bath just before you rang and it must be getting cold. I'm afraid I'll have to go.'

On her feet, she carried her mobile to the slightly ajar bathroom door and anxiously bit down on her lip as she waited for his reply. The comment he'd made about her having a sexy voice had unravelled her.

'Well, then, you must go and take your bath. But know this... I don't think I'm going to be able to sleep at all tonight, since I will have in my mind the arresting image of you naked, soaking in a bath of scented bubbles. I hope when I ring again tomorrow night you'll end the conversation on a far less provocative note? Goodnight, Natalie. Sleep well.'

By the time Natalie had roused herself from the trance she'd fallen into, her bathwater and the scented bath foam she'd poured into it were too cold to contemplate immersing herself in. Resigning herself to going without, she pulled out the plug and once again got lost in thoughts of Ludo as she watched the water spiralling urgently down into the drain...

It had been a far from easy journey to his homeland for Ludo. The inner turmoil of his thoughts had made it impossible for him to relax.

The private plane he'd chartered was the epitome of the luxury he'd long come to expect when he travelled. As far as that was concerned there had been nothing to complain about. The cabin crew had been ultra-professional and attentive, and the flight had been smooth without any disconcerting turbulence. But even though the sight of Natalie at the airport, in a pretty multicoloured maxi-dress, with her shining hair, had quickened his pulse, it had still been difficult to raise his spirits.

Ludo had immensely enjoyed and indeed looked forward to the nightly telephone conversations he'd had with Natalie, but when she'd sat beside him on the plane, every now and then attempting to engage him in light conversation, he hadn't found it easy to respond in the same cheerful fashion he'd been able to adopt on the phone. In fact his mood had deteriorated more and more the closer they'd got to their destination.

The phone conversation he'd had with his mother earlier that morning had been a double-edged sword. While it had been a joy to hear her voice, and to be able to relate some good news to her, it didn't assuage the onerous weight of guilt and pain that still dogged him over his brother's death. Clearly overwhelmed and excited about the prospect of seeing Ludo again after three long years, his mother had had an emotion in her voice that had almost made it hard for him to breathe, let alone speak. There had been no words of reprimand or blame to make him feel guiltier than he was already, and somehow that had made the prospect of seeing her and his father again even more difficult.

Naturally they'd wanted to send a car to bring him and Natalie back to their spacious villa, but Ludo had carefully and respectfully declined the offer. He'd told her that he and Natalie were going to stay at his own waterside villa and take a valuable day's rest before they drove out to see them. Even though his absence had been a prolonged one, he'd need a little more time to acclimatise himself to the fact that he was home again, as well as time to take stock.

His mother had naturally been curious about Natalie. 'What's she like?' she'd asked excitedly. 'Are you happy with her, my son?'

All Ludo had told her was that Natalie was a 'charming, good-natured girl' and that he was sure they would love her. He'd deliberately squashed down the wave of remorse that had crashed through him because he was inventing a scenario that wasn't true.

For some strange, inexplicable reason, at the back of his mind the tentative hope had surfaced that some good might come of being with Natalie despite his deception. He hadn't just enjoyed their nightly phone conversations, he had started to *rely* on them. She'd always been so reassuring, and if he'd had a bad day his spirits had been buoyed by the idea of talking to her. He'd never experienced such a strong connection to a woman before. And the memory of the sexy, ardent kiss that he'd shared with her back in his office a week ago had definitely got him believing that having her with him in Greece might help alleviate some of the stress that would inevitably come his way.

But he also knew it would take more than one kiss or a reassuring conversation to ease the grief and anxiety he was feeling about returning home again.

Finally, just before they'd reached the cosmopolitan

Greek island they were heading for, Natalie had shaken him out of his morose mood with an unexpected comment.

'As you know, I'm not undertaking this trip purely because I'm in love with the idea of going to Greece, or because I need a holiday. I'm doing it because you offered me a deal that was impossible to refuse. While I'm not exactly looking forward to playing your fiancée, I respect the fact that you paid my father a much more realistic price for his business than you initially offered. And because of that I fully intend to honour my part of the bargain. However, it's a little off-putting that you don't seem to want to talk to me. If it's because you're having second thoughts about bringing me with you, I want you to know that I'm perfectly willing to get on the next flight home just as soon as it can be arranged.'

It was as though she'd dashed a bucket full of ice water in his face. For one thing, it didn't do his ego a whole lot of good to hear her confess that she wasn't looking forward to playing his fiancée and was willing to go home if he'd changed his mind. Turning in his seat, he studied the troubled but defiant expression on the lovely face before him with a stab of remorse.

'That is most definitely *not* what I'd prefer, *paidi mou*. Forgive me for not being a more amiable companion. It is nothing to do with my not wanting to be with you. It is purely a private dilemma that has been preoccupying me.'

Folding her hands in her lap across the pretty colourful fabric of her dress, Natalie lifted her huge grey eyes to his. 'Is that dilemma to do with returning to

Greece for the first time since your brother died? The last thing I want to do is distress you by asking you to talk about it, but don't you think it would help us both if you opened up a little? I'm sure it's going to seem very strange to your parents if I haven't got a clue about what your brother was like or how you felt about him.'

Ludo stared. What she said was perfectly true. He now saw that he hadn't given his impromptu plan nearly enough consideration. As painful and uncomfortable as it might be, he had no choice but to talk to Natalie about Theo.

Linking his hands together, he felt his heart race a little as he attempted to marshal his thoughts. 'Very well, then. I will tell you something of my brother Theo. Where do I begin? He was a giant of a man—our very own Rhodes Colossus... Not just in build—he was six foot four—but in character and heart too. Ever since he went to medical school to train as a doctor he knew he wanted to specialise in taking care of children.' He allowed himself a briefly strained smile. 'So that's what he did. He became a paediatrician. At the clinics he attended, or on the wards, the kids just loved him. More than that, when he told them he would make them better they totally believed him...as did their parents. More often than not he was able to keep that heartfelt promise. Pretty soon his services were in demand not just in Greece but all over Europe.'

Natalie's answering smile was unreserved and encouraging. 'It sounds as though he was quite a man. You and your parents must have been so proud of him.'

'Everyone was. He might have been my brother, but it was a privilege to know him, let alone be related to him.'

'Was he married? Did he have children of his own?'

The flush of pink that Ludo realised was a given whenever she was remotely embarrassed or self-conscious was very much in evidence again.

'No.' He hefted a sigh. 'He used to tell us all he was married to his work. He may not have been a father biologically, but he was father to many children when they were in his care.'

'I wish I'd been able to meet him.'

'If you had, you would never have given me a second glance.' The painfully wry comment was expressed before Ludo had a chance to check it.

Natalie's perfectly arched brows lifted in bewilderment. 'Why would you say that? You must know you have many appealing qualities—and I'm not referring to your wealth.'

'My brother was admired for his kind and unselfish nature as well as his desire to help heal children afflicted by illness or disability. Compared to him, my own achievements are a lot less worthy and nowhere near in the same league.'

'I can't believe you mean that. Not everyone has the skill of creating wealth like you do, Ludo—wealth that no doubt helps create jobs and opportunity—and I'm sure a lot of people wish they had. I don't doubt your family is as proud of you as of the son they sadly lost.'

'My parents will tell you they are, but my brother was a tough act to follow. He was a son in a million… irreplaceable.'

Natalie fell silent. The sadness in her eyes took Ludo aback. He regretted being so candid with her. He had never craved anyone's sympathy and never would, yet her unstinting kindness undid him.

Quickly searching for a new topic to divert her, he said, 'I should have asked you this before, but how did your parents take the news you were coming on this trip with me?'

He was disturbed by the idea that she might have put herself in an awkward position with her family. He didn't want them to give her a hard time over it. No doubt it would taint the experience for her if they did. Where he came from family were the number one priority, and he completely understood Natalie's devotion to her own. Clearly she didn't want to worry or shame them by taking off with a man they didn't even know. Even her father had only met him that one time in his office, and the occasion would hardly have let him warm to Ludo in any way.

As he silently observed her, Ludo felt his heartbeat quicken at the increasing evidence of her thoughtful and caring nature. It didn't hurt that she was rather beautiful too… To his surprise, the dour mood that had plagued him since the start of the trip lightened.

'My dad was very worried at first,' Natalie confessed. 'When I told him you'd substantially increased what you paid for the business he feared you'd only done it to try and blackmail me into becoming your lover.'

Her porcelain cheeks suddenly acquired the most radiant shade of pink Ludo had ever seen. But, surprisingly, he found he wasn't offended by the idea that her father had feared he was blackmailing his daughter, because he understood the older man's natural concern. It would surely take a hard-hearted father *not* to be concerned. Ludo was pleased that Natalie had frankly admitted it, because it gave him the opportunity to set her straight.

'I have been known to be ruthless in my bid to seal a deal, but I am no blackmailer, Natalie. Besides, does your father really think I'd need to resort to that in order to make you my lover?' Gently touching her lips with his fingertips, he was intrigued to know her response. 'I wouldn't, would I, Natalie?'

CHAPTER SIX

HER EYES WIDENED to incandescent twin full moons.

'Of course you wouldn't. I'm quite capable of making up my own mind about whether I take a man as a lover or not, without being coerced by the promise of money or—or whatever.'

Frowning and pursing her lips, she let her long hair slip silkily round her face, as though to shield her from closer scrutiny, and it made Ludo want to brush it back for her with his fingers. He would have done exactly that had she not started talking again.

'I told him I thought that despite your wealth and position you were most likely a decent man. I told him you'd suggested that if I spent some time with you in Greece I could benefit from learning important business skills that would help me in the future.'

'And you didn't mention that I'd asked you to assume the role of my fiancée?'

Hectic colour once again suffused her features. 'No…I thought it best not to mention that part.'

'I'm not sure whether I should take your declaration about me as being "most likely" a "decent man" as a compliment or not. The way you said it leaves me with the feeling that perhaps you doubt it.'

'I don't.'

In her haste to reassure him Natalie automatically laid her hand over his. Never before had the simple touch of a woman's hand inflamed Ludo to the point of wanting to haul her onto his lap and make love to her there and then, but that was what he felt at the sensation of her cool soft skin against his and the alluring drift of her pretty perfume.

'Even though you said you didn't want me to pay you back,' she continued, 'I haven't forgotten your generosity in paying for my train fare. Not many people would have been so quick to help out a complete stranger, and that absolutely illustrates how decent you are.'

The tension in his shoulders started to ease. He wouldn't normally care what a woman thought of his character if he was contemplating taking her to bed, but with Natalie he found he definitely craved her good opinion. The nightly phone calls they'd shared had played a big part in changing his attitude, especially when she'd talked about being concerned for family and friends, even the guests who stayed at the bed and breakfast. Her store of kindness knew no limits, it seemed.

'I confess to being reassured. What about your mother? What did she think of you going to Greece with me?' he asked interestedly. 'Did you tell her who I was, *glykia mou*?'

'Yes, I did.'

'And what did she say?'

To Ludo's great disappointment, she withdrew the

slim hand that still lay over his and lightly shrugged a shoulder.

'She told me to be careful…then she told me to tell you that she was very sorry to hear about your brother. She'd heard of him, you see. She told me about his reputation for being an incredible paediatrician and that the Greek community held him in the highest regard.'

Learning that Natalie's mother was Greek had been one thing. But discovering that she'd heard of his brother as well as of his shocking demise was deeply unsettling. He was also disturbed that she'd advised her beautiful daughter to 'be careful'. She could only mean one thing. Presumably, in her eyes, Ludo wasn't held in the same high regard as his brother had been. *No change there, then.* His lighter mood evaporated like ice beneath a burning sun.

'Hopefully that will reassure her that you are in good hands,' he commented dryly, 'even though it sounds like she mistrusts me. Why else would she warn you to be careful?'

'Every mother who cares about her grown-up daughter worries about who they're associating with… especially when it comes to men.'

'Well, my beautiful Natalie, I will do my best to allay her fears and send you home completely intact.'

Smiling ruefully, he signalled to the male flight attendant standing nearby and without hesitation ordered a glass of Remy Martin brandy.

On their arrival at his stunning waterside villa, Ludo's housekeeper Allena and her husband Christos came out to greet them. As he found himself embraced by two of the warmest hugs he'd had in a very long time Ludo was almost overcome by the couple's genuine pleasure at seeing him again. It made him realise just how much he'd missed their familiar faces and unreserved regard.

They were a little more politely restrained when he introduced them to Natalie, but their smiles couldn't hide their pleasure and curiosity. *He didn't doubt they'd heard on the grapevine that he was bringing his fiancée home.* As a wave of guilt descended yet again, he filed it away irritably and refused to think about it. Wasn't it enough that he'd fulfilled his parents' wishes and come home?

After Allena had told him that she'd prepared something special for their dinner that night, and that there were cool drinks waiting for them out on the terrace, Christos lifted their luggage from the car and he and his wife transported it into the villa to dispatch it to their rooms. Relieved that he could have Natalie to himself for a while, in the privacy of his own home, Ludo guided her through the open-plan living room out onto the large terrace to take in the view. He couldn't deny the sense of pride it gave him to know that she would adore it.

The shimmering azure sea glinting in the midafternoon sun just a few feet from the door was like a sheet of sparkling glass it was so still and perfect. And the warm scented breeze that blew in to caress her skin was infused with the most heavenly scent of bougainvillaea. With delight Natalie saw that the radiant red and pink flowers were generously draped over every dazzling white wall in sight. It was hard to believe she hadn't wandered into a dream. For a long time she had yearned to come back to Greece, and to find herself here in this breathtaking idyll with a man as handsome and charismatic as Ludo Petrakis made the experience seem even more like the most incredible fantasy.

'What a gorgeous view! It's just wonderful! It's even more stunning than I'd hoped it would be,' she breathed, letting her hands rest on the sun-warmed railing of the stone-pillared balustrade.

Her companion smiled fleetingly. 'Many people call it the Jewel of the Aegean.'

'It must be,' Natalie concurred.

Ludo shook his head. 'Personally, I think that title should go to *my* island.'

'What do you mean, *your* island?' She wasn't sure why, but underneath her ribs Natalie's heart bumped a little faster. It was already racing due to Ludo's enigmatic smile. Her only regret was that she wished his smiles weren't quite so rare…

'It is called Margaritari, which is the Greek word for pearl.'

'That's beautiful. And this island? It's somewhere that you're particularly fond of?'

His chiselled profile was facing out to sea as she asked him this, and a sudden breeze lifted some dark golden strands from his hair and blew them across his forehead. As Natalie stared, mesmerised, a muscle flinched in the side of his carved cheekbone and he went very still.

'I was so enamoured of it that I bought it. Sadly, I

am not so enamoured of it any more, since my brother died there in the boating accident.'

As she reeled from the shocking admission Ludo left her side to make his way to a cane chair positioned next to a slatted wooden table and sat down.

'I hardly know what to say.' Immediately she moved to the other side of the table, so that she could see his expression. 'What a devastating blow for the accident to have happened on the waters of your own island.'

It was almost unbearable to think of Ludo being consumed not only by grief but also by guilt. Did he blame himself for the accident? Was that why he sometimes looked so troubled and didn't believe he was as well regarded as his brother Theo had been?

'It was…it *is*.' He didn't bother to try and disguise the painful emotion that gripped him. It was written all over his face. 'I had often urged him to take a holiday and make free with the island for as long as he wanted. It is so private there that only people I personally invite are allowed to stay. It is a magical place, and I'd hoped it would work its magic on him and help him relax. He rarely took time off from his work and my parents often expressed their concern that he looked so tired.'

Restless again, Ludo shot to his feet and strode round the table. He stopped directly in front of Natalie, and the look in his diamond-chipped blue eyes was so full of torment it made her catch her breath.

'He finally took up the offer and went to stay there. One day he took a boat out and it capsized. It was hard to understand how it had happened… Theo was a good sailor. But I found out afterwards that there were strong gusts of wind that day. Apparently they must have caught the mast and turned the boat over before he could do anything about it. He was a good swimmer, but the coroner told us that if he had been particularly fatigued his reactions would have been slow, and that's why he had been dragged under the boat and drowned.'

'Ludo, I'm so sorry…really I am.'

'A thing like that…a loss so grievous…the pain of it never goes away.'

It was a purely humanitarian instinct to offer comfort that made Natalie bridge the short distance between them and embrace him. At first she sensed his body turn rigid as the trunk of an oak, immovable, with no give or softness in it whatsoever. Her stomach sank to her boots as she thought she'd done the wrong thing. But before she could retreat self-consciously Ludo captured her shoulders and crushed her lips beneath his in a searing, passionate kiss that stole her breath and rendered her limbs weak as a new-born babe's.

The leap of unexpected raw desire that shot through her in response was like a lightning bolt appearing out of a cloudless blue summer sky. She emitted a hungry groan that she could scarce believe was her. It was coupled with a delicious languorous ache that suddenly stole over her like a fever, and Natalie couldn't help but kiss him back with equal ardour, loving the feel of his hard, honed body beneath her explorative fingers so much that she didn't at first register his palm spreading over her breast or sense that he was aroused.

Stunned that she'd let things progress quite so far, she immediately started to draw away. But Ludo held her fast, lifting his head to gaze down at her with a sensual, rueful smile that made her heart thump hard.

'Where do you think you are going?'

The commanding tenor of his captivating voice made it impossible for her to move.

'I shouldn't have done that.' Even though she'd intended to withdraw, his languourous sexy gaze continued to transfix her.

With his hands now resting lightly on her hips, Ludo made no concession to the comment other than to subject her to a provocative study of her eyes and lips.

'You did absolutely the right thing, *paidi mou.* Make no mistake about that. I was in a dark place and your warm, very welcome embrace brought me out into the light.'

'Then I don't regret it.' Proffering a tentative smile, Natalie found she could neither move nor look away, and didn't wish that she could.

'That pleases me very much.' His hand reached out to capture a long strand of her glossy brown hair and he wound it round and round his fingers, as though mesmerised by the treasure he'd found.

If his housekeeper hadn't appeared on the patio just then Natalie wondered how long he would have kept her there, just playing with her hair and staring at her as if he'd like to do so much more...

'Excuse me, Mr Petrakis.' Allena's charming faltering English was no doubt in deference to his guest. 'Your rooms are ready.'

'*Efharisto,* Allena,' Ludo replied, reluctantly freeing the coil of hair he'd captured and stepping round to Natalie's side.

Feeling her face grow hot at being caught out in what could have been a highly awkward situation, she turned slowly. Her lips still ached and throbbed from the passionate kisses she'd exchanged with Ludo, and the expensive musky cologne he used that smelled of pure sex clung to her skin, as though to ensure she would never forget the encounter. Just in time she remembered there was no need for any awkwardness or embarrassment as she was supposed to be Ludo's fiancée. But the inflammatory thought didn't help to cool the heat that still tumbled like an unstoppable raging river through her bloodstream...

'Come.'

Placing his hand beneath her elbow, the man at her side led her back into the pleasantly cool villa and up a flight of white marble stairs. Determinedly holding on to the fact that Allena had said 'rooms', and not 'room', Natalie tried not to feel so tense. Even though she found herself intensely attracted to Ludo, it was still overwhelming to imagine being in his bed. For one thing, her experience of such a scenario was extremely limited. In fact one might legitimately say it was non-existent. No wonder she was tense. And if that weren't enough to contend with tomorrow she would be introduced to his parents as his intended bride-to-be! What if they saw immediately that she was merely putting on an act and she was no such thing?

'This room is for you.'

Gesturing that she should enter the light and spacious

room ahead of him, Ludo was quiet as Natalie endeavoured to take in her luxurious surroundings. Her heart
raced when her gaze fell on the imposing carved bed
in front of her. With its sash curtaining of sumptuous
gold silk and matching counterpane scattered with an
array of scarlet and gold-braided cushions, it was a bed
fit for a princess. More than that, Natalie thought, it was
a bed created for the perfect *seduction*…

Realising that Ludo was intimately observing her reaction, she didn't let her gaze linger a moment longer
than necessary on the imposing bed. Frowning, she ex-
amined the art on the walls instead. It didn't help matters when she saw that the framed scenes depicted some
of the most sensually charged stories in Greek mythol-
ogy. There was an elegant print of *The Awakening of
Adonis* by John Waterhouse, and two skilfully executed
oil paintings of the beautiful Aphrodite and Andromeda. Andromeda was depicted in the part of the legend
where she was chained to the rocks before Perseus came
to rescue her from the sea monster.

Studying the pictures of the two bare-breasted
women, Natalie felt the blood slow and thicken in her
veins as though it were treacle. Ever since she'd first laid
eyes on Ludo she seemed to have developed a height-
ened awareness of her womanhood—of needs that had
lain dormant for too long without true opportunity for
release. It was extremely disconcerting that they should
come to the fore now.

She turned away and a far less provocative scene met
her gaze, utterly stilling the anxious thoughts domi-
nating her mind just then. Emitting a heartfelt sigh of

pure pleasure, she stared transfixed at the awe-inspiring vista presented before her. The generously proportioned French windows stood open to reveal the most breathtaking view of the sparkling, still aquamarine sea. An exquisite breeze imbued with the arresting tones of bougainvillaea and pine in drifted intoxicatingly just at that very moment. Overwhelmed at her good fortune in being able to experience such beautiful natural delights, Natalie turned round to share her joy with her host.

'I'm almost speechless. This is one of the most incredible views I've ever seen. I feel so lucky.' She smiled, then added quickly, 'To be here, I mean.' Her smile started to slide off of her face when she saw the knowing look in Ludo's arresting blue eyes.

'Because you are here with me or because you have fallen in love with my country?' he teased.

'I've always been in love with Greece,' she murmured, crossing her arms over the soft linen bodice of her dress. 'This is my mother's country too, remember?'

'I did not forget, my angel. Did you think I had?'

He had gradually been moving towards her as he spoke, and now he stood in front of her with a scorching glance hot enough to melt her innermost core. Nervously, Natalie smoothed a less than steady hand down the front of her dress. 'You said—you told me that this was my room? I have to ask…do you intend to share it?'

'No, Natalie, I do not.' His flawless blue eyes glinted enigmatically. 'The only room you will share with me—and then only if you invite yourself—is *mine*. It is right next door to this one and the door will always be open during the night, should you feel inclined to visit me, *glykia mou.*'

It wasn't what she had expected him to say at all. For a long moment, even though her mind teemed with all the possible reasons she could think of as to why he didn't simply announce he was expecting her to act like his fiancée from day one and sleep with him—especially after their explosive kiss downstairs—Ludo's matter-of-fact answer perturbed her.

'That's fine,' she answered tetchily, immediately on the defensive. 'As long as you don't take it for granted that I *will* visit you.' Two hot flags of searing heat scorched her cheeks. 'We are only *pretending* to be engaged after all.'

Chuckling softly, Ludo lightly pushed back the slightly waving strand of hair that glanced against her cheekbone, and the movement reacquainted her with the tantalising drift of his provocative cologne.

'What a charming young woman you are, *glykia mou.* Yet, charming as you are, I hasten to remind you that we made a bargain, did we not?'

Lifting her chin, Natalie scowled, even as her heart thundered at her own daring. 'Yes, we did. But as far as I can recall our bargain didn't involve casual sex. We only agreed that I would come to Greece with you and *pretend* to be your fiancée. There was nothing said about our having intimate relations.'

'Are you saying that you are not attracted to me?'

'Clearly, after the kiss we shared downstairs, that would be a lie. But just because I find you attractive it doesn't mean I'm going to sleep with you at the drop of a hat!'

'No...?'

Even as he sardonically uttered the word Ludo overpowered her with an ardent embrace and once again captured her lips. As her mouth opened to receive the hot invasion of his tongue and his arms possessively encircled her narrow waist Natalie couldn't help whimpering with pleasure. Immediately his action acquainted her with the intoxicating heat radiating through his linen shirt, as well as the steely hardness of his strong, hard-muscled body. If he continued to drug her into submission with his arousing kisses, much as she secretly revelled in the seductive attention, she realised she wouldn't have a prayer of denying him that nocturnal visit—and the implications of such an action *terrified* her.

Dragging her lips determinedly away, she tried to shape what she hoped was a blasé smile. 'Do you think I might have some time to myself to unpack? Perhaps when I'm done I could join you for that cool drink your housekeeper said was out on the terrace?'

'You certainly know how to drive a hard bargain, angel. Was that your intention? To drive me crazy with desire so that I will give you anything you ask for?'

'You make it sound like I have some kind of plan. I definitely don't. The only reason I'm here at all is because you agreed to pay my father a fairer price for his business. You kept your end of the bargain before we left England and now I'm keeping mine. Other than that

I have no expectations…except perhaps to enjoy a holiday. It's been a long time since I've had a proper break.'

The stunning Adonis in front of her threw up his hands in frustration. 'Then go and unpack your things and meet me out on the terrace as soon as you can. Just so that you know—my own intention is to monopolise every moment of your time while you are here, Natalie…so much so that when the time comes for you to leave the very notion of parting from me and my country will break your heart!'

Striding to the door, he didn't spare her a single glance before angrily departing. Staring after him, Natalie moved over to the sumptuous silk-covered bed and sank down onto it, clutching her hands over her chest in bewilderment and shock.

He was not a man to be easily subdued when frustrated. When a long cold shower didn't help temper his thwarted desire, Ludo strode out onto the private balcony adjacent to his bedroom in an attempt to lose himself in the breathtaking Mediterranean view that for the past three years he had denied himself. Vying with the tantalising images of Natalie he had in his mind, memories of his childhood and youth inevitably came flooding back.

Inhaling a deep breath, he endeavoured to get a better grip on his emotions. He had just started to relax a little when on the horizon glinting in the sunshine he glimpsed a small white sailing vessel. It was about the same size and proportion of the boat that Ludo's brother had used whilst staying on Margaritari. *Why didn't I*

insist on providing him with a bigger and sturdier ves-
sel? If I had it would have had a much better chance of
staying afloat in those gusting winds than the one Theo
used...the one Theo drowned beneath...

But even as his heart pounded with renewed sorrow and regret Ludo couldn't help remembering his big
brother's amused voice saying, 'You need more than one
sailor to handle a bigger boat, little brother, and I want to
be by myself on this holiday. I'm surrounded by people
every working day of my life, and often during the night
too if I'm on call. A small boat will do me just fine!'

Rubbing his chest with the heel of his hand, Ludo
freed a heartfelt sigh. Some way, somehow, he was
going to have to come to terms with what had happened to his brother properly, or the crowd of 'what ifs'
and 'if onlys' would burden him for the rest of his life.
He couldn't let that happen. If he did, then Theo's inspi-
rational and admirable example of how to live a good
and useful life would be buried along with his memory.

Once again he sought to divert his troubling thoughts
with the memory of the honeyed heat of Natalie's sexy
mouth and the feel of her slim, shapely body in his arms.
Allowing himself a brief smile of anticipation, he wondered if tonight would be the night when she paid that
visit to his room. The hope that she would made him realise that it had been at least an hour since he'd left her
to her own devices—ostensibly to unpack and maybe
to take a reviving shower after their travels, like he had.
Surely she must be finished by now?

He'd noted that all she'd brought with her was one
small suitcase and a tote. Women in Ludo's experience

usually brought far more than that when going on holiday with him—but then he already intuitively knew that Natalie was unlike most of the women he was acquainted with. She was neither self-centred nor vain, and if he was right she wasn't trying to impress anybody either.

When he knocked on her door a couple of times and she didn't appear, he immediately turned on his heel and hurried downstairs to see where she had got to.

CHAPTER SEVEN

WITH HER INSIDES churning at the prospect of facing Ludo again after he'd stormed from the room, Natalie made herself unpack and hang up her clothes. This wasn't the way she'd envisaged her stay in Greece starting out.

In the streamlined, beautifully accessorised marble bathroom she took a quick cooling shower and then, in a bid to lift her spirits, selected one of her favourite dresses to wear. It was a burnt orange halter-neck in a flatteringly soft fabric that trailed elegantly down to her feet, and she teamed it with some pretty Indian bangles and flat Roman-style sandals. With the timeless Mediterranean glinting in the sun behind her, wearing the dress helped her feel as though she really *was* on holiday…at least so long as she didn't think about Ludo being angry with her, or the myriad of potentially difficult connotations of agreeing to pose as his fiancée.

What had he meant by his declaration that by the time she came to leave the very idea would break her heart? It had sounded as though he was furious that she would dare to deny him *anything*. It had already occurred to Natalie that he was probably a man who used physical gratification as a way to soothe deep private pain. Hav-

ing been denied his chosen way of gaining some relief,
it wasn't hard to understand why he'd reacted so furiously. The death of his brother and his own self-imposed
exile from his home had to be weighing heavily on him.
But, whatever Ludo's meaning, Natalie had heard pain
and longing in his voice and that alone already had the
power to break her heart.

Turning into the cavernous arched hallway that led to
the dining room, kitchen and the herb garden so lovingly
attended by Allena and her husband, Ludo discovered
exactly where his guest had gone. She was immersed in
animated conversation with Christos, and he saw with a
start of pleasure that she was wearing the most beautiful burnt orange-coloured gown. Her long hair was arranged in a loose fashion on the top of her head, so that
a few silken tendrils drifted free to frame her face, and
the halter-necked design of the dress revealed her long
slim neck and slender shoulders. The flowing material
was the perfect foil for her stunning womanly form.

As if intuiting his presence Natalie turned, and the
rose-tinted blush that heated her cheeks rendered her
pretty as a picture. Ludo's lips shaped a deliberately
slow and appreciative smile. 'So this is where you are.
And I see that you have dressed for dinner. You look as
lovely as Aphrodite herself. Come…let me look at you.'

Catching hold of her hand, he made her pivot slowly
so that he could study every facet of the gown and her
lovely, lissom shape. Behind them, Christos discreetly
made his way out into the garden with a knowing smile.

'You remind me of a beautiful water-nymph in that

dress,' he commented, the timbre of his voice turning unwittingly husky.

'Aren't they supposed to be graceful, ephemeral creatures?' Her luminous grey eyes teasingly sparkled. 'You can't be comparing me to one of those, surely? When I was a child my dad always told me I was about as graceful as an elephant with two left feet.'

'I'd ask you if he was blind but, having met him, I know that he isn't.'

'No…I suppose he was just being realistic.'

'And you have carried the belief that you are not graceful around with you since you were a child?'

'It was just playful family banter. It doesn't mean that he didn't love me.'

As Natalie once again managed to bewitch him with her beautiful smile and sparkling eyes Ludo impetuously drew her against him, suddenly needing to hold her so he could once more experience the pleasure of having her in his arms, her exquisite feminine curves pressed up close to his body. It seemed that every time he touched her, every time he so much as *glanced* at her, a fire spread throughout his blood that wouldn't easily be extinguished. At least not until he made her his. Then and only then, when she gazed up at him with the same fever of longing and lust that he now experienced, would he attest to feeling remotely satisfied.

'He should have told you every day how beautiful, how precious you were to him,' he murmured, brushing a gentle kiss to the side of her velvet-soft cheek.

'He might never have said those exact words,' Natalie demurred, 'but I knew he felt the sentiment behind them. I'd hate you to get the wrong impression about him. Honestly, behind his bluff, confident exterior is a man who cares deeply about his loved ones.'

Happy to stay right where he was, with his hands resting lightly on the gentle flare of her slender and yet pleasingly curvaceous hips, Ludo stared hungrily back into the soft grey eyes and thoughtfully reflected on her comment.

'I seem to remember when we first met you questioned whether you were a kind and devoted daughter. In my opinion, from what I've observed so far Natalie, you most definitely *are*. But I think you take on far too much responsibility for your father. Is it your fault that he acquired the destructive habits that resulted in him being forced to sell his business?'

'Of course it isn't.'

Frowning, Natalie abruptly stepped away, and Ludo couldn't help regretting the impulse that had made him mention her father's debts. But he honestly felt aggrieved on her behalf. It was one thing being a good son or daughter, but quite another feeling responsible for every mistake a parent made. He sighed, and then, because she looked so enchanting, immediately found a smile.

'Please don't believe I am telling you how to think or feel. I am only concerned that you do not regard yourself enough. Also, it has been a lifelong habit of mine to be frank, and I know my earlier display of temper must have upset you.'

Moving nearer, he gently curled one of the long loose tendrils of hair that glanced against her cheek behind her ear. At first her answering smile was tentative and uncertain. But then, like the sun emerging from behind a rain cloud, the warm curve of her lips became quite simply exquisite.

'I'm not upset. The tensions of any journey can make a person snappy and on edge. But I'd like to be frank too, Ludo. I'm a firm believer that a worry shared is a worry halved. I know that you're still grieving for your brother, and you're worried about facing your parents after not seeing them for so long, but might it help you to talk about your concerns with me? Whatever you say, I promise I would never betray a confidence. I'd just listen and hopefully give you some support.'

'Of course you would.' His expression was sombre. 'It's probably what you do for all the waifs and strays and wounded hearts that come your way, isn't it? The bed and breakfast that you run with your mother is probably like a local, more comfortable branch of the Samaritans.' His lips twisted for a moment. 'And who wouldn't welcome a vision like you to talk to?'

He didn't mean to be cruel, but he couldn't quell the bitterness that suddenly surfaced in him. Why couldn't there have been someone like Natalie around when he'd heard the news that Theo had died? Someone he would have felt safe breaking his heart in front of? Someone who wouldn't judge him or see a chance to advance themselves in some way by their association with him?

He shook his head. 'I'm sorry, Natalie. But now is not the time for me to bare my soul. I am not saying I've completely closed the door on the possibility, but just not right now.'

She treated him to another understanding smile, and for a few captivating moments Ludo allowed himself simply to bask in it, as though it were warm rain after a cold, dry spell.

'Anyway,' she said, 'Christos was telling me about your garden—that it's full of orange and lemon trees. Can I see it?'

'It will be my pleasure to show you the garden, *glykia mou.*'

Cupping her elbow, Ludo couldn't help the glow of pride that swept through him that Natalie should be interested in the garden. The beauty and bounty of nature had always been one of his passions, right from when he was a boy, but apart from his mother, who had often talked about the healing power of it, he had rarely encountered women who felt the same way as he did.

Outside, Christos touched the tip of his straw hat in acknowledgement as Ludo and Natalie appeared. Speaking in Greek, he commented, 'You came at the right time to enjoy the oranges and lemons, Mr Petrakis. If you had left it much later the fruit would not have been at its best.'

'I know. And, by the way, thank you for all your hard work tending the gardens, Christos. I am convinced it is your magic touch that makes everything grow so abundantly.'

'It is my pleasure to be of service.'

Ludo was gratified to know that his devoted and respected employee was still happy to be working for him. When Christos and his wife retired he would make sure to provide them with a lovely home and garden so that he could continue enjoying his craft. Moving on, still cupping Natalie's elbow, Ludo guided her onto the meandering red stone path that led to the verdant green where the trees and fruit flourished so abundantly. Even before the trees came into view the air was drenched with the intoxicating scent of ripened fruit.

Breaking away from him, the woman by his side enthusiastically clapped her hands. 'This scent is incredible!' Her bright shining eyes and joyful enthusiasm were so engaging that for a moment Ludo was struck dumb.

'Walk on,' he invited smilingly, 'and you will see the fruit that is responsible.'

It was like walking into the Garden of Eden. Both the perfume and the sight of lush oranges and lemons hanging heavily from slim branches amid a bejewelled floral carpet of emerald-green was nothing less than wondrous. What added to her wonderment and pleasure was that her handsome companion seemed so much more relaxed than he had been earlier. It had given her heart when he'd told her he hadn't completely closed the door on baring his soul to her. A passing warm breeze lifted the gold lock of hair that glanced against his forehead, and in that instant he suddenly looked so carefree and young that she could imagine him in a gentler time, long before the unbearable tragedy of losing his beloved brother and separation from his homeland had etched indelible scars on his heart that likely would never be erased.

'It takes my breath away.' Shaking her head, she spontaneously held the palm of her hand over her heart.

'It makes me wonder what on earth I could have done to deserve being treated to such a sight.'

Without comment, Ludo walked over and took her by the hand. Unsure of what he was going to do, Natalie felt her heart drum hard as he led her across the grass to a fulsome lemon tree, plucked a plump yellow fruit from one of the branches, then tugged her hand towards him.

'Open your palm,' he instructed.

She obeyed, and he gave the lemon a hard squeeze so that the skin split and ripe juice spilled out into her hand like sparkling nectar, filling her nostrils with the sharp fresh scent of the sun-kissed fruit. As Ludo took his hand away Natalie moved her hand back and forth beneath her nose. 'It's glorious!' She smiled. 'It must be the freshest scent in the world.'

'If you add a teaspoon of sugar to the juice and rub your hands together I'm assured you'll have the best method of softening your skin that you could find.'

'How do you know that?'

With his sky-blue eyes squinting against the sunlight, Ludo grinned with pleasure.

'I heard about it from my mother. I used to watch her apply lemon juice and sugar to her hands after she'd washed the dishes. All I can tell you is that her hands were always soft as a child's. Don't take my word for it. When you get the chance give it a try.'

'I will.'

'Now, let's go over to the fountain and you can rinse your hands.'

At a magnificent solid-stone fountain, with its crystal-clear waters gushing from the upturned sculpted jug of a young shepherdess, Natalie rinsed her hands, bringing them up to her face to cool her sun-kissed cheeks. She knew it wasn't just the sun that had warmed them. Ludo Petrakis had cast the most mesmerising spell over her. A spell that right then she had no desire to ever be free of... 'That's better.' She smiled.

'Then I think we should go in to eat. Allena has prepared us something special, and if my guess is right it will probably be my favourite *moussaka,* followed by some *baklava.* I hope you have a sweet tooth, Natalie?'

'I do have a sweet tooth, and *baklava* happens to be a favourite of mine.'

Ludo's glance was slow and assessing, and in the ensuing momentary silence Natalie almost held her breath, wondering what he was thinking. She soon found out.

'It is very gratifying to know that you can yield to temptation, *glykia mou,*' he drawled. 'Because right now the temptation of *you* is sorely testing me.'

When he reached for her hand once again she let him clasp it without hesitation, loving the reassuring warmth of his touch and realising she could very easily become addicted to it.

Turning, Ludo led her back down the stone path and into the house...

After enjoying the superb moussaka and fresh three-bean salad that Allena had served them, also the delicious syrup-drenched baklava, they took their coffee out onto the terrace, where Ludo had first taken Natalie on their arrival. It was now almost full dusk, and the glass-like surface of the Mediterranean gleamed not with sunlight but with the bewitching, serene light of the moon.

Natalie leaned back in her rattan chair and sighed contentedly. About to share her thoughts on the beautiful scene with her companion, she saw that his eyelids were closed, and didn't know if he'd fallen into a light doze or was simply lost in thought. The journey on the plane had certainly been fraught with tension for him, knowing he was going back home for the first time since his brother's funeral. For now, she decided to keep her thoughts to herself so as not to disturb him.

It was certainly no hardship to relax with all the breathtaking beauty on display, and Natalie couldn't help but include Ludo in that description. More and more she was starting to believe that he was right. It *would* break her heart to leave this place…to leave *him*. The thought made her sit up with a jolt. The impulse she'd followed in accepting his deal to come with him was dangerously beginning to backfire on her. And tomorrow he was going to introduce her to his parents as his *fiancée*. As much as she was enamoured of this wonderful country, and longed to have the time to explore some of it, Natalie wondered if she really could go through with the pretence Ludo had suggested after all.

The sudden unexpected movement of his hand over a hard-muscled thigh in his cream-coloured chinos alerted her to the fact that he wasn't dozing at all, but just sitting quietly.

Reaching forward to collect her cup of coffee from the table, she ventured, 'Ludo? Are you all right?'

'Of course I'm all right. Why do you ask?'

'I was just concerned about how you were feeling. Ever since I told you that my mum had heard about what happened to your brother I've had the sense you've been retreating little by little. You hardly talked at all on the journey here. I didn't mean to upset you by telling you what she said.'

Lifting his hand to his forehead, Ludo rubbed a little, his blue eyes glinting warily as a cat's when confronted by some potential sudden danger.

'I sometimes think that Greek people round the world have an uncanny sense of knowing what's going on with each other even if they've never met. I shouldn't have been surprised that your mother had heard of the tragedy, but I was. If I seem to have shut down a little it's because any reference to my brother inevitably brings back great sadness and regret for me. I am also going to have to face my parents tomorrow and explain to them why I ran away after the funeral.'

Natalie swallowed hard. 'Ran away?'

'Yes. I packed my bags and left straight after the funeral without giving them any real explanation. I couldn't deal with their grief. It cut me like a knife to see them so heartbroken…not knowing what to do anymore. They had always been just like my brother Theo—steady and dependable. As if nothing, not even an earthquake, could shake their unified solidity.' He shook his head, agitatedly combing his fingers through his golden sun-streaked hair. 'And instead of supporting them through that terrible time and providing solace I chose to escape. I wanted to try and blot out the past and all that had happened by losing myself in my work and trying my damndest not to think about it.'

'And did that help?'

'Of course it didn't help!' Furious with himself, with Natalie, and perhaps with the whole world too, Ludo shot up from his chair, breathing hard. 'I discovered you can run away as far as you like—even to the remotest place on the planet—but you can't leave your sorrow and grief behind. Wherever you go, the pain travels with you. All running away did for me was add to my already unbearable sense of guilt and inadequacy. The realisation that as a son I had totally failed my parents— the people I love the most. They devoted their lives to raising me and Theo and look how I repaid them. It's unforgivable.'

The anguish in his voice immediately made Natalie get to her feet. 'You didn't do it deliberately, Ludo. It wasn't planned. You were hurting too, remember? It was a totally understandable reaction.'

Dropping his hands to his lean straight hips, he trapped her gaze with the sheer desolation in his eyes. 'The only way I can make it up to them is by introducing you as my fiancée, Natalie. That's why you have to do this for me. It is not enough that I return home by myself.'

'Why?' She stepped round the table to face him. 'Why isn't it enough? You're their beloved son, Ludo. A son any parents would be proud of. And people forgive those they love. Even when they've done the so-called "unforgivable".'

'Do they indeed?' His burning blue eyes gleamed

cynically. 'I wonder how you have become such an optimist. It is my experience that forgiving someone who has hurt you, and hurt you badly, is the hardest thing of all.'

'But if you see that you only hurt yourself more by not forgiving them, then maybe it's not so hard. For instance, when my dad walked out on my mum and me, I felt so heartbroken and betrayed that I thought I'd never trust him again. How could he do such a thing to us? I thought he was a liar and a cheat and deserved never to be happy again! For a long time I didn't even want to see him. But through it all my mum wouldn't hear one bad word said about him and she urged me to forgive him. Trust me, it wasn't easy… But it had to be done if I was ever to have any peace, because it was killing me holding all that blame and hurt in my heart. Then, when he had his heart attack, the decision to forgive him for everything was easy. I'm so glad I realised it, because now our relationship is closer than ever.'

Her heart was galloping as she came to the end of her impassioned speech—a speech that had asserted feelings she hadn't expressed to anyone before. Not even her mum.

Combing her fingers shakily through her hair, Natalie was appalled at herself. 'I'm sorry' she murmured, 'We were talking about your parents. I only wanted to illustrate that I believe if you really love someone that love never dies. I don't doubt for one second that your parents have already forgiven you, Ludo. My mother once told me that the love for your child surpasses any other and lives on even when a parent dies.'

Now her face was burning. The man in front of her had neither moved nor tried to interrupt her. Instead, the long, considered glance he was giving her suggested he was thinking hard, hopefully finding some solace in her assertion that a parent's love never died, no matter what their offspring had done. Natalie could only pray that it was true.

Beneath the white linen shirt he was wearing Ludo's broad athletic shoulders lifted in an enigmatic shrug that revealed very little about what he felt, and her anxiety skyrocketed—she had blundered in where maybe she shouldn't have.

'Whether my parents forgive me or not, we will find out tomorrow. But right now I intend to go for a very long walk so I can reflect on our reunion.'

'Would you like me to go with you?'

One corner of his mouth lifted slightly towards a high bronzed cheekbone. 'No. This is one walk that I must take on my own. If you want some entertainment ask Allena to show you what we have available. And if you think of anything else you need, just ask her. If you feel that you want an early night, go ahead. Don't trouble to wait up for me. We can talk again in the morning over breakfast. *Kalinihta,* Natalie. Sleep well.'

Stepping closer, Ludo almost absentmindedly brushed her cheek with his warm lips, and as he turned and walked away the warmth from his body stirred the air, mingling with the scent of bougainvillaea draped heavily over the terrace walls, as if the flowers too registered his leaving and couldn't help but be saddened by it.

CHAPTER EIGHT

HE LIKED THE night. Even more, he liked the night air of his country. No matter where a person went on the island, they breathed in air that was drenched with an eclectic variety of sensual aromas. Some of the most pervading scents were of olives and pine, bougainvillaea and jasmine, crusty bread baked in traditional fire ovens. And wherever people ate the delicious aroma of roasted meats and the freshest fish imaginable would tempt even the most jaded of appetites. But more than the tempting food and scents that lured tourists to the country time and time again Ludo loved the sight and sound of the Mediterranean and the Aegean best of all. It had always calmed and centred him, no matter what worry might be plaguing him at the time.

But the day he'd heard that Theo had drowned in the waters off Margaritari was the day that Ludo had come to *despise* the sea. How could he ever take pleasure in it again after it had so cruelly taken his brother from him?

Walking along the near deserted beach, he stopped to gaze up at the bewitching crescent moon that hung in the inky dome above him.

'Make a wish on the crescent moon,' his mother had

often told him and his brother when they were boys. 'If you do, it is bound to come true, my children.'

Well, Ludo had wished to be as rich as Croesus. No doubt Theo had made a much more humanitarian plea to be of service to those less fortunate than himself. Even as a young boy he had exhibited uncommon kindness and patience. But, no matter how wealthy or powerful he became, Ludo knew he would instantly give up every single euro he had if he could have his brother back.

Once again, a familiar arrow of grief pierced him as though he were on fire and, rubbing his chest in a bid to try and ease the pain, he made himself walk farther on down the beach. One or two tourists greeted him, and after reluctantly acknowledging them he quickly moved on. He wasn't in the mood to be sociable tonight.

Having removed his canvas shoes as soon as he'd stepped onto the sand, and despite the sorrow and regret that weighed him down, he briefly luxuriated in the sensation of sun-baked golden grains on the soles of his feet. The thought came to him that he should have brought Natalie. Why had he turned down her offer to accompany him? He should know by now that her presence soothed him. Soothed him and *aroused* him.

He suddenly felt a strong urge to hear her voice, to listen to the encouraging advice that seemed to come to her so naturally. What if he let down his guard and admitted he no longer wanted to endure the fears and concerns that plagued him on his own? What if he asked Natalie to *share* them? Would she be willing to do that for him?

But even as he mulled the idea over in his head Ludo

remembered how she had urged him to believe that his parents had already forgiven him for his negligence. It had dangerously raised hopes that would be cruelly dashed if they had not. Then where would he be? His so-called success meant nothing if he didn't have their unconditional love and respect.

His thoughts returned to Natalie. Would she have taken up his suggestion and had an early night? During their meal that evening she'd shielded a yawn from him more than once. She was probably looking forward to a good night's sleep—while he undoubtedly faced another torturous night wrestling with his fears about how tomorrow would go.

Damn it all to hell! Why couldn't he have engineered a simpler existence than the one he'd chosen? Instead of obsessively working himself into the ground and trying to accumulate even more wealth, what he wouldn't give right now to be wooing the love of his life—as his father had done when he'd met his mother—to be anticipating building a home and family together and perhaps living a good part of the year on Margaritari as he'd once dreamed he would? It hit him how tired he'd grown of the endless travelling that filled most of his year. What he really wanted to do was to spend some proper time with family and friends, to immerse himself again in the simple but solid values that shone like a beacon of goodness and common sense in a world that frequently moved too fast, where people restlessly went from one meaningless pleasure to the next in search of that most elusive goal of all…*happiness.*

The truth was that, for Ludo, the dog-eat-dog business world that he'd so eagerly embraced had all but lost its appeal since Theo died. He might have sought refuge in it when he'd exiled himself from his parents, but the exercise had failed miserably. All it had shown him was how emotionally barren his life had become. He was just kidding himself that he wanted to keep on travelling down the same soulless path. In truth, Ludo had missed his home and country much more than he'd realised.

Unbidden, a mental vision stole into his mind of Natalie holding out her hand beneath the lemon tree, so that Ludo might demonstrate the ripeness of the fruit. There was a strangely alluring innocence about her that grew more and more compelling every time he saw her. But it was playing merry havoc with his libido. Just thinking about her graceful slender figure, her river of shining hair and big grey eyes, made him feel near *desperate* to take her between his sheets and passionately seduce her.

Would she ever feel inclined, or indeed brave enough, to invite herself into his room one of these nights, as he'd suggested? Ludo didn't know why, but despite their almost instantaneous connection he'd intuited that he shouldn't seduce Natalie just to fulfil his own hungry desire for gratification. He should give her time to realise that her own needs were just as great as his. When she came round to the fact of her own free will, the heat between them would be nothing less than *explosive,* he was sure.

But it didn't help to dwell on the tantalising prospect. Kicking at the sand with another frustrated sigh, he found himself ambling towards the seashore.

He wasn't the only one to be won over by Natalie's charms. During dinner her genteel manners and ready smile had clearly formed a bond between her and Allena. Given the opportunity, would a similar bond ever be forged between Natalie and his own mother? Irritably reminding himself that their engagement was nothing but a bittersweet ruse, born of a desire to convince his parents to see him in a better light, Ludo emitted a furious curse. Reaching down, he picked up a small jagged rock that was half buried beneath the sand and threw it into the foaming moonlit waves lapping onto the shore.

Natalie had been so tired that she'd fallen asleep on the bed fully dressed. She'd tried hard to wait up for Ludo, but when the evening had worn on and he still hadn't shown she'd regretfully made her way upstairs to the bedroom.

After staring out at the moonlit sea from the terrace for what seemed like an eternity, thinking how tragic it was that the revered and beloved Theo had perished there beneath the waves, she'd found herself overwhelmed by a sense of sadness she hadn't been able to dispel easily. Lost in her poignant daydream, she'd experienced a moment of real panic, imagining Ludo walking alone by the seashore, with nothing but sorrow and regret accompanying him. She should have insisted that she join him, even if he'd got angry. It would have been worth the risk to make sure he was all right.

Finally, unable to fight what felt like sheer exhaustion, Natalie had crossed the room to the lavish bed, sat down to remove her sandals and before she knew it, had lain down curled up in a foetal position and fallen fast asleep.

She didn't have a clue what time it was when she woke the next morning, but the sun beaming in through the open patio doors was glorious. When she sat up and saw that she still wore the pretty orange dress she'd had on last night she shook her head in disbelief. That had never happened before. But then yesterday had been full-on, with all the travelling and its accompanying tension—that tension increasing when Ludo had chosen to go for a moonlit walk on his own last night and she hadn't seen him return.

Hurriedly stripping off the colourful dress, Natalie headed straight into the bathroom. But not before nervously wondering if Ludo thought her ungracious or rude for not waiting up for him. After all, it was hardly the behaviour of the supposedly devoted fiancée his parents were expecting to meet today, was it? The realisation of what she had pledged to do hit her again like a head-on collision. But the shock that eddied through her also acted as a spur for her to hurry up and present herself to her host. She realised she had a lot of questions to ask about their proposed visit to his family home.

A smiling Allena informed Natalie that Ludo was out on the terrace, waiting for her to join him for breakfast. Drawing in a long, deep breath, she hovered in an arched doorway that was draped with blossom, silently observing him as he lounged in a cane chair with his knees drawn up against his chest and his arms loosely wrapped round them.

His attire today consisted of a casual white linen shirt and rust-coloured chinos. His feet were bare. With the stunning vista of the sparkling ocean glinting in the sun before him, his sun-kissed golden hair and long limbs made him resemble a beautiful dancer in repose, and her heartbeat skittered nervously. She was utterly mesmerised by the breathtaking picture he made.

Turning suddenly, he took her completely by surprise with his greeting. How long had he known she was standing there?

'*Kalimera,* Natalie. I trust you slept well?' he drawled, smiling.

The stunning sapphire eyes that crinkled at the corners when he utilised his smile rendered her temporarily speechless.

Quickly gathering her wits, she replied, 'I slept like a log, thanks. In fact I was so tired last night that I fell asleep fully clothed and didn't wake up until about half an hour ago. I hope I haven't kept you waiting too long?'

'I was expecting you to arrive at any moment—so, no. You didn't keep me waiting too long. And even if you did it was worth the wait. You look very lovely in that dress.'

The simply-cut cornflower-blue dress that Natalie wore had short sleeves and a pretty sweetheart neckline, embroidered with the tiniest of white daisies, and the folds of the skirt draped softly down to her knees. She loved it because her mother had bought it for her trip to Greece, professing it to be modestly respectable but pretty enough to win her the 'right' kind of attention. There was only one man whose attention she wanted to win, Natalie privately acknowledged, and that was the real-life Adonis sitting in front of her.

'Thanks. My mum bought it for me.'

'Ahh… Now I see why you chose to wear it today. It's exactly the kind of dress that a Greek mother would buy for her young and beautiful daughter. A dress she can confidently wear to a family gathering with friends and relations. It is suitably virginal and will definitely make the right impression,' he teased. 'Now, why don't you come to the table and help yourself to some yogurt and honey for breakfast?'

Still reeling from his comment that her dress was 'suitably virginal', Natalie hurriedly pulled out a chair opposite him and sat down—anything to stop Ludo seeing that she was blushing painfully. As she scooped some yogurt into a cereal bowl from the generous ceramic dish in front of her she was in no hurry to meet his omniscient gaze.

'I waited up for you for quite some time last night,' she told him. 'What time did you get in?'

'About one or two in the morning.' He shrugged. 'Who knows? I was hardly keeping track of the time.'

'Did it help to clear your head, going for such a long walk?'

'Perhaps.' His reply was painfully non-committal.

'It's a tremendously brave thing that you're doing, Ludo—coming back home after three years and facing what happened,' she told him encouragingly. 'Your parents must be so happy at the prospect of seeing you again.'

'You are an eternal optimist, I think.'

'Maybe I am.' Natalie frowned. 'But I'd rather be-lieve in hope and resolution than be cynical.'

'You should try some honey with your yogurt. I am sure you know it is traditional.'

Suddenly his piercing blue eyes were boring into hers and she forgot what she'd been going to say.

'Here…'

Leaning towards her, he scooped up a teaspoon of the richly golden nectar. Just when Natalie expected him to stir it into her helping of yogurt he touched the spoon to her lips for her to sample it instead. Her body tightened and the tips of her breasts tingled fiercely at the sensual nature of the gesture. Obediently and self-consciously she licked the honey off the spoon. The whole time she was hotly aware that Ludo was staring at her.

'Hmm,' she responded, emitting a soft sigh. 'It's de-licious.'

Her expression was no longer self-conscious but laced with helpless invitation. The man was driving her crazy! Natalie might not be experienced in the art of seduction, but she was getting close to desperate for Ludo to seduce *her*. In turn, he gave her an amused slow smile that made her want to rip off his shirt, dis-card the pretty blue dress that he'd declared 'suitably virginal' and all but drag him across the table and insist he make love to her…

The thought made her bite her lip to prevent herself from giggling because it was so outrageous. It was also diametrically opposed to anything she'd ever contem-plated in her life before.

'You're such a goody-two-shoes when it comes to

men, Nat,' a friend had once teased her. 'Haven't you ever met a man you simply just *had* to have?'

Not until she'd set eyes on Ludo Petrakis, she hadn't…

'You looked like you were about to laugh. What was so funny?' Ludo asked, depositing the spoon he'd used for the honey on a saucer.

'A crazy thought came into my mind, that's all,' she admitted warily.

'Want to share it with me?'

'No.' Tucking her hair behind her ear, she shrugged carelessly in a bid to deflect his curiosity. 'At least not right now. Can you tell me a little bit more about your parents before I meet them? And is it possible to stop off somewhere on the way to buy your mother a gift? I'd really like to get her something. Does she like flowers?'

'Of course—but she has a large garden full of flowers. You don't have to worry about getting her a gift. Your presence as my fiancée will be gift enough, Natalie.'

Feeling suddenly deflated, she frowned. Her brow puckered. 'But I'm not your fiancée, am I? We're only pretending that I am.'

The muscle that flinched in the side of his smooth tanned cheekbone indicated his annoyance. 'I know that.'

'At any rate, it's polite to take a gift when someone invites you into their home for the first time, isn't it?'

He sighed. 'If it means that much to you, angel, then we will stop off at a place I know and purchase a nice vase that she might put her own flowers in. Will that suffice?'

Feeling marginally better, Natalie somehow found a smile. 'Thank you. It does. Will you tell me a bit about what your mother is like? I'd really like to know.'

Ludo's expression instantly relaxed, as though the topic couldn't help but fill him with pleasure.

'She is a beautiful woman and a wonderful mother and she loves to put people at ease when they visit her. What else can I tell you?' His blue eyes twinkled in amusement. 'She is an incredible cook and an accomplished seamstress—she was a dressmaker before she met my father. He utterly relies on her, you know? But he wouldn't thank me for telling you that. He is a typical "man's man" and proud of it. Now, can you do something for me before we talk further?'

'What would that be?'

Her heart jumped a mile high as her gaze fell into his dazzling blue irises. She was still aroused. It was surely an impossible challenge to hold his glance for long and not reveal her desire? With his elbows resting on the table, Ludo leaned in a little closer—so close that she could count every single long golden lash that fringed his eyelids.

'Can you try not to look so adorable when you smile?' he asked huskily. 'It makes me want to wipe the smile clean off your face with a hot, languorous kiss that would very likely lead me into removing that pretty virginal dress your mother bought you and more besides.'

Just in time Natalie suppressed a groan. 'I don't think— I mean, I think we should—we should—'

'Give it a try?'

Swallowing hard, she reached for a white paper napkin and touched it to her lips, lightly dabbing at them. 'I think we should stay on a safer subject, don't you?'

'Even if it's nearly killing me to have you look at me with those innocent grey eyes and not tell you in graphic detail what I'd like us to do together in bed?'

'That's how I make you feel?' Her voice had dropped to a shocked whisper.

'You have no idea,' he growled, then abruptly got to his feet and drove his long fingers through his hair. 'But no doubt it will keep. We have to make the journey to see my parents very soon, and I suppose we should concentrate on getting ready.'

'How long will it take us to get there?'

'About an hour.'

'Where exactly do they live?'

'About four kilometres from Lindos, but the area is quite rural in comparison to the town. Thankfully, it's also close to the beach.'

'And that's where you grew up?'

Once again Natalie registered wariness in Ludo's eyes. He was still apprehensive about seeing his parents, and probably fearing the worst about their reception of him. She wished she knew a way to help put him more at ease.

He turned away to gaze out at the sea. 'Yes…it is where my brother Theo and I grew up. We had a truly magical childhood, living there. We were so free— which should be the right of all children, in my view. Most days we ran down to the beach to play before school. Then we'd run home in anticipation of our breakfast.'

'You had breakfast? I know that many Greeks don't… apart from drinking coffee, I mean.'

'My mother believed it was important for children to start the day with some food in their bellies.' With a wryly arched brow, he turned back towards her. 'She gave us soft cheese spread on sesame-seeded *psomi* to eat.'

'I love that bread. My mum still makes it now and then, especially when we have friends to dinner.'

Joining him, Natalie was mindful of not disturbing his poignant and unexpectedly heart-warming train of thought and couldn't deny the warmth it instigated in her own heart that he would share the memory with her.

'You will have to tell my mother. She is sure to want to know all about it.' Lifting his palm, Ludo briefly pressed it to her cheek, as if he didn't trust himself to let it linger. 'I think it's time that we went. If there is anything else you wish to ask me you can ask it on the journey.'

In the next instant he'd moved swiftly away to the open patio doors, and before she could reply he disappeared inside.

CHAPTER NINE

THE TRADITIONALLY BUILT white house that was so familiar to Ludo loomed up before them minutes before the Range Rover reached the end of the rutted undulating track they'd been travelling on. Although the architecture was typical of many homes in the locale, it was unusually tall and imposing. Built on the crest of a hill, it could be seen for miles.

The unmade track was very soon replaced by a smooth driveway lined with fig trees that led directly to the house's white-stone arched terrace. Behind the dwelling the deceptively calm waters of the Aegean created the most stunning iridescent backdrop, and even though he knew the house and the view well, it still made Ludo draw breath at the beauty of it.

But he didn't contemplate the scene for very long. Parking the car, he felt his stomach churn at the prospect of his first encounter with his parents after three long years. Was it possible that they would ever forgive him for his desertion at a time when they'd most needed him…particularly his mother? If they didn't, then he would simply just have to wish them well and walk away again—even if it broke his heart.

'Ludo?'

Beside him, Natalie's soft voice halted his painful reflection, reminding him he wasn't going to have to do this on his own. He remembered thinking about the possibility of sharing his worries with her last night and the tension in the pit of his belly eased a little.

'It's going to be all right.'

She smiled, and he reached out for her small hand and squeezed it in gratitude. It struck him afresh how pretty and innocent she looked today in the simple blue dress her mother had bought her. The conservative sweetheart neckline revealed not the slightest décolletage, yet in his opinion a sexy black cocktail dress couldn't have been nearly as alluring or beguiling.

'I'm sure you are right. If anyone has the ability to convince me of that it is you, *agapiti mou*. Let's do this, shall we?' His voice was gruffer than he'd meant it to be, but the relinquishing of his guard had left him feeling curiously vulnerable.

As he stepped down from the Range Rover onto the patterned marble drive he glanced towards the entrance of the house. With his heart beating double time he saw his parents walking towards them. Wearing an elegant blue tunic over white palazzo pants, her dark blonde hair shorter than he'd seen her wear it before, his mother Eva looked as effortlessly elegant as ever, if a little thinner. She was holding on to his father's strong muscled arm.

Unusually, his father was wearing a suit, as if to instigate some formality into the proceedings and perhaps to remind his errant son that he was a long way from being forgiven and accepted…at least by *him*.

Acutely aware that emotions were probably running high in all of them, Ludo returned his gaze to his mother and saw her smile tentatively, as if unsure how he was going to receive her. That uncertain look on her beautiful face twisted his heart. Yet because his father's expression was so serious he hesitated to throw his arms round her as he longed to.

He needn't have worried. Releasing her husband's arm, Eva Petrakis stepped onto the mosaic tiles where Ludo stood and wholeheartedly embraced him. Her still slender body trembled as he hugged her back without hesitation, his senses awash in a sea of childhood memories of her unstinting love and affection for him and his brother. Oh, how he had missed her!

With her hands resting lightly but firmly on his arms, as if she was reluctant to let him go, she stood back to scan his features. In Greek, she told him how worried she'd been about him, and that every night when she went to bed she'd prayed he was safe and well and planning on coming home soon…home where he belonged.

In return, Ludo murmured his sincere apology and regret. She smiled, gently touching his face. Then she told him that she knew far more of how he felt than he'd realised. There was no need for him ever to feel sorry about his actions again. She understood and had never blamed him for them, so neither should he blame himself. As hard as it had been for her and Alekos to accept, they had now reconciled themselves to the fact that it had been Theo's time. It was their profound belief that he was home with God now…

Leaning towards him, she planted a warmly affectionate kiss on Ludo's cheek and, lowering her voice, told him that he should give his father a little more time to realise what a great gift it was for them to have him home again. 'Be patient,' she advised sagely.

Observing his father across her shoulder, Ludo saw that sorrow and time had indeed taken their toll on him. There were deep grooves in the forehead of his handsome face, and his curling dark hair was more liberally sprinkled with salt and pepper strands than it had been three years ago. But without a doubt he still emitted the same formidable energy that Theo had envied so much.

'If I live to be my father's age and still have the strength and energy to accomplish as much in one day as he can,' he'd often declared, 'then I'll know the Petrakis gene pool hasn't failed me!'

Swallowing down the lump that swelled in his throat at the bittersweet memory, Ludo moved away from his mother and determinedly went to stand in front of the man who had been responsible for raising him.

'Hello, Father,' he greeted him. 'It has been too long, yes?'

Even though he was absolutely sincere—because events and the passage of time had rendered the already considerable distance between them a veritable chasm—his words couldn't help but sound awkward and strained. Instead of embracing the older man, as he might normally have done, he held out his hand. Alekos Petrakis didn't take it. Ludo's tentative hopes for a reconciliation splintered like shattered glass.

'So you have deigned to come home at long last?' his father remarked coldly. 'I had hoped you would grow into a man to equal your brother Theo in conduct and character, but your absence these past three years has demonstrated to me that I hoped in vain. I do not recognise you, Ludovic, and it grieves me sorely that I do not.'

Ludo reeled. It felt as though he'd been punched hard. 'I am sorry you feel like that, Father. But Theo has his path and I have mine.'

The shame-filled break in his voice catapulted him back to being the small boy who'd longed to have his father regard him as highly as he did his big brother, and he couldn't help flinching in embarrassment as well as pain. The older man's admission had all but floored him. Didn't he see *any* good in him at all? Were the only people who had any kind of belief in his worth the two women who stood patiently waiting for him to join them?

'*Had,*' his father corrected him. 'You said Theo "has" his path. Your brother is no longer with us, remember?'

Ludo silently cursed the unfortunate blunder. The accusing look in his father's brown eyes cut him to the quick. Hardly able to bear it, he turned away, seeing with a jolt of surprise that his mother Eva had moved up close to Natalie and was exchanging a reassuring smile with her. Natalie held out the slim glass vase she had insisted on buying as a gift and his mother graciously accepted it. Remembering that she'd advised him to be patient with regard to his father, he determinedly quashed any further thoughts of failure and remorse and returned to the women.

'He doesn't want to know me,' he murmured, glancing ruefully at his mother, then at Natalie.

'He just needs a little more time, my son,' she answered in English. 'You both do. Time to get to know each other again.' Carefully setting down the delicate vase on a wrought-iron table behind them, Eva reached for his hand and gently squeezed it. 'Now, we have all been dreadfully remiss. You have not introduced us to your beautiful fiancée, Ludo, and I'd like you to remedy that. She has just given me the most beautiful vase as a gift and I am taken aback by her generosity.'

Without hesitation Ludo caught hold of Natalie's hand and gripped it firmly. An instantaneous bolt of electricity flashed between them and for a long moment his glance cleaved to hers. He wished they were somewhere more private, so he could show her *exactly* how she made him feel. It was a revelation that he seemed to need her so much. At the same time he knew it was important to make the proper introductions.

'Mother, this is Natalie Carr—and Natalie…this is my mother, Eva Petrakis.'

'*Kalos orises,* Natalie. Although I'm told that you are half-Greek, I will speak to you in English because my son tells me you do not speak Greek at home with your mother. It is a shame you do not speak it, but I'm sure that will change given time. I cannot tell you how long I have waited for the moment when I would welcome my soon-to-be daughter to our home, and it comes as no surprise to me to find that you are so beautiful. My son has always had the most exquisite taste.'

Natalie found herself affectionately hugged by the elegant and friendly Eva in a waft of classic Arpège perfume. She smiled because it was the same fragrance that her mother wore, and it made her feel immediately at home.

'*Yia sas.*' Using one of the few greetings in Greek she *did* know, she said hello. 'It's so nice to meet you, Mrs Petrakis. Ludo always talks about you with such affection.'

She stole a glance at the man standing silently by her side, quite aware that he'd become even more uneasy since that short conversation just now with his father. The older man seemed formidably stern to her. She would dearly love to know what had transpired between them, and guessed it wasn't good.

His mother, on the other hand, was clearly a different proposition. She seemed much more forgiving and approachable. And even though Natalie wasn't really the 'soon-to-be daughter' she'd longed for, strangely she wasn't embarrassed that it wasn't the truth. All she could think right then was that Ludo needed her help. More than that, she'd made a contract with him that she was bound to follow through on. He'd kept his part of the bargain by giving her father a better deal for his business, and now she had to act the part of his fiancée convincingly…at least until the time came for her to return to the UK.

The thought was a harsh and sobering one.

'Ludo has always been my baby.' Eva smiled, her gaze lovingly meeting her son's. 'He was always such a mischievous little boy, but I loved that he was so playful and liked to have fun. Our friends and neighbours adored him. They called him the golden-haired Petrakis angel.'

Beneath his lightly tanned chiselled features Ludo reddened a little. The realisation that his mother's tender little speech had embarrassed him made Natalie warm to him even more, because she guessed how much the fond declaration must secretly please him. After what had happened three years ago he must be all but *starving* for a demonstration of his parents' love and affection—along with their forgiveness.

'Come with me, Natalie.' Firmly grasping her hand, Eva started to walk Natalie over to the man who stood silently and a little broodingly, observing them all. 'I want to introduce you to my husband—Ludo's father—Alekos Petrakis.'

'*Yia sas.* It's a pleasure to meet you, Mr Petrakis.'

She tried hard to inject some confidence into her tone but it wasn't easy. Not when she had the distinct feeling that the man with the unflinchingly direct brown eyes was not an easy man to fool. But to Natalie's surprise he warmly captured her hand between his much larger palms and his pleased smile seemed utterly genuine.

'*Kalos orises,* Natalie. So you are the woman who is brave enough to take on my son Ludovic?'

Her heart thumped hard as she started to reply. 'You never know, Mr Petrakis—maybe Ludo is the brave one? We haven't known each other for very long. When he gets to know me a little better he might discover that I have a few unappealing traits that can't help but irritate him.'

To her surprise, Alekos threw back his leonine head and laughed heartily. But before he could make a comment, Ludo usurped him.

'I doubt that very much, my angel. You have too many traits that please me to counteract my being irritated by any less appealing ones. Plus, you are very easy on the eye…do you not agree, Father?'

Natalie hardly dared to breathe. What was clear to her was that Ludo was holding out an olive branch to his stern parent…trying to disperse some of the tension between them with light humour. She prayed his father would recognise that was what he intended. The older man gave a slight downward nod of his head to indicate yes, and the dark eyes flicked appreciatively over Natalie's face.

'Your wife-to-be is certainly bewitching.' He smiled, and Eva Petrakis' coral-painted mouth curved with a delighted smile of her own. Linking her arm with her husband's, she looked searchingly at Natalie and frowned. 'Why are you not wearing an engagement ring? Has my charming son not purchased one for you yet?'

Touching his hand to Natalie's back, Ludo let it slide downwards so that he could encircle her waist. His fingers firmed against her ribcage beneath her dress, and she couldn't deny that his warm touch helped her feel more secure.

'We were waiting until we arrived in Greece to select one.'

His dazzling blue eyes emitted a silent signal for her to agree with him.

'In fact I intend to call a jeweller friend of mine in Lindos about it tomorrow.'

'And I presume you have asked Natalie's father for

her hand in marriage?' Alekos challenged with a frown. 'You know it is the custom.'

Ludo pulled her closer into his side. Had he sensed her tremble just then? Suddenly their pretence at being engaged was presenting more problems than she'd anticipated. Out of the blue, Natalie recalled her mother's stories of her childhood in Crete. An engaged couple's parents also had to have a period of getting to know one another before their children were wed. Why hadn't she remembered that when she'd agreed with Ludo to masquerade as his fiancée? More importantly, why hadn't *he*?

'It all happened so suddenly...what we feel for each other, I mean.'

Incredibly, Ludo was gazing into her eyes as though he meant every word he was saying. Her heart galloped as hard as a racehorse out of the starting gates and her mouth turned dry as sand. It was as though she'd suddenly been plunged into some fantastical dream.

'We have barely had time to think about anything other than the fact we want to be together,' he explained. 'When we return to the UK I will be formally asking Natalie's father for her hand, just as soon as we can arrange a meeting.'

'And afterwards you must come back to us, so that we may have an engagement party for you. If Natalie's parents would like to be there—as I am sure they will—you must ring me straight away so that we can organise things, my son.' His mother's voice was both happy and eager. Her beaming glance fell on Natalie. 'I know it has all been rather sudden for you, my dear, but do you have any idea at all about a date for the wedding?'

'We were thinking that later on in the year might be better. Perhaps autumn,' Ludo interjected smoothly, robbing her of the chance to reply.

It was just as well, Natalie thought. She was far too stunned that he should be anywhere near mentioning a date when in reality they both knew that the event wasn't even going to take place. Just as soon as they were alone again they were going to have to have a very serious talk, because right now events were taking on all the urgency and speed of an ambulance crew racing hell for leather to an emergency, and she wasn't confident she could halt them.

The deceit was making her feel intensely uncomfortable...not to mention *guilty*. Yet despite her unease, Natalie felt a sense of heartfelt disappointment that she *wasn't* engaged to Ludo, wasn't going to marry him. The undeniable revelation that she was head over heels in love with him made it hard to project even the most temporary appearance of composure.

'So you are going to adhere to the traditional time for a marriage, when the olive harvest is gathered in?' Ludo's father was nodding his approval of the idea. 'I think that is a very wise choice. It will help people see that you are a man of principle, Ludovic...a man to whom family values are still important.'

He might almost have added *after all* to that statement, Natalie thought, tensing anxiously. The immediate sight of a muscle jerking in the side of Ludo's sculpted cheekbone told her he had read his father's declaration in the same way and vehemently resented it. In the next instant he confirmed it.

'So you do not believe I was a man who had principles and family values before, Father?' he ground out tersely.

Natalie's stomach plunged at the sudden potential for familial disaster.

'I speak as I find,' Alekos answered stiffly. 'If you ever indeed had both those qualities, then you clearly lost them when your brother died.'

With a furious curse Ludo spun away from Natalie to stand in front of his father. She flinched. His pain at being so cruelly judged by his own flesh and blood was agonisingly tangible.

'Why?' he demanded, glaring. 'Because you conclude I left without reason? Did you never ask yourself *why* I needed to put so much distance between us? Did you not guess how much I was hurting, too? When Theo died I would have given anything for the accident to have happened to *me,* not him! *He* was the one everyone regarded as a good man—a son to be proud of—and he was! He was amazing, and the work that he did was of benefit to hundreds...maybe thousands of families. Whereas I—'

Suddenly he was staring down at the ground, shaking his head in bewilderment and rage. 'I directed my talents to making money...a *lot* of money. It's almost like a dirty word to you, Father, isn't it? I'm not worthy enough to be thought of as good, even if I *can* help people by creating jobs. And you know what? I learned how to become rich from *you.* It takes blood, sweat and tears to make it in this world—you taught me that. Work hard and the world will be your oyster—then you can have anything you want. That was your mantra all through our childhood. But when Theo became a doctor you decided to make a distinction between what was good and what was bad. And you did it because you liked the kudos and admiration you got from your friends due to your son being a renowned doctor.'

Breathing hard, Ludo scraped his fingers through his hair. 'Well, I am what I am, and it hardly matters what you think of me now. But you should know that Theo was the best friend I could ever have wished for. He was my ally, too. I'll always remember him not just for being my brother but for the love and support he gave me throughout our time together. *He* was the wise man who told me it would only cause me more pain if I fought against your prejudice when you always made it clear that you preferred him to me. "Just be yourself," he told me. "Follow your heart wherever that may lead you. You need no one's approval…not even Father's." I only came back here to see my mother. I truly regret that I added to her suffering after Theo went, and if there is anything I can do to make it up to her it is my solemn promise that I will.'

'I never sought compensation from you, Ludo. But you have already lifted my heart and my spirits by coming back to me and bringing me a soon-to-be beloved daughter.'

Eva Petrakis pulled him into her arms and hugged him fiercely. Then she moved across to Natalie and gently touched coral-painted fingertips to her cheek. Her pretty blue eyes were moist with tears.

'Not only has my dear son returned to me, but he has brought me the daughter that I have long prayed for. One day I hope she will grant my dearest wish and present me with my first grandchild.'

The sound of birdsong, and in the distance of the waves crashing onto the seashore, faded out to be replaced by an almost dizzying white noise in Natalie's head. She didn't seem to have the ability to feel anything but shock and distress after Ludo's poignant outburst. And now, after what his mother had just said, she hardly trusted herself to string a coherent sentence together. All she knew was that the woman standing in front of her with such hope and trust in her eyes didn't deserve any more heartache or pain. But then neither did her son...

'I think we have stood out here in the midday sun for long enough.' Eva smiled. 'We should all go inside for a while, and I will see to some refreshments for us. I assume you are staying for lunch? But of *course* you are! We have so much to celebrate. This is turning out to be a very good day indeed.' Frowning at her husband, who hadn't moved so much as an inch since his son had publically berated him, she said, 'Come with me, Alekos. I think we should have a little talk before we join the children.'

As they moved towards the open patio doors that led inside the house Ludo gripped Natalie's hand hard—as though it were a lifeline in the choppiest of stormy seas. He made a point of deliberately ignoring his father's gaze completely.

CHAPTER TEN

LUDO HAD STAYED ominously quiet so far on the return journey to his villa, and Natalie knew why. Although his mother had tried hard to get the two men to make peace with each other during a delicious prolonged lunch they had both stubbornly resisted her efforts. Ludo was angry with his father for not understanding or forgiving his need to escape after his brother's funeral, and in Natalie's opinion Alekos was holding on to an old perception of his son that he either couldn't or *wouldn't* change.

At any rate, the conversation that had taken place had mostly been between herself and Eva Petrakis, and by the time it had come for the two couples to say their goodbyes father and son were barely even making eye contact.

The situation couldn't have been sadder. After Ludo's impassioned outburst, confessing his feelings, there should have been some resolution between him and his father—or at least a willingness on both their parts to forgive what had happened between them so that they could make some headway into forging a better relationship in the future.

But in spite of her compassion, and her concern for

Ludo's dilemma, Natalie found she couldn't ignore her own needs. She wanted to make it clear to him that she wasn't blindly going to go along with whatever he wanted to make his life easier just because he'd paid her father more for his business. He'd asserted he was no blackmailer, but he *did* have a reputation for ruthlessly winning deals, and she didn't want to end up feeling a fool.

As they drove on towards the villa, Natalie couldn't remain silent any longer. 'I know that the situation at your parents' was very difficult for you,' she told him, nervously clutching her hands together in her lap, 'but it wasn't easy for me either. I can see now why you brought me with you and made that deal with me. It's easier to confront a situation like you have with your father when you have someone else in your corner—someone to help act as a sort of buffer between you. But my big concern is that you're thinking of me purely as one of your business deals, and all you want is the outcome you desire without taking into account *my* feelings.'

She saw Ludo's shoulders tense immediately and his hands firmed on the steering wheel. He momentarily took his eyes off the road to consider her bleakly.

'Is that really the impression you have of me, Natalie? That I only think of you as a business deal I want to win at all costs and don't regard you as a person with needs of your own?'

The surprised and hurt tone in his voice made her anxious that she'd got his motives completely wrong. Her face coloured hotly.

'You *do* regard me, then?' Her voice dropped to a near whisper even as her eyes filled with tears. 'I mean...you do care about what I feel?'

'The fact that you have to ask tells me that you do not think I do. I think it is probably best if we finish this conversation back at the house.'

Scowling, he trained his gaze firmly back on the road, and Natalie turned hers away to stare forlornly out of the window.

It was dusk when they reached the villa. Still quiet, Ludo held the door open for her to precede him. As they entered the spacious open-plan lounge with its sea of marble flooring she was about to speak when he abruptly brushed past her and swept up the marble staircase.

'Ludo, where are you going?'

Because of their conversation in the car, Natalie's felt almost sick with fear that he was going to tell her to go home...that he no longer required her help. She made a snap decision to pursue him, seeing with surprise that he was ripping open the buttons of his linen shirt and taking it off as he went. The arresting sight of his bare, taut, tanned musculature and athletic shoulders sent her heart bumping not only in alarm but with a dizzying sense of excitement too. What on earth was he doing?

Not quick enough to reach him, she saw him get to his bedroom and stride inside without even turning to see if she followed. Taking a deep breath, she cautiously rapped her knuckles against the door. Even though it was partially open she wouldn't risk walking in unannounced.

'Ludo? I know you're probably not in the mood for talking, but you're starting to worry me. I don't want the conversation we had in the car just now to come between us and make us stop communicating. Can I come in?'

'Of course. Unless you want us to converse with each other from either side of the door.'

Smoothing a nervous hand down the front of the blue dress he had professed to like so much, Natalie pushed the door wider and walked inside. Ludo was standing in front of the large silk-canopied bed that dominated the room and seemed to be making a deliberate point of tracking every step of her cautious approach.

'Why did you take off your shirt?' It hadn't been the first thing she wanted to ask him, but she asked anyway because she was curious.

'I wanted to get rid of the taint of disapproval from my father. Unfortunately it's apt to cling and cast a shadow if I keep it on. I didn't want that.'

Even as he discarded the crumpled garment onto the bedspread he glanced at Natalie with a provocative smile. His magnificent sculpted torso was bare, and his rust-coloured chinos were riding low enough on his well-defined lean hips for her to glimpse the column of darker hair that led even lower down. She forced herself not to be so swayed by his arresting male beauty that she wouldn't be able to discuss things sensibly.

'So it's not because I made you angry by asking if you regarded our arrangement as purely a business deal you had to win?'

'It didn't make me angry, but it did upset me coupled with the fact that our reunion lunch with my parents was spoilt by my father glaring at me across the table like I was public enemy number one. It's not hard to understand why I'm on edge and would prefer to just forget about the whole thing.'

'But it won't help if you simply put what happened to the back of your mind.' Natalie sighed. 'It won't be as easy to discard as your shirt, Ludo. The memory will surface again and again if you don't try and deal with it properly. If you want to talk about it then I'm a good listener.'

'So you would still listen to my troubles even though you are suspicious of my motives?'

Her heart twisted with regret that she'd expressed that. 'I've just had to contend with you telling your parents that you're buying me an engagement ring tomorrow and there will be a wedding in the autumn, when none of that is remotely true. But now that I've met your parents and seen how much they mean to you I think I'm astute enough to know that you mean no harm by the deception. If you want to talk to me about things I really am willing to listen and try and help if I can.'

'It might not be true that we're getting married in the autumn, but I still intend to buy you an engagement ring. Our engagement will hardly be convincing if I don't. I take it even if you don't agree you will still keep your part of the deal?'

Pursing her lips at the suggestion of doubt in his tone, Natalie nodded her head. 'I will. But right now I'd like you to open up to me a little and tell me how you *really* feel about things.'

Ludo scowled. 'You think I'll feel better if I get

things off my chest? Is that what you're saying? Don't you think I've done enough of that today? You saw how my father dealt with it. It only made things even worse between us.'

'He's probably feeling just like you are right now. Instead of feeling justified that he was so stubborn, I bet he wishes he could turn back the clock and have the time over again to make things right. You're his *son*, Ludo. I'm sure he loves you very much.'

The man in front of her was still wearing a mistrustful scowl. 'I don't want to discuss this any further. What I want to do is have a drink. Preferably a *strong* one.' Feeling uncomfortably cornered, he rubbed an irritable hand round his jaw.

'And that's going to solve everything, is it?' Shaking her head in dismay, Natalie frowned. It was quite unbelievable how stubborn he could be. Clearly he must have inherited the trait from his father.

'No. It's not. But it's going to help me feel a hell of a lot better than I do right now after that debacle of a family reunion!'

He dragged the heel of his hand across his chest and his riveting sapphire eyes glistened furiously. But the anger that had appeared as suddenly as a flash flood out of a clear blue sky dispersed just as quickly, and this time his gaze transfixed her for an entirely different reason. It was smouldering with unmistakable *lust*.

'That is,' he drawled, 'unless you can think of another way of making me feel better, Natalie....'

She swore she could count every single beat of her heart as she stood there. In the past few seconds her ability to hear every sound that echoed round that stylish and spacious bedroom, right down to the waves breaking onto the shore outside, had somehow become preternaturally sharp, as had the rest of her senses.

Lifting her hair off the back of her neck to help cool her heated skin, she murmured, 'I can't. But that doesn't mean I want you to drink. Alcohol is what my father resorted to when he couldn't deal with his despair—and take it from me, it only made things worse. Is that what you want, Ludo? To feel worse than you do already? Much better to talk things out than to let your feelings fester and make you ill.'

'It must have been a great boon to your father to have a daughter like you. So wise for someone so young... and so forgiving.'

Natalie felt the heat rising in her cheeks, because she didn't know if he was being sincere or sardonic. 'When you love somebody you naturally want to do everything you can to help them when they need it.'

'I agree. But what if sometimes you need *their* help even more? Do you think that makes you a bad person?'

'Of course not.' Tucking her hair behind her ear with a less than steady hand, she realised that Ludo might have taken her well-meant reply about helping someone you love as a criticism of his own actions when he'd departed after his brother's funeral instead of staying behind to help his parents deal with their grief. She'd be mortified if he believed that. 'Ludo, I hope you don't think I was being insensitive. I was only trying to explain what motivated me to help *my* dad.'

'Is it even possible that someone like you could be insensitive? I don't think so. Come over here.'

'Why?'

He shrugged a shoulder. 'I want to talk to you. I also want to apologise for making you think I don't regard your feelings.'

Gesturing for her to move closer, he gave her a smile that was indisputably slow and seductive. Natalie did as he asked—she couldn't resist him. But her legs were shaking so badly she hardly knew how she managed it.

When they were face to face Ludo lifted his hand and slid it beneath the heavy silken weight of her long hair, letting his palm curve warmly against her nape. His touch and the intimate closeness of his body electrified her into stillness. So much so that her nipples stung with an almost unholy ache for him to touch them. Never before, in all her twenty-four years, had she experienced such wanton, primitive desire for a man—and the force of it shook her hard.

'I said I would only expect you to share my bed if you invited yourself into my room,' he reminded her huskily, his burning blue gaze shamelessly scorching her.

'Is that why you said you wanted to talk to me?' She found herself mesmerised by the alluring sculpted shape of his lips and the heat that reached out to her from his half-naked body. It was impossible to keep her nerves steady.

'Do you know how long I've waited for a girl like you to come into my life?' he asked.

'What do you mean by that? Do you mean you hoped

to meet someone ordinary who doesn't move in the same exalted circles as you do?'

'You are far from ordinary, *glykia mou*…and I don't care where you come from or what kind of circles you move in. I'm simply telling you that I want you.'

'Why?' She barely knew why she even asked, because the answer was shockingly apparent as his eager hands shaped her bottom through her dress and brought her body flush against his. Behind the button fly of his chinos she sensed his heat and his hardness—and he didn't try to hide it to spare her blushes.

'I think there's been enough talking. I'm sure you knew that when you knocked on my door and asked if you could come in…'

A shuddering sigh of need left Natalie's throat as Ludo reached for the zip at the back of her dress, dragged it downwards and stripped the garment off her shoulders. Just when she thought he might be going to kiss her he slid his fingers beneath the straps of the daring black lace bra that she'd bought for this trip, hardly knowing why she should select such an uncharacteristically impractical item. It was a million miles away from her usual safe utilitarian style.

Ludo yanked down the delicate silk and lace to bare her breasts. With a bold glance that challenged her to deny him he cupped her and brought his mouth firmly down onto a stinging erect nipple. His hot wet tongue caressed her flesh and his teeth bit, sending shooting spears of molten lightning straight to her womb. The pleasure-pain was so intense that she grabbed on to his head with a groan. A few sizzling seconds later he

looked up and with a devil-may-care glance dragged the
rest of her dress down to her feet and helped her step
out of it. As Natalie tremblingly kicked off her shoes he
kept her steady by holding firmly on to her hips. When
she was done, he deftly unhooked her bra and let it fall
to the floor.

'Do you know how beautiful you are? You are like a
goddess,' he declared, sweeping his gaze appreciatively
up and down her semi-nude figure. 'So beautiful that it
hurts me to look at you.'

Ludo meant every word. She had the most exquisite shape, highlighted by an impossibly tiny waist and
gently flaring hips. And with her river of shining hair
cascading down over her pert breasts she reminded him
again of mythological depictions of Athena and Andromeda. His attempt to make peace with his father
earlier had been anything *but* a success, but being here
with Natalie like this, fulfilling the fantasy that he'd
been gripped by since first seeing her on the train to
London, was going a long way to helping him set aside
his personal pain.

Her luminous grey eyes widened as he stooped to position one arm beneath her thighs and the other round
her back. The texture of her matchless smooth skin was
like the softest velvet, and the experience of holding
her semi-naked body in his arms was one of the keen-
est pleasures he had ever known. With her luxuriant
hair brushing tantalisingly against his forearm and the
scent of her perfume saturating his senses like a hot
and thirsty sirocco, she was a woman to weave serious
sexual fantasies about.

But it wasn't just Natalie's looks that made her appeal
to him more than any other woman he'd been attracted
to before. There was an air of innocence about her that
was utterly refreshing after the parade of hard-nosed
businesswomen, models and gold-diggers he'd dated
from time to time. He'd known his parents would love
her…how could they not? She was just the kind of girl
they'd always hoped he would meet. And behind his desire, behind the hope he dared not give a name to, there
was a nagging sensation of being jealous of any other
man who had known her intimately. Had they realised
at the time what a prize they'd won for themselves?

Pushing his jealousy aside, he tipped Natalie back
and carefully lowered her onto the opulent silk counterpane. As he stood beside the bed, taking the opportunity
to survey her loveliness, she returned the compliment by
letting her gaze avidly roam him. The hunger in her eyes
was unmistakable, and it hardened Ludo even more.

Natalie caught her breath. The well-defined biceps
beneath Ludo's naturally bronzed skin intensified the
desire that had been building in her blood all day. She
was suddenly impatient for him to join her, so that she
might know first-hand the raw power that his strong,
fit body exuded so effortlessly. The man was temptation personified, and it never failed to strike her how
perfectly proportioned and beautiful he was.

As soon as her glance fell into that sea of sapphire-
blue once more he gave her a dazzling and knowing
smile and dropped down next to her on the bed. The
need for conversation redundant, he moved over her
with graceful fluidity and straddled her hips with his

strong, long-boned thighs. When he sat back on his haunches to undo his chinos her ability to think clearly utterly fled. All Natalie knew was that she wanted Ludo as much as he wanted her—if not *more*. Yet she momentarily closed her eyes when he dispensed with his trousers and the navy silk boxers that he wore underneath simply because she couldn't stem her anxiety over not being able to please him as much as a man of his experience might be expecting her to...

How could she when she'd never gone all the way with a man before?

Would he be furious with her when he found out? She'd long realised she must be in quite a minority to be still a virgin at twenty-four.

Her nervousness immediately evaporated the instant Ludo touched his lips to hers. The man's deliciously expert kisses were to *die* for. When she responded eagerly, her own lack of expertise didn't seem to matter one iota. Winding her arms about his strong neck, she gave herself up to the passionate embrace with all her heart, and didn't tense when he caught the sides of her lace panties and rolled them down over her thighs. The only feelings that washed though her right then were excitement and lust, and when he returned to claim her mouth in another avaricious kiss Natalie couldn't help but wind her long slender legs round his hard, lean waist. It all seemed so natural and so right.

'Let me love you,' he entreated against her ear, murmuring low.

With her hands resting on the strong banks of his

shoulders, she gave him a tremulous smile. 'There is nothing I want more,' she admitted softly.

Somewhere along the line he had retrieved a foil packet from his trouser pocket and he briefly sat back on his haunches to deal with protection. But not before Natalie allowed herself a curious glimpse. With a contented sigh she rested her head back on the sumptuous silk pillow and readied herself to receive him.

She bit down hard on her lip at his first eager invasion, and couldn't deny the initial sting of pain that she experienced—but when Ludo's muscular body suddenly stilled in surprise she pulled him against her to encourage him to continue, kissing him. There would be plenty of time for that particular awkward discussion later, she thought. Right now all Natalie wanted was to be made love to by the man she now knew without a doubt was the thief of her heart. A man who on the surface appeared to have everything that was supposed to signal success in the world...wealth, property, business acumen second to none, as well as movie-star good looks.

But in truth, she reflected, he was clearly lacking the one thing he perhaps craved above all else—the thing most people yearned for. Unconditional love and acceptance. From family, friends and colleagues, and—given time—*the person they fell in love with.* Even though that last part of her realisation made her pulse race, Natalie knew she wouldn't deny her lover anything. Not now, when she'd just surrendered her most precious gift to him.

Pressing himself deeper and deeper inside her, Ludo wound his fingers through hers as they began to move as one, his breathing becoming more and more laboured as he succumbed fully to the passion that drove him so hungrily to seek release.

For Natalie, the tide of molten heat that had consumed her from the moment he'd welcomed her into his room was now at its peak, and the power of it was like a ferocious drowning sea, sweeping her away to a heart-pounding place of no return…

Wrapping her in his arms as he lay spent beside her, Ludo felt his mind teeming with questions. His heart thudding, he lightly twined a long strand of her silken hair round his fingers and asked, 'Why didn't you tell me that this would be your first time?'

Meeting his glance with her big grey eyes, Natalie gave him a long, considered look. 'Would you have still made love to me if I'd admitted it?'

'You are far too irresistible for me *not* to have. But I would have tried to be a little more gentle…more considerate.'

'I loved it that you were so passionate, Ludo. I may not have much experience, but even so I have desires— just like you.'

His heart thudded a little less hard but he was still confounded by her frank response. Confounded and enthralled. He'd never met a woman like her. 'What made you wait so long to give yourself to someone?'

She blushed, and because she looked so adorable Ludo couldn't help planting a light kiss on her forehead.

'My mother always told me to wait until the time was right…until I was sure that the man I gave my virginity to was worthy of it. Well, today was the day I knew the time was right and the man more than worthy.'

'See what you've done, my angel?'

'What do you mean? What have I done?'

'You have made me want you all over again.'

With a shameless grin, Ludo impelled her firmly onto his aroused manhood, proud and pleased that she fitted him like the most exquisite satin glove.

'Except this time, although I will be no less passionate, I will endeavour to go more slowly…to take my time and savour you more so that you may experience the utmost pleasure.'

Her long hair cascaded down over her naked breasts like a waterfall and her beautiful eyes widened to saucers. 'Like lessons in love, you mean?'

With a throaty laugh of sheer delight, he stilled any further inclination she might have to talk by capturing her lips in a long and sexy, heartfelt kiss…

CHAPTER ELEVEN

EVEN THOUGH THE afternoon at his parents' had not gone as well as he might have dared to hope, it had been one of the most wonderful evenings of his life. Natalie had Ludo in a spin. The air of innocence that he'd sensed about her from the beginning had been proved to be right. But he was stunned at just how far that innocence had extended. More than that, at the fact that she would willingly surrender that innocence to *him*. In spite of the upsetting altercation with his father earlier, he was walking on air—and predisposed to take his lover out to dinner.

He no longer cared that the locals would see him and know that he'd returned, or indeed if they made private unflattering judgements about him. It was strange, but with Natalie by his side Ludo felt as if he could deal with just about *anything*—even the painful realisation that he would probably never have his father's love and regard.

His favourite local restaurant overlooking the moon-lit bay was heaving with tourists and locals alike tonight, and as soon as he and Natalie walked in heads turned to observe them. Deciding it was because his partner looked so ravishing in her mint-coloured dress and the cream pashmina that she'd draped round her shoulders, Ludo felt a strong glow of pride eddy through him.

'*Kopiaste*…welcome. Come in and join us,' the restaurant staff eagerly greeted them. Accustomed to getting a table wherever he went, whether he'd booked ahead or not, Ludo decided not to go elsewhere when he was told they were fully booked tonight but would not dream of turning him and his beautiful partner away. He smilingly kept hold of Natalie's hand and waited patiently while a space in one of the most attractive parts of the restaurant was hastily made available and an extra table was laid. The friendly *maître d'*, whose family Ludo had known for years, attended them personally, and on his instruction a young waiter and waitress brought appetising plates of *mezes* and some complimentary *ouzo* to their table in celebration of his return home.

But although the staff behaved impeccably Ludo could see in their eyes that they were having difficulty containing their curiosity. He had read the speculation in the Greek press three years ago about why he'd left the country so abruptly following his brother's funeral. The picture they'd painted of him had not been a good one…

'Everybody seems so pleased to see you,' Natalie commented, her grey eyes shining.

'Of course.' Ludo couldn't help being wry. 'Money talks.'

'Please don't be cynical. Not tonight. I'm feeling so happy and I want to stay feeling that way…at least until the evening is over.'

Reaching for her small elegant hand, he could have bitten off his tongue for bringing that wounded look to her eyes. 'I fear my cynicism about people has become a habit. But it doesn't mean that can't change,' he added, smiling.

'No, it doesn't,' she agreed and, lifting his hand, brushed her soft lips across his knuckles.

'You are a dangerous woman, Natalie Carr,' he responded, deliberately lowering his voice. 'A small kiss and one approving glance from your bewitching grey eyes and I'm undone. All I really want to do now is take you home and teach you some more lessons in love.'

Her pretty cheeks coloured, just as Ludo had known they would.

'Well...I know I have a lot to learn. But, as tempting as that sounds, I'd really like something to eat first. What do you recommend?'

He didn't even bother to glance at the leather-bound menu he'd been given. He knew it like the back of his hand. There had been many occasions in the past when he and his brother Theo had dined here. He deliberately set the heartrending memory aside to concentrate on Natalie.

'Leave it to me.' He smiled, and immediately signalled for the *maître d'*, who had made sure to stay close by in readiness to take his order.

That night Natalie fell asleep in Ludo's arms, with the sweet scent of night-blooming jasmine drifting in through the open windows of the bedroom. It seemed that everything that had happened was taking on the

magical qualities of a dream, and she wished that life
might imitate that dream forever.

When she woke early the next morning, with her
head on Ludo's chest, Natalie couldn't resist spend-
ing several minutes just breathing in his unique warm
scent and observing the handsome features that looked
more peaceful and vulnerable than she'd ever seen
them. There was nothing remotely threatening or untrustworthy about him, she concluded. He had a good
heart. Why couldn't his father see that? She refused to
believe her perception was coloured rose just because
she only saw the good in Ludo, and because she was
head over heels in love with him.

Hugging herself at the reason why she suddenly felt
so light and free, she planted the softest kiss on the blade
of his chiselled jaw and regretfully left the lavish warm
bed. Leaving him to sleep on, she dressed in a pair of
light blue denims and a white cotton shirt, then made
her way downstairs in search of some coffee and perhaps some delicious Greek bread to go with it. Making
love certainly built up an appetite, she thought. She was
absolutely starving!

She was drinking her second cup of coffee, courtesy
of Allena, when Ludo walked out onto the patio to find
her. He too was wearing jeans, but with an ice-blue shirt
that emphasised the stunning hue of his incredible eyes.
She noticed that he hadn't had a shave, and his jaw was
shadowed with bristles. There was no question that it
suited him. The less groomed look made him appear
dangerous and sexy as hell, Natalie decided, the tips of

her breasts tingling fiercely at the delicious memory of his ardent lovemaking last night...

'Good morning,' she said with a smile, her hands curved round her still steaming cup of coffee.

'Kalimera.' He strode round the table and with a grin removed the cup of coffee and put it down on the table. Then he gently but firmly hauled her to her feet. 'I was worried when I woke up and found you gone,' he intoned huskily, moving her body intimately close to his.

'There was no need. I only came down here for a cup of coffee and some bread. My appetite is at its sharpest in the morning.'

'Really? Then why did you desert me? I would have willingly satisfied your hunger if you'd stayed in bed with me.'

Feeling as though she'd strayed to the edge of a cliff and was about to plunge headlong over the precipice, Natalie dug her fingers into Ludo's hard lean waist as if her life depended on it. 'You're a very bad boy,' she said softly, unable to help the slight quaver in her voice.

He lifted an amused eyebrow. 'If I'm bad, it's because you're always tempting me, Miss Carr. Promise me you'll never stop being the one temptation I can never resist?'

He kissed her hard, angling her jaw so that he could deepen the scalding contact even more. Natalie was dizzy with desire and longing for him. Her blood pounded hotly through her veins as though she was on fire. When he laid his hand over her breast beneath her shirt she couldn't help wishing with all her heart that she had indeed stayed in bed with him this morning, instead of leaving him to go in search of coffee.

'Excuse me, Mr Petrakis, your father is here to see you.'

Allena's slightly nervous but respectful voice had them both turning abruptly in shock and surprise. Ludo's features suddenly turned unnaturally pale. With his blue eyes briefly conveying a silent apology, he moved away from Natalie to go and stand in front of his housekeeper.

'Where is he?' he asked her.

Allena told him that she'd taken him into the living room and was about to make him some coffee.

'Tell him I'll join him in a minute.'

When Allena had returned inside Natalie went straight over to Ludo and instinctively reached for his hand. He flinched as though abruptly woken from a dream. It was easy to see that this unexpected turn of events had caught him on the raw, and she wondered what he was thinking.

'Are you all right?'

'Not really.' He freed his hand from hers to drag his fingers through the already mussed golden strands of his hair. 'Whatever he wants to say to me, it can't be good.'

'You don't know that yet. Why don't you just go in and talk to him, help put your mind at rest, instead of standing out here worrying?'

He scowled, already turning away from her. 'Like I said, whatever he has to say to me, it can't be good. It never is. Go and finish your coffee, Natalie. No doubt I'll be back soon.'

She watched him go as though he were about to present himself in front of a firing squad, and silently prayed that whatever Alekos Petrakis had to say to his son it wouldn't make him despise himself even more than he already did over the tragic events of three years ago.

His father had his back to him when Ludo entered the living room, and he realised that he was twisting and turning a long string of tasselled orange marble worry beads known as *komboloi* that had been passed on to him by his own father when he was young. The sight jolted him into stillness for a moment. It had been a long time since he'd seen him use them. The last time had been at his brother's funeral.

Sucking in a deep breath to steady himself, he announced his arrival with, 'Hello, Father. You want to see me?'

The older man hastily slid the beads into the pocket of his immaculate suit jacket and turned round. Once again it shocked Ludo to see the deep new lines of worry that furrowed his brow.

'Ludovic. You were not about to go out, I trust?'

'Not immediately, no.' Ludo did indeed have plans for himself and Natalie that morning, but it wouldn't hurt to delay them.

'Good. Shall we sit down? I believe that your excellent housekeeper is bringing some coffee.'

They moved across the room to the two lavish gold couches positioned either side of a carved mahogany table. Almost right on cue Allena appeared with a tray of coffee and a dish of small *baklavas*. Thanking her,

Ludo reached forward to hand his father a cup and saucer and poured him his beverage. It was such a simple, commonplace gesture, but somehow he had a sense that it had more significance than he perhaps realised.

Stirring a generous spoonful of sugar into his coffee, Alekos asked, 'Where is your charming fiancée this morning?'

'She's waiting for me outside on the patio.'

'As much as it would please me to have her join us, I think it best that she does not. At least not until we have had some private time together...do you agree?'

Taken aback that his father would even *consider* his opinion, Ludo lightly shrugged a shoulder. 'I agree. There is no point in including her in our conversation if things are going to be unpleasant.'

Alekos Petrakis gravely shook his head, as if he couldn't quite believe what he had just heard. 'Am I such an ogre that you automatically expect things to be *unpleasant* between us? If you do, then all I can tell you is that I truly regret that.'

Stunned into silence, Ludo watched him wipe away the tear that had trickled down over his weathered bronzed cheek. Never before had he known his father to weep, or indeed to be sentimental in any way. What on earth was going on?

'You had better tell me what you want to say, Father. I'm sure you must have some particular reason for coming here to see me today.'

Returning his cup and saucer to the table, Alekos Petrakis sighed heavily and linked his hands together across his lap. 'I came here to tell you that I love you, my son. And to express my deep regret that for all these years you did not know it. Your mother and I had a long talk last night after your visit, and she made me see how foolish and stubborn I have been…how *blind* I have been about you. It was fear that made me that way. Fear of losing you.'

His mouth drying, Ludo stared. 'What do you mean, fear of losing me?'

Alekos's dark eyes met and cleaved to his. 'We have never told you, but you were born premature and we nearly lost you. The doctors worked day and night to save your life. One day our hopes would be high that you were going to survive, and the next…' After a helpless catch in his voice he made himself continue. 'The next day we'd prepare ourselves to bury you. We were told by the doctors that even if you lived you would never be strong. When you did survive, and we brought you home, your poor mother watched over you day and night like a hawk, and I somehow convinced myself that it was *my* fault you were so weak…that I had in me bad seed. What other reason could there be? Theo was big and strong—why weren't you?'

Rising to his feet, Alekos pulled out a handkerchief to mop his brow. 'My logic was ridiculous. I see that now. Your mother always told me that Theo might be the big and strong son but you—*you* were the handsome and clever one. I wish I had seen that when you were a boy, Ludovic, because your mother turned out to be absolutely right. But whether you are handsome and clever, or big and strong, it does not matter. What matters is that you know I am proud of you and love you as deeply and strongly as I loved your dear brother. Can you forgive a very foolish old man for the stupidity of the past so that he may build a happier relationship with his beloved son in the future?'

Already on his feet, Ludo strode round the table and embraced his father hard. It was as though the dam that had been closed against the forceful sea of emotion behind the gates of his heart had suddenly burst open, and the relief it brought made him feel as if he could breathe freely again.

'There is nothing to forgive, Father. I too have made a grave mistake in believing that you didn't care for me as much as you did my brother. I also have a stubborn streak, and sometimes believe I am right when I am wrong. I deeply regret walking away after Theo died. I convinced myself that you had no time for me, that my achievements were not as worthy of regard as his were, and that if I stayed it would be like rubbing salt into the wound of losing him.'

'He would be cross with us both for being so stubborn and wasting so much time in feeling aggrieved, no?'

Grinning, Ludo stepped out of the embrace and slapped his father on the back. 'He would. But he'd also be happy that we have at last made amends. So will my mother when you tell her. Nothing would make me happier than knowing that she feels more at peace about our relationship.'

'I have a question for you,' said Ludo's father.

'What's that?' Old habits died hard, and Ludo

couldn't help tensing a little in anticipation of what he was going to ask.

'I wanted to ask you about Margaritari...your island. What do you intend to do about it now? It has been a long time since you have allowed people to stay on it, and it seems such a shame to leave such a beautiful place to lay in waste when it could bring people pleasure. Nor should you let what happened to Theo destroy your own pleasure in it, Ludo.'

'I admit that I've missed visiting the island. It is like no other place on earth. When we visited it as children Theo and I knew it was special. That's why as soon as I had the chance I bought it.'

His father looked thoughtful. 'Then go and visit it again. Take Natalie and go and create some happy memories there to alleviate the sorrowful ones. For what it's worth, my son, I really think you should take my advice.'

Ludo thought he should, too. But first there was something important he had to do...something that involved purchasing an engagement ring.

As if reading his mind, Alekos put his arm round his shoulders and said, 'Now, let us go and find your beautiful fiancée. I want to reassure her that you and I no longer bear any grudges. I also want to tell her that I am proud my son has been guided by his heart and not his head in choosing such a lovely woman to be his wife. Which reminds me—weren't you two supposed to be getting an engagement ring today?'

Not missing a beat, Ludo replied, 'We were—we *are*.'

'Good. Then later on tonight we must meet up again,

so that your mother and I can see the ring, and then go out to dinner and celebrate.'

Natalie was over the moon when Ludo appeared with his father and they told her that all previous tensions or grudges between them were no more. Following the wonderful revelation that both men were now willing to forgive and forget, she made the discovery over more coffee and *baklava* that Alekos Petrakis had a wicked sense of humour as he regaled her with illuminating tales from his boyhood and the mischief he had got up to.

'I was not always the upstanding citizen you see before you today!' he confessed laughingly.

But even as she enjoyed his jokes and stories Natalie couldn't help feeling a little down. It was clear that Alekos was regarding her as his son's *bona fide* wife-to-be, and yet again she couldn't help feeling hurt because it wasn't true. How would he and his charming wife Eva react when they found out that her engagement to Ludo was nothing but a sham? That as soon as they left Greece in all probability she'd be going back to work in the bed and breakfast she ran with her mother, never to see their charismatic son again...even though in secret she loved him with all her heart?

When Alekos had bade them goodbye, making them promise they would drive over that evening to show them the engagement ring they had chosen, Natalie felt almost sick with guilt and regret.

In complete contrast to the blues that had descended on *her*, Ludo was uncharacteristically relaxed and happy. 'Will you do something for me?' he asked, impelling her into his arms as they returned inside the house after waving his father goodbye.

Her nerves jangled a little and her mouth dried. Her gaze was wary. 'What's that?'

His blue eyes sparkling, as though nothing was amiss or possibly *could* be, he replied, 'I want you to go upstairs and find something pretty to wear. Perhaps the beautiful dress you wore on our first night here? I'd like to get some photographs of us together when we buy the engagement ring.'

Natalie blinked and stared. 'Don't you think this charade has gone far enough, Ludo?'

'I don't know what you mean.'

'Are you honestly saying you want to keep up the pretence that we're engaged? It's going to break your father's heart when he learns that it's not true, and, personally, I *really* don't want to be responsible for that. He's a good man, and you've just made up with him after years of hardly speaking to each other. How do you think he's going to feel when he finds out you've been playing him for a fool?'

His hands dropping away from her waist as if he'd been mortally stung, Ludo flashed her a piercing blue gaze like the precursor to an all-out thunderstorm.

'Again I have to ask you—have you forgotten the deal we made before we flew out here?'

Her heart knocking painfully against her ribs, Natalie shook her head sadly. 'I've forgotten nothing, Ludo... including giving you my word that I'd pretend to be your fiancée unless things became too difficult or untenable.

I have to tell you that that's exactly what they've become. *Untenable*.'

With her head held high and her heart pierced by unbearable sorrow, she headed for the marble staircase without sparing him a second glance.

CHAPTER TWELVE

THE BEDROOM DOOR was flung open just as Natalie was hauling her suitcase onto the bed in order to pack. With the heel of her hand she hastily scrubbed away the scalding tears that had been blurring her vision and spun round to find Ludo standing in the doorway, with his arms crossed over his chest and an enigmatic smile hitching his lips.

She was immediately incensed. 'I can't believe you think the situation is remotely amusing! The fact that you do tells me you're not the man I thought you were.'

'I am far from amused that you think my father too good a man to be deceived about our engagement. Anything *but*.'

'Then what are you smiling about?'

Inside her chest Natalie's heart ached with distress. All she wanted to do right now was board the next plane back to the UK and spend some time reflecting on what she could do to prevent herself from ever being so gullible again.

Slowly, Ludo started to walk across the room towards her. When he was almost a foot away Natalie caught the familiar sensuous drift of his cologne and her insides cartwheeled. How would she ever come to terms with not seeing him again? Her feelings for him were no five-minute wonder, here today and gone tomorrow, she was crazy about him—despite his using her to help achieve his own ends. It didn't matter that he'd made a deal with her, or that he'd followed through on his part of the bargain—she now found she couldn't meet hers. How could she when even contemplating such a painful idea had suddenly become impossible?

'You've been crying,' he observed.

There was a look in his eyes that momentarily stole her breath.

'Yes, I've been crying.' Sniffing, she pulled out a crumpled tissue from her jeans pocket and blew her nose.

'Why?'

'Can't you guess? I'm crying because you were right, Ludo…it *is* going to break my heart to leave you. I also don't want to leave Greece. I didn't want to go home so soon, but now I'm going to have to. I thought I could do this but I can't…not after learning how much it means to your mother that you've met someone special and are engaged, and not after listening to your father today and seeing how much he loves you. I can't do it because I'm not mercenary and I don't want to hurt people. If you want to sue me for reneging on our deal then go ahead. There's nothing I can do about that.'

'You said that it would break your heart to leave me. Did you mean it?'

Sounding amazed, Ludo moved in a little closer and

smiled. Feeling heat pour into her face, Natalie swallowed hard and stared.

'Yes. I'm not trying to put you in an awkward position, but I mean it.'

'How does telling me such an incredible thing put me in an awkward position?'

'I don't want you to feel you have to do anything about it. It's bad enough that people are going to be hurt because I'm not going to be able to continue to carry out my part of our bargain.'

'You mean my parents?' His expression was grave.

'Of course I mean your parents'

'What about me, Natalie? Do you not consider that I might be hurt if you don't adhere to our bargain and agree to be my fiancée?'

'You mean if I don't *pretend* to be your fiancée?'

'I no longer want you to pretend.'

He moved in even closer—so close that his warm breath fanned her face. Every plane and facet of the handsome features that were so dear to her made her heart ache anew, because after today she might never see them again.

Then, suddenly registering what he had just said, she turned rigid with shock. 'What did you say?'

'I said I no longer want you to pretend to be my fiancée. I want us to get engaged for real.'

'You're joking.'

'No, I'm not. I want us to become officially engaged with a view to getting married. I'm deadly serious.'

At the end of this declaration he tenderly gathered Natalie's face between his hands and brought his lips passionately down on hers. There was nothing she could do but eagerly respond. The lessons in love that he had given her had made her an addict for his touch, for the slow, tantalising kisses that rendered her so weak with need that she couldn't think straight…couldn't even remember her own name when he made love to her.

She was so glad his arms were round her waist when she could finally bear to tear her lips away from his or she might have stumbled.

'This really isn't some kind of a joke, is it?' she asked huskily, staring up into the incandescent sea of blue that never failed to mesmerise her.

'No. It isn't a joke. I would never be so cruel. I mean every word I've said. I don't want a pretend engagement, Natalie, I want a real one. So there is no longer any need for you to worry about deceiving my parents. I genuinely want you to be my wife, *agape mou*. When I buy an engagement ring for you today I want it to be for real.'

'But why would you want that?'

'Do you really need to ask? Have you not already guessed?' He exhaled a wry breath, then, smiling warmly down into her eyes, said, 'I love you Natalie… I love you with all my heart and soul and I don't think I can even bear the thought of living without you. That's why I want to marry you.'

For several heart-pounding seconds his passionate declaration stunned her into silence. Then, gathering her wits, she tenderly touched her palm to his cheek and smiled back.

'I love you too, Ludo. I wouldn't consider marrying

you if I didn't. You swept into my life like a whirlwind and turned everything I thought about myself and what I wanted upside down. I know it might sound ridiculous, but I had more or less resigned myself to being single for the rest of my life, because I couldn't imagine marrying anyone for anything less than true love.'

'That is what I thought, too. I longed to find someone real and true who would be my friend and my companion as well as my lover… The idea that a woman might only marry me for my money was a genuine fear of mine.'

'I would never marry you for your money, Ludo.' Natalie frowned. 'I'm an old-fashioned girl who believes that there's someone for everyone—that when two people fall in love it's written in stars.' Her cheeks reddened self-consciously. 'And I believe it was written in the stars that day we met on the train and you paid for my ticket. Especially when you turned out to be the man who was buying my father's business! People sometimes read me wrong because I have a side to me that's very pragmatic, but I've had to be. When my dad left I had to be a support and friend to my mother, as well as help her to get a business up and running so that we had an income. But I'm still an incurable romantic. Anyway, I learned early on in my life, from what happened with my parents, that money is no guarantee of living happily ever after with someone. Not unless their love for each other is more important than anything material.'

Tipping up her chin, Ludo stole a brief, hungry kiss. When he lifted his head to gauge her reaction, he seemed delighted by the fact that she was blushing again.

'I told you once that you have a very sexy voice, remember? As much as I would love to listen to you talk some more, *glykia mou*, we have a special appointment at my friend's jewellers in Lindos. He is closing the shop for the afternoon so that we might take our time in choosing a ring. He is the most sought-after designer and will create something utterly exquisite for you. That may take a few weeks, and we will have to wait for it to be made, but my intention is to buy you a beautiful ring that we can take with us today, so that the world knows we intend to marry. That being the case—we should be making our way over there now.'

'That seems awfully expensive, Ludo. Surely just one ring will do?'

He stole another kiss and playfully pinched her cheek. 'In the circles I've moved in you are unlike any other woman I have ever known, my love. Most of those women have their eye on a man who can keep them in the style they believe they deserve, and they do not much care if he is a good person or even if they really like him…as long as he is rich. But with you, Natalie, I already know you love me for myself and not for the material things I may provide. Therefore I'd be pleased if you indulge me in this matter today.'

'If it means that much to you, then I will.'

'Good.'

'Ludo, can I ask you something? Something we haven't really talked about?'

His hands resting lightly on her hips, he gave her a briefly wary nod. 'What's on your mind?'

Because it wasn't an easy question to ask, and she was slightly dreading hearing the answer, Natalie grimaced. 'Have you—have you had many lovers before me?'

'No. Not many. So few, in fact, that none of them are even memorable. They weren't exactly good choices. But I'm not interested in revisiting my past, Natalie.' He sighed. 'I'm much more interested in what's going on right now and the lovely woman who is standing in front of me...the woman who has so miraculously told me that she loves me and that it would break her heart to leave me.'

'It's true.' It was her turn to reach up and plant a soft kiss on his bristled cheekbone. 'She *does* love you, Ludo...with all her heart. And if you really want a photograph of us to mark the occasion of our engagement I'll go and put on that dress you like so much and tidy my hair.'

'Natalie?'

'Yes?'

'Do you mind going into the bathroom to dress instead of staying in here? Because if you stand here and disrobe I might not be able to resist the temptation to help you.'

'If you do that we'll never get to the jewellers today.'

'You are right. We had better focus on the matter in hand. I'm sure there'll be plenty of time later for the other things I'd like to focus on.'

With a boldly lascivious gleam in the sapphire eyes

she had so come to love, Ludo reluctantly freed her from
his embrace, turned her round and gave her a little push
in the small of her back. He was still chuckling when
she hurried into the bathroom and shut the door.

The heavily perfumed air was just as hypnotic and spell-
binding as Ludo remembered, and it throbbed with the
soporific sound of bees and insects. Blessedly devoid
of the noise of traffic—there was none on the island,
and the only means of reaching it was by boat—if there
was one place in all the world where a person couldn't
help but relax and unwind from day-to-day stresses then
Margaritari was that place.

He'd taken his father's advice about returning to the
island and creating some happier memories, and had
brought Natalie with him to do just that. He had also
shared with his father his conviction that he felt he'd become a better man for having met and fallen in love with
her, and hoped with all his heart that they would enjoy
a marriage as long and as happy as Eva's and Alekos's.

Barefoot, he started to follow the crescent-shaped
arc of lush golden sand, thoughtfully gazing out at the
calm blue waters gently rippling beside it and sending
up a silent prayer of thanks for his good fortune. He
had made his peace with his father and he was in love
with the kindest, most beautiful girl in the world. And
he didn't care who knew it.

Right now Natalie was back in the simple but elegant
stone cottage he'd had built for his own use, telephoning
her father. He hadn't forgotten that his cultural tradition
demanded that he ask him for her hand in marriage, but

first Natalie wanted to talk to Bill Carr in private and tell him why she wanted to marry Ludo. They were madly in love…it was as simple as that.

He hoped her father would not try and talk her out of it in the belief that he was leading her on…that he might not follow through on his declaration to marry her…that he was untrustworthy. Snapping himself out of the old habit of fearing he was not as well regarded as others, he stopped walking and stood quietly staring out to sea at the vast incandescent horizon that stretched out before him. Sadly he remembered his brother Theo. Even though he had died too young, and so tragically, somehow Ludo knew that he was pleased he had made up with their father and had met Natalie and fallen in love with her. He had a strong sense that his beloved brother wished them well…

'Ludo!'

He turned at the sound of the voice that thrilled him like no other, his heart thrumming in anticipation of what she might be going to tell him. He prayed the news was good.

Natalie was running towards him across the sand, barefoot and beautiful in the mint-coloured sarong he had bought her at the market in Lindos, her lovely long hair cascading over her shoulders like a shining water-fall. In her hand she was carrying a small bunch of ole-ander and lavender. As she drew level he made himself resist taking her into his arms and gave her the chance to get her breath back first.

'He gives us both his blessing, and says that you can ring him when we get back to the cottage.' Her grey eyes shining, she grinned. 'He also said I'm to tell you that you're a lucky man…a *very* lucky man.'

'Does he think I don't know that already?' Impatient to hold her, Ludo hauled his wife-to-be against his chest, the heady scent of the small floral bouquet she held drifting hypnotically beneath his nose. 'So, he gives us his blessing and does not mind that you are to become Mrs Ludo Petrakis?'

'As long as it's what I want, then he's more than happy. In fact he's going round to my mum's tomorrow to tell her the news himself. Apparently she's invited him to stay for dinner.' Natalie's brow furrowed a little. 'I suppose it's good that they're talking properly… Anyway, my dad says it's only right that if he gives us his blessing to be married he should be the one to tell her.'

'He sounds to be in good spirits. Is his health any better?'

'Much. You have no idea how much it helped him when you agreed to pay him that extra sum for the business. He says he's buzzing with ideas for a new one. I just hope he doesn't get too carried away and overdo it.'

'And why have you brought these flowers to the beach, *agape mou?* If you want to admire them they are all around us in the coves and by the rock pools… the garden is also full of them.'

'I know. That's where I picked these from. To tell you the truth, I wanted us to say a little prayer for your brother and cast them out to sea in his memory,' Natalie answered softly. 'Do you mind…?'

'Do I *mind*?' Ludo shook his head from side to side in wonderment. 'It is so like you to think of something like this. I'm so proud to know you, Natalie…and prouder still that you are soon to be my wife.'

'Let's do it, then.' Gazing lovingly up into his eyes, she gently stepped out of their embrace and crouched down beside the seashore.

He willingly dropped down beside her. 'Let us remember Theo Petrakis…'

Quietly murmuring a prayer in Greek, Ludo repeated it for Natalie afterwards in English. When he was done, he gestured to her to let her know, and one by one she let the delicate flowers float out into the ocean….

Being on the island was like being on honeymoon. Every night, after making passionate love with the man she loved, Natalie would fall into a blissful sleep in his arms, and every morning, soon after waking, she'd run down to the sea to take a refreshing dip in cool tranquil waters not yet warmed by the sun. Then she'd hurry back to the cottage to have breakfast with Ludo out on the terrace.

They had been on the island for almost a week now, and he had lost that wary look that conveyed his cynicism about the world—a look he'd seemed to wear habitually when they'd first met. He was looking younger every day. Even his brow was less furrowed, as if all his cares had fallen away. Natalie couldn't help but sigh contentedly.

Sitting opposite her at the rattan table, Ludo lowered his aviator sunglasses and his sublime sapphire eyes couldn't help but dazzle her.

'What is it?' he wanted to know.

'I was just thinking how much more relaxed you look than you did when we first met. It must be this place. It's magical, isn't it?'

'There is definitely a touch of paradise about it. I almost have to pinch myself when I remember that I own it.' Straightening in his chair, he tunnelled his fingers through his hair, as if coming to some momentous decision. 'In fact, it is so like paradise that I have decided it's not right to keep it just for myself and family and friends. I've been thinking about building some more accommodation, so that the families of sick children on the surrounding islands might come here for a rest or a holiday when they need it. Of course they wouldn't have to pay for the privilege. I thought I could set up a foundation in Theo's name. What do you think?'

'What do I *think*?' Natalie's heart was racing with excitement and pride. 'I think it's a wonderful idea. Could I help you set it up? If I'm not going to be working at the bed and breakfast any more after we're married I'd like something useful to do...something that I could believe in.'

'Of course you can help. That is...until we have our first child. I'm a strong believer in a mother being there for her children as they are growing up if she can be. How do you feel about that, *glykia mou*?'

'I agree.' Reaching across the table, she smilingly squeezed his hand. 'I want to be there for *all* our children as they grow up. As long as their father is there for them as much as possible, too.'

With a delighted smile, Ludo raised her hand and turned it over to plant a lingering warm kiss in the centre of her palm. 'We very definitely have an agreement. You said *all* our children? That implies we will have more than one or two?'

Natalie dimpled. 'I was thinking maybe three or four?'

'And I'm thinking I'm going to be a very busy man for the next few years if you are planning *that* kind of agenda, my angel. In which case I suppose there's no time like the present to get started on carrying it out!'

* * * * *

'Surely I can do this,' Mia whispered. 'I've come so far since those days—surely I can do this?'

She closed her eyes, but nothing could stop those memories as she allowed herself the luxury of picturing Carlos O'Connor in her mind's eye. Luxury? Or was it a torment?

How could she forget the satanic edge to his looks that was so intriguing—irresistible, but at the same time capable of making you feel you were playing with fire?

Or not remember the way he laughed sometimes and that wicked sense of humour?

Or those times when no one would have suspected he was at the helm of a multinational construction company? Times when he'd exchanged his suits for jeans and a T-shirt and indulged his favourite pastimes: sailing, riding, flying. In fact he was rarely formal, when she thought about it.

But, above all, how could she ever forget lying in Carlos O'Connor's arms?

Lindsay Armstrong was born in South Africa, but
now lives in Australia with her New Zealand-born
husband and their five children. They have lived in
nearly every state of Australia, and have tried their
hand at some unusual—for them—occupations, such
as farming and horse-training: all grist to the mill for
a writer! Lindsay started writing romances when their
youngest child began school and she was left feeling at
a loose end. She is still doing it and loving it.

Recent titles by the same author:

WHEN ONLY DIAMONDS WILL DO
THE GIRL HE NEVER NOTICED
THE SOCIALITE AND THE CATTLE KING
ONE-NIGHT PREGNANCY

Did you know these are also available as eBooks?
Visit www.millsandboon.co.uk

THE RETURN
OF HER PAST

BY
LINDSAY ARMSTRONG

First published in Great Britain 2013
by Mills & Boon, an imprint of Harlequin (UK) Limited.
Harlequin (UK) Limited, Eton House, 18-24 Paradise Road,
Richmond, Surrey TW9 1SR

© Lindsay Armstrong 2013

ISBN: 978 0 263 90024 8

Printed and bound in Spain
by Blackprint CPI, Barcelona

THE RETURN
OF HER PAST

PROLOGUE

MIA GARDINER WAS home alone and preparing dinner for her mother when the storm hit with very little warning.

One minute she was rolling pastry, the next she was racing around the big old house known as West Windward and home to the wealthy O'Connor family, closing windows and doors as raindrops hammered down on the roof like bullets.

It was when she came to close the front door that a dark, damp figure loomed through the outside gloom and staggered towards her.

For a moment her heart leapt into her throat in fright, then she recognised the figure.

'Carlos! It's you. What are you doing—Carlos, are you all right?' She stared up at him, taking in the fact that he had blood pouring down his temple from a nasty-looking cut. 'What happened?' she breathed and clutched him as he swayed where he stood.

'A branch came down as I was crossing from the garage to the house. Hit me on the head,' he said indistinctly. 'That's quite a storm,' he added.

'You're not wrong.' Mia put her hand on his arm. 'Come with me. I'll fix your head.'

'What I need is a strong drink!' But he swayed again as he said it.

'Come,' she said, and led him through the house to the housekeeper's sitting room. It opened off the kitchen and was small but comfortable.

Mia cleared her mother's knitting off the settee and Carlos O'Connor collapsed gratefully onto it. In fact he lay down and groaned and closed his eyes.

Mia was galvanised into action. Half an hour later she had cleaned and dressed the cut on his head whilst not only rain but hail teemed down outside.

Then the lights went off and she clicked her tongue, mainly because she should have expected it. They had frequent power failures in the district when the weather was stormy. Fortunately her mother kept some kerosene lamps handy but in the dark she tripped around until she located them. Then she lit a couple and brought one into the sitting room.

Carlos was lying unmoving, his eyes were closed and he looked very pale.

She stared down at him and felt a wave of tenderness flow through her because the truth of the matter was that Carlos O'Connor was gorgeous. All the lean six foot plus length of him, the dark hair, testament to his Spanish heritage, that he often pushed out of his eyes, those grey eyes that sometimes glinted wickedly at you...

She'd had a crush on Carlos since she was fifteen—how could you not? she sometimes wondered. How could anyone be immune to that devastatingly sexy aura? He might be ten years older than her eighteen years but surely she could catch up?

Not that she'd seen an awful lot of him over the past five years. He didn't live on the property but she believed he'd grown up on it; he lived in Sydney, but he did come back from time to time. Usually it was only for a couple of days but he rode, not only horses but quad bikes, and because Mia was allowed to stable her horse on the property, and because she kept a weather eye on his horses when she was home, they had a bit in common.

She'd had some marvellous gallops with Carlos and if he'd ever divined that sometimes he made her heartbeat triple he'd never given any sign of it.

At first her daydreams had been simple and girlish but over the last couple of years she'd graduated from alternating between telling herself to forget all about Carlos O'Connor—he was a multi-millionaire, she was only the housekeeper's daughter—and some rather more sophisticated daydreams.

Still, he was way out of her league. What could she offer him over the gorgeous beauties who sometimes accompanied him on his visits?

'Mia?'

She came out of her daydream with a start and saw that his eyes were open.

'How do you feel?' She knelt down beside him and put the lamp down. 'Do you have a headache? Or double vision? Or any strange symptoms?'

'Yes.' He thought for a moment.

She waited, then, 'What? Tell me. I don't think I can get a doctor to come out in this—' she gestured up towards the cacophony on the roof above '—but—'

'I don't need a doctor,' he murmured and reached for her. 'Just this. You've grown up, Mia, grown up and grown gorgeous...'

Mia gasped as his arms closed about her and somehow, she wasn't sure how, she ended up lying beside him on the settee. 'Carlos!' she remonstrated and tried to sit up. 'What are you doing?'

'Relax,' he murmured.

'But—well, apart from anything else, you could have a fractured skull!'

'If I did, quiet and warmth and comfort would be recommended, don't you agree?' he suggested gravely.

'I...you...perhaps but—' Mia broke off helplessly.

'That's exactly what you could provide, Miss Gardiner. So would you mind not wriggling around like a trapped pilchard?'

'A trapped pilchard?' Mia repeated in outraged tones. 'How dare you, Carlos?'

'Sorry. Not the most complimentary analogy. How about a trapped siren? Yes, that's better, don't you agree?' And he ran his hands down her body, then cuddled her against him. 'Pilchard. I must be crazy!' he murmured.

Mia took a breath to tell him he was crazy but suddenly she was laughing. Then they were laughing together and it was the most wonderful thing that had ever happened to Mia.

So much so, she lay quietly in his arms and when he

started to kiss her, she didn't resist. She was powerless to be unaffected by the amazing rapture he brought to her as he kissed her and held her. As he told her she had the most luscious mouth, skin like silk and hair like midnight.

She was made conscious of her body in ways she'd never known before as delicious ripples of desire ran through her. She was deeply appreciative of his easy strength and his long clean lines, the width of his shoulders and the way his hands brought her so much pleasure.

In fact she started to kiss him back and, when it was over, once again she lay quietly against him, her arms around him and she was deeply affected by everything about him. Not only that but conscious that it wasn't impossible for him to be attracted to an eighteen-year-old—why else would he be doing this? Why else would he tell her she'd grown up and grown gorgeous?

Surely it couldn't be concussion?

Two days later Mia drove away from the O'Connor estate and set her course, so to speak, for Queensland, where she'd been offered a university place.

She'd said goodbye to her parents, who'd been proud but just a little sad, but she was secure in the knowledge that they loved their jobs. Her father had a great deal of respect for Frank O'Connor, who'd built his construction company into a multi-million dollar business, although he'd recently suffered a stroke and been confined to a wheelchair, leaving his son Carlos in charge.

It was Carlos's mother Arancha, a diminutive Spanish lady, a beauty in her earlier days but still the epitome of style, who had given her only son a Spanish name and it was she amongst the O'Connors who loved the Hunter Valley estate of West Windward passionately.

But it was Mia's mother who actually tended the homestead, with all its objets d'art, priceless carpets and exquisite linens and silks. And it was her father who looked after the extensive gardens.

To some extent Mia shared both her parents' talents. She loved to garden and the greatest compliment her father had given her was to tell her she had 'green fingers'. She also took after her mother in her eye for decorative detail and love of fine food.

Mia was conscious that she owed her parents a lot. They'd scrimped and saved to give her the best education at a private boarding school. That was why she always helped as much as she could when she was home with them and she knew she was fulfilling their dream by going to university.

But as she drove away two days after the storm, her thoughts were in chaos, her head was still spinning and she didn't look back.

CHAPTER ONE

'CARLOS O'CONNOR WILL be attending,' Mia Gardiner's assistant Gail announced in hushed, awed tones.

Mia's busy hands stilled for a moment—she was arranging a floral display. Then she carried on placing long-stemmed roses in a standard vase. 'He is the bride's brother,' she said casually.

Gail lowered the guest list and stared at her boss. 'How do you know that? They don't have the same surname.'

'Half-brother, actually,' Mia corrected herself. 'Same Spanish mother, different fathers. She's a couple of years older. I think she was about two when her father died and her mother remarried and had Carlos.'

'How do you know *that*?' Gail demanded.

Mia stood back, admired her handiwork but grimaced inwardly. 'Uh—there's not a lot that isn't known about the O'Connors, I would have thought.'

Gail pursed her lips but didn't disagree and studied the guest list instead. 'It says—it just says Carlos O'Connor and partner. It doesn't say who the partner is. I thought I read something about him and Nina

French.' Gail paused and shrugged. 'She's gorgeous. And wouldn't it be lovely to have all that money? I mean he's got a fortune, hasn't he? And he's gorgeous too, Carlos O'Connor. Don't you think so?'

'Undoubtedly,' Mia replied and frowned down at the tub of pink and blue hydrangeas at her feet. 'Now, what am I going to put these in? I know, the Wedgwood soup tureen—it sounds odd but they look good in it. How are *you* going, Gail?' she asked rather pointedly.

Gail awoke from her obviously pleasurable day-dream about Carlos O'Connor and sighed. 'I'm just about to lay the tables, Mia,' she said loftily and wafted away, pushing a cutlery trolley.

Mia grimaced and went to find the Wedgwood tureen.

Several hours later, the sun went down on Mount Wilson but Mia was still working. Not arranging flowers; she was in the little office that was the headquarters of the Bellbird Estate.

It was from this office in the grand old homestead, the main house on the estate, that she ran the reception function business, Bellbird Estate, a business that was becoming increasingly well-known.

Not only did the old house lend its presence to functions but its contents delighted Mia. It contained lovely pieces of old furniture, vases, lamps, linen and a beautiful china collection—including the Wedgwood tureen.

She catered for wedding receptions, iconic birthday parties—any kind of reception. The cuisine she provided was superb, the house and the gardens were lovely but perhaps the star of the show was Mount Wilson itself.

At the northern end of the Blue Mountains, west of Sydney, it had been surveyed in 1868 and had gradually acquired a similar reputation to an Indian 'hill station'—English-style homes with cool-climate English gardens in alien settings, this setting being bush and rainforest.

And anyone's first impression of Mount Wilson had to be how beautiful it was. Yes, the road was narrow and clung to the mountainside in tortuous zigzags in places but the trees in the village—plane trees, limes, elms, beeches and liquid ambers, were, especially when starting to wear their autumnal colours, glorious. There were also native eucalypts, straight, strong and reaching for the sky, and native tree ferns everywhere.

The glimpses of houses through impressive gateways and beyond sweeping driveways were tantalising, many old and stone with chimneys, some smothered in creepers like wisteria, others with magnificent gardens.

All in all, she'd thought often although she kept it to herself, Mount Wilson shouted money—new money or old money but *money*—and the resources to have acres of garden that you opened to the public occasionally. The resources to have an estate in the Blue Mountains, a retreat from the hurly-burly of Sydney or the heat of its summers....

And tomorrow Juanita Lombard, Carlos O'Connor's half-sister, was marrying Damien Miller on Mount Wilson—at Bellbird, to be precise. Damien Miller, whose mother, rather than the bride or her mother, had booked the venue without mentioning who the bride was until it was too late for Mia to pull out without damaging her business reputation.

Mia got up, stretched and rubbed her back and decided enough was enough; she'd call it a day.

She didn't live in the main house; she lived in the gardener's cottage, which was in fact a lot more modern, though unusual. It had been built as an artist's studio. The walls were rough brick, the plentiful woodwork was native timber and the floors were sandstone cobbles. It had a combustion stove for heating, a cook's delight kitchen and a sleeping loft accessible by ladder.

It was an interior that lent itself well to Mia's photography hobby, her images of native wildlife and restful landscapes, enlarged and framed, graced the walls. It also suited her South American poncho draped over a rail, her terracotta tubs full of plants and her chunky crockery.

It was also not far from the stables and that was where she went first, to bring her horse, Long John Silver, in from the paddock, to rug him and feed him.

Although it was summer, there were patches of mist clinging to the tree tops and the air was chilly enough to nip at your fingers and cheeks and turn the end of your nose pink. But the sunset was magical, a streaky symphony of pink and gold and she paused for a long moment with her arms around Long John's neck to wonder at life. Who would have thought Carlos O'Connor would cross her path again?

She shook her head and led Long John into his stall. She mixed his feed and poured it into his wall bin, checked his water, then, with a friendly pat and a flick of his mane through her fingers, she closed him in.

That was when she came to grief. She'd collected some wood for her stove and was taking a last look at the sunset when, seemingly from nowhere, what she'd kept at bay for hours enveloped her—the memories she'd refused to allow to surface ever since she'd known who would be at tomorrow's wedding flooded back to haunt her.

'Surely I can do this,' she whispered. 'I've come so far since those days—surely I can do this?'

She closed her eyes but nothing could stop those memories as she allowed herself the luxury of picturing Carlos O'Connor in her mind's eye. Luxury? Or was it a torment?

Whatever, how could she forget that night-dark hair that sometimes fell in his eyes? That olive skin his Spanish mother had bequeathed, yet the grey eyes that came from his Irish father and could be as cool as the North Sea or so penetrating his glance made you mentally sit up in a flurry and hope like mad you had your wits about you.

How could she forget the satanic edge to his looks that was so intriguing; irresistible but at the same time capable of making you feel you were playing with fire?

Or not remember the way he laughed sometimes and that wicked sense of humour?

Or the times when no one would have suspected he was at the helm of a multi-national construction company. Times when he exchanged his suit for jeans and T-shirt and indulged his favourite pastimes—sailing, riding, flying. In fact he was rarely formal when she thought about it. But above all how could she ever forget lying in Carlos O'Connor's arms?

She stood perfectly still for a long moment, then she reached into her pocket for a tissue and mopped herself up, determined that she would recover her equilibrium before tomorrow.

Mercifully, when she woke early the next morning, it was to see that at least the weather was fine; the sun had just started to climb into a cloudless sky. She had all sorts of contingency plans for wet weather but it was a relief not to have to resort to them.

She got up, dressed swiftly in jeans and an old shirt and brewed herself a cup of tea, which she took out into the garden. She loved the garden, all five acres of it, and although Bellbird employed a gardener it was Mia who supervised what went in and came out, something that led her into frequent discord with the gardener, Bill James, a man in his sixties who'd lived all his life on the mountain. Bill and his wife, Lucy, lived in another cottage on the property.

Lucy James was away at the moment. She made an annual pilgrimage to spend a month with her daughter and her six grandchildren in Cairns. To Mia's regret, Bill drove Lucy up to and back from Cairns but only ever stayed a couple of days with them.

That left Mia in the position of having to cope with Bill living on his own and hating it until Lucy returned. If he was cranky when his wife was present, he was ten times crankier when she wasn't.

Still, it had been a huge stroke of luck how she'd come to be able to start her reception business at Bellbird in the first place. She'd met the two old ladies, sisters and spinsters and now in their late eighties, who owned Bellbird, at Echo Point.

It had been her first visit to the Blue Mountains' premier tourist attraction, from which you could look over the Three Sisters and the Jamison Valley.

From the viewing platform she'd gazed out over the scenery and been enchanted by the wondrous views.

The elderly sisters had sat down on the bench beside her and struck up a conversation. Before long she'd learnt about the estate on Mount Wilson, the fact that the sisters now lived in a retirement home in Katoomba, which they hardly had a good word to say for. And the fact that they were looking for a use for their estate.

Mia had explained that she'd come up to the Blue Mountains with the idea of opening a function business—and things had progressed from there. Of course the sisters had had her vetted but what had started out as a business venture had blossomed into a friendship and Mia often visited them in their despised retirement home that was actually very luxurious and well-run. And she often took them bunches of flowers and snippets of gossip about the mountain because she could well imagine what it must be like living away from Bellbird.

If there was one area of concern for her regarding the estate it was that her lease was renewed annually and due for renewal shortly. Her two spinsters would be perfectly happy to renew it but had let drop that they were under some pressure from their nephew, their closest relative and heir, to think of selling Bellbird and investing the money for a higher return than the estate was earning them.

On the morning of the Lombard/Miller wedding, things at Mount Wilson were looking pretty grand. The gardens were in spectacular form and so was the house, Mia noted, as she reluctantly went indoors and did a thorough inspection.

The ceremony was to be conducted by a marriage celebrant in an elegant rotunda in the garden, whilst the meal was to be served in the huge main dining room that easily seated the estimated seventy-five guests. It was a spectacular room with a pressed iron ceiling and long glass doors that opened onto the terrace and the main rose garden.

Dancing would be in the atrium with its cool tiled floor, and tables and chairs were dotted around the main lawn.

'Well, it all looks good,' Mia said to the newly arrived Gail—she lived on the mountain only a few minutes' drive away. 'And here come the caterers. OK! Let's get started.' And she and Gail gave each other a high five salute as was their custom.

In the time she had before the wedding party arrived Mia took a last look into the wedding suite—where the members of the bridal party would dress and be able to retire to if need be. And, content that it was all spick and span, she jogged to her own quarters, where she took a shower and dressed herself for the event.

She studied herself thoughtfully in the mirror when she was ready. She always contrived to look elegant enough to be a guest but a discreet one, and today she was wearing a slim short-sleeved jade-green Thai silk dress with fashionable but medium heels in matching leather and a string of glass beads on a gold chain. She also wore a hat, more of a fascinator, to be precise. A little cap made from the same Thai silk with feathers and a froth of dotted voile worn on the side of her head.

He probably won't recognise me, she reassured herself as she stood in front of her cheval mirror admiring her reflection, and particularly the lovely fascinator, which seemed to invest her with more sophistication than she usually exhibited.

But even without the hat she was a far cry from the kind of girl she'd been in those days. Always in jeans, always outdoors, always riding when she could get away with it. Her clothes—her hair alone must look different from how she used to wear it. She grimaced.

Her hair was a sore point with her. Nearly black, it was wild and curly, yet it never looked right when it was cut to be manageable. So she wore it severely tied back when she was being formal, something she'd not done when she was younger.

Nothing, she had to acknowledge, had changed about her eyes, though. They were green and Gail had once told her her eyelashes were utterly to die for and so was her mouth. She also possessed a pair of dimples that she wasn't a hundred per cent keen on—they didn't seem to go with the sophisticated woman of the world she liked to hope she resembled.

She turned away from the mirror with a shrug and discovered, to her horror, that she was trembling finely because she was scared to death all of a sudden.

No, not all of a sudden, she corrected herself. Ever since she'd realised who the bride was, she'd been pretending to herself that she was quite capable of dealing with the O'Connor family when, underneath that, she'd been filled with the desire to run, to put as much distance between them as she could.

Now it was too late. She was going to have to go through with it. She was going to have to be civil to Arancha O'Connor and her daughter Juanita. Somehow she was going to have to be normal with Carlos.

Unless they didn't recognise her.

She took a deep breath and put her shoulders back; she could do it.

But all her uncertainties resurfaced not much later when she moved the Wedgwood tureen with its lovely bounty of hydrangeas to what she thought was a better spot—her last act of preparation for the Lombard/ Miller wedding—and she dropped it.

It smashed on the tiled floor, soaking her feet in the process. She stared down at the mess helplessly.

'Mia?' Gail, alerted by the crash, ran up and surveyed the mess.

'I'm s-sorry,' Mia stammered, her hand to her mouth. 'Why did I do that? It was such a lovely tureen too.'

Gail looked up and frowned at her boss. At the same time it dawned on her that Mia had been different over the last few days, somehow less sure of herself, but why, she had no idea. 'Just an accident?' she suggested.

'Yes. Of course,' Mia agreed gratefully but still, apparently, rooted to the spot.

'Look, you go and change your shoes,' Gail recommended, 'and I'll clean up the mess. We haven't got much time.'

'Thank you! Maybe we could get it fixed?'

'Maybe,' Gail agreed. 'Off you go!'

Mia finally moved away and didn't see the strange look her assistant bestowed on her before she went to get the means to sweep up what was left of the Wedgwood tureen.

The wedding party arrived on time.

Mia watched through the French windows and saw the bride, the bridesmaids and the mother of the bride arrive. And for a moment she clutched the curtain with one hand and her knuckles were white, her face rigid as she watched the party, particularly the bride's mother, Arancha O'Connor. She took a deep breath, counted to ten and went out to greet them.

It was a hive of activity in the bridal suite. Mia provided a hairdresser, a make-up artist and a florist and in this flurry of dryers and hairspray, perfumes both bottled and from the bouquets and corsages, with the swish of petticoats and long dresses, laces and satins, it seemed safe to Mia to say that no one recognised her.

She was wrong.

The bridal party was almost ready when Arancha

O'Connor, the epitome of chic in lavender with a huge hat, suddenly pointed at Mia and said, 'I know who you are! Mia Gardiner.'

Mia turned to her after a frozen moment. 'Yes, Mrs O'Connor. I didn't think you'd remember me.'

'Of course I remember you! My, my, Mia—' Arancha's dark gaze swept over her comprehensively '—you've certainly acquired a bit of polish. Come up a bit in the world, have we? Although—' Arancha looked around '—I suppose this is just an upmarket version of a housekeeping position, really! Juanita, do you remember Mia?' She turned to her daughter. 'Her parents worked for us. Her mother in the kitchen, her father in the gardens.'

Juanita looked absolutely splendid in white lace and tulle but she frowned a little distractedly. 'Hi, Mia. I do remember you now but I don't think we really knew each other; I was probably before your time,' she said. 'Mum—' she looked down at the phone in her hand '—Carlos is running late and he'll be coming on his own.'

Arancha stiffened. 'Why?'

'No idea.' Juanita turned to Mia. 'Would you be able to rearrange the bridal table so there's not an embarrassingly empty seat beside Carlos?'

'Of course,' Mia murmured and went to move away but Arancha put a hand on her arm.

'Carlos,' she confided, 'has a beautiful partner. She's a model but also the daughter of an ambassador. Nina—'

'Nina French,' Mia broke in dryly. 'Yes, I've heard of her, Mrs O'Connor.'

'Well, unfortunately something must have come up for Nina not to be able to make it, but—'

'Carlos is quite safe from me, Mrs O'Connor, even without Ms French to protect him,' Mia said wearily this time. 'Quite safe, believe me. And now, if you'll excuse me, I'll get back to work.' She turned away but not before she saw the glint of anger in Arancha's dark eyes.

'It's going quite well,' Gail whispered some time later as she and Mia happened to pass each other.

Mia nodded but frowned. Only 'quite well'? What was wrong? The truth was she was still trembling with suppressed anger after her encounter with Arancha O'Connor. And it was impossible to wrest her mind from it.

Her skill at blending the right music, her talent for drawing together a group of people, her adroit handling of guests had deserted her because Arancha had reduced her from seasoned professional to merely the housekeeper's daughter.

'But *he's* not here!' Gail added.

'He's running late, that's all.'

Gail tut-tutted and went on her way, leaving Mia in her post of discreet observer but feeling helpless and very conscious that she was losing her grip on this wedding. Not only that but she was possessed of a boiling sense of injustice.

She'd actually believed she could show Arancha that she'd achieved a minor miracle. That she'd begun and prospered a business that had the rich and famous flocking to her door. Moreover she could hold her own amongst them; her clothes bore designer labels, her taste in food and décor and the special little things she brought to each reception was being talked about with admiration.

But what had she proved? Nothing. With a few well chosen words Arancha had demolished her achievements and resurrected her inferiority complex so that it seemed to her she was once more sitting on the sidelines, looking in. She was no closer to entering Arancha and Juanita's circle than she'd ever been. Not to mention Carlos's…

She'd believed she could no longer be accused of being the housekeeper's daughter as if it were an invisible brand she was doomed to wear for ever, but, if anything, it had got worse.

From a dedicated cook, a person to whom the smooth running of the household—the scent of fresh clean linen, the perfume of flowers, the magic of herbs not only for cooking but infusions as well—from that dedicated person to whom all those things mattered, her mother had been downgraded to a 'kitchen' worker.

Her father, her delightfully vague father who cared passionately about not only what he grew but the birds and the bees and anything to do with gardens, had suffered a similar fate.

She shook her head, then clamped her teeth onto her bottom lip and forced herself to get a grip.

That was when the snarl of a powerful motor made itself heard, not to the guests but to Mia, whose hearing was attuned to most things that came and went from Bellbird, and she slipped outside.

The motor belonged to a sports car, a metallic yellow two-door coupé. The car pulled up to a stone-spitting halt on the gravel drive and a tall figure in jeans jumped out, reached in for a bag, then strode towards her.

'I'm late, I know,' he said. 'Who are you?'

'I…I'm running the show,' Mia replied a little uncertainly.

'Good, you can show me where to change. I'm Carlos O'Connor, by the way, and I'm in deep trouble. I'm sure I've missed the actual ceremony but please tell me I haven't missed the speeches!' he implored. 'They'll never talk to me again.' He took Mia's elbow and led her at a fast pace towards the house.

'No, not the speeches,' Mia said breathlessly, 'and now you're here I can delay them a little longer while you change. In here!' She gestured to a doorway on the veranda that led directly to the bridal suite.

Carlos turned away from her. 'Would you let them know I'm here?'

'Sure.'

'*Muchas gracias.*' He disappeared through the doorway.

Mia stared at the door with her lips parted and her eyes stunned. He hadn't recognised her!

Which was what she'd hoped for but the awful irony was she hated the thought of it because it had to be that she'd meant so little to him she must have been almost instantly forgettable…

She swallowed, then realised with a start that she

still had a wedding to run and a message to deliver. She straightened her hat and entered the dining room and discreetly approached the bridal table, where she bent down to tell the bride and the groom that Mr O'Connor had arrived and would be with them as soon as he'd changed.

'Thank heavens!' Juanita said fervently and her brand new husband Damien agreed with her.

'I know I didn't need anyone to give me away,' Juanita continued, 'but I do need Carlos to make the kind of speech only he can make. Not only—' she put a hand on Damien's arm and glinted him a wicked little look '—to extol all my virtues but to liven things up a bit!'

Mia flinched.

'Besides which, Mum is starting to have kittens,' Juanita added. 'She was sure he'd had an accident.'

'I'd have thought your mother would have stopped worrying about Carlos years ago,' Damien remarked.

This time Juanita cast him a speaking look. 'Never,' she declared. 'Nor will she ever rest until she's found him a suitable wife.'

Mia melted away at this point and she hovered outside the bridal suite to be able to direct the latecomer to the dining room through the maze of passages.

She would have much preferred to delegate this to Gail, not to mention really making Gail's day, no doubt, but she was not to be seen.

After about five minutes when Carlos O'Connor still had not appeared, she glanced at her watch with a frown and knocked softly on the door.

It was pulled open immediately and Carlos was

dressed in his morning suit and all present and correct—apart from his hair, which looked as if he'd been dragging fingers through it, and his bow tie, which he had in his hand.

'I can't tie the blasted thing,' he said through his teeth. 'I never could. Tell you what, if I ever get married I will bar all monkey suits and bow ties. Here!' He handed Mia the tie. 'If you're in charge of the show, you do it.'

Typically Carlos at his most arrogant, Mia thought, because she was still hurt to the quick.

She took the tie from him with a swift upward glance that was about as cold as she was capable of and stood up on her toes to briskly and efficiently tie the bow tie.

'There.' She patted it briefly. 'Now, *if* you wouldn't mind and seeing as you're already late as it is, this wedding awaits you.'

'Wait a moment.' A frown grew in Carlos's grey eyes as he put his hands on her hips—an entirely inappropriate gesture between guest and wedding reception manager—and he said incredulously, 'Mia?'

She froze, then forced herself to respond, 'Yes. Hi, Carlos!' she said casually. 'I didn't think you'd recognised me. Uh…Juanita really needs you so…' She went to turn away but he detained her.

'What are you mad about, Mia?'

She had to bite her lip to stop herself from blurting out the truth, the whole truth and nothing but the truth. Chapter and verse, in other words, of every reason she had for…well, being as mad as she could ever recall.

She swallowed several times. 'I'm having a little

trouble getting this wedding going,' she said carefully at last. 'That's all. So—' She tried to pull away.

He slipped his hands up to her waist and said authoritatively, 'Hang on. It must be—six—seven years— since you ran away, Mia.'

'I didn't…I…well, I suppose I did,' she corrected herself. 'And yes, about that. But look, Carlos, this wedding is really dragging its feet and it's going to be my reputation on the line if I don't get it going, so would you please come and make the kind of speech only you can make, apparently, to liven things up?'

'In a moment,' he drawled. 'Wow!' His lips twisted as he stood her away from him and admired her from her toes to the tip of her fascinator and all the curves in between. Not only that but he admired her legs, the slenderness of her waist, the smoothness of her skin, her sweeping lashes and delectable mouth. 'Pardon my boyish enthusiasm, but this time you've really grown up, Mia.'

She bit her lip. Dealing with Carlos could be difficult at the best of times but she well recognised him in this mood—there would be no moving him until he was ready to be moved.

She heaved an inward sigh and mentally gritted her teeth. All right, two could play this game…

'You're looking pretty fine yourself, Mr O'Connor,' she said lightly. 'Although I must say I'm surprised your mother hasn't found a wife for you yet.'

'The last person I would get to choose a wife for me is my mother,' he said dryly. 'What brought that up?'

Mia widened her eyes not entirely disingenuously but

in surprise as well. And found she had to think quickly.
'Probably the venue and what's going on here,' she said
with an ironic little glint. 'Mind you, things are about
to flop here if I don't pull something out of the hat!'
And she pulled away, successfully.

He stared at her for a long moment, then he started to
laugh and Mia felt her heart pound because she'd gone
for so long without Carlos, without his laugh, without
his arms around her...

'I don't know what you expect me to do,' he said
wryly.

'I don't care what you do, but if you don't come and
do *something*, Carlos,' she threatened through her teeth,
suddenly furious although she had no idea if it was
with him or with herself, or the situation, 'I'll scream
blue murder!'

CHAPTER TWO

'FEELING BETTER?'

Mia took another sip of brandy and looked around. Everyone had gone. The bridal party, the guests, the caterers, they'd all gone. The presents had all been loaded carefully into a station wagon and driven away.

Gail had gone home in seventh heaven because she'd not only seen Carlos, she'd spoken to him. And the wedding had been a success. It had livened up miraculously as soon as Carlos had made his speech and Juanita had thrown her arms around Mia and Gail and thanked them profusely for their contribution to her special day as she'd left.

Carlos had driven away in his metallic yellow car and Mia had kicked off her shoes and changed her Thai silk dress for a smock but, rather than doing any work, she'd sunk into an armchair in the foyer. Her hat sat on a chair beside her. She was perfectly dry-eyed but she felt as if she'd been run over by a bus.

It was quite normal to feel a bit flattened after a function—she put so much into each and every one of them—but this was different; this was an emotional flat liner of epic proportions. This was all to do with Carlos and the fact that she'd been kidding herself for years if she'd thought she'd gotten over him.

All to do with the fact that the feel of his hands on her hips and waist had awoken sensations throughout her body that had thrilled her, the fact that to think he hadn't recognised her had been like a knife through her heart.

That was when someone said her name and she looked up and moved convulsively to see him standing there only a foot or so away.

'But...but,' she stammered, 'you left. I saw you drive off.'

'I came back. I'm staying with friends just down the road. And you need a drink. Point me in the right direction.'

Mia hesitated, then gestured. He came back a few minutes later with a drinks trolley, poured a couple of brandies and now he was sitting opposite her in an armchair. He'd changed into khaki cargo trousers and a grey sweatshirt.

'Feeling better?' he asked again.

She nodded. 'Thanks.'

He frowned. 'Are you sure you're in the right job if it takes so much out of you, Mia?'

'It doesn't usually—' She stopped and bit her lip.

'Doesn't usually affect you like this?' he hazarded.

She looked down and pleated the material of her smock. 'Well, no.'

'So what was different about this one?'

'I don't know.' Mia shrugged. 'I suppose I didn't think any of you would recognise me.'

'Why the hell wouldn't we?' he countered.

She shrugged. 'I've changed.'

'Not that much.'

She bridled and looked daggers at him before swiftly veiling her eyes. 'That's what your mother tried to tell me. I'm just a souped-up version of the housekeeper's daughter, in other words.'

'I didn't say that,' he retorted. 'Since when did you get so thin-skinned, Mia?'

She took a very deep breath. 'I'm not,' she said stiffly.

'I can't work out whether you want us to think you have changed or not.'

'Don't worry about it, Carlos,' she advised coolly. 'In fact, thank you for getting me a drink but I'd be happy if you went back to your friends. I have a lot to do still.'

'Short of throwing me out,' he replied casually, 'which I doubt you could do, you're going to have to put up with me, Mia, until I'm ready to go. So, why don't you fill me in on the missing years? I'm talking about the years between the time you kissed me with considerable ardour then waltzed off to uni, and now.' His grey gaze rested on her sardonically.

Mia went white.

'I'm waiting,' he remarked.

She said something supremely uncomplimentary beneath her breath but she knew from the autocratic set of his jaw that he wouldn't let up until he got the answers he wanted.

'All right!' She said it through her teeth but he intervened.

'Hang on a moment.' He reached over and took her glass. 'Let's have another one.'

With the deepest reluctance, she told him about the intervening years. How her mother and father had retired and were living in the Northern Rivers district of New South Wales. How they'd started a small tea shop in a country town that was becoming well known, not only for the cakes her mother baked but the honey her father produced and the herbs he grew.

How she'd finished university, spent some months overseas; how a series of catering jobs had finally led her to taking the plunge and starting her own business.

'And that's me up to date,' she said bleakly and added with irony, 'how about you?'

He avoided the question. 'No romantic involvement?'

'Me?' Mia drew her finger around the rim of her glass. 'Not really. Not *seriously*. I haven't had the time. How about you?' she asked again.

'I'm...' He paused and grimaced. 'Actually, I'm currently unattached. Nina—I don't know if you've heard of Nina French?' He raised a dark eyebrow at her.

'Who hasn't?' Mia murmured impatiently. 'Top model, utterly gorgeous, daughter of an ambassador,' she added.

'Yes.' He nodded. 'We had a relationship. It fell through. Today, as a matter of fact.'

Mia choked on a sip of her drink. 'Today?'

He nodded.

'Is that why you were late?' she asked incredulously.

He nodded. 'We had a monumental row just before we were due to set out—to be here on time.' He shrugged. 'About fifty per cent of our relationship consisted of monumental rows, now I come to think of it.'

'Oh. I'm sorry,' Mia said. 'But that probably means a…a grand reunion.'

'Not this time,' he replied perfectly coolly, so coolly it sent a little shiver down Mia's spine.

He was quiet for a time, rolling his glass in his hands. 'Otherwise,' he continued, 'I've worked like a Trojan to fill my father's shoes since he had that stroke. He died a few months ago.'

'I read about that. I'm sorry.'

'Don't be. It was a release—for all of us, I guess. After the stroke he became embittered and extremely hard to live with. He was always a hard man. I never felt I was living up to his expectations before he became ill but even less so afterwards.'

He sat back and tasted his drink. 'I've even branched out in new directions, successfully, but—' he paused and shrugged '—I can't help feeling he wouldn't have approved or that he would have thought of a different way of doing things.'

'I didn't know him much,' Mia murmured.

'The thing is—' Carlos drained his drink and looked out into the sunset '—I don't know why I'm telling you this; maybe weddings generate a desire to understand things—or maybe monumental rows do it—' he shrugged '—but I don't know if it's thanks to him and his…lack of enthusiasm for most things, including me, that's given me a similar outlook on life.'

Mia frowned. 'What do you mean?'

'There's something missing. Hard to put my finger on it, though.'

'Maybe you'd like to take a year off and live amongst some primitive tribe for a change? Is it that kind of an itch?'

He grimaced. 'Not exactly.'

'Then it could be a wife and family you're lacking,' Mia said in a motherly sort of way and was completely unprepared for what came next.

He studied her for a long moment, his eyes narrowed and very intent. Then he said, 'You wouldn't like to take Nina's place?'

Mia's eyes widened and her mouth fell open. 'What do you mean?'

'You wouldn't like to get engaged to me? Not that I was engaged to Nina, but—' He gestured.

She swallowed, choked again on a sip of her drink and came up spluttering.

He eyed her quizzically. 'An unusual reaction,' he murmured.

'No. I mean yes. I mean…how could you?' She reached for a napkin from the trolley and patted her eyes and her mouth. 'I don't think that's funny,' she told him coldly.

He raised a dark eyebrow at her. 'It wasn't meant to be. I'm in rather desperate need of a—what should I call it?—a shield at the moment. From Nina and the whole damn caboodle of them.' He looked irritated to death.

'Them? Who?' Mia queried with a frown.

'The set she moves in, Juanita too, my mother and all

the rest of them.' He gestured. 'You saw them all today.'
He paused, then smiled suddenly. 'In comparison, the
housekeeper's daughter is like pure sweet spring water.'

Mia moved abruptly and went white to her lips. 'How
dare you?' she whispered. 'How dare you patronise me
with your ridiculous proposal and think you can make
me laugh about being the housekeeper's daughter?'

'Mia—' he sat up '—it may be seven years ago but
you and I set each other alight once—remember? Perhaps it didn't mean a great deal to you, but it happened.'

'M-may not have meant m-much to me?' Mia had
trouble getting the words out. 'What are you saying?'

'You ran away, remember?'

'I…Carlos, your mother warned me off,' Mia cried,
all her unspoken but good intentions not to rake up the
past forgotten. 'She told me I could never be the one
for you, no "housekeeper's daughter" would be good
enough to be your wife. She told me you were only
toying with me anyway and she threatened to sack my
parents without references if I didn't go away.'

'*What*?' he growled, looking so astounded Mia could
only stare at him wide-eyed.

'You didn't know.' It was a statement rather than a
question.

'I ended up in hospital that night, remember? When
I got home you'd gone. Listen, just tell me how it happened,' he ordered grimly.

Mia stared into the past. 'She came home first, your
mother,' she said slowly. 'The storm had passed but I
was still—' she hesitated a moment '—I was still lying
on the settee. I hadn't heard her. You were asleep. She

was…she was livid.' Mia swallowed and shivered. 'She banished me to the service quarters after I'd told her what had happened and she rang for a medevac helicopter. I don't know when you woke up. I don't know if you had concussion but the next day was when she warned me off.'

'What about your parents?'

'I never told them, not what had happened with you. But I had just received an offer of a place at a Queensland university. I hadn't been sure I'd take it— it would mean I'd be a long way from my parents— but that's what I told them—that I'd made up my mind to do it. I left two days later,' she said bleakly. 'You hadn't come back. I didn't even know if you would. But I couldn't risk them losing their jobs.' She looked at him long and steadily. 'Not both of them at the same time. I just couldn't.'

He closed his eyes briefly. 'I'm *sorry*. I had no idea. I must have been quite groggy because I don't remember much about the medevac. But I did go back to West Windward after all sorts of tests and scans and—' he shook his head impatiently '—palaver to determine whether I'd cracked my skull but you'd gone. That was when she told me you'd got a place at a Queensland university, that your parents were so proud of you and what an achievement it was for you. So I congratulated them and *they* told me they were so proud of you and there seemed to be no trauma attached to it.'

Mia patted her eyes again with the napkin. 'They were proud of me.' She shrugged. 'Did you never…' she paused, then looked at him directly '…did you never consider looking for me to check it out?'

He held her gaze for a long moment, then he said, 'No.'

'Why not?' she whispered.

He looked away and rubbed his jaw. Then he looked directly into her eyes. 'Mia, it occurred to me I could only mess up your life. I wasn't ready for a relationship so all I could offer you was an on/off affair, especially if you were up in Queensland. I'd only just taken over from my father so my life was in the process of being completely reorganised.'

He shrugged. 'I could have kicked myself for doing it—' He stopped abruptly as she flinched visibly.

'Hell,' he said. 'I'm *sorry* but—'

But Mia had had enough. She jumped up precipitately. 'So, if your mother hadn't warned me off, *you would have*?'

'No.' He said it decisively and he got to his feet and reached for her. 'No.'

As she jumped away she tripped and would have fallen if he hadn't grabbed her. 'Listen to me,' he ordered as he wound his arms around her. 'Just listen.'

Mia ignored him and struggled to free herself.

'Mia,' he warned, 'since when did you think you could beat me in a damn fight? Be still and listen.'

'There's nothing you can say I want to hear,' she gasped.

He eyed her narrowly, her flushed cheeks and her eyes dark with pain, her hair coming loose. 'OK.' He shrugged. 'Then how about this?'

And before she had a chance to identify what he was leading up to, he bent his head and claimed her mouth with a kiss.

She went limp in his arms, from sheer surprise about the way he did it, the way he moved his hands on her body. The feel of him, steel-hard against her softness, was mesmerising. And her lips parted beneath his because she simply couldn't help herself.

When it was over her head was resting on his arm, her hair flowing over it, her eyes huge, very green and stunned, her lips parted in sheer shock—shock that he had done it, shock that she had responded after his news of what had to amount to a betrayal.

'Don't look like that,' he said.

'Why did you do it?' she whispered.

'It's a traditional way to stop a fight between a man and a woman,' he said dryly. 'Didn't you know?'

Her lashes fell and it occurred to him that he'd hurt her again—like some ham-fisted clod, he thought with distaste. 'Mia, I would never have warned you off because you were the housekeeper's daughter.'

'Oh, Carlos, you may be able to deceive yourself but—'

'Listen,' he broke in savagely, 'yes, I'd have told you there was no future for us *then* but it had nothing to do with who you were. I have never,' he said through his teeth, 'shared my mother's delusions of grandeur.'

It flashed through Mia's mind, an image of herself during the day and how, once again, she'd keenly felt her position on the sidelines, despite her designer clothes and her undoubted skills. How she'd proven

to herself today that she still had a long way to go in
the self-confidence stakes, how she might always be
a fringe-dweller compared to the O'Connors and the
ubiquitous Nina French.

But above all how much it *hurt* to know that Carlos
would have warned her off himself…

As for his proposal?

'I think you must be mad,' she said with bitter can-
dour, 'if you really believe I'd want to get engaged to
you. After all that—have you any idea how cheap your
mother made me feel?'

He closed his eyes briefly, then released her and
handed her her glass. She blinked and took a sip of
brandy.

Carlos stared at her for an eternity, then he said
abruptly, 'How old are you now?'

She narrowed her eyes. 'Why?'

'Why not—twenty-five?'

She nodded.

'Has there been *anyone*?'

Two spots of colour entered her cheeks and she put
her glass down on the trolley with a snap. 'That's none
of your business, Carlos.'

'I think it is. I think it must have been a ghastly experience. My mother—' He gestured and shrugged.

'I'm a little surprised you believe me,' Mia broke in.

'My mother,' he repeated dryly, 'has persistently
meddled in all our lives but not in a way that's actually hurt anyone like this before. What happened to
my father came as a big shock to her too and may have

made her…may have unbalanced her a bit.' He paused and grimaced. 'Whatever, I can't let this go.'

'There's nothing you can do. I…one…gets over these things.'

'That's the problem, I don't think you have. I strongly suspect you're a twenty-five-year-old virgin, Mia.'

Mia gasped and jumped up. 'Will you…will you just go away?' she flung at him. 'To…to think,' she stammered, 'that *I* thought you were the nicest of the O'Connors.'

He lifted a wry eyebrow. 'The best of a bad bunch?'

'Yes! No. Oh!' Mia clenched her fists and ground her teeth and suddenly it was all too much for her again and she kicked her shoes off and ran out onto the veranda, onto the lawn and down towards her cottage.

Of course she came to grief—it was that kind of day.

She didn't see the sliver of glass she stepped onto although she yelped in pain.

Carlos was right behind her, and he said her name on a harsh breath and simply picked her up and turned as if to take her back to the big house.

'No, no,' she said raggedly. 'I don't want to bleed all over the house.'

'Where then?'

'Down there, my cottage. I've got a first aid kit. Oh, I'm bleeding all over *you*.'

'Don't worry about it. Here we are. Stand on one foot while I open the door and get the lights.'

A few minutes later Mia was sitting lengthwise on her settee with a towel under her foot. Carlos had turned all the lights on and, following her instructions, had found the first aid kit in the bathroom.

'I'm a good doctor, by the way,' he said as he laid out tweezers, a bowl of antiseptic, cotton wool and dressings.

'How do you know?' Mia peeled off her stocking.

'I've had no complaints to date.'

'How many people have you actually "doctored"?' she asked. 'Is it deep?'

He studied her heel. 'Deep enough. But I can't see anything in it and we should be able to keep it from bleeding until tomorrow when we can get you to a proper doctor. It might need a couple of stitches. You'll have to keep off it for a while.'

He dabbed it liberally with cotton wool dipped in antiseptic, then he dried it and applied a dressing.

'There.' He sat back. Then he reached for her and took her in his arms. 'And you're a good patient,' he said into her hair. 'Feeling OK?' He held her away and studied her face. 'You look a bit pale.'

Mia grimaced and, without giving it a second thought, laid her head against his shoulder. 'I'll be OK. I feel a bit stupid. I always check the lawn for broken glass; when people drink you never know what they can end up doing with their glasses. I *never* sprint across it barefoot.'

'Why did you?' He kissed the top of her head and it felt like the most natural thing in the world to Mia.

But she sighed. 'I was running away from you, Carlos.' She lifted her head and looked him in the eye. 'For a few minutes I really hated you. And thinking back makes me feel that way again.'

'Then don't think back,' he advised and traced the outline of her mouth. 'It always was one of the most delicious mouths I've ever seen.'

Mia was conscious of a growing clamour in her nerve-endings, delicious but at the same time disturbing, as her awareness of him grew. Awareness of how surprisingly strong he was; he'd carried her with ease. Awareness of all the old sensations being in his arms could arouse, the feel of his body against hers, the pure male scent she used to love so much when they rode together, of the cotton of his shirt mingled with a hint of musk.

Awareness and memories of his hands, so sure when he'd kissed and touched her tonight and once before, even if he was suffering from a concussion on that occasion.

It was that last thought that brought her up with a start. She had to remember that Carlos was dangerous to her mental health!

Correspondingly, she pushed herself away from him and changed tack deliberately and completely. 'This accident couldn't have happened at a worse time. I've got wall-to-wall functions over the next week. I really need to be on my feet!'

'Tomorrow?' he queried.

'No, not tomorrow but from the day after.'

He looked at her with some irony. 'Don't you have any contingency plans? Are yours the only pair of feet available?'

Mia sank back. 'Well, no. There's Gail.'

'Ah, Gail,' Carlos murmured with a sudden glint of amusement in his grey eyes. 'Now, I met Gail. She very kindly introduced herself to me and offered me any assistance I might need.'

Mia looked briefly heavenward.

Carlos noted this with a twist to his lips. 'I did form the impression, however, that, despite being young and impressionable, Gail is a fairly practical person. Possibly a hard worker as well.'

Mia closed her eyes on her inward irritation, then opened them to say honestly, 'You're right. Forgive me, Gail,' she added in an aside.

'So you can give the orders and Gail can carry them out. Problem solved.'

Mia cast him a glance liberally laced with a mixture of frustration and exasperation and, in lieu of being able to trust her voice, merely nodded.

Carlos contemplated her for a long moment, then he said, 'I see.'

Mia blinked. 'What? What do you see?'

'It's not visible to the naked eye.'

She blinked again. 'How do you see it then?'

'It wasn't that kind of an "I see".' He stood up and gathered the first aid accoutrements together and took them to the bathroom. 'It denoted understanding,' he said, coming back.

Mia made a kittenish sound of frustration. '*Understanding of what*?'

'Your state of mind. I get the impression mine is the last advice you'd want to take,' he said with a flourish. 'That kind of understanding.' He moved into the kitchen area. 'Would there be anything to eat in your establishment, Miss Gardiner?'

Mia, who didn't at that moment know whether to laugh or cry—laugh because he could be so crazy at times, cry because he read her so well—said faintly, 'Look in the fridge,' and swallowed a lump in her throat. 'Uh…I'm sorry, I did bleed all over you but cold water is good for getting blood out.'

'You don't say?' He looked down at himself and swore softly. 'I see what you mean. OK, I'll scrub what I can.'

She had to laugh when, after he'd washed the blood-stains away, he found her apron hanging on a hook on the wall and donned it.

'There.' He smoothed it down. 'Presentable.' He opened the fridge door and apparently approved of what he saw. He withdrew a bowl of pasta marinara already prepared and just requiring heating up. There was a small salad also made and under cling wrap.

Lastly he took out a bottle of white wine with a shrug. 'Is there any point in being virtuous *and* sober at this end of the day?'

'Virtuous?' she queried.

'You could hardly call us decadent.'

'Well, no.' Mia paused as Carlos put the pasta in the microwave and set out some cutlery on her little round kitchen table.

Within minutes they were eating and sharing some of the wine.

Mia ate from a tray on her knees; she was still ensconced on the settee with her feet up. They talked desultorily—he was the one who'd promoted the conversation by asking her some questions about the reception business.

'So,' he said at one point, helping himself to more pasta, 'in the case of a bridal party like today, you actually provide a hairdresser and a make-up person so all the dressing et cetera takes place up here—very sensible. It'd be a long drive all kitted out in a wedding dress. But how do the brides cope with a strange hairdresser? I had a girlfriend once who left me to follow her hairdresser to Townsville.'

Mia wound her last mouthful of pasta around her fork and couldn't help grinning. 'The hairdressers and make-up girls work in salons in Sydney, so the bridal party have a couple of appointments with them *before* the big day to work out hairstyles and so on.'

He looked at her with admiration. 'That's pretty inspired, Miss Gardiner.'

She shrugged. 'It's just a question of—' she paused and looked thoughtful '—of helping Mount Wilson to work its magic, I guess.'

'Mmm…' He pushed his bowl away and got up to take the tray from her. 'Who owns the place?'

She told him and then, unwittingly, voiced her concern. 'They're in their eighties now,' she said slowly, 'and they seem to be going downhill a bit. They're getting forgetful and—I guess it's only natural but I think they're worried about Bellbird. They have a nephew who's their heir. He wants them to sell it and invest the money where they'd get a higher return. Of course—'

she gestured '—it's entirely up to them but I might be looking for somewhere else one day. Which would be a pity but—we'll see.'

'Are you attached to the property?' he asked after a moment. 'It's not only a business proposition for you?'

Mia sighed and reached for her wine glass. 'I love it,' she said dreamily and with a faraway look in her eyes. 'I'd love to own it. I'd love to pretend I was a lady from another era who had this summer residence in the hills and a garden I could open to the public if the whim took me. I'd love to call this place home.' She looked at Carlos, smiling. 'Mount Wilson residents can because they have roots here; they have a bit of history behind them.' She smiled at her glass and drained her wine. 'Yes, I think I'd love to play ladies up here at Bellbird. I'd also love to have ten kids.'

He blinked at her. 'Ten?'

She waved a hand. 'No, not really, but some. I love kids.'

She paused and recalled one of her early fantasies— having Carlos's children. She grimaced inwardly but, as had happened to her before, she couldn't help wondering if she ever would have kids now, if she couldn't fall in love again.

'I think maybe it was because I was an only child— that's why a large family appeals. It shouldn't,' she said humorously. 'The last picnic day I had nearly ruined me.'

'Picnic day?' he queried.

'Twice a year I invite some kids from a youth club in an inner city area up for a picnic—well, a sausage

sizzle really. Eight- to ten-year-olds. The last lot were
especially spirited. They…um…ran riot, you could say.
That's what Bill said, anyway.' Her eyes glinted with
laughter. 'He also said if he'd ever seen a bunch of hood-
lums in the making they were it.'

'Bill?'

'Oh, didn't I mention him? He's the gardener. He
and I have a…difficult relationship, although he's a
wonderful gardener. It's just that I rather fancy myself
as a gardener too.' She shrugged. 'At least my father
thought I had green fingers and if anyone should have
known, he would have.'

Carlos was sitting in one of her ladder-back kitchen
chairs. He had his hands behind his head and was tilt-
ing the chair. 'That's…quite a daydream,' he said after
a long moment.

Mia dimpled. 'Daydream being the operative word.
But I guess we all have daydreams.'

'Yes.' He sounded distracted and almost as if he was
examining his daydreams and not finding them satisfactory or perhaps not finding any at all.

'Do you have any…well, ambitions or future plans,
if not daydreams?' Mia heard herself asking curiously.

He thought for a long moment with a frown in his
eyes. 'I have one,' he said at last. 'Not so much an ambition but one thing I keep a long-term eye on, you could
say. Someone I would hate to see steal a march on me.'

'That sounds more like a vendetta than an ambition,'
Mia commented. 'Who?'

'Talbot Spencer.'

She blinked. '*The* Talbot Spencer?'

He looked at her dryly. 'Is there another? Yes, him.'

'But he's a builder, like you. I mean…I don't mean you actually build things with your hands these days but his is also a multi-million dollar construction company, isn't it?'

'It is and we've been competing against each other for contracts for years. He's also tried to buy me out a couple of times. That's one reason why I have a thing about him.'

'He's a playboy, isn't he?' Mia frowned as she ran through her mental resources on the subject of Talbot Spencer. Then her eyes widened. 'I suppose you could be called one too, though.'

'Thank you, Mia,' he said sardonically.

'Well—' she gestured '—cars, boats, planes, horses and women. You both seem to qualify.' She paused and pictured Talbot Spencer in her mind's eye, not that she'd ever met him but she'd seen him pictured. Not quite as tall as Carlos and fair-haired, he was still interesting-looking.

'So what was the real needle between the two of you? The cut-throat world of business?'

Carlos leant his chin on his hand and he took so long about it she thought he wasn't going to answer, then he said, 'A woman.'

Mia's lips parted. 'He stole a…a girlfriend from you?'

Carlos shook his head. 'Not from me; it was my best friend's girl. Talbot's a few years older. My friend and I were still at university, whereas he was a seasoned bachelor. She was at uni too. She fell for him and gave my friend his marching orders.' He fiddled with the tablecloth. 'She was a country, convent-schooled girl. Anyway, to cut a long story short, Talbot got her pregnant, paid for her abortion and turned his back on her.'

'Oh, no,' Mia murmured.

'Oh, yes. She was devastated and guilt-ridden over the abortion and she tried to end it all. It took years for her mental scars to heal and my friend went through the mill with her. For which I will never forgive Talbot and he knows it and he knows why. That's why he'd like to grind O'Connor Construction into the ground... Why the hell am I telling you this, Mia?'

She had to smile. 'I don't know. It's been quite a day, one way and another. Maybe that's why.'

'You're not wrong. Uh...where's the bedroom?'

Mia waved a hand in the direction of the loft. 'Up there.'

He stood up. 'That's the only one?'

She nodded.

'Mind if I take a look?'

Mia tried to remember how tidy she'd left her loft, then shrugged. 'Go ahead.'

Five minutes later he looked down at her. 'It's going to be me up here, you down there, Miss Gardiner. Tell me what you need and I'll bring it down.'

Mia sat bolt upright. 'What do you mean? You can't be serious!'

'But I am.'

'Carlos—'

'Mia—' he interrupted firmly '—you cannot honestly expect me to abandon you up here on the top of a mountain with not a soul within reach. How come you live so alone like this in the first place?' he asked irritably.

'I don't. There's another cottage where Bill and his wife live, but she's away at the mo...' She broke off and bit her lip.

'Away at the moment?' he supplied.

Mia nodded.

'Then you're going to have to put up with me because probably the furthest you'll be able to go is hop to the bathroom. There's no way you're going to be able to get up this ladder, for starters.'

And, so saying, he tossed down a pair of pyjamas for her plus a pillow and a duvet.

Mia drew a deep breath as she gathered what he'd thrown down. 'All right, maybe I couldn't do that but otherwise I can manage. Thank you very much for the offer, though; it's really kind of you but I don't need it.'

'Mia...' He came down the ladder and sat on the end of the settee. 'Mia,' he repeated, 'I'm not going to ravish you or even seduce you. Believe me.'

They stared at each other until she said tonelessly, 'I didn't think you were. I just don't like feeling beholden—to anyone.'

'Or are you afraid that even if we're not into ravishment and seduction,' he said dryly, 'you might get to liking me again?'

Mia opened her mouth but Long John Silver chose that moment to make his presence felt. He neighed shrilly several times.

Mia's hand flew to her mouth.

'Your horse?' Carlos queried.

'Yes. I forgot all about him! He hasn't been fed or rugged or put in his stall for the night. Oh!' She made to swing her legs down but sanity prevailed. 'I'm not going to be able to do it, am I?' she said hollowly.

'No.' Carlos got up. 'But I can. I can also get some more wood for the fire.'

'What about…aren't you staying with friends, though? Won't they be wondering where you are?'

He pulled a mobile from his pocket. 'I'll ring them. Any more objections?' he asked with sudden impatience.

She lay back with a sigh. 'No.' She sat up immediately, though, with anxiety etched into her expression. 'Be careful with Long John. He can bite.'

'Surely you don't put up with that?' Carlos raised an incredulous eyebrow at her.

'Oh, not me,' Mia assured him. 'Usually only strangers. Well, Bill, but I wouldn't be surprised if Bill provokes him.'

'Thanks for the warning,' he said dryly. 'Anything else I need to be warned about? Like killer cats or pet snakes in the loft?'

She had to laugh. 'No. Oh…' She grimaced and hesitated.

'Spill it,' he ordered briefly.

'Well, I didn't lock up. The main house, I mean. Not that we usually have any crime up here, but I don't like to leave it all open.'

'Just tell me what to do. Come to think of it, I left my car unlocked.'

Mia explained how to lock up the house.

'Wish me luck,' he said wryly and stepped out into the night.

Mia stared at the closed door and was conscious of never feeling more confused.

Bewitched, bothered and bewildered, she thought, and closed her eyes. How could she possibly kiss Carlos O'Connor when he had admitted there had never been a future for them?

A few minutes later she decided to take advantage of his absence and she got up painfully and hopped to the bathroom.

When she got back to the settee she was colourfully arrayed in her tartan pyjamas and she snuggled under the duvet.

Perhaps the wine on top of a couple of brandies was helping to dull the pain in her heel, she reflected, but it wasn't too bad.

Her last thought was that it certainly wasn't going to keep her awake and she fell asleep without intending to, without even realising it, on a day of mixed emotions like no other in her life.

Carlos came back eventually, all chores done, but Mia didn't even stir when he added some wood to the stove.

He stood looking down at her for a long time. At the almost ridiculously long lashes against her cheeks. At her thick dark hair that she'd braided, making her look younger, as did—he smiled—the tartan pyjamas. At her mouth—it *was* one of the most luscious mouths he'd seen and if he looked at it long enough it was hard not to want to kiss it.

What would happen if he did kiss that delicious mouth again right now? Lightly at first at the same time as he stroked her cheek.

Would she sigh a warm little puff of air, then reach out to wind her arms around his neck? Would she invite him to lie beside her and accept his hands on her body in all those softly rounded or slender places?

He moved restlessly and shoved his hands in his pockets as he was struck by the irony of it, this compulsion that came over him from time to time to have and to hold Mia.

He gritted his teeth but pulled up a kitchen chair and continued to watch her as she slept.

Truth be told, he was having trouble linking the two Mias—the one from his past and this one. Although he remembered clearly being aware of the shy schoolgirl crush she'd had on him he'd ignored it, quite sure it would go away but, before it had happened, a freak storm had intervened, he'd got clobbered on the head by a falling branch and when he wasn't sure what was what, he'd been beset by the certainty that all he wanted was to have and to hold Mia Gardiner.

Then sanity and reality had returned and he'd come back to West Windward kicking himself, although still not a hundred per cent sure what had actually happened between them.

Only to find the problem was solved. Mia apparently had accepted that he'd been concussed and gone on her way to a Queensland university, making her parents very proud.

But it hadn't happened like that, he reminded himself grimly.

How had she managed to throw off as much of the shadow of it all as she had?

He thought of his mother with grim forbearance. Arancha was—Arancha, fiercely loyal to her family, no matter the cost and no matter—he grimaced—how misplaced her sentiments might be.

It was a problem that had escalated with his father's death, one he'd inherited. It had struck him once or twice that maybe grandchildren would be the balm Arancha needed, only to wonder with a touch of black humour what kind of chaos his mother could create as an interfering grandmother.

Fortunately Juanita stood little nonsense from her mother but could Damien stand up to her? Come to that, Juanita stood little nonsense from Damien, he reflected wryly, and wondered if his new brother-in-law had understood what he was getting himself into.

None of which, it occurred to him, was of any help to him in this contretemps. How could he make it up to Mia for his mother's cruelty? Not only that, but *his* thoughtless declaration today that he could have kicked himself for what he'd done. And the admission that he would have deemed it right to warn her off too? Not only all that, but not checking out with her that she was all right seven years ago.

Yes, she might have made a success of her life but, beneath that, there obviously lurked the stigma of being branded 'the housekeeper's daughter'. And it was obvious that it still hurt.

What about the attraction there had been between them? Maybe only a teenage crush on her part and a concussion-fuelled moment of madness on his but there all the same. Yet, once again he'd held her and kissed her and she'd responded.

He studied her with a frown, sleeping so peacefully and looking quite unlike the high-powered executive she was in reality.

It must take considerable organisational skills and flair to hold receptions on Mount Wilson. The logistics alone—just about everything had to come from Sydney—were mind-boggling.

Not only that, the foresight to appreciate that the special magic of the mountain would make it irresistible to people for their special days. So, yes, it wasn't inappropriate to call her a high-powered executive.

Even though she slept in tartan pyjamas and looked about sixteen when she did.

He stretched and at the same time felt his mobile phone vibrate in his pocket. He took it out and studied it.

Nina…

He switched it off and put it back in his pocket.

Gorgeous, exotic Nina who ticked all the right boxes for his mother. Model looks, father an ex-politician rewarded for his services with an ambassadorship, uncle married to an Englishwoman who was a Lady in her own right.

Nina, who could be the essence of warmth and charm or cool and regal depending on how the mood took her. Nina, who aroused in most men the desire to bed her, yet who could be incredibly, screamingly insecure.

He stared at the flickering shadows on the wall behind the settee and listened to the crackle of the fire.

What was he going to do about Nina?

She was the one who'd called off their relationship in the middle of the row—he couldn't even remember how it had started now—they'd had before Juanita's wedding.

Well, yes, he could remember, he realised, not exactly how it had started but what it had been about. It was something that had been brewing through all of Juanita's wedding preparations. It all had to do with Nina's desire that *they* get married, something he'd not, for reasons all too clear, although belatedly to him, been willing to do.

And yet he'd allowed things between them to carry on when he'd known he shouldn't but his pride had got in the way.

He'd allowed the good times to define their relationship and he'd cut himself off from her when she was being impossible—she always came back to him as if he was the only spar she had to cling to in the storm-tossed sea of life. He had no doubt that was what she was ringing him for.

But could they go on like this?

He lowered his gaze to the girl sleeping so peacefully on her settee. And he was reminded suddenly of the ridiculous proposal he'd made to her—that she take Nina's place. What had prompted that? he wondered.

Could he blame her for being angry and insulted by it? No…

But what germ of an idea or perception had prompted him even to think it?

The feeling that Mia wouldn't cling, she wouldn't employ emotional blackmail to hold him? That she wouldn't be impossibly nice in between being a bundle of bizarre hang-ups?

If anyone should have some bizarre hang-ups, Mia Gardiner should, he reflected, directly due to the behaviour of himself and his mother.

CHAPTER THREE

MIA WOKE THE next morning to the sound of running water.

She moved under her duvet but she was so snug and comfortable, apart from a slight throbbing in her foot, she was reluctant to get up, reluctant even to open her eyes.

As for the water she was hearing, could it be rain? They had been forecasting rain for a few days...

But no, it didn't sound like rain on the roof, it sounded just like her shower.

Her lashes flew open and she sat up with a gasp as it all came tumbling back into her mind. It had to be Carlos in her shower.

Right on cue, she heard the bathroom door open and he padded through the kitchen wearing only his khaki trousers and drying his hair with a towel.

'Morning,' he said. 'Do you happen to have a razor I could borrow?'

She blinked. 'Only a tiny one. I get my legs waxed.'

He rubbed the dark shadows on his jaw. 'Then you'll

have to put up with me like this. What's your favourite tipple first thing in the morning?'

Her eyes widened. 'Tipple?'

'Champagne? Vodka and fresh orange juice? I personally subscribe to a Bloody Mary.'

He dropped the towel and reached for his shirt lying over a chair. 'You believed me, didn't you?' He shook his head. 'No wonder you're so suspicious if you harbour these dissipated views of me.'

Mia closed her mouth and tried to dampen her look of no doubt naive surprise. Then she confessed with a grimace that she had believed him for a moment. 'But I gather you meant tea or coffee? If so, tea, please, black, no sugar and one slice of raisin toast with butter.'

'Done,' he replied, pulling his shirt off after realising it was inside out. 'Mind you, there are times when champagne is a great way to toast in the morning.'

Foolishly, she realised too late, Mia raised an eyebrow at him. 'When?'

He studied her, his lips twisting. 'When a man and a woman have a night to remember, to celebrate.' His grey eyes flicked over her in a way that left her in no doubt he was visualising a night to remember with her.

Mia blushed—it felt as if from her toes to the top of her head. And hard as she tried to tear her gaze away from his, she couldn't do it as wave after wave of colour ran through her and her senses were alive and leaping. 'Oh.'

'That hadn't occurred to you, obviously,' he said with a glint of wicked amusement in his eyes now.

'No,' she said slowly, but her thoughts were running

riot. She had to get a grip on her responses to him! 'It may not be standard behaviour for housekeepers or their daughters,' she told him tartly.

He frowned. 'You really do have a chip on your shoulder, don't you, Mia?'

She bit her lip but decided she might as well soldier on. 'Yes,' she said starkly and pushed aside the duvet. 'But I don't want to discuss it, thank you, Carlos. I would *really* like to go to the bathroom.'

He put down his shirt again. 'Sure.' And, before she had time to resist, not that she would have been able to anyway, he came across, picked her up and deposited her outside the bathroom door.

Mia ground her teeth but was at a loss to be able to do anything about it.

He still didn't have his shirt on when she made her way out of the bathroom, but there was a steaming cup of black tea and a slice of raisin toast waiting for her on a tray. There was also a neat pile of clothes on the settee. A pair of jeans and a T-shirt as well as a selection of underwear.

'Don't,' he warned as he saw her eyeing the undies with a pink tinge of embarrassment creeping into her cheeks.

'Don't what?' she managed.

'Don't be embarrassed or go all prim and proper on me,' he elucidated. 'I've seen a few bras and panties in my time so I'm not going to become all excited and leap on you.'

'Ah.'

He eyed her. 'And there's still no way you could have gone up the ladder.'

Mia changed tack mentally and said sweetly, 'Thank you, Mr O'Connor.'

He looked surprised for a moment, then picked up his shirt but clicked his tongue as he stared at it.

'What?' Mia asked through a mouthful of toast.

'More blood on it!' He took it over to the sink and rinsed one of the sleeves.

'I'm doubly sorry,' Mia said, actually managing to sound quite contrite as she sipped her tea.

He looked across the kitchen at her with a spark of curiosity in his eyes. 'If that's what a sip of tea and a slice of toast can do for you I'm tempted to think a full breakfast could work miracles.'

Mia had to laugh. 'I don't know about that but I do love my first cuppa.'

He rinsed his shirt sleeve, squeezed it out and turned it right side out again.

That was when Mia frowned as she stared at his back. Her gaze had been drawn to it anyway because she'd suddenly been possessed of an irrational desire to be in a position to run her hands up and down the powerful lines and sleek muscles of it.

'Hang on,' she said slowly. 'What have *you* done to yourself? Your back—there's a black and blue patch on your back.'

'Ah.' He squinted over his shoulder. 'Can't see it but that wasn't me, that was your blasted horse.'

Mia's hand flew to her mouth. 'But I warned you.'

'And I told him I'd been forewarned and he'd be stupid to try anything.' He raked his hair with his fingers. 'We obviously don't speak the same language.'

Mia started to laugh helplessly. 'I'm sorry. I'm sorry,' she repeated. 'I know it's not funny—'

'You expect me to believe that?' he broke in politely.

'You know what I mean! But anyway, you'd better let me put something on it.'

He brought his own tea over and sat down on the coffee table. 'Don't worry about me. Let's see your foot.'

Mia was still shaken by giggles but she stuck her foot out obediently. He unwound the bandage and lifted the dressing off carefully.

'Hmm...still bleeding a bit. Look, I'm going to my friends' to get a change of clothes, then I'll be back and I'll take you to the nearest clinic.'

'You don't have to.'

He got up to fetch the first aid kit. 'Don't start, Mia,' he warned over his shoulder. 'By the way, it's raining.'

Mia glanced out of the window and rubbed her face as she noted the grey, gloomy view. 'I thought it was earlier. At least we don't have a function on today.'

'At least,' he agreed.

They were both silent while he redressed her foot until she said out of the blue, 'We always seem to be bandaging each other.'

He looked up. 'I was just thinking the same thing. History repeats itself.'

'What...what would your father have thought if you'd married someone like me?'

He frowned. 'What makes you ask that?'

'You said his influence was a sort of negative one. Do you know why he was like that?'

Carlos smiled, a tigerish little smile. 'I think it had something to do with the fact that he'd done all the hard work, he'd built the company up from the dirt, whereas I'd, to his mind, had it easy. The right schools, university, the means to—' he gestured '—do whatever I wanted.'

Mia thought for a moment. 'That doesn't mean to say you couldn't be an achiever. It looks as if you've nurtured his dreams and his company and taken them on to even greater heights.'

He shrugged. 'Yes, I have. I doubt if even that would have given him much pleasure.' He looked into space for a moment. 'I don't see why you're wondering about this in connection with us.' He searched her expression narrowly.

'I wondered if he'd disinherit you if he didn't approve of whoever you married.'

'I've no doubt he'd have found something to disapprove of, whoever it was.' He paused and looked into the distance with his eyes narrowed as if some chord had been struck with him but he didn't elaborate.

'Why do people get like that?' Mia asked.

He linked his fingers. 'I think it's the struggle. The almighty battle to pull yourself up by your bootstraps. Coupled probably with a sense of ambition that's like a living force.' He looked down at his hands. 'I could be wrong. But no, he wouldn't have disinherited me. That's the other thing that…weighed, you could say, with my father—my mother.'

Mia blinked. 'How do you mean?'

'She would never have stood by and let him disinherit me.' He grimaced. 'I'm not sure he entirely appreciated the fact that, while she would defend him with her dying breath, she would do the same for me. She's very strong on family loyalty.'

Mia stared into space and listened to the rain on the roof. Then she shivered.

'Mia, what exactly happened that night?'

Her startled gaze jerked back to his. 'You don't remember?' she breathed incredulously.

'I remember...feeling like hell and suddenly being possessed of the strongest urge to hold you in my arms. As if it would make me feel a whole lot better. It did.' His lips twisted. 'Then I remember laughing about something but not exactly what it was and—'

'You called me a pilchard,' she broke in.

He blinked. 'Why the hell would I do that?'

'You actually told me to stop wriggling around like a trapped pilchard.'

Mia said it seriously and her expression was grave but she couldn't maintain it as the expression in his grey eyes went from puzzled to incredulous then gleamed with laughter.

'I'm surprised you didn't find a pilchard to clobber me with! Hopefully I retrieved things?'

'You called me a siren next. Then you kissed me.'

'I remember that.' His gaze fell to her mouth and Mia trembled inwardly. 'But that's all,' he said after a long moment.

A moment when her fingertips tingled as if she was

actually touching them to his skin, as if she was running her fingers through the night-darkness of his hair and trailing them along the blue shadows of his jaw.

If she did that, would he grasp her wrist and kiss her knuckles, would he flick open the buttons of her tartan pyjama top and touch her breasts?

The mere thought of it made her nipples harden and a rush of heat run through her body. She moved restlessly and said hurriedly, 'That is all.'

'Nothing else?' he asked, scanning her pink cheeks with a frown.

'No. You fell asleep and I just stayed there. I didn't want to wake you.' She gestured. 'To be honest, I didn't want to move. I think I must have dozed too because I didn't hear your mother drive in.' She hesitated. 'Why do you ask?'

'So it was only a kiss and an embrace?'

She stared at him. 'Did you think there was…' her voice shook '…more?'

'Not as I remembered it, but…' He frowned. 'For you to be so upset and still so affected by it, I'm now wondering.'

Mia drew a vast agitated breath. 'You think I've made a mountain out of a molehill?'

'No.' He closed his eyes briefly and took her hands.

She wrested them free. 'You do. Oh, will you just go away and leave me in peace, Carlos O'Connor? To think that I once thought I had a crush on you—'

She broke off and her hand flew to her mouth.

'It's all right. I knew.' He stood up—and someone knocked on the door.

'You decent, Mia?' Bill James called out. 'I'm home, just thought to let you know—oh!' He stopped abruptly as Carlos swept open the door.

Bill was in his sixties, white-haired, stocky, tanned and with a distinctly roman nose. His bushy white eyebrows all but disappeared beneath his cap as he took in every detail of the scene before him.

Mia in her pyjamas, Carlos just starting to pull his sweatshirt on.

'Blimey,' he said. 'I'm sorry. I had no idea. I'll go.'

'I'll come with you,' Carlos said. 'I've just been given my marching orders. See you later, Mia. Think you can manage in the meantime?'

'Yes,' Mia said through her teeth, then was forced to back down somewhat. 'Uh…my horse. He needs a feed. Bill, would you mind? Just be careful—'

'Tell you what, Mia,' Bill broke in, 'it's time you got rid of that horse—he's a menace.'

'I couldn't agree with you more.' Carlos put out his hand and introduced himself to Bill, and they left together as if they were lifelong friends, closing the door behind them.

Mia stared after them, then picked up her pillow and hurled it at the door.

'I can't believe you've done all this,' Mia said later as the sports car nosed its way into Bellbird's driveway and pulled up at the main house. It was pouring.

'Taken you to the doctor?' Carlos raised a quizzical eyebrow. 'Would you rather I'd left you to bleed to death?'

Mia clicked her tongue. 'I wasn't going to!'

'The slightest pressure and it was still bleeding,' he commented.

Mia looked down at her bandaged foot. She now had three stitches in her heel and she had a crutch.

'No, not that. Thank you very much for that,' she said stiffly. 'I obviously couldn't have driven myself. No, I mean ringing Gail last night so—'

'Look, Mia,' he said evenly, 'when I came to lock up last night I noticed Gail's number in a prominent position on the wall in your study and I decided the sooner she knew you were incapacitated the better. I was going to tell you when I got back to the cottage but you were fast asleep. What's wrong with that?'

'Gail,' Mia said precisely, 'will be absolutely agog to think that you spent the night with me and will be imagining all sorts of wild and improbable things. You don't know her. She is also incapable of keeping things to herself so it will be all over the mountain. And Bill is just as bad,' she added forcefully.

'Who cares?' Carlos replied this time. 'You and I know the truth, that's all that matters, and anyway, in this day and age, nobody thinks twice about that kind of stuff. OK. I presume you will want to see Gail?'

Mia nodded.

'Then we'll do this the easy way.'

She looked questioningly at him but he simply got out of the car and came to open her door. He then scooped her out of the seat and carried her into the house. 'You know, if I owned this place,' he remarked at the same time, 'I'd add some undercover parking. Your office?' he asked.

'Yes. Oh, hi, Gail,' she added. 'And you remember Mr O'Connor?'

'Mia!' Gail said dramatically as she fluttered around them. 'Are you all right? Mr O'Connor, good to see you again. Bring her this way, Mr O'Connor—I've put a cushion under her desk for her to put her foot on and I've made some coffee. I'm sure we could all do with some!'

It was over lunch that Mia asked, 'Gail, are you sure you can handle all this? You'll have to do everything I normally do for the next few days as well as the stuff you usually do.'

Gail hesitated. 'There is my sister, Kylie. She's only fourteen but she's pretty good around the house. I'm sure she could help and she's on school holidays at the moment.'

'Kylie!' Mia sat up. 'That's brilliant. Will your mum mind?'

'No way. Anything to take Kylie's mind off boys at the moment will be very welcome.' Gail cast her gaze skywards as if she was at least forty with a boy-mad daughter of her own.

'All right.' Mia selected a smoked salmon sandwich. 'Thanks for making lunch, Gail.'

'No problemo.' Gail poured their tea. 'Uh—is Mr O'Connor coming back?'

'He didn't say—rather, all he said was, "I'll be back". By the way, Gail—' Mia took a sip of tea '—I misled you a bit yesterday. My parents used to work for the O'Connors, that's how I knew about Juanita and her family.'

Gail put the teapot down slowly. 'So you used to know him?' she said.

'Yes.' Mia flinched inwardly to see Gail staring at her with patent, revamped curiosity and regretted embarking on these tangled explanations. She'd only done so because she'd felt guilty about not precisely lying to Gail the day before but not being exactly honest and open either. Had she also thought it mightn't look so bad, the fact that Carlos had spent the night in the cottage with her, if they knew each other?

She bit her lip and could have kicked herself but decided she had to soldier on. 'I was only the housekeeper's daughter and I didn't think they'd recognise me. That's why—' She broke off and shrugged.

'So that's why he came back after the wedding was over,' Gail said slowly. 'How lucky was that? I mean your foot.'

I only cut my foot because he antagonised me enough to make me run away from him, Mia thought but did not say. 'Yes. Yes, it was lucky,' she murmured.

'You know what?' Gail rearranged her teacup and saucer, 'I think he'll keep coming back,' she confided.

Mia looked at her uneasily. 'Oh, I don't know about that.'

'I do.' Gail smiled mysteriously. 'But I won't say another word.'

'Gail!' Mia stared at her assistant with deep frustration written large into her expression. 'You can't just say things like that and leave them up in the air.'

'OK, if you want it spelt out.' Gail got up as if she thought she might have to take evasive action. 'There's chemistry,' she announced.

'What?' Mia frowned.

'There's a little crackle of tension in you when he's around and he enjoys picking you up and carrying you around. Not only that, he enjoys the fact that it annoys you. I can see a wicked little glint in his eye when he does it.'

Mia stared at her assistant open-mouthed.

'You did want to know, didn't you?' Gail enquired, looking the picture of injured innocence.

'Yes. No. You're quite wrong, Gail. I—'

But with a perky, 'We'll see!' over her shoulder, Gail left the office.

Mia glared after her. Next she glared at the last salmon sandwich on the plate but decided to eat it anyway. Then she sat back with a deep sigh, feeling moody and without grace.

Of course being confined to hopping around on one foot, even with a crutch—which was not that easy to manage—was enough to make her feel helpless but it was also an emotional helplessness. It was like a roller coaster ride.

What had she believed would happen between her and Carlos all those years ago?

At the time she'd had no expectations, it had all happened out of the blue and—yes, she had to concede, she'd wondered if it was all due to his concussion. But she'd also thought it wasn't impossible for him to be attracted to her.

Then had come the horrible confrontation with Arancha, and the weeks after she'd left West Windward when she'd cherished the little seed of hope in her heart that Carlos would find her and tell her his mother was wrong, he needed her, he wanted her, he loved her.

But as the weeks had grown into a month, then two, and she'd felt that fragile little seed die and she'd... hated him?

No, she thought, that was the funny part about it. If anything, she'd hated herself because she couldn't hate him, although she'd certainly hated his mother.

But the other funny thing was when she'd refused to allow herself to wallow in self-pity and started living again, socialising and dating and so on, it didn't happen for her. There had been no real attractions and the half-baked ones she'd thought might turn into the real thing never had. And that was down to Carlos.

'OK.' Gail came into the office, delving into her purse for her car keys.

Carlos had not returned after dropping Mia off from the doctor, although he'd said he'd be back and he'd stay the night. Consequently, Mia had asked Gail to make up two of the never used bedrooms in the main house.

Gail had cast her a narrowed look and said, 'Much snugger in the cottage, but it's up to you.'

'Yes,' Mia had replied with something of a snap.

'Look, I'm sorry I've got to go before he gets back,' Gail said now as she jangled her keys, 'but everything is under control and Bill is here. It's not such a big event tomorrow, only thirty for lunch, a garden club on their annual day out so they'll be raving about this garden— and I'll bring Kylie with me to lend a hand. Sure you'll be OK? I would stay until he comes but it's my Girl Guides night tonight so I can't be late.'

'I'm fine, promise, don't worry. And I've plenty of bookwork to occupy me.' Mia leant over her desk and touched Gail's hand. 'Thanks, pal. I don't know what I'd do without you!'

Gail beamed with pleasure.

Mia sat back and listened to her drive off, then smote her forehead with the heel of her hand because she'd been going to ask Gail to feed Long John Silver and put him away for the night but she'd forgotten. Gail was good with Long John.

Only a moment or so later, however, she heard a car drive up and assumed it would be Carlos, but frowned suddenly because his car had a distinctive engine note. She discovered she was right; it wasn't Carlos, it was her neighbour, Ginny Castle, and her twelve-year-old son Harry.

'Come in, Ginny,' Mia called in response to Ginny's knock. 'In the study.'

Ginny, a bustling redhead, came through, talking nineteen-to-the-dozen, as was her habit.

'Just heard you've got stitches in your foot, Mia, love—you really should be more careful!—but anyway, with Bill and Lucy away, how about if we took Long John home until you're up to scratch again? Harry can ride him over and I can bring all his clobber in the ute.'

'Ginny, you're a darling!' Mia said with very real gratitude. 'I was going to ask Gail to feed and rug him before she left but she was obviously in a hurry and anyway, I forgot. And actually Bill is home, but he and Long John don't get along.'

'Not a problem. Got anyone to feed and water *you*?' Ginny asked and laughed richly.

'Someone is coming, thanks all the same.'

'Then we'll get going before it gets dark.' And she shepherded Harry out in front of her.

'Just be careful, Harry,' Mia called. 'He can bite.'

Harry evaded his mama and stuck his head back round the office door. 'Not me, he doesn't!'

'How come?' Mia enquired.

'Because the last time he tried it I bit him back. See you, Mia.'

Mia was still laughing and experiencing a warm glow a few minutes later when the phone rang.

She answered it but when she put it down many minutes later she was pale and shaken-looking and she dropped her head into her hands.

'What's wrong?'

She jumped and realised Carlos must have driven in without her hearing him. It was raining again. He stood in the doorway in jeans and a tweed jacket and he was frowning down at her.

'Are you in pain?'

'No. Not much. Well, maybe a little heart-sore,' she said with an attempt to smile. 'I'm about to lose Bellbird. But I did know it might be on the cards so...' She shrugged.

He said nothing, then he reached for a cardigan lying over the back of a chair and handed it to her.

Her eyes widened. 'What's this? I'm not cold, not yet, anyway.'

'You could be. We're going out.'

'Where? No, I mean I don't feel like going out.' She regarded him with a frown and said something silly but she was feeling bruised and battered. 'Don't think you can call all the shots, Carlos.'

'Will you stop being tedious, Mia?' he shot back. 'We're going out to dinner whether you like it or not. Why you shouldn't like it is beyond me. You're not up to cooking and I'm still a P-plater when it comes to—'

'A *what*?' she interrupted.

'A pupil when it comes to cooking, like a learner driver.'

'Last night—'

'Oh, I can drive a microwave,' he said with a wave of his hand, 'but I don't happen to feel like anything microwaved tonight. I feel like something hearty, like an inch-thick steak with English mustard hot enough to make my eyes water. Like hot chips, crisp on the outside and soft and fluffy inside, like grilled mushrooms.'

He paused, then continued. 'Maybe a side salad, but not one with all those weird leaves—I'm very conventional when it comes to my salads. I like iceberg lettuce. And when I've finished that I'd like a nice piece of cheese, some cheddar, perhaps, and then something light and sweet but not too sweet, like lemon meringue and not a lot, just a slice followed by real coffee, Kona perhaps, from Hawaii.'

They stared at each other. He was resting his fists on the other side of her desk.

'Oh,' was all Mia could think of to say. But a moment later, 'My mother makes the best lemon meringue.'

He grinned fleetingly. 'The Northern Rivers might be a bit far to go. But we could try Blackheath.' He straightened. 'It's raining again. Would you like me to carry you to the car?'

'No,' she said hastily. 'I mean—' she got up and reached for her crutch, cast a quick upward glance at his expression—and there was a wicked little glint of pure amusement in his eyes, damn him! '—I mean I can manage.'

'Good.' He watched her for a moment more, then turned to lead the way and open the doors.

It was a small, dim little restaurant in Blackheath he took her to but when he asked what she'd like to order she could only stare blindly down at the menu in front of her.

'All right, I'll order for you,' he murmured.

A couple of minutes later she had a glass of golden wine and in due course his steak and a herb omelette for her arrived.

Good choice, she thought with the only part of her brain that seemed to be functioning, *I couldn't have coped with anything heavier.*

In the end she finished the omelette and ate her roll

before she finally sat back and said with a tinge of surprise, 'I didn't know I was hungry.'

He finished his steak.

'How was it?' she queried. 'As mouth-watering as you described it earlier?'

He grimaced. 'I got a bit carried away, but almost. So, they're not going to renew the lease?'

'No. My two lovely old ladies have handed over their affairs, including their enduring power of attorney, and they've signed Bellbird over as well, to their nephew.' She fiddled with her napkin. 'And he's decided to put it on the market.'

'I'm sorry.'

Mia lifted her glass and cupped the bowl of it in the palm of her hand, the stem between her fingers, as she watched the liquid swirling around. 'But that's not the only problem,' she said finally. 'I did have written into the lease should this happen that I needed at least six months' notice because I had to be able to take forward bookings.' She paused. 'Even six months is not very long; some people have wanted to book from year to year. Some weddings are planned nine—' she gestured '—twelve months in advance.'

'So you'll have to cancel some forward bookings you took over the six months mark?'

She shook her head. 'I didn't take any over the six months mark, although I have a lot under it. But the nephew wants to contest the six months' notice.'

Carlos narrowed his eyes. 'Does he have a leg to stand on?'

Mia sighed. 'I don't know. He's threatened me with

the fact that his aunts may not have been in their right minds when they signed the lease, that I may even have exerted undue influence on them. I think—' Mia twirled her glass and sighed '—I get the feeling he's in financial straits and he really needs to sell Bellbird.'

'*He* may have been the one who exerted undue influence,' Carlos said meditatively.

'I wondered about that, but the thought of going to court...' She shook her head. 'I may not have much choice, though. *I* could get sued for leaving some of the closer functions in the lurch.'

He sat back and placed his napkin on the table. 'Apart from that, are you confident you'll find somewhere else and be able to get a business up and going again?' he asked.

Mia shook her head. 'Not confident. I've got butterflies in my stomach—terrible fears would be more accurate—that I won't be able to, but I'll push on. Somehow.'

He said, as he pushed his plate away, 'Not a great couple of days.'

'No,' she agreed. She rubbed her forehead, then collected her loose hair in one hand and drew it in a thick rope over her shoulder.

'I like your hair loose.'

Mia looked up and their gazes caught and held across the table. And something in the way he was looking at her ignited a rush of awareness in her as well as sending her pulse racing.

Heavens above, she thought, it would be so easy to seek solace and comfort, from a cruel blow on top of everything else, in his arms. It would be not only that but something she craved, she acknowledged, still staring into his eyes and feeling herself drowning in their grey depths.

But she had to break this spell. She made herself look away and blink a couple of times.

'Mia.' He said her name very quietly.

'Tell me more about Nina.'

She bit her lip, then thought, why shouldn't she ask about her?

'I don't know why you're looking like that,' she said evenly.

He raised an eyebrow. 'Like what?'

'As if—' she paused '—as if I'm being ridiculous.'

His lips twisted. 'If I did, it was because I don't see the connection—thank you,' he said to the waitress delivering their coffee.

She blushed and tripped as she walked away.

This time it was Mia who expressed unspoken irony—she looked heavenward.

'We seem to be at cross purposes,' Carlos said lazily, sitting back and looking even more amused.

Mia controlled herself with difficulty. 'You don't see the connection? OK! Let's put it in black and white,' she said tartly. 'You've virtually come straight from Nina French's arms to being—to looking—to...' She stopped helplessly.

'To being possessed of the desire to have and to hold you?' he supplied and sat forward to rest his elbow on the table and his chin on his fist. 'You know, it's a funny thing but that desire seems to exist on its own.

It seems to have a life of its own. It doesn't seem to be susceptible to anything else that's going on all around it—if you know what I mean.'

'I…' Mia stopped, frowned at him, looked away, then looked back as if jerked on a string. 'I'm not sure what you do mean,' she said uncertainly.

'Simple. Since I got clobbered on the head by a falling branch, I only have to be in your company to want you. In my bed, in case there's any misunderstanding. Whatever the other circumstances of my life happen to be.'

Mia was dead still for a long moment, then she clicked her tongue in sheer frustration and stood up, ready to walk away. 'You're impossible! Actually you're crazy, Carlos O'Connor. What you're describing—the way you're describing us makes it sound as if we exist in a bubble. It doesn't sound *real*,' she said intensely.

There was silence for a long moment, then she said quietly, 'That's why I want to know about Nina. And if *she's* real for you.'

He stood up and it stunned her to see that he *was* suddenly grimly serious. 'Nina and I are washed up. I never should have let it go on for so long but my dearest wish is for her to find someone who understands her better than I did. Someone who anchors her and loves her even when the impossible things about her make it…almost impossible to do so.'

Mia blinked several times and sat down.

He stared down at her for a long moment and she was shocked by the harsh lines scored into his face, then he sat down himself.

'I'm sorry,' Mia said quietly but her throat worked. 'I didn't realise it was so painful for you.'

'Painful?' He picked up his glass and studied it. 'I wish to hell I knew what it actually was.'

Mia opened her mouth, then decided to keep her thoughts on that subject to herself. 'Shall we go?' she said tentatively. 'We're the only ones left and they might be wanting to close up. I'll just visit the powder room.'

'Sure.' He signalled for the bill and when she came back he helped her out to the car. It was still raining.

'Damn,' Mia said as they drove along.

He looked questioningly at her.

'I've got a garden club coming for lunch tomorrow. They're really keen to see the Bellbird gardens.'

'It could be a whole new world tomorrow,' he said wryly.

Mia smiled. 'It's what I need. But I doubt there'll be much change, although the sun may shine. By the way, Gail made up two beds in the main house for tonight—'

'Oh,' he interrupted, 'didn't I tell you? I've made different arrangements for tonight. Gail's coming to stay with you after her Girl Guides session ends.'

Mia's mouth fell open. 'No, you didn't tell me. Neither did Gail—she didn't say a word to me. Not about tonight.'

'She didn't know before she left work this afternoon. I didn't get around to making these other arrangements until quite late.' He looked across at her. 'I didn't think you'd mind.'

'I…well…' She stopped helplessly.

'You don't sound too sure and you look cross,' he

observed. 'In light of your extreme agitation on the subject last night, I'm surprised.'

Mia gritted her teeth. 'It's just that I like to know what's going on. When did you get in touch with Gail?'

'While you were in the powder room.'

'You...I...*how* did you get in touch with her?'

'I rang her last night, remember? So I've got her number in my mobile phone. Anything further you'd like to know, Sergeant Gardiner?' He turned into Bell-bird's driveway just after, as it happened, Gail did and they followed her tail-lights up the driveway.

'*Why*?'

'I've decided to go back to Sydney tonight—hell, I forgot about Long John. I'll drive down—'

'You don't have to,' Mia said.

'But you can't let him starve. That could make him worse than ever.'

'He won't starve—I've given him to someone to look after.'

'Someone he won't bite, I hope, but how do you know he won't bite *this* person?'

'Because *this* person bit him back,' Mia replied and dissolved into laughter. 'I'm sorry,' she said finally, still giggling, 'I think it's all been a bit much for me but it does have its funny side. And don't you dare carry me out of this car and inside. I can manage. Take care in Sydney.' She patted his arm, and struggled out with her crutch.

'What's so funny?' Gail asked as they met at the front door. 'Are you laughing or crying?'

'I don't know.' Mia rubbed her face. 'Well, yes, I do. You were right—it's much cosier down at the cottage, Gail, so shall we go down there and start a fire and have a drink? As someone once said, what's the point in being sober *and* virtuous at this end of the day?'

'Who said that? Shakespeare?'

'No—just someone I know.' Mia climbed into Gail's car and stowed her crutch. 'Not that I'm unsober. I've only had one glass of wine. Mind you, now I come to think of it, maybe I don't have anything to drink after last night.'

'Just as well it's me.' Gail climbed into the driver's side and she hauled a bottle of wine out of her bag. 'Don't know why but I thought to pop this in with my PJs.'

'Gail, you're a treasure.' Mia leant over to kiss her assistant on the cheek. 'You wouldn't believe the kind of day I've had. Or the last couple of hours, anyway. Oh, Gail, I've got some bad news.'

'Wait,' Gail advised as she drove down the track to the cottage. 'I know a bit of it, anyway.'

'How? Don't tell me Carlos told you!'

Gail nodded. 'He said you could be feeling a bit delicate so I was to take care of you on his behalf till he gets back.'

Mia stared at Gail in the gloom of the car. 'He said that?'

'Yep.' Gail coasted to a stop, switched off and doused the lights.

'He takes a lot upon himself,' Mia said indistinctly, in the grip of an emotion she found hard to name—

anger at his high-handed ways? Helplessness? Or the faintest whisper like a tiny echo in her heart that told her how wonderful it would be to have Carlos to turn to, for advice, for mental support? To help her to shore up her shaken defences?

'If I had Carlos O'Connor on my side,' Gail said with a certain militancy but almost as if she'd read Mia's mind, 'and thinking of me, I'd be a bit more gracious about it than you are, Mia. Now, will you come in and get warm and maybe a bit unsober?'

CHAPTER FOUR

THE SUN CHOSE to shine on the garden club lunch the next day and Gail, with the help of her sister Kylie, managed brilliantly.

Mia spent most of the day sitting in her office talking on the phone and working on the computer. She'd tossed and turned all night under the twin weights of losing Bellbird and what she thought of as the irrefutable knowledge that Carlos was still in love with Nina, much as he might wish otherwise.

Trying to seek legal advice as well as trying to find a venue she could transfer functions to did not do anything to cheer her up.

She had another twenty-four hours before she had to make a response to Bellbird's new owner but she couldn't make up her mind whether to go to court or not.

Finally, late afternoon, when all the guests had left, the clear air lured her out into the garden. She hopped over to a bench and sank down. The sunlight was warm on her skin; she was wearing a soft green summer dress that matched her eyes. And, because she'd not been on show, her hair was only lightly tied back.

The gardens were beautiful. The rain had freshened them up, there were bees and dragonflies hovering over the flowers, there were delicate scents on the air, there was the unique aura of Mount Wilson, and there were bellbirds calling.

Don't cry, she warned herself as she closed her eyes and gave herself over to the magic of the estate.

It was the roar of Carlos's car that roused her from her reverie.

She opened her eyes and watched it pull up at the main house. She saw Carlos get out and stretch, then walk inside.

Carlos, she thought with a sudden pang as well as an accelerated heartbeat. Despite all her own catastrophes, she'd not only tossed and turned overnight, she'd had Carlos and Nina French at the back of her mind all day.

It had sounded—from what he'd said last night— as if they couldn't live together but they couldn't live without each other. It had sounded like a relationship fraught with tearing, deep emotion, like a battlefield, but she got the feeling that while those tearing emotions might hurt deeply, the other side of the coin could be heights such as they'd never known with anyone else.

But, whatever it was, in comparison, her own romantic dealings with Carlos had sounded trivial.

She had to forget about him. He never was for her and he never would be.

It was the clink of glass that drew her out of her reverie this time and she opened her eyes again to see Carlos crossing the lawn towards her with a tray bearing a jug and a couple of glasses.

He was wearing jeans, boots and a blue-and-white striped shirt with the neck open and the sleeves rolled up. He looked impossibly attractive with his dark hair and olive skin, with his height and wide shoulders, his lean body...

'Hi!' she said, taking a very deep breath. 'Welcome back, but if that's alcohol I think I should abstain.'

He grinned. 'Gail told me you and she demolished a bottle of wine last night. No, it's fresh fruit juice, not at all spiked.'

He put the tray down on a wrought iron table and sat down next to her on the bench. 'How's the foot?'

'Not bad. I'm getting the hang of the crutches now—there's a bit of an art to it. I—' she hesitated '—I wasn't sure if you were coming back. You didn't need to. I'm being very well looked after.'

'Good.'

'Thank you all the same—' she interrupted '—for all your help. I don't want to seem ungracious.'

'Ungracious?' He looked quizzical.

'That's what Gail said I was.' She bit her lip.

'So Gail's giving you lessons in tact and diplomacy?' he hazarded. 'Should be interesting.'

Mia regarded him for a long moment with an expression of deep hostility. 'Between the two of you,' she said bitterly, 'it's not surprising I'm feeling like a nervous wreck. *I am not ungrateful for your help*, Carlos,' she said, emphasising each word. 'That's all I'm trying to say.'

'Good,' he replied comfortably and handed her a glass of fruit juice. 'Lovely out here, isn't it?' He looked around.

'Yes,' she said on a little sigh. 'Hear the bellbirds?'

He listened. 'Yes. How was your day?'

Mia sighed. 'Pretty disheartening. I haven't come up with an alternative yet and I can't make up my mind whether to go to court or not, but—' she gestured and squared her shoulders '—tomorrow's another day—I think it was Scarlett O'Hara who said something like that.'

'No doubt after Rhett told her he couldn't give a damn.' He looked amused. 'Uh…I have some better news for you. I've bought it.'

'Bought what?' she asked automatically.

'This place.' He waved a hand.

Mia choked. Even the bellbirds seemed to stop calling in the long moments before she could gather her wits to reply. Then she turned to him, her face suddenly pale, her eyes huge, dark and uncomprehending.

'What do you mean? What are you talking about?'

He put his hand along the back of the bench behind her. 'I bought Bellbird,' he said slowly and precisely.

'*Bought it*?' she echoed huskily, still looking stunned. 'Why?'

He withdrew his arm and sat forward with his hands between his knees. 'So you can stay on. You can lease it from me for as long as you want. But there were other reasons. I had this vision planted in my mind of a girl in a long white dress, carrying a big hat and playing ladies on a hill station. A girl with heavy, midnight-dark hair and green eyes. Wait,' he murmured as Mia stirred. 'Let me finish.'

He thought for a moment. 'A girl I admired and—'

'And felt sorry for,' Mia said out of a clogged throat. 'Please don't go on.'

He put a hand on her knee. 'No, I don't feel sorry for you, Mia. There's something about you that doesn't go with sickly sentimental stuff like that. But I do like to repay my debts.'

'You don't owe me anything.'

'Yes, I do,' he countered. 'Between myself and my mother, we must have created hell for you. I also—' he paused '—need to apologise for the possibly flip-pant way I described the effect you have on me from time to time.'

Mia blinked.

'Not that it doesn't happen,' he added dryly. 'But you're right, there's something a bit unreal about it.'

Mia flinched inwardly and immediately called her-self a fool. Why did it hurt? She'd told herself only hours ago he wasn't the one for her; he'd never been. And her beleaguered mind turned to the fact that he'd bought Bellbird.

'I can't believe you bought it,' she said shakily.

He shrugged. 'It's a little bit of heaven. Who wouldn't want it if they could have it? Besides—' all of a sudden he sounded cold and grim '—there's not a lot I can do about a nephew exerting undue pressure on his elderly aunts but the details of the sale include

me taking over your lease and deducting a compensa-
tory amount from the sale price.'

Mia blinked. 'I don't know what to say. I wish you
hadn't.' It was a sentiment that slipped out unexpectedly
but it was true, she realised. Despite everything she felt
for the property and her business, she wished he hadn't.

'Why?'

She interlaced her fingers. 'It makes me feel beholden to you.'

He swore beneath his breath.

She hesitated and in the grip of a maelstrom of emotions, she rubbed her face distractedly. 'It also puts me
in an impossible position.'

'What does?' There was a distinct coolness in his
voice now.

Mia put a hand to her mouth. 'To think you bought
Bellbird because of me and therefore I should, out of
gratitude, do anything you want.'

'Perish the thought,' he said harshly. 'You don't really believe I'm going to blackmail you into anything,
do you?'

She was silent.

'But—' he paused '—if you didn't want to stay, you
could have your six months to get you out of any con-
tractual difficulties and then—' he grimaced, folded
his arms across his chest and stretched his legs out
'—we would come to our final parting of the ways,
Mia, at least with me knowing I'd done as much as
I was allowed to, to compensate for what happened
seven years ago.'

Mia jumped up, her eyes flashing, and fell over as her injured heel hit the ground.

Carlos was on his feet immediately and he picked her up and held her in his arms as she struggled.

'Whoa!' he admonished. 'What the hell do you think I'm going to do? Here.' He handed her the crutch and put his hands on her hips until she steadied.

Then, to her fury, he tidied her hair with his hands and pushed it back over one shoulder. 'I see what you mean about the crutch,' he said as he straightened the collar of her dress. 'Not only are you one-legged but you're one-handed—awkward.'

Mia breathed deeply and Carlos sat down again and drained his glass.

'Go on, I'm all ears,' he drawled.

'Look, please don't think I'm not grateful—'

'Here we go again,' he murmured. 'You're a good teacher, Gail.'

'All *right*,' she said through her teeth with sudden tears streaming down her face. 'I will *never* forgive your mother for what she did, how she made me feel. I will never forgive *you*—' she broke off and realised that it might have come seven years late but it was true '—for not checking up on me, even if it had been to come and say, "Mia, I *could only mess up your life*."'

'Mia—'

But she waved him to silence. 'Nor will I ever forgive your mother for coming back into my life and patronising me all over again. This—' she gestured to take in Bellbird '—can't change that and if I did stay on I'd feel terrible because I'd still feel the same way. Don't you see?'

'All right.' He stood up and put the glasses back on the tray. 'But you'd be well advised to stay for the six months. Protracted legal dealings can cost a fortune. Don't worry.' He looked down at her sardonically. 'I won't trouble you at all.'

Mia discovered she was trembling all over and she still had tears rolling down her cheeks. 'Look, I'm sorry if I…if…'

'Forget it,' he said. 'Better to know where we stand. You hold your crutch.'

Mia looked up at him. 'What do you mean?'

'This, no doubt for the last time, Mia.' And he picked her up effortlessly and started to stride across the lawn with her.

Mia was struck dumb because, apart from kissing her, he couldn't have done anything that affected her senses more drastically. To feel herself cradled against his hard, toned body, to inhale that tantalising smell of sweat and fresh cotton sent ripples of desire and need through her.

Then he compounded it as they reached the house.

He set her carefully on her feet, waited until she was steady on her crutch, then he kissed her full on the mouth with his hand cupping her head.

'Take care, Miss Firebrand,' he advised with an ironic little glint in his eye. 'Take care.'

He made sure she was steady again and walked away to his car.

It was Gail who came out to stand beside Mia as Carlos accelerated down the drive. It was Gail who put her arm around Mia's shaking shoulders and led her inside.

CHAPTER FIVE

Six weeks later Mia put down the phone and stared into space, her mind reeling.

She was still at Bellbird, having, after serious thought and some legal advice, written Carlos a stilted little note to the effect that she would be grateful to stay on for the six-month term of her original lease. She'd got a reply agreeing to her request, written and signed by his secretary.

Gail happened to be passing the office doorway with a pile of snowy tablecloths in her arms but she paused and raised an interrogative eyebrow at her boss.

'That was Carol Manning,' Mia said in a preoccupied manner.

Gail waited a moment, then, 'Do I know Carol Manning?'

'Uh…no, sorry.' Mia tapped her teeth with her pencil. 'She's Carlos O'Connor's secretary.'

Gail advanced into the office and dumped the tablecloths on a chair. 'What's he want?'

'A lunch for forty next week. They're holding some kind of a conference on the two preceding days and have decided to wrap things up with a lunch.'

'Not a great deal of notice,' Gail observed. 'He's lucky you had the day free.'

'He...' Mia paused. 'He had something else planned, a cruise on the harbour, but the long range forecast is for showers and high winds now—in Sydney, that is, it's only a coastal low pressure system, apparently. It should be OK up here. I can't help wondering why he didn't choose another venue, though.'

Gail grimaced. 'Why should he when he owns the best venue there is?'

Mia smiled dryly. 'In a nutshell,' she murmured. 'I still wish he'd gone somewhere else.'

'I can understand that.' Gail picked up her tablecloths. 'Considering the way things ended between you two. Not that I've asked any questions, but you only had to have eyes.'

'Gail, you've been a tower of strength and I really appreciate the fact that you haven't asked any questions,' Mia said warmly. 'I just...I'm just not sure how I'll be.'

'You'll be fine! At least you can walk on two feet now. OK—' she dumped the tablecloths on a chair again and sat down opposite Mia '—let's help you to be fine; let's slay 'em. Let's give them the best darn lunch they've ever had. Is there any kind of theme to the conference—did this Carol Manning mention anything pivotal?'

'Horses,' Mia said succinctly. 'O'Connor Construction is planning to build an equestrian centre that should accommodate stabling, tracks for thoroughbreds, tracks for trotters, dressage plus a vet hospital, swimming pools for horses, you name it. Thus, at the conference there'll be a variety of people from vets to trainers to owners to jockeys, but all horsey.'

'I'm quite a fan of horses,' Gail observed, looking thoughtful.

'I am too.' Mia chewed the end of her pencil this time. 'Gail, you're a genius. I've just had the most amazing idea.'

'I don't see how that makes *me* a genius.'

'It was your "pivotal" point that did it. You may not know it, but one of the most famous horse races in the world is the Kentucky Derby.'

'Well, I did know that.'

'Good.' Mia turned to her computer and her fingers flew over the keys as she did some research. 'The other thing about it is the fact that it's laden with tradition. You drink mint juleps at Churchill Downs on Kentucky Derby day, you eat burgoo—'

'I've heard of mint juleps but what on earth is burgoo?'

'It's a concoction of beef, chicken, pork and vegetables,' Mia read from her screen, 'and they play Stephen Foster's "My Old Kentucky Home" while you do. Then there are the roses.'

'We've got plenty of roses,' Gail put in.

'I know.' Mia thought of the rose gardens outside in full bloom. 'The tradition is that the winner, the horse, is draped in a blanket woven with five hundred and fifty-four roses. We probably—' she looked up at Gail '—don't have to use that many roses, then again we do need a horse.'

'Not a live one. Certainly not Long John—he could go about biting all manner of people,' Gail objected.

'Nooo—but I can't think what else to substitute. Apart from that, though, wouldn't it be something to serve a horsey crowd mint juleps and—' she pointed to her screen '—feed them burgoo from an authentic recipe—and have the waiters and waitresses dressed in jockey silks?'

Gail blinked. 'The mint juleps sound a bit dangerous if you ask me.'

'The guests are coming by coach so we don't need to worry about drink-driving. A horse, a horse,' Mia said rapidly, 'my kingdom for a horse.'

'My mother's got one; it's a wooden rocking horse, it's nearly as big as the real thing and it's in beautiful condition for an antique. It's Mum's pride and joy.'

'Oh, Gail, do you think she'd lend it to us?'

'We can only ask. What else do we need?'

'Stephen Foster music, but I'm sure I can find that. All right.' Mia sat up. 'I won't have time to think straight.'

'Five hundred and fifty-four roses?' Bill James said incredulously. 'You must be mad, Mia. Clean off your rocker, more like it.'

'If you'd let me finish, Bill,' Mia said with a slight edge, 'I was just telling you that's the number they use in the actual Kentucky Derby to decorate the winner's blanket.'

'They, whoever they are, sound as nutty as fruitcakes

too, if you ask me,' Bill interjected. 'Five hundred and fifty-four. For a horse blanket!'

'Bill—' Mia breathed heavily '—we won't use *nearly* as many but we will use *some*—so be prepared.' She eyed him militantly.

Bill snorted and then eyed *her*. 'You're getting snippety, Mia. Not only that, you're looking peaky. If I were you, I'd get that boyfriend of yours back.'

Mia went to speak but choked instead and finally turned on her heel, the good one, and marched away.

To her dismay, she found herself tossing and turning in her loft the night before the O'Connor lunch, despite her earlier conviction that, with the forthcoming event to think about, she would be too busy to think of anything else.

Finally she got up, climbed down her ladder, put some more wood into the stove and brewed herself a cup of chocolate.

In the six weeks since she'd last seen Carlos, she'd had days when she was sure, quite convinced, in fact, that she'd done the right thing. Even accepting the six months had gone against the grain with her. It had made her feel like the recipient of charity. It made her, as unreasonable as it sounded, but she couldn't help it, feel like the housekeeper's daughter again.

But on other days she thought she must have been a little mad to have knocked back the opportunity to stay on at Bellbird.

Why couldn't she have buried her pride? After all, it had been her dream only a few weeks ago. Even now, as she resolutely looked for new premises to move to when her lease was up, it was tearing her apart to think of leaving.

But that's nonsense, she thought as she sipped her chocolate. It's only a place.

And he's only a man, but like it or not I've had a crush on Carlos for a long time, and probably always will....

She stared into the fire and shivered, not from cold, but from fear. She was feeling scared and young because she was confused, because she was sometimes tempted to think she could love Carlos much better than Nina French had.

In fact loving Carlos, or the thought of it, was something that plagued her waking hours as well as her dreams.

It was mad. No sooner had she told him she could never forgive him, no sooner had she told him she wished he hadn't bought Bellbird, than she'd started to feel bereft and in a particular way.

She missed him. She shook secretly with desire for him. She missed the way he charmed people, like Gail's mother. She desperately missed the way he forked back his hair, how his eyes could laugh at her while his expression was grave. The feel of him when he carried her in his arms...

The next morning Mia dressed carefully in a skirt and blouse.

She'd tied her hair back but used a lilac scarf to lessen the severity of the style.

Then, having checked with the caterers that everything was going well with the 'burgoo'—she gave it a taste test—she took a last tour of the dining room.

Pride of place on a dais was Gail's mother's rocking horse, looking spectacular under its 'rose blanket', which was a work of art, even if nothing like five hundred and fifty-four roses had been used. And in the centre of the room there was an ice carving of a mare with her foal at her foot.

'My Old Kentucky Home' was playing softly in the background and waitresses in jockey silks and caps were waiting to serve mint juleps.

Then the guests arrived and Mia held her breath as they filtered into the dining room but she was reassured by the gasps and delighted comments, and she sought out Gail across the room with her eyes and they gave each other the thumbs-up sign.

There was no sign of Carlos, although Carol Manning had introduced herself. 'He should be here any minute,' she said with some obvious frustration. 'He's often late.'

'I know, he was late for his sister's wedding,' Mia said and bit her lip. 'Uh…he didn't come by bus?'

'Bus! When you have the kind of car he drives, no,' Carol Manning responded and looked more closely at Mia. 'So you're Mia Gardiner? How do you do? I must say—' she looked around, wide-eyed '—I can understand why Mr O'Connor decided to have you do this lunch. It's inspired. Ah, here he is now.' And she nodded to the entrance of the dining room.

Carlos was standing in the doorway, looking around.

He wore a beautifully tailored grey suit, a pale blue shirt and a navy tie. Then, with a faint smile twisting his lips, he came across the room and, for an instant, Mia felt like fainting under the almost overpowering impact of his good looks, his masculinity and what he used to mean to her.

'Well done, Miss Gardiner,' he said. 'Very well done. How's the foot?'

'Fine now, thank you, Mr O'Connor,' she murmured. 'I'll leave you to it. Enjoy your lunch.' And she moved away smoothly.

'So here you are.'

Mia looked up with a start. She was in her cottage having seen, or so she thought, the last of the lunch guests off.

It had clearly been a highly successful function. Carlos had been nowhere to be seen, nor had his car.

'I thought you'd gone,' she said.

'Or hoped I had? Never mind. I actually went to see Gail's mother.' He sat down at the kitchen table.

'What on earth for?' Mia frowned.

'Gail told me she wove the rose blanket so I went to thank her.'

'That was nice,' Mia conceded.

'You sound surprised.'

'No, I've always known you can be nice.' Mia said flatly, then added on a rush of breath, 'What do you want, Carlos? We've got nothing more to say to each other.'

He raised an eyebrow. 'You may not have but it looks

to me as if you've lost weight. Finding it a bit hard to maintain a stance so full of righteous indignation, Mia?'

She gasped. 'How dare you? It's not that!'

'Then what is it?'

'I mean, I haven't lost weight,' she corrected herself belatedly, but it was a lie. She was not prepared to admit as much to Carlos, however.

'According to Bill, not only don't you look well but you're cranky and hard to work with.'

Mia opened her mouth, closed it, then, 'Hard to work with?' she repeated furiously. 'If anyone is hard to work with it's Bill. Have you any idea how I have to nurse him through Lucy's month with her grandkids?' She broke off, breathing heavily.

He watched the way her chest heaved beneath the black blouse, then looked into her eyes. 'If it's any comfort,' he said quietly, 'I'm like a bear with a sore head at times too.'

Her lips parted. 'Why?' she whispered.

'Whatever the rights and wrongs of it, I want you. I thought you might be in the same difficulty.'

She was transfixed as she turned pale then pink in a way that virtually shouted from the rooftops that she was.

'I…I…' she stammered and couldn't go on.

He moved a step closer but that was when her phone rang. It was lying on the kitchen table and she was all set to ignore it but she saw her mother's name on the screen and picked it up to answer.

Her tears were impossible to control when she ended the call and she was white to the lips.

'What?' he asked. 'What's happened?'

'My father. He's had a stroke. Oh, I've got to go but it could take me hours to get off the mountain, let alone up to Ballina.' She wrung her hands.

'No, it won't.' He pulled his own phone out and punched in some numbers.

Half an hour later Mia was on her way down the mountain beside him in his fast car and when they reached Sydney Airport she transferred to a waiting helicopter he'd organised.

'There'll be a car at the airport to take you to the hospital,' he told her just before she boarded the chopper.

'I can't thank you enough!'

'Don't worry about it,' he recommended.

She turned away to climb aboard, then turned back impulsively and kissed him swiftly. 'Thanks,' she said from the bottom of her heart.

A week later her father, who'd been moved to the Lismore Base Hospital, was recovering.

It was going to take some months of physiotherapy for him to be as mobile as he had been, but all the signs were good. And her mother had returned from the shell-shocked, frightened, trembling person she'd been at first to her usual practical and positive self.

'I think we'll lease the tea room out,' she'd told Mia. 'You know, apart from the birds and the bees and growing things, your father has always had another ambition—to drive around Australia. I think the time has come, when he's recovered, to buy a caravan and do it.'

'Why not?' Mia had responded.

Her mother had then looked at her critically and told her she looked as if she needed a break.

Mia agreed with her but didn't tell her she actually felt as if she'd been run over by a bus. Instead she mentioned that she planned to have a couple of days off before she returned to Mount Wilson, since Gail seemed to be coping well and now had Lucy James to help her out.

Mia's mother had looked unconvinced about the efficacy of 'a couple of days' but she'd urged Mia just to do it.

Mia took herself to Byron Bay, south of the Queensland border and the most easterly point of the Australian mainland.

She booked herself into a luxury motel just across the road from the beach and she slept for hours on her first day.

Then she took a stroll down the beach at sunset.

It was a beautiful scene, a pink cloud-streaked sky, the sheen of pewter laid across the placid low-tide water and the lighthouse an iridescent white on the dark green of Cape Byron.

She rolled her jeans up and splashed in the shallows. Her hair was loose and wild. She had a turquoise T-shirt on and she'd tied a beige jumper round her waist by its sleeves. On her way back she stopped to untie it and pull it on as the pink of the sunset slipped from the sky and the air cooled.

That was when she noticed a tall figure standing on the beach below the surf club.

A tall figure she could never mistake—Carlos.

She didn't hesitate. She pushed her arms into the sleeves of the jumper as she walked over to him.

'I didn't know you were here, Carlos.'

'I wasn't. I've only just arrived. Your mother told me you were here.'

'Oh, Carlos! You spoke to my mother?'

He nodded. 'And your father. I went to see them.'

'They would have loved that. Thanks a million. Where are you staying?'

He took her hand and touched the side of her face, then pushed her hair behind her ears. 'With you, Mia. With you if you'll have me.'

She took a breath and a faint smile curved her lips. 'Just as well it's only across the road then,' she said serenely.

'I like the way you do that,' Mia murmured.

She was lying naked across the king-sized bed and her body was afire with his touch as he left no part of her unexplored.

'But I think I need to be held before I…I don't know what, but something tempestuous is liable to happen to me, Carlos,' she went on with a distinct wobble in her voice.

He laughed a little wickedly and took her in his arms. 'How's that?'

'Oh, thanks.' She wound her arms round him and kissed the strong tanned column of his neck. 'You know, I can't believe this.'

'Believe what?' He cupped her bottom.

'How good it is to be here in bed with you,' she said on a genuine note of wonderment. She leant up on one elbow and looked at him seriously. 'It's not too tame for you, is it?'

'Tame?' he replied equally as seriously and removed his hands from her hips to cup her breasts. Her nipples hardened as he played with them and she took several ragged little breaths.

He looked into her eyes. 'Tame?' he repeated as she writhed against him and bit her bottom lip. 'It's the opposite, but are you ready for me, Mia?'

'More than that, dying, actually. Oh!' she gasped as he turned her onto her back and eased his body onto hers. And she was ready to welcome him so that in moments the rhythm of their lovemaking increased and there was absolutely nothing tame about the way they moved together and finally climaxed together—it was wild, wanton and wonderful.

In fact Mia couldn't speak for a few minutes afterwards as she lay cradled in his arms, her body slick with sweat, her hair a cloud of rough black silk on the pillow. And she made a tiny sound when he moved— a sound of protest.

'It's OK,' he reassured her and pulled the sheet up. 'I'm going nowhere.'

She relaxed.

Mia sat cross-legged on the beach early the next morning, sifting sand through her fingers as she watched Carlos body-surfing into the beach.

She'd given up on her hair and hadn't even bothered to pin it back. She wore short white shorts and her turquoise T-shirt, she was barefoot and, because of a playful breeze, she'd pulled on Carlos's sweatshirt.

It was miles too big for her but it not only made her feel warm, it was like having his arms around her.

She was smiling at absolutely nothing at all.

'Hi.' He stood in front of her, droplets of water still sliding down his sleek tanned body, and picked up his towel as he studied her dimples. 'Something funny?'

'No,' she assured him. 'Oh, you'll want your top.' She started to take his sweatshirt off.

'Keep it on,' he said. 'I'll use the towel—now you're laughing!' He looked around. 'What is it?' He sat down beside her.

'It's me,' she told him.

He grimaced. 'What's so funny about you?'

'You know those stereotyped women you see on TV and in the movies who float around radiantly on cloud nine after someone has made love to them?'

'Uh-huh.' He rubbed his hair with the towel and looked at her quizzically. 'Not...?' He didn't finish.

'Yep.' She nodded vigorously. 'That's who I remind myself of this morning. Or those smiley faces on computers.'

'The smiley trail?' He started to laugh and pulled her into his arms and lay back on the sand with her. 'You're crazy,' he teased.

'And you're wonderful,' she replied, sobering. 'There is something else your lovemaking has achieved, though.'

'I hesitate to ask,' he said ruefully.

'I could eat a horse,' she told him. 'I'm *starving*.'

'Ah—' he sat up with her still in his arms '—now there we are of the same mind. Let's go.'

They got back to their room and Mia showered while Carlos ordered breakfast.

When she emerged, breakfast had not arrived but a bottle of champagne stood in an ice bucket on the coffee table next to two flutes and a flask of orange juice.

'Oh,' she said, recalling their conversation about morning-after champagne celebrations. 'Dangerous and delightful.'

Carlos had showered at the beach and he wore khaki shorts and a white shirt. His hair was still damp and hanging in his eyes. His feet were bare but he was enough to make her heart beat faster and then, when he came and ran his hands down her body, over her colourful cotton sarong, all the fire he'd aroused in her the night before came back to her and she trembled and put her arms around his waist and laid her head on his chest.

'You shouldn't,' she said huskily.

He traced his fingers down the side of her neck and cupped the smooth curve of her shoulder. 'Shouldn't?' He said it barely audibly.

'Touch me. It sets off all sorts of chain reactions.'

She felt his slight jolt of laughter and he kissed the top of her head. 'You're not alone.'

There was a knock on the door.

They drew apart, both laughing.

* * *

It was a glorious day.

She spoke at length to her parents, then they drove up to the lighthouse after lunch and were rewarded as they gazed down at the wrinkled blue ocean to see a pod of humpback whales making their way back to the Southern Ocean after their sojourn in the tropical waters of Queensland.

'There's something about them that always makes me feel emotional,' she said of the whales as they sat on a bench from where they could see not only the ocean to the east of Cape Byron but the protected beaches to the west as well as Mount Warning, and Julian Rocks out in the bay.

'I think it's because they're so big and it's such an amazing journey.' He put his arm around her shoulders. 'Don't cry.'

She sniffed. 'I'm not crying, not really.'

'How about—' he stretched out his legs '—we go out for dinner tonight?'

'Uh…we could. Any special reason?'

He meditated for a moment. 'There's a band playing at the restaurant next door to the motel,' he said, 'so we could eat and dance.'

'Sounds good.'

'But I have an ulterior motive,' he went on. 'I think I would like to see a really glamorous version of you, all dressed and tizzied up, and be confident in the knowledge that when I got you back to our room I'd be able to undo it all.'

Mia choked. 'That's...diabolical.'

He took his arm from her shoulders and sat forward, taking her hand. 'You'd enjoy it, I promise.'

'I...possibly,' she conceded. 'Always assuming I could sit still and eat my dinner with that on my mind. However—' she paused dramatically '—there's one problem.'

He raised an eyebrow at her.

'I didn't bring any smart clothes with me.'

'Ah. Well, look, while I make some calls, why don't you undertake some retail therapy?'

Mia pursed her lips. 'You really think I should?'

'I really do. I've discovered that next to sex—and sometimes even over and above sex—retail therapy does wonders for girls.'

Mia almost went cross-eyed as she struggled not to make a thoroughly exasperated feminist retort to this.

'You don't agree?' he asked.

Mia looked at him. He was still in his khaki shorts and white shirt. The breeze was lifting his hair and the fine white cotton of his shirt.

He looked big, utterly relaxed and sinfully attractive with one dark eyebrow raised quizzically at her. As if he knew exactly what was going through her mind....

She shrugged. 'I don't mind a bit of retail therapy.' She waited for a moment but he said nothing. 'And of course Byron is not a bad spot for it,' she added.

'Bravo!'

Mia blinked. 'What for?'

'Not responding to the bait,' he drawled and put his arms around her.

Mia frowned, squinted, then gave way to laughter. 'How could I? Nothing on earth is going to stop me from going shopping now!'

He kissed her and they got up and strolled back to the car, hand in hand.

Byron Bay, with its village atmosphere and plethora of boutiques and restaurants, was a charming place for a spot of retail therapy.

It was in a glamorous little boutique that Mia found the dress. Chalk-blue in a crinkly fabric, the bodice was sleeveless and moulded to her figure, with tantalising cut-outs from under the arms to the waist. The skirt billowed down her legs with a long slit up one side. A pair of high blue suede sandals could have been made for the outfit so she bought them too.

Then she found a hairdresser and not only had her hair done but her finger and toenails painted a dark blue. It was the hairdresser who directed her to a lingerie shop where she purchased a pair of divine high-cut panties in blue satin and lace. The dress, on account of its cut-outs, had a built-in bra, but, because she was really on a roll, she also bought a sleek ivory silk nightgown that came with a black silk kimono embroidered with ivory birds of paradise that she fell in love with.

She took herself back to the motel, deeply satisfied with her session of 'retail therapy' but wondering how she was going to hide a certain glint in her eye from Carlos. Then she decided she didn't care. She was quite happy to share her euphoria with him.

He wasn't there.

There was a note on the table to the effect that he'd got a call from a business associate who'd found out they were both in Byron, and he'd gone to meet him for a drink. He was, the note said, ready for dinner and he'd meet her at the restaurant next door to the motel.

'It'll give you the time and privacy to do your own thing,' the note finished.

She stared at it and discovered she didn't want the time and privacy to do her own thing. She wanted nothing more than to sit down with him, maybe share a glass of champagne with him, and talk.

Yes, and show him her purchases, perhaps even model them for him, but anyway, she didn't want to be alone.

She dropped her carrier bags on the bed and sat down on it with a sudden sigh. So much to think about; when had this happened? How had she let it happen without any trace of a fight? Why did she hear something like warning bells ringing in her brain?

CHAPTER SIX

SHE WAS READY on the dot of seven.

She was not a hundred per cent happy about walking the short distance to the restaurant on her own. Not that she was afraid of being mugged or anything like that; she suddenly felt more dressed up than most people would be, an out of place sort of feeling. She turned to the kitchenette to pour herself a glass of water but a sound from the sliding glass door that led out to the garden and the pool arrested her, and she swung back on her beautiful new heels.

It was Carlos.

He wore a dark suit, a pale shirt and a navy tie.

He looked completely serious, even inscrutably so in a way that highlighted his dark looks.

And they stayed poised like that for what seemed like an eternity, staring at each other across the wide expanse of the bed.

It was an extraordinary moment for Mia. Not only the furnishings, the painting of orchids on the wall, the fall of the curtains seemed to be imprinted on her consciousness, but everything about Carlos too.

How wide his shoulders looked beneath the suit—how different he looked in a suit, come to that, she thought. Far more impressive than his father ever had.

But, at the same time, it registered with her that there was an air of mystery about him. As if he was a man she only knew a small part of, and she shivered suddenly.

He stirred at last and put out a hand.

She hesitated for a moment, then walked forward to take it.

'You look sensational,' he said barely audibly as the beautiful dress settled around her legs.

She moistened her lips. 'So do you.'

'I came to get you.'

'I'm glad you did.'

'So am I.' He pulled her a touch closer. 'Someone on a white horse with wings could have whisked you up and away over oceans and continents.'

A smile trembled on her lips.

He raised an eyebrow at her. 'Is that what you were worried about?'

'Hardly,' she murmured. She looked down at herself. 'I felt a little out of place. And maybe a bit shy about walking into a restaurant on my own. So that's why I'm glad you came.'

'Good.' He drew her even closer then, right into his arms. 'Am I allowed to kiss you?'

'That depends.' She brought her hands up against his chest.

'On what?' he drawled.

'If it's a gentle salutation you have in mind, that's permitted. I—'

But he interrupted her and bent her backwards over his arm with his other arm around her hips. 'How about this?'

Mia maintained her decorum with an effort. 'If you don't wreck my hair and my make-up, it's fine. If you do—'

'You'll never speak to me again? You'll scream blue murder?' he suggested with a wicked glint.

'No, I'll get changed and go for a jog along the beach. And I'll buy a hamburger for dinner.'

Surprise saw Carlos O'Connor straighten and Mia started to laugh.

'Is that what you really want to do?' he asked, looking startled.

'After all this?' She pushed herself a little away from him and gestured down her figure expressively. 'I wasn't really serious.'

His lips twisted. 'It would be fun, though. We could take a blanket. We could take some wine. It's a full moon tonight. It's mid-week, it's not school holidays, so there aren't many people on the beach and, anyway, I know of a secluded spot.'

Mia put her hands on her hips. 'You…are serious?'

He leant back against the door and folded his arms. '*You* were the one who brought it up.'

'I know, but—' she looked down at herself again '—all this!'

'You could wear it tomorrow night.' He straightened. 'We could just reverse things.'

'Are we staying another night, though? I didn't…I mean, I didn't know.' She broke off.

'I believe Gail is coping brilliantly,' he remarked, 'so why not?'

Mia shrugged. 'You're right. So much for believing I was indispensable.'

'How about it, then?'

She looked up at him. 'Why not? So long as you promise not to seduce me to some other venue tomorrow.'

'I promise we can dress up all over again tomorrow night.'

'Thank you.'

'This is rather lovely,' Mia pronounced as she snuggled up against Carlos in the depression they'd scooped in the sand against a bank and lined with a car rug he kept stored in the boot of his car.

They'd finished hamburgers with the lot: lettuce—iceberg specially requested—pineapple, beetroot, tomato, onion and cheese. There had also been chips. They'd bought a bottle of wine and some plastic glasses to drink it from.

The moon had cleared Cape Byron and was sending down a white light on the sea, and the stars looked within reach.

They were both dressed warmly against the night air.

'Be nice to put all this in a bottle,' she said suddenly.

'We wouldn't need to if we got married. We could do it time and again.'

Mia took an unexpected breath and tensed. 'Carlos, I don't know what to say.'

He picked up her hand and threaded his fingers

through hers. 'Look, it's a thought. What else did you have in mind? An affair?'

'If...I hadn't thought that far ahead. I don't really know what to think. It happened—' she pulled her hand free and gestured a little helplessly '—so out of the blue.'

'Really?' he said with an audible tinge of scepticism.

Mia bit her lip. She sat up suddenly and rested her chin on her knees. 'Maybe not,' she conceded, and paused as she suddenly recalled the horribly embarrassing fact that he'd known about her crush on him.

She grimaced. 'Look, all right, there was always some attraction but—' she hesitated, then said bleakly and honestly '—I've taken a bit of a battering lately.'

'You're not operating on full power, full mental capacity?' he suggested. 'Is that what you're trying to say?'

She shrugged. 'Something like that.'

'And that's why you fell into my arms without so much as a murmur of opposition?'

Mia glanced over her shoulder but she couldn't read his expression. A little shiver ran down her spine all the same. 'Well...'

'Not because you really wanted it, because you couldn't help yourself or anything like that? Not because it was *us* and nothing else was going to work?'

There was no doubting the mockery in his voice now.

Mia trembled within. 'I'm sorry if I've offended you,' she said slowly and carefully.

'Because—' he sat up abruptly '—you needed some space to lick your wounds? Is *that* it, Mia?' he shot at her.

She stumbled to her feet. 'Yes. Probably. I haven't had time to analyse it but you don't have to make it sound so awful.'

He stood up behind her. 'How would you put it?' he asked harshly, putting his hands on her shoulders and spinning her round to face him.

She tripped over her feet and had to cling to him for a moment. 'As…as needing some warmth, some consolation,' she stammered. 'What's wrong with that?'

'It's a lie,' he said and gripped her shoulders again. 'That's what's wrong with it. You need me, we need each other now and nothing else is going to make sense.'

Mia could feel her temper rising. 'You can't dictate to me like this, Carlos. I'll make up my own mind.' And she pulled away.

He reached for her but she warded him off and ran down the beach towards the water's edge. 'Stay away from me, Carlos,' she warned.

He took absolutely no notice of her and she ran a bit further, quite unaware the tide was coming in until a rogue wavelet broke around her ankles and her feet sank into the sand. She put out her hands to steady herself but fell over, just in time to be doused by another wavelet.

'Mia, be careful!' Carlos lifted her up and set her on her feet. 'You're all wet and sandy. What did you think I was going to do to you?'

'*Kiss me,*' she said through her teeth. 'Kiss me and hold me and touch me until I don't know if I'm on my head or my heels and then persuade me to elope! But that's not fair, Carlos. I don't want to marry you.'

'Sure?' He asked it quite casually as he lifted her

and set her down further up the beach and out of the way of the incoming tide.

'No, of course I'm not sure,' she said irritably as she looked down at the sodden mess she was. 'There'd be lots of quite nice things about being married to you. None of them are the real reason for marriage, though.'

'Quite nice things such as Bellbird, such as playing ladies and imagining yourself on an Indian hill station? Such as kids when you want them and as many as you want?'

She clicked her tongue. 'Those were dreams. I never really expected them to come true.'

'All right, how about this, then? Such satisfactory sex you can't stop smiling?'

Mia bit her lip and inwardly cursed Carlos.

He went on. 'As for those real reasons you quote— I imagine being madly in love for ever and ever is numero uno?' He raised a dark eyebrow at her.

She nodded reluctantly.

'How are you supposed to know it's going to happen?' he enquired.

Mia stared up at him. 'It can happen. You sound as if you don't believe in it, but it happened for my parents.'

'It happened for my parents,' he said dryly. 'But *I* happen to think it's something that grows between two people. Do you see it happening for you? Has anyone got as far as this with you, Mia?'

'This?' she said uncertainly.

'Yes, this. I'm going to take you back to the motel now. I'm going to strip off your wet sandy clothes and put you in a warm shower. When you come out I'm going to put you into bed with an extra blanket to keep you warm and heap up the pillows. Then I'm going to brew some of the excellent coffee they've provided.'

Mia simply stared up at him.

'When we've had that,' he went on, 'if we feel like it, we can make slow, exquisite love to each other. Or the wild and wanton variety we had last night. Or we can just go to sleep together.

'Incidentally,' he added, 'I love the way you curl up in my arms and go to sleep. I love the way you even smile in your sleep.'

'I don't…I do?' she said huskily.

'You do. Look—' he shoved his hands into his pockets '—you could catch cold like this.'

She shivered right on cue.

Fortunately they hadn't driven to the beach. They'd just collected the rug from the car, so Mia didn't have to worry about the mess she would make in his car; the motel and the thought of shedding damp sand all over the place was another matter.

'Put your shoulders back, tilt your chin and just do it, Mia,' he advised. 'It probably happens all the time. Besides which, they're bound to have vacuum cleaners.'

She cast him a look that told him he might pay her funny little compliments but he needn't think he was forgiven for anything. In fact she was in just the right mood to do as he suggested, put her shoulders back and tilt her chin—at him, though.

'All right. Not so bad?' he said as he unlocked their door and she stepped into the room. 'Next step,' he said as she nodded reluctantly. 'Straight into the shower. You can rinse yourself and your clothes off,' he recommended with just a hint of amusement.

Mia went to say something along the lines of it all being his fault anyway but she resisted the temptation and marched into the bathroom and closed the door pointedly.

He opened it immediately.

She whirled round, her eyes sparkling a furious green.

'I just wanted to apologise and assure you I now have no intention of laying a finger on you,' he drawled. 'As for marrying you, it was only a thought, not a threat.' And he closed the door gently.

Mia rinsed her clothes thoroughly before showering and washing her hair. By the time she'd done all this the bathroom was well and truly steamed up and her skin was rosy. The only problem that remained was the fact that she had nothing to wear; she'd not taken that into account in her high dudgeon.

Her shoulders slumped as she stared at herself in the steamy mirror. What was she fighting about anyway? she wondered disconsolately. No one could force her to marry them. All she had to do was remove herself.

But… She sighed suddenly and closed her eyes. She was inextricably tied up with Bellbird for the next few months, something Carlos well knew.

What would it really be like to be married to Carlos

O'Connor? Of course there was only one way to find out, wasn't there? And was he right—love grew?

She wrapped a thick white towel around herself and opened the bathroom door.

Carlos was lying on top of the bed wearing only his boxers, resting his head on his elbow. There was a tray with a coffee plunger and cups on the bedside table next to him. There were pencil-thin little packets of sugar in a brown pottery bowl on the tray and some locally made cookies in cellophane wrappings.

He said nothing, just watched her advance towards the bed and his expression was entirely unreadable.

Mia reached the foot of the bed before she spoke. 'I don't know what you're thinking, Carlos, but I hate this kind of bickering. I mean, I don't like myself for... for going along with it so I'll just say this. I'm not sure of anything anymore. I can't make any decisions right now...and—' she pointed towards her pillows '—would you mind passing me my nightgown? By the way,' she sniffed, 'your coffee smells wonderful.'

His expression softened suddenly and he sat up and held out a hand to her.

She hesitated, then walked round the bed and took it. 'Hop in,' he invited.

'This towel is wet.'

'Ah.' He reached under her pillows and withdrew her nightgown, not her new one but an unexceptional sky-blue silky one with shoestring straps and kites all over it.

She loosened the towel and he told her to lift up her arms.

She did so obediently and he slipped the nightgown over her head and smoothed it down her body.

'There, all present and correct,' he murmured and studied the kites. 'Could even be fairly topical.'

'What do you mean?' She looked down.

'Assuming you lift the embargo you placed on me—' he ran his fingers through her damp hair '—we—'

'I placed no embargo on you,' she broke in.

'You told me, through gritted teeth,' he contradicted, 'that I had a habit of kissing you and holding you and touching you until you didn't know if you were on your head or your heels.'

Mia drew an exasperated breath. 'All the same…I mean, that's not an embargo.'

'No,' he agreed. 'Still, no decent guy would fail to realise you disapproved of not knowing if you were on your head or your heels, and therefore desist.'

Mia stared at him almost cross-eyed as she tried to work out what he was getting at. 'What has this got to do with my nightgown?' she asked finally in a heavily frustrated voice.

'Kites,' he replied succinctly.

She blinked.

'I see you still don't understand.' He put his finger on her chin and smiled at her. 'We could reach for the sky like your kites—if we were friends and lovers. That's why it seemed topical.'

Mia stayed perfectly still for about half a minute. That was as long as she could maintain her sobriety and prevent a smile from curving her lips.

'You're quite mad, you know,' she told him.

'Maybe,' he agreed perfectly seriously, 'but am I forgiven?'

'Yes.'

'Come in then.'

She climbed into bed and said in a heartfelt way, 'That's much better.'

'Better?'

'Than fighting. Don't you think?'

'Yes.' He put his arms around her but she didn't see the faint frown in his eyes as he looked over her head.

A couple of hours later, Mia was fast asleep but once again Carlos found himself watching her as she slept.

They had made love, not the wild, wanton variety but it had been warm and sensuous all the same. She was generous and delicious as a lover and she came down from the heights in a way that aroused his protective instincts.

In fact, it occurred to him that he wouldn't like to think of her vulnerability at those times in another man's hands. Someone who didn't realise she gave it her all, like she did so much in her life.

He'd got up when he'd found he couldn't sleep and gone outside into the garden. He'd heard the surf pounding on the beach and the breeze sighing through the Norfolk pines that lined the road. He'd listened to it for a time before he'd come back inside and pulled on a sweatshirt and pushed an armchair over towards the bed.

And, as he watched, he thought back to her as a girl. A girl who'd loved nothing better than to ride like the wind whenever she came home. Almost as if, he mused, her horse and the breeze through that tangled mop of dark hair released her from the constraints of her boarding school.

She'd been a shy child—you wouldn't have known she was there until you caught glimpses of her on the estate.

Then, when she was about fifteen, he reckoned, they'd started riding together when he was home. It had happened quite coincidentally and not often but after a while he'd noticed on the odd occasion that she coloured slightly when he spoke to her.

He'd done nothing other than limiting his visits to West Windward if he knew she'd be home, said nothing and hoped it would go away for her.

Only to get hit on the head by a falling branch in a wild storm and to discover Mia Gardiner was no longer a kid. Not only that, but she was a luscious eighteen-year-old and eminently desirable.

She was still luscious and desirable but there was a lot more to it now. She was clever, she was spirited, she'd fashioned a successful career for herself that didn't depend on her looks—if his father had been alive to see Mia Gardiner now, he would approve of her much more than he'd ever approved of Nina French.

He grimaced as this thought came to him. Contrary to his wife's opinion on the matter, Frank O'Connor had deemed Nina French to be a lovely clothes horse with an empty head and without the internal fortitude to make a good wife and mother.

Not that his father's sentiments had surprised him. But they had, unfortunately, he reflected, sent him down a path he was now very much regretting. In fact he was not only regretful but guilty, he thought sombrely.

Of course the irony of it all hadn't failed to strike him either. Nina had very much wanted to marry him. Mia did not.

He stared across the bed at a dim rim of light below the bathroom door. Why had he brought marriage into the equation like throwing a hat in the ring?

What kind of a marriage did he envisage with Mia, anyway?

A peaceful one. A marriage to a woman who was practical, clever, resourceful and artistic. Someone who loved kids—his mother should appreciate that, always assuming he could ever get his mother to appreciate anything about Mia.

A marriage with her living at Bellbird and him coming and going as he saw fit. None of the highs and lows of his relationship with Nina—none of the insidious feelings that marriage to Nina would be like a never-ending grand opera. And of course Mia being forever grateful for the way he'd redeemed himself, and his family.

He set his teeth because it was an unpleasant thought. But there had to be something more to it all, he reflected. The answer that came was not much help to him.

There was something about Mia Gardiner that got under his skin.

CHAPTER SEVEN

MIA WOKE THE next morning with no idea what to expect.

But, unaware that Carlos had been up half the night wrestling with his demons, she was surprised to find him fast asleep despite the sunlight filtering into the room, courtesy of the curtains they'd forgotten to close.

She watched him for a while and wondered why she should not exactly be uneasy about what today would bring but have a question mark in her mind.

Last night had ended well, she thought, and felt a rush of colour in her cheeks. *Ended well* was a strange phrase to use to describe an encounter that had left her on cloud nine and aware of her body in ever new and divinely sensual ways.

What if Carlos wanted to talk about marriage again? How would she respond in the cold light of day?

She shook her head and decided to go for a swim, thinking that maybe it would wash away all her uncertainties.

She slipped out of bed and padded to the bathroom, where she put on her black-and-white bikini and her white terry robe. When she came back into the room he was still fast asleep.

She blew him a kiss.

It was a fabulous morning. A high blue sky had followed the burnt orange of dawn as the sun rose and the surface of the water was glassy. It was about half tide and long gentle breakers were rolling in to the beach, perfect for body-surfing.

Mia dropped her robe, ran into the water and dived cleanly beneath the first breaker she came to.

Half an hour later, she emerged to find Carlos sitting on the beach wearing board shorts but looking moody.

'Hi.' She picked up her towel. 'The water is amazing. Don't you want to go in?'

'I do and I don't. Would you mind not dripping all over me?'

Mia clicked her tongue and hid a smile. 'Sorry.' She spread out her towel and sat down on it. 'I'll come with you if you like.'

'You think I might need my hand held?' he asked with some animosity. 'I've been surfing since I was six.'

She put her hand over his. 'Not that kind of a hand. The hand of friendship, I meant. Some days when you wake up feeling sour and cranky, it helps.'

She lifted his hand and kissed his palm, then folded his fingers over it and gave him his hand back. 'There!'

And she got up and ran down the beach and back into the water.

He wasn't far behind her.

* * *

'You're a genius,' Carlos said later, over breakfast. 'I got up fully prepared—' he paused and buttered his toast '—to be mean and miserable today. Now look what you've done.' He smoothed some marmalade onto the toast.

They were eating at a beachside café renowned for their breakfast. They both wore jeans and T-shirts. Mia had tied her hair back with a floral scarf.

'I'm glad,' she said, and smiled.

'Still on the smiley trail,' he commented.

'Still on the smiley trail,' she agreed but sobered. 'What are you doing today?'

'Why?'

'I thought I'd go up to Lismore and see my parents, but you don't need to come.'

'I would come but in fact I've got some guys to see this morning—you'd be amazed who ends up in Byron,' he said a shade ruefully. 'But they're actually involved with the equestrian centre, so it's a good opportunity. Take the car.'

'Oh, I thought I'd hire a car.' She poured some coffee and sniffed appreciatively. 'More delicious coffee.'

'This is grown in the area, around Newrybar, I believe. Take the car,' he repeated.

'I've never driven a sports car.'

'So long as you can drive a manual you'll be fine.' She hesitated.

'Mia, do you have any idea what an honour this is?'

'Honour?' She looked around bewilderedly, at the

wooden table and benches, at the other breakfasters and the beach over the railing.

'Not this place,' he told her. 'But I have never offered my car to a woman to drive.'

She stared at him with parted lips. Then she had to laugh. 'If you think that makes me feel any better about it, you're mistaken.' She paused. 'But thanks, anyway.'

'Don't forget we've got a date tonight,' were his last words to her before she set off for Lismore.

'I won't! Thanks again,' she called back and with a surge of exhilaration swung his beautiful little car into the street.

Mia arrived back late afternoon, safe and sound from her trip to Lismore and without putting so much as the tiniest scratch on his car.

She was happy with the state of mind she'd found her parents in and the news that her father would be leaving hospital shortly.

She was greeted on her return with the news that Carlos had gone to Queensland.

'Gone to Queensland?' she repeated to the receptionist who had waylaid her. 'Are you serious?'

'Just over the border by helicopter to look at an equestrian centre. Apparently he's developing one down south and he wanted to see if he could get any ideas from this one. He asked me to explain that to you, Miss Gardiner, and to assure you he'll be back in time for your dinner date this evening.'

'Oh. Well, thanks.'

* * *

That had been a few hours ago and Mia was now almost dressed for dinner, although there was still no sign of Carlos.

She was sitting at the dressing table contemplating her hair.

Whereas this time yesterday she'd had a most elegant and intricate style wrought by a hairdresser, she'd washed her hair twice lately, once last night after getting rolled over in the wet sand and once this morning after her swim. Therefore her hair was no longer sleek; it was wild and curly. With an inward sigh she decided there was only one solution—to tie it back severely.

But she stayed where she was when she'd finished, staring at her image unseeingly as she fiddled with her brush and recalled her parents' unspoken curiosity on the subject of her and Carlos.

Assuming she had to explain things to them, she thought, what would she say? *He actually asked me to marry him but I said no.* Why? *Because I still sense... I don't know...I can't forget what he said or how he looked when he talked about Nina in the restaurant at Blackheath that night.*

Why? Because it struck me—and he didn't so much ask as suggest we get married—that it was a testing the waters sort of proposal. A thought, not a threat, maybe another unreal aspect of our relationship.

And, for all the happiness he's brought me, there's still a shadow of something in him, be it Nina or...

Her eyes widened suddenly as Carlos strolled in and stood behind her so she was looking at his reflection.

'Hi,' he said. 'Penny for them?'

'What do you mean?' she asked huskily.

'I was watching you from the doorway before you caught sight of me. You were deep in serious thought.'

Mia stood up and smoothed her dress down. 'I was beginning to think you'd forgotten about me.'

'No.' He caught her in his arms. 'I've been thinking about you all day, it so happens. And half the night,' he added a shade dryly.

She cupped his cheek. 'Is that why you woke up in a bad mood?' she asked wryly.

'It was myself I was cranky with. Hey—' he looked down at her '—what have you done to your hair?'

She explained.

'But I like it wild and curly.' He raised his hands and started to take out the clips.

'Carlos!' She stopped.

'Mia?' He raised an eyebrow at her and continued to take out the clips.

She grimaced. 'I guess it's a waste of time asking you to desist?'

'Yes. There.' He presented her with a little bundle of clips and ran his fingers through her loosened hair.

'Is there anything else you don't approve of?' she queried.

'About you?'

'Yes, me. I just thought I ought to be prepared in case you decide to wreak further havoc with my appearance.'

'No,' he said simply as he looked her up and down. 'Well, much as I am looking forward to removing your lovely blue dress and allowing myself the pleasure of parting your thighs, running my fingers over your breasts and round your hips, I'll wait.'

Mia all but choked. 'I'm glad to hear it,' she said with difficulty.

He raised an eyebrow again at her. 'You don't approve?'

'Oh—' she tossed her head '—I approve. That's the problem. But if you can wait, so can I.'

And she turned on her heel and walked away from him.

He caught her and turned her in his arms. 'On second thoughts,' he growled, 'I don't think I can. We've still got time.'

She took a ragged breath.

'We've—' he looked at his watch '—got nearly an hour. Half an hour until the table is booked, half an hour or a bit less to be fashionably late.'

'Carlos,' she breathed but she couldn't go on—for several reasons. She had no idea what she'd been going to say and it was impossible to think straight as he ran his hands from the rounded curves of her shoulders down her arms.

He still wore the jeans and shirt he'd put on after their swim, clothes he'd been wearing all day, and she was assaulted by the pure man smell she'd always loved about Carlos, musk and cotton and something that was so masculine she just loved it.

Then he found the zip of her dress and the material parted down her back and the dress pooled on the floor at her feet.

He made a husky sound of approval in his throat as

she stood before him wearing only her blue silk and lace panties and her beautiful high blue sandals. And his grey gaze lingered on her slim waist, on her thighs and on the smooth hollows at the base of her throat where a telltale nerve was beating a tattoo.

Then he moved forward and cupped her breasts and bent his head to tease her nipples with his tongue and teeth.

Mia went rigid as wave after wave of sensation and desire crashed through her body, and he picked her up and laid her on the bed.

This time there was no time for any more formalities, this time they were both ignited to a fever pitch and desperate for each other. This time it took Carlos as long to come down from the heights as it did Mia.

'That,' he said eventually and still breathing heavily, 'is a record. In as much as we could still shower, get dressed again and be on time for our reservation.'

Mia chuckled. 'We could also sit down and die at the table. I think I'd rather be late.'

He rearranged the pillows, then pulled her back into his arms. 'OK?'

She nodded.

He kissed the tip of her nose. Then he looked into her eyes wryly. 'Realistically, I suspect we're not going to make dinner.' He looked a question at her.

'You suspect right,' she told him. 'I don't feel like getting all done up again.' She snuggled up to him. 'I just feel like staying here.'

He smoothed some strands of hair from her cheek. 'Why not?'

So that was what they did—stayed in bed, with Carlos watching television with the sound turned down and Mia dozing next to him.

Then, at about eleven o'clock, they decided they were starving so they got up and dressed in jeans and sweaters and ran down the motel stairs to the ground floor, hand in hand, and out into the moonlight.

They found a small packed restaurant vibrating with blues music and serving late dinners.

Mia had pasta, Carlos had ocean-fresh prawns and they drank Chianti. Every now and then they got up and joined the crowd on the minuscule dance floor until last orders were called, then they walked to the beach.

'Still OK?' He swung her hand. 'Still on the smiley trail?'

She stopped walking and looked up at him. 'Yes.'

He responded to her rather intent look with a quizzical one of his own. 'You were going to say?' he hazarded.

Mia licked her lips. *I was going to say yes, I will marry you, Carlos. I couldn't not marry you. It would be like sentencing myself to purgatory. I almost got it out but I can't quite bring myself to say it. Why can't I?*

She said, 'What will we do tomorrow?' and inwardly called herself a coward.

He studied her expressionlessly for a long moment, then he shrugged and they started walking again. 'If you think Gail can spare you for another day we could drive up to the Goldie and have a look around.'

'You mean the Gold Coast?'

'Uh-huh.'

'All right. As for Gail—' she dimpled '—she is in seventh heaven—and she's doing marvellously well. She's got her mother helping and Bill's wife, Lucy. I'm proud of her.'

'You probably trained her well,' he commented. 'Ready for bed? Again?' he asked whimsically.

'Considering it's three o'clock in the morning, yes!'

But they didn't go anywhere the next day. Instead they swam and lazed around and enjoyed each other's company.

That evening they were seated at a table for two in the luxurious restaurant next door to their motel. Mia was wearing her new blue dress.

'Third time lucky,' she'd said to Carlos earlier, when she was dressed and ready to go.

He smiled down at her. 'You look marvellous. So does your hair.'

She'd left her hair loose and riotous. 'You know,' she said to him, 'you could make my life much simpler.' She paused and looked suddenly rueful.

'I have been trying to make that point,' he replied as he shrugged into the jacket of his navy suit, worn with a crisp white shirt and a navy tie. His dark hair was thick but orderly and secretly he took her breath away.

'I meant my hair. I wouldn't have to worry so much about it.'

He closed in on her and tilted her chin with his fingers. 'That should be the least of your worries,' he said softly, but scanned her significantly from head to toe.

'Now you've really got me seriously concerned,' she said with an anxious expression. 'Did I speak too soon?'

'About getting to dinner in your new blue dress?' He let his words hang in the air, then took her hand with a wicked little smile in his eyes. 'Get me out of here, Miss Gardiner, just to be on the safe side.'

They dined on lobster and they drank champagne.

Mia was just making up her mind whether to have dessert when she looked up from the menu to see Carlos staring past her, looking pale and with his expression as hard as a rock.

She didn't have to turn to see what had engaged his attention so dramatically. Nina French swept up to their table and there was no mistaking her or, after a startled moment, the man she was with—Talbot Spencer.

Nina was eminently photogenic but in the flesh she was breathtakingly beautiful, with the finest skin, velvety blue eyes and long smooth-flowing corn-gold hair. She was wearing a floral sheath dress that clung to her figure and was held up by shoestring straps so that it just covered her breasts. High nude platform shoes complemented her legs. Above all she had a tiny smile curving her lips, not of triumph or mockery, but a genuine smile.

Talbot wore a suit and Mia had to admit that, fair and freckled, he was also dangerously attractive, although in a way she couldn't quite put her finger on.

It was Nina who broke the startled silence. 'Hi there, Carlos. This is a surprise. I guess you know Talbot, but please introduce me to your friend.'

Carlos stood up and probably only Mia noticed that

his knuckles were white as he put his napkin on the table. 'Nina, Talbot,' he drawled. 'You're right, this is a surprise. Didn't know you two knew each other. Uh… this is Mia Gardiner. Mia,' he went on, 'and I are contemplating getting married, so wish us luck.'

The silence that crashed down around them was deafening.

Nina's expression spoke volumes although she said not a word. She looked horrified; her face actually crumpled and her beautiful blue eyes filled with tears.

It was Talbot who broke the silence. 'That's an interesting way of putting it. Do let us know the outcome of your contemplations. We're off back to Sydney tomorrow—maybe we could get together down there? Nice to meet you, Mia! Come, Nina.'

Nina swallowed, then turned obediently and followed him out of the restaurant.

Carlos sat down but immediately stood up. 'Let's get out of here,' he said tersely.

'Th-the bill,' Mia stammered.

'Don't worry about it, they know me. Ready?'

It wasn't to the beach he took her. They drove up to the lighthouse instead. In silence.

It was cool and dark, the moon hidden by a thick blanket of clouds.

'It's going to rain tomorrow, the end of our idyll, Mia. In more ways than one, I suspect.' He turned to her and slid his arm along the back of her seat. 'Go ahead, say it. I can guess anyway—how *could* you, Carlos?'

Mia cleared her throat. 'Yes,' she agreed huskily, 'I was, and I'm still going to say it. How could you?'

He raised a sardonic eyebrow at her. 'It isn't true? I've certainly been contemplating marrying you, Mia. I could have sworn you might even have been having second thoughts about it.'

Mia bit her lip and tried desperately to gather some remnants of sane rational composure around her. 'Carlos,' she said as she battled more tears, 'do you think linking up with Talbot Spencer was a calculated move on Nina's part to get back at you for breaking up with her?'

'Yes, I do,' he said dryly.

'Have you spoken to her since you broke up?'

'No.'

'Has she tried to speak to you?'

'Mia, she was the one who broke it off,' he said tersely. Then he shrugged. 'She's left messages,' he said sombrely, and added, 'I've been overseas most of the time.' He took a breath and said through his teeth. 'Anyone but Talbot!'

'I don't think so.' Mia closed her eyes and tried to concentrate. 'I think whoever it was, you'd hate the idea of it because—' she gestured helplessly '—there's still something between you two. From the way she looked, there certainly is for *her*. But whatever, none of this is about *me*, don't you see? I've been like a sideshow to the main attraction through all this and it's not something I care to be any more.'

Despite her tear streaks he could see the determination in her eyes and the set of her mouth, and he cursed inwardly.

'Mia…' he paused, and his tone was harsh as he continued '…there's something you don't understand. I will probably always feel guilty about Nina unless I can see her genuinely happy with another man.'

'Guilty?' Mia whispered. 'Why?'

'Because she quite inadvertently became a hostage in my war with my father.'

'You're right. I…I don't understand,' Mia stammered.

Carlos rubbed his face. 'He didn't approve of her.'

Mia did a double take. 'He must have been the only one!'

He grimaced. 'Possibly. But because I thought he was running true to form, finding fault with my choices simply on principle, I wanted to prove him wrong.

'But he was right. Well—' he shrugged '—I don't know if she'll ever make a good wife and mother, but underneath the initial attraction, and you'd have to be a block of wood not to be attracted to her,' he said with obvious bitterness, 'we were never really compatible, Nina and I, only I refused to admit it because I couldn't bear to think my father was right and I was wrong.'

Mia stared at him incredulously.

'And in the process,' he continued bleakly, 'I guess I gave Nina a false sense of security—if not that, I obviously led her to believe that whatever she did, I'd always be there for her. In a way she was entitled to think I'd marry her. And for that I will always feel guilty. And now she's fallen into Talbot's clutches.'

He raked a hand through his hair, then, as she shivered, he took his jacket off and put it round her shoulders.

Mia hugged herself beneath his jacket and came to a decision. 'I...I can't help thinking—I'm sorry but I still believe you haven't got over her and maybe you never will.'

'Mia—'

'No,' she interrupted. 'Please, you must listen to me. I can't be a party to breaking Nina French's heart, or taking you to a place you don't really want to go, not in *your* heart.'

There was a long silence as they looked painfully into each other's eyes. Then he said, 'It's been good, though?'

Mia thought back over the last few days and nodded. 'Yes, yes, it's been lovely.' She wiped her eyes on her wrists.

'Don't cry.' He slipped his jacket off her and pulled her into his arms. 'Don't cry, please.' He kissed the top of her head. 'I feel bad enough as it is.'

'You don't need to.'

'I can't leave you like this.'

'Carlos, you can—for once in my life I didn't bring a tissue or a hanky!' she exclaimed frustratedly.

'Here.' He pulled a clean navy hanky out of his trouser pocket.

She mopped up and blew her nose. 'What was I saying? Yes, you can.' Mia paused and dredged the very depths of her soul for the right words, the right key to handle this, to bring it to a closure that would release not only her, but Carlos without him realising how much she loved him.

'Have you ever seen the Three Sisters?'

Carlos blinked. 'At Echo Point?'

'Mmm-hmm…' She nodded.

'Well, yes.' But he looked mystified.

'I used to feel a bit like them.' Mia dabbed at her eyes again. 'Sort of frozen and petrified. As if I could never break the bonds of what happened at West Windward.'

She hesitated, still searching for the right words. She stared out to sea, but all she could see was a dark blue world.

'Now, thanks to you, I feel different,' she said slowly. 'I feel I can go ahead. It's funny because she'd absolutely hate the thought of it, but what you've done for me is remove the stamp your mother put on me that kept me trapped like that.'

He was silent. But the lines and angles of his face spoke volumes too; he looked harsh and forbidding but at the same time tortured.

'But—' Mia took a deep breath '—this is a real parting of the ways for us. You do see, don't you?' she pleaded.

'You don't believe you're sending me back to Nina, do you?' he asked roughly.

Mia put a finger to his lips. 'That's not for me to do,' she said huskily. 'Only you can work that out. But I think you *have* to work it out. I just want you to know you don't have to worry about me.'

He took her hand and kissed her palm and, as she had done only the day before, closed her fingers over her palm.

'I can only do this one way, Mia.'

She looked a question at him with silent tears slipping down her cheeks.

'Now, tonight. I'll take you back to the motel, then drive on to Sydney. I can organise transport back for you whenever you want it.'

She licked the tears off her lips. 'That's fine. Thanks.'

'Mia—'

'No, you mustn't worry about me.'

'You're crying again,' he said harshly.

'Most women probably have a man they remember with a tear and a smile. The one that got away,' she said whimsically. 'But, believe me, it's the way I want it.'

He stared into her eyes and found them unwavering. He closed his eyes briefly.

She leant over and brushed his lips with hers. 'Still—' she managed a brief but radiant smile '—we don't need to prolong things.'

They didn't.

Carlos drove them back to the motel, consulted over the bill, and it only took him ten minutes to pack. He changed into jeans and a tweed jacket.

Then it was all done and Mia stood straight and tearless in her lovely blue dress before him. 'Bye, now,' she said barely audibly. 'Please just go, but—*vaya con dios*.'

His face softened at the Spanish salutation and he hesitated, closed his eyes briefly and said, 'You too, Mia. You too.' Then he was gone.

Mia stayed where she was for a few minutes, too

scared to move in case she fractured and broke like glass. But of course it didn't happen.

You just go on, she thought as she lay down on the bed and pulled a pillow into her arms. You just go on and hope the pain goes away. You just know you couldn't go through the hoping and the dreaming—and the slamming back to earth again.

The Pacific Highway between Byron Bay and Sydney was at times narrow and tortuous, almost always busy. Not an easy drive at the best of times. Late at night in wet conditions behind the monotonous click of the windscreen wipers with spray coming up off the road from oncoming traffic, it required skill and concentration.

It didn't stop Carlos from thinking that he'd displayed little skill in his dealings with Mia. After the encounter with Nina and Talbot, who could blame her for withdrawing from the lists?

After revealing that Nina had known what she was doing in linking up with his enemy and after their tit-for-tat exchange and the way Nina had looked was enough to make anyone believe there was unfinished business between them.

Was there? he wondered suddenly. Other than the explanation he undoubtedly owed Nina? Could he ever go back to that emotional roller coaster he'd shared with Nina French?

It struck him suddenly that he might have if he hadn't run into Mia again. He might have allowed the familiarity of their routine to draw him back to her; the guilt he felt towards her might have made him do it.

The irony was that now he knew he couldn't go back to her, the reason for it—Mia, who smiled in her sleep—was apparently prepared to sleep with him but not to marry him.

Could he blame her? No. Her shock on hearing how he'd used Nina in the war with his father—had that recalled memories of the way she'd been treated back at West Windward?

Had those fears ever left her—that it could happen to her again in some way? Would they ever leave her? Yes, she'd slept with him, but had she ever really opened her heart to him?

She certainly hadn't shown any great excitement at the thought of racing to the altar with him.

But here he was, racing back to Sydney to stop Nina French from getting entangled with Talbot Spencer—why?

Because he had a guilt complex? No doubt about it.

Because he needed to exorcise himself of the demons that his father as well as Nina had left him with so he could go back to Mia without any baggage.

But how to do that? If she really meant it was over?

CHAPTER EIGHT

FOUR MONTHS LATER Mia sat at her desk on her last day at Bellbird.

She'd held her last function the day before and a van now stood outside the house, ready to remove all the equipment she'd hired on a year to year basis, tables, chairs, trolleys and linen. Another truck had removed the commercial kitchen equipment and all the crockery and cutlery.

Her office was unusually tidy. All her paperwork was filed and boxed, all her notes on the wall had gone.

All that was left, in fact, was her phone, a pen and a pad.

It had been a successful four months in that she'd managed to fulfil all her obligations. She had quite an extensive file of references for her next venture but, as it turned out, the glowing terms for her entertaining skills in those references were not going to be much help to her at all as things stood at the moment.

She'd neither seen nor heard from Carlos. All her dealings had been with his secretary, Carol Manning, and no more functions had been booked for O'Connor Construction.

She'd held her breath and felt like fainting for a moment when she'd been idly scanning a newspaper and seen an article entitled: O'Connor Wedding Goes Without Hitch Despite Weather.

Carlos and Nina, a voice of doom had said in her head. But when she'd opened her eyes and forced herself to read, it wasn't Carlos O'Connor who'd got married—it was his mother!

She'd read on, astounded. 'Arancha O'Connor, widow of construction billionaire Frank O'Connor, had remarried in an elegant ceremony despite highly inclement weather, with her son Carlos and her daughter Juanita by her side. Her new husband,' the article continued, 'was a chef, and he had made the wedding cake.'

Mia had choked on nothing to the extent that Gail heard her coughing and came and banged her on the back, then brought her a glass of water.

'What?'

'I don't believe it!'

'Don't believe what?' Gail asked.

'His mother has married a chef!'

'Always handy to have a chef in the house,' Gail had commented. 'Whose mother?'

Mia took a mouthful of water. 'Carlos.'

'Oh, him.' Gail had shrugged. Carlos had never regained his stellar status in her estimation. 'I remember her. Small, dark, big hat. Almost regal.' She'd looked at Mia curiously. 'Is there anything wrong with marrying a chef, though?'

'Yes. No, of course not, not in the normal course of events, but—' Mia had stopped, breathing heavily.

'That explains that. Yes and no. Clear as mud.'

Mia had to laugh. 'She…she could be quite snooty.'

Now, a few weeks after Arancha's wedding and the day before Mia left, not even Gail was with her.

She'd moved down to Sydney and taken up a position in a top hotel restaurant.

Bill and Lucy were staying on as caretakers and keepers of the garden; Bill was looking forward to having his autonomy handed back to him.

Not even Long John was with her; she'd given him to Harry Castle, the only person apart from her and Gail the horse didn't bite.

Now don't get maudlin, she warned herself as the last of the trucks drove off and she had the place more or less to herself. *What I'll do is—play ladies*.

She stood up and looked down at herself. She was wearing a long, full floral skirt with a white broderie anglaise blouse. Her hair was tied back in one thick, heavy bunch at the back. She even had a wide-brimmed lacy straw hat which a guest she hadn't been able to trace had left behind.

She also had a Royal Albert tea service, patterned with roses, one of Bellbird's heirlooms; she did have tea and a lemon on the tree beside the back door and she did have a kettle.

Ten minutes later, she'd pulled a wicker chair onto the front veranda, she had a small round wicker table beside her and a cup of lemon tea on it as she watched the late afternoon sun cast its lengthening shadows over the summer gardens of Bellbird and Mount Wilson. Her hat lay on a second chair.

She sipped her tea then put her cup down. Breathe this in, she told herself. *May some dim deep memory of the lovely peace of Bellbird always be with me.* She closed her eyes. *May the association it will always hold with Carlos bear no bitter memories for me.*

A car drove up.

She had to be dreaming, but didn't she know the sound of that engine off by heart? Didn't he *always* manage to kick up the gravel when he stopped?

She opened her eyes and it was Carlos.

Her hands flew to her mouth. 'It is you!' she whispered. 'I thought I must be dreaming.'

He propped a foot against the bottom step and leant against the rail. He wore cargo pants and a navy shirt. His dark hair was wind-blown; he must have had the car roof down at some stage. And, just at the sight of him, her heart started to beat heavily and her pulse raced. And for a moment she could smell the sea air, hear the surf and see in her mind's eye the wrinkled ocean below the lighthouse on Cape Byron....

He said, 'I couldn't let you go without making sure you were OK.'

He stopped and took in the lovely china on the wicker table beside her, the hat, and he half-smiled. 'Playing ladies?'

She grimaced. 'Being silly really, but yes.'

'Where are you going, Mia?'

'I...' She took a breath. 'To my parents for a while.'

'I thought they were driving around Australia.'

'They are. So their house is empty. I can stay as long as I like. But it'll only be until…' she plaited her fingers '…I get organised again.'

He watched her twining fingers as a faint frown grew in his eyes.

'So nothing definite in the pipeline at the moment?'

'Uh…one or two. These things take time to set up, though, Carlos.' She tried to look casual and unfazed as she said it but the truth of the matter was she had absolutely nothing in the pipeline.

Hard as she'd tried to get motivated and to move her life and her career forward, she hadn't succeeded—not something she was prepared to admit, however.

'By the way, I read about your mother!' she said in a bid to change the subject completely.

'She surprised the life out of us but they seem to be blissfully happy, even if he is only a chef, although—' he looked amused '—she insists he's a "celebrity" chef.' He rubbed his jaw ruefully. 'And she's like a different person. Much more contented.'

'I was going to say good,' Mia murmured with a tiny smile, 'but on second thoughts I won't say a word. Uh—how's Juanita?'

'She's fine. She's pregnant. Another cause for contentment in our mutual parent.'

Mia smiled. 'That's great news.'

'How are you getting to your parents' place?'

'I bought myself a four-wheel-drive station-wagon. I can fit all my stuff into it. I haven't got that much.'

He raised an eyebrow. 'Not Long John, though. Will you send him by horse transport?' He grinned suddenly. 'That should be jolly. Does he bite other horses as well as people?'

She dimpled and told him about Harry Castle.

'That's better,' he said.

Mia looked enquiringly at him. 'What?'

'I haven't seen those dimples for a while.'

'They…must come and go. Oh, by the way, I've left an inventory of all the china and stuff. You probably should go through it with me now.'

'No. It doesn't matter.'

'But there's some beautiful stuff.'

'Help yourself if you want any of it. And so can Bill and Lucy, for that matter, Gail's mother too.'

'That's nice but don't you…you don't care about it, do you?' she hazarded with a look of something like pain in her eyes at the thought of Bellbird being summarily stripped of its treasures, even if they were going to people she knew. Not that they were worth a fortune or anything like that, but they were old and they were lovely.

Carlos straightened and folded his arms. 'Mia, you didn't want Bellbird. You couldn't have made that plainer. So it's going on the market again. As soon as you leave.'

It was like an arrow going through her heart. She gasped and went white.

He swore under his breath. 'What did you think I'd do with it? What do you think I ought to do with it?' he asked harshly.

'You told me it was nice enough for that to be sufficient reason to buy it.'

'Not if you're not going to live on it.'

'Carlos, I thought it would be safe with you,' she said passionately. 'Safe from people who'd tear the house down and put up something modern. Safe from developers and sub-division. You never know when that can happen.'

'It's not going to happen up here in the foreseeable future, Mia.'

She subsided but started plaiting her fingers again.

'You're not having second thoughts, are you?'

She swallowed and turned her head away.

'Mia, look at me,' he commanded softly. 'Are you?'

'No.' She said it barely audibly but quite definitely.

'Then what are you so upset about? Just leaving here?'

'I…I was doing fine until you turned up. Indulging in a little gentle melancholy, perhaps—' she grimaced '—but mostly under control. Tell me about *you*.'

He came up the steps, lifted her hat off the chair and sat down, putting the hat on the floor beside him. 'Nina married Talbot.'

Mia moved convulsively. 'Why?' she whispered. 'Why did you let her? Why was there no publicity?'

'You'd have to ask her why,' he said dryly. 'As for letting her, how could I stop her? And, lastly, they tied the knot overseas; in fact, they've moved overseas.'

Mia stared at him. 'But she looked so devastated. That night at Byron.'

'Nina's good at that.'

'But she looked so…I can't put my finger on why,

but she looked so nice, I mean, as if she's a thoroughly nice person!'

'She is, most of the time. But buried under that is a too-beautiful-for-her-own-good girl who's been spoilt rotten.' He shrugged. 'You never know, Talbot may just be the one to cope with her. She may even be the one to bring out the best in him. Strangely, I saw them at the airport recently. They looked—' he gestured '—happy.'

'Are you sick at heart?' Mia asked. 'Surely you can tell me.'

He picked up her hat and twirled it around. 'To be honest, I'm relieved. I know I wasn't at first, but Talbot always brought out the worst in me.' He thought for a moment. 'I don't know if she was on the rebound, I probably will never know, but one thing I do know, *I* couldn't have made it work for us. If I hadn't known that intrinsically I wouldn't have held out against marrying her for so long.'

Not quite the same as saying he didn't love her, nor did it mean he didn't still love her, Mia thought, and wondered what would be worse—to know Nina was unhappy with Talbot, or happy?'

She got up and walked to the edge of the veranda. The hydrangeas that rimmed the veranda and had looked so good in the Wedgwood soup tureen were dying off now. In general, the gardens were on their last summer legs, as Bill put it.

She looked out and shaded her eyes against the sun and she could suddenly visualise the gardens being allowed to run wild, the property being sub-divided, the house being altered or simply neglected and she thought she couldn't bear it…

'Would you…w-would you…' her voice shook '…would you consider going into a business partnership with me, Carlos?'

She heard the startled hiss of his breath and steeled herself for rejection, scorn, anger or all three.

'What do you mean?' he said harshly.

She turned round slowly and swallowed twice as she tried to marshal her thoughts. 'I made a small success of the business I ran here, I guess you could say, but it was always a bit of a battle. I only managed to start it with a bank loan and I was always having to plough most of the profits into loan repayments and lease payments. But with a partner, especially one who owned the place, I could really—' she twisted her hands '—go onto bigger and better things.'

'Like what?'

'Like upgrading the furniture and fittings. They're starting to get shabby. Like live music, such as a classical quartet for functions, or live jazz or live modern, but really good stuff. Like children's birthday parties.' She paused.

He frowned.

'I mean special parties with a marquee, a carousel, castles, fairies or, for boys, cowboy themes and pony rides. We could set it up in the west paddock. I have a theory that real class attracts real money and I think I could make the Bellbird Estate more than pay its way for you by going really upmarket, but with imagination and…well…' she looked a bit embarrassed '…flair.'

All she could hear in the silence that followed were the bellbirds calling.

'Another thought I had was a honeymoon suite. There's a marvellous view from the east paddock. You could build a luxury cottage for the bride and groom to spend their first night in, with open fireplaces and gourmet meals. Is—' her eyes were wary '—there any point in me going on?'

'All right,' he said at last. 'If that's how you want it, so be it. I'll get the paperwork drawn up.' He stood up and handed her the hat. 'You can unpack, Miss Gardiner.'

Mia stared up at him with her heart in her mouth because something was radically different about him. It was as if a shutter had come down and she couldn't read him anymore except to see how cold his eyes were now.

'Carlos,' she said involuntarily, then stopped and bit her lip.

'Mia?' He raised an eyebrow. 'You were saying?'

'I…no, nothing,' she stammered.

'Nothing,' he repeated. He lifted a hand and touched his knuckles to the point of her chin. 'Nothing's changed, I guess. I'll be in touch. Or Carol will.' And he moved past her, jogged down the steps and, minutes later, his car roared away.

'What have I done?' Mia asked aloud. 'Oh, what have I done?'

CHAPTER NINE

SIX MONTHS LATER Mia and Gail were engaged in a conference about an upcoming function—a christening.

Mia had not so much pinched Gail from her upmarket job, she'd welcomed her back with open arms. Gail had been miserable down in Sydney.

The first thing Mia had done, after gathering herself together following her encounter with Carlos on the day before she'd been supposed to leave, had been to advertise and send out flyers to previous customers to the effect that the Bellbird Estate was reopening shortly after some renovations and with some new attractions.

For the next couple of months her life had been spent on the redecorating trail and consulting with architects, designers and builders.

The house had been finished first and it was gratifying to find she was almost booked up for the first month.

Then the honeymoon suite had been completed and their first couple to spend the first night of their marriage in it were so impressed they'd wanted to stay on.

The children's party arena and marquee wasn't quite

finished but was on its way. They'd called it Noah's Ark and, as well as a wooden ark you could fit thirty kids into, there were all sorts of wooden and plush animals, teddies, rocking horses, wombats and koala bears and Mia's favourites, white unicorns, all two by two.

But through it all she hadn't laid eyes on Carlos.

He'd been as good as his word; he'd been, despite keeping an eye on all her ideas, good to work with, except she hadn't worked with him at all. It had been done entirely at second hand through his secretary, Carol, and a variety of construction staff.

Mia had wondered if she'd be expected to cater for any O'Connor Construction functions but she had not.

Now, though, she was about to be thrown in at the deep end, as she thought of it. She'd been asked to put on the christening party for Juanita's baby.

'Make that babies,' she said faintly to Gail when she put the phone down on Carlos's half-sister. 'She's had twins!'

Gail started to laugh. 'It's all right; I don't suppose they'll have to have twin parties. But tell me what she wants.'

'Well, the actual baptism is to take place in the local church. Then she wants a light luncheon here in the house or garden, depending on the weather. And then, because there'll be quite a few kids, she wants them to go down to Noah's Ark.'

'You've been wanting to give Noah a test run. Now's your chance. How long have we got to prepare for this bash?'

'A month. We don't have to worry about a christening cake—the twins' step-grandfather will make it.'

Gail grinned mischievously. 'I told you it was handy to have a chef in the family.'

'So you did.' Mia rotated her pencil between her fingers and fell silent.

'How about their uncle?' Gail asked after a time.

Mia looked up with her eyebrows raised.

'Carlos?' Gail elucidated somewhat sardonically. 'The guy you got yourself all tied up in knots about, remember?'

'I didn't,' Mia said mechanically.

Gail simply stared at her.

'Oh, all right!' Mia closed her eyes in patent irritation. 'There's no "how about it" at all. I haven't seen or heard from him for months. For all I know, he could have married a...an Eskimo.'

'Now that I very much doubt,' Gail pronounced and stood up. 'He's too tall for an igloo. But it could be best to shore up your defences well and truly.'

Mia stared up at her with her heart suddenly in her eyes. 'How do you do that?' she asked out of a dry throat. 'How do you do that?'

'Tell yourself that, whatever he might like to think, you had good reasons for what *you* did.'

'But...but if you're not sure you did?'

'Mia—' Gail planted her fists on the desk and leant on them '—you've got to go with your gut feeling. And if it tells you things are not right, they're not.' Gail straightened.

'How come you're so wise?' Mia asked with just the glint of a tear in her eye.

Gail shrugged. 'My mum says it's easy to be right about other people's problems. And now I'll leave you to design this christening.'

The weather forecast for the day of the christening was not that good—wet and windy.

Mia grumbled under her breath as she read the details the day before but made the usual decision not to take any chances with sodden food, sodden effects or sodden guests.

She'd already partially decorated the dining room to be on the safe side and decided she needed to finish it off.

Rather than going for pastel pinks and blues, she'd used stronger colours and silver ribbons in bunches. For the rest of it she'd relied on magnificent bunches of flowers.

But some of the ribbons were coming undone and she fetched the ladder and climbed up to retie them.

It was a labour intensive job, getting up and down the ladder and moving it around the room as well as stretching her neck. Which might have been why she came to grief opposite the doorway to the hall.

She must not have had the ladder properly balanced because, as she started to climb down, it wobbled, she lost her footing and, with a startled cry, began to fall.

At first she didn't recognise the pair of arms that caught her. It flashed through her mind that it must be Bill, for once in his life, where she was concerned, anyway, in the right place at the right time.

Then recognition seeped through her pores—Carlos.

'Mia,' he growled, 'you could have broken your back or your head—couldn't you be more careful?'

'Carlos—' she said faintly; he still had her in his arms '—that's funny, isn't it?'

'What's funny?'

'I haven't seen you for months but, once again, it's in an injury situation. Well, no.' She slipped out of his arms. 'I'm fine! Thanks to you. But what are you doing here? The christening isn't until tomorrow,' she said foolishly.

He cast her a frowning look. 'I know that. I came to see you.'

It was her turn to frown. 'Does that mean you're driving back to Sydney, then up again tomorrow?'

He shook his head. 'I'm staying here.'

Mia's mouth fell open.

'Oh, not in your loft,' he drawled, 'but, according to what Gail told Carol, not that Gail knew why Carol was asking, the honeymoon suite is vacant tonight so I thought I'd give it a try. I also thought it was time to have a guided tour of all the changes and improvements.'

'By all means,' Mia heard herself say. 'I was wondering when you would want to see what you'd paid for.'

They stood back and studied each other.

Mia's heart was still beating rapidly beneath the pink blouse she wore with jeans, her cheeks were flushed and her hair was coming loose.

She thought he was taller than she remembered, then realised it was because she was barefoot. She put her hands to her cheeks, then looked around for her shoes.

'I'm sorry I'm so disorganised,' she gabbled, finding herself in complete disarray. 'Actually, I'm not really disorganised. I'm just…' She stopped helplessly and put a hand to her throat. 'Why did you want to see me?'

'We don't need to talk here, do we?' he countered.

Mia licked her lips. 'Where would you like to go?'

'Show me Noah's Ark first.'

'It was only finished a week or so ago,' Mia said as he looked around. 'So I'm really looking forward to giving it a trial run.' She grimaced. 'That doesn't mean to say I'm experimenting with Juanita's guests; it's all safe and sound—I just hope the kids will like it.'

Carlos picked up a wooden giraffe and a smile twisted his lips. 'They will.'

'There are things for older children to do.'

'You've done well, Miss Gardiner.'

She looked up at him. 'Is something wrong?' she asked because he seemed like a stranger to her, because she seemed to be fluttering like a trapped butterfly around him, but there was no light in him, just a very different Carlos O'Connor.

'You could say so.'

'What?' Her eyes were wide and dark and supremely anxious. 'What is it?' She put a trembling hand on his sleeve. 'Tell me.'

He covered her hand with his briefly. 'Just tired, I guess. I only got home from a European trip this morning. OK, now for the much-vaunted honeymoon suite. Lead on.'

Mia hesitated, not entirely convinced he was being honest. 'All right. I'll have to get the keys from the main house, then we can drive your car down.'

Fortunately, Gail had gone into Katoomba on an errand, so as Mia collected the keys she didn't have to attempt any explanations. She did collect a small basket of dairy products, fresh rolls and fruit to take down to the honeymoon suite.

'So,' she said a few minutes later, 'this is it.'

Carlos looked around at the spacious, uncluttered sheer elegance and luxury of the suite, at the stone fireplace and the lovely art on the walls.

Mia moved over to the windows and swept back the curtains and had to smile because the magnificent view down Mount Wilson in the late afternoon sunlight always had that effect on her.

She turned to Carlos. 'It doesn't look like it at the moment, but there's rain predicted for tomorrow. Uh… you'll probably want to have a rest. If you want a snack I brought some fresh rolls, some cheese and other stuff but—' she moved into the galley-style kitchen and opened an iridium fridge '—there should be a gourmet pack here. Yes. Some smoked salmon, anchovies, olives. Uh…beer, wine and champagne as well as spirits.'

She opened another cupboard and revealed a coffee-maker. 'And there's tea and coffee, and here—' She stopped because he walked up to her and took her hand.

'You don't have to sell the place to me, Mia,' he said quietly.

'You did pay for it. And I haven't shown you the bedroom.'

He shrugged. 'Sit down. Glasses?'

Mia hesitated, then pointed to a cupboard.

'Champagne OK with you?' He raised an eyebrow at her.

'Well, one probably won't hurt,' she temporised, then, at the look of irony in his eyes, put her hands to her cheeks as she felt herself blush and, in disarray again, sat down on a stool at the breakfast bar after nearly knocking it over.

He said nothing as he removed the foil from the champagne cork and unwound the wire. It popped discreetly and he poured the bubbly golden liquid into two cut-glass flutes.

'Cheers.' He slid a glass towards her and sat down diagonally opposite her on another stool.

'Cheers!' Mia raised her glass, then took an urgent sip. 'Oh.' She started to slide off the stool. 'I can put together a snack, won't take a moment.'

'Mia, no.'

She stilled.

'Tell me something,' he went on. 'Are you happy?'

She stared at him. 'I…I'm doing fine.'

'Not quite the same thing,' he observed, then gestured, 'except that in your case it might be.'

'What do you mean?'

He looked down at his glass. 'Six months ago I came up here to ask you again to marry me.'

Her lips parted and her eyes were stunned.

'I was going to tell you about Nina—I did, but only part of it,' he went on. 'I was going to suggest we put all the past behind us, not only her but West Windward. I was going to remind you of Byron Bay if you still had reservations.' He stopped and studied her and she shivered for some reason

'Only to discover,' he went on, 'that the one thing that really affected you was the concept of Bellbird being sold. That shocked you to tears and spurred you into making a partnership offer, that's all. That's, incidentally, what made me wonder if "doing fine" in a career and business sense is all that matters to you.'

Mia made a small sound in her throat—a sound of protest.

'Or is it that you still can't forgive me for West Windward, Mia? And my mother? Is that why you could be the way you were at Byron but then all you had to offer me was a business proposition?'

She licked her lips. 'Carlos, did you think all *you* had to do was tell me about Nina and Talbot and I'd fall into your arms? Is that what you're trying to say? I hadn't seen or heard a word from you for *four* months.'

He rubbed his jaw. 'No,' he said at last. 'But I couldn't find the words to tell you that I did try to stop her going off with Talbot. I did try to explain to her what had happened with my father—she was justifiably horrified. She asked me—' he paused, looking tortured '—what I was going to do to wreck *your* life. I don't know if she had any inkling that I'd already damaged it or if it was simply a shot in the dark, but it had a powerful effect on me.'

Mia stared at him, transfixed. 'What do you mean?'

'It made me think maybe my best bet was to avoid you. It made me doubt my judgement, even my sanity. She may never realise it, she may never have intended it as such, but she completely destabilised me with that one little question.'

'So you stayed away?'

'I stayed away—it was also what you wanted,' he reminded her. 'But the day before you were due to leave I knew I couldn't live with myself if I didn't see how you were. But that,' he said with palpable irony, 'led me down the rocky road to hell.'

Mia blinked. 'I was upset to think of Bellbird being sold,' she whispered, 'but I still believed it wasn't over between you and Nina. I couldn't decide what would be worse for you, to see her happy with Talbot or unhappy.'

'No,' he said, 'it is over, it is done with. I'm happy to see her happy, at last.'

Mia closed her eyes. And a surge of something she'd never known before ran through her, a powerful urge to clear her soul of all its secrets.

Her lashes flew up. 'There's one thing you don't understand about me, Carlos. Yes, I may be single-minded in a business sense. Yes, it means a lot to me to succeed because the more I do the fainter the memory of being branded the housekeeper's daughter grows. But it doesn't stop there.'

'What about Byron?' he asked tautly.

'Byron was lovely,' she said with the first sign of

tears in her eyes. 'But you got the shock of your life that night. So did Nina.' She drained her glass. 'I can't forget it.'

He made an involuntary movement towards her, then stilled and poured more champagne.

'Thanks,' she said huskily. 'I told you once I wasn't going to be used to break Nina's heart. Well, I'll never know about that but—' she stopped and drew a deep breath, then trembled as the shutters of her mind fell away and for the first time she really understood her own secrets '—you mean far too much to me to s-see you—' her voice broke '—tied to someone you don't love deeply.'

'Mia,' he said roughly.

But she held up her hand. 'The other thing is—' She stopped and sighed and soldiered on. 'The other thing is…I have an enormous inferiority complex.' Her eyes were wet and dark. 'I didn't really understand it myself, but Juanita is so sure of herself, for example. And Nina, that night. She was so poised—until you told her we were getting married. Poised and classy. It's not how I see myself, not around you. It's something that holds me back without me realising it.'

She rubbed her face. 'So you see, Nina is not the only one with complexes.'

He stared at her incredulously. 'Say that again?'

'No, Carlos—' she sniffed '—you heard.'

'I may have but it's hard to believe.'

'It shouldn't be, you—'

'I caused it?' he broke in.

'It might just be the way I'm made,' she said miserably.

He studied her for a long moment, her wet spiky lashes, that luscious mouth, her wayward hair, the lovely trim figure, and knew he had to pull out all the stops because he'd made all sorts of mistakes with this woman and it was killing him. Killing him to think Bellbird meant more to her than he did.... But how to right those mistakes? If only he could get her to laugh with him. Maybe the simple truth? It had all the makings of comedy. Well, a farce anyway...

'These have been the hardest six months of my life,' he said.

She looked at him with a faint frown.

'I've fulfilled one of my father's dreams, to have construction sites on the four corners of a major city intersection, to have O'Connor Construction billboards plastered on all four corners.'

'Oh. Congratulations.' But she looked at him uncertainly, not sure what his tone meant or where this was leading.

'Thanks.' He shrugged. 'It didn't help.'

'What do you mean?'

'It didn't help me to view him more affectionately. If anything I was more annoyed than ever. And it's a nightmare scenario, traffic-wise. Then there's my mother.'

Mia's frown grew.

'Yep.' He moved his glass. 'I've always taken her with a grain of salt.' He grimaced. 'What I mean to say is, I've recognised what motivates her, family loyalty above all, and I've dealt with the consequences without too much angst. Except in your case and then it was too late.' He studied his glass and pushed it away, as if it was annoying him too. 'But lately she and her "celebrity" chef husband have been irritating the life out of me. Turns out he's as much of a raving snob as she is, hard as that is to imagine.'

Mia blinked. 'A chef?'

A crooked grin twisted his lips. 'You're as bad as she is, as he is. Yes. He cannot remain silent on any topic relating to food and beverage. He's positively painful on the subject of what wines go with this, that and the other. On what is the correct way to cook this, that and the other, on the best restaurants, not—' he shook his forefinger '—only in Australia but the whole world.'

'Oh, dear.'

He eyed her keenly. 'As you say. Then there's Juanita. As a single half-sister she always had quite a bracing personality but she could be a lot of fun. As a married matron and mother of twins she's insufferably smug, another snob and—' He broke off and gestured. 'I don't know how Damien puts up with her.'

Mia put her hands on the island bench. 'Carlos—'

But he waved her to silence. 'Hang on. Then there's the construction industry in general. Now, I may have had issues with my father but I'm actually a passionate engineer and builder—or I was.' He looked supremely sombre.

'Not anymore?' Mia hazarded.

'I couldn't give a damn if I never built another thing.'

'Carlos—' she paused '—I'm not a hundred per cent sure you're serious.'

'I am, and there's more. I've lived like a monk ever since Byron Bay because I haven't been able to have you, Mia.'

Mia took an unexpected breath.

He waited a moment, then he slid his hand across the island bench and touched her fingers with his.

For a moment she was frozen, hardly even breathing, her eyes huge.

'Really?' she said at last.

He nodded.

'You…you tried?'

He nodded again. 'A couple of times. With disastrous consequences. How about you?'

'Oh, I didn't want to so I didn't even think of trying,' she assured him, then she broke off and bit her lip.

The pressure of his fingers increased on hers. 'Do you think that means…anything?'

'Carlos…' She took a breath.

'Mia, I can't live without you,' he said. 'It's killing me. All the mistakes I made are killing me. As for your complexes—' he closed his eyes briefly '—please throw them away because they mean nothing to me. And please take me on—you can redecorate me, renegotiate me but if you don't restore me I'm in serious trouble. And that's the plain, unvarnished truth.'

Her lips trembled and, hard as she tried, she couldn't stop herself from starting to smile.

Carlos got up cautiously and came round the island

bench. He stopped in front of Mia and tilted her chin up gently. And there was a question in his eyes.

'Oh, look,' Mia whispered. 'I'm not sure why, but I think I've always loved you, Carlos, and I always will.'

'Is there anything wrong with that?' he queried.

'No. Not anymore. I don't seem to have any fight left in me,' she conceded. 'I've missed you so much.'

He pulled her into his arms. 'Same here. More than you could ever know. Mia—will you marry me?'

'Yes. Yes, I will,' she said and found she couldn't stop smiling.

'They're back, your dimples,' he said unsteadily.

'That can only be because you're back,' she told him.

'Thanks for that.' And he started to kiss her.

Quite some time later they stirred in each other's arms. They'd moved from the island bench to a settee in the lounge area, one that overlooked the view—a view that was dominated by some magnificent purple thunderheads.

'I told you rain was forecast,' she said as she nuzzled into his shoulder.

He stroked her hair. 'Juanita will be upset—upset that she can't control the weather.'

Mia gave a spurt of laughter although she said, 'Now that's unkind. She's not that bossy. Is she?'

He shrugged and traced the line of her jaw with his finger. 'She has actually run into one spot of bother with Damien. Over naming the twins.'

'Oh, tell me about it, and about them! All I know is that it's a boy and a girl.'

His fingers traced a path down her neck to the little hollows at the base of her throat. 'True. And Juanita wants to name them Charlotte and Henry—if that isn't aspiring to the aristocracy I don't know what is. But Damien wants to call them Barbara and Banjo. His grandmother who he's very fond of is a Barbara—I don't know where he got Banjo from—apart from Banjo Paterson. Up until I last saw them yesterday, the issue was still to be decided.'

Mia had to laugh. 'They're leaving it a bit late.'

'Mmm,' he said, sounding preoccupied and his fingers slid down to the top button of her blouse. 'I'm a godfather, by the way. You'll probably have to help me out a bit there.'

But Mia had other things on her mind as he flicked open the button, and then the next and the next and slipped his hands around her back and released her bra.

She took several ragged breaths but didn't protest as he drew her blouse off and then helped her out of her bra.

Nor did she protest when he said, 'What we need is a bed.'

'This might be a good place to remedy that.' Her dimples appeared. 'You ain't seen nothing yet, Mr O'Connor,' she teased. 'Not until you see the bedroom.'

'OK, lead on.' He picked her up.

What he said next was somewhat different.

'Holy…mackerel!' He looked around the honeymoon suite bedroom, a symphony of white and green with a huge bed piled with cushions, an exquisite original painting of flowers taking up almost all of one wall, deep pile carpet, a padded velvet headboard and a beautiful crystal chandelier.

Mia laughed softly. 'Think I might have gone overboard?'

'Not at all.' He put her down on the bed and together they tossed aside all the silken cushions, then they shed their clothes and Mia could not doubt his desperate hunger for her, nor hers for him.

And when they crashed back to earth, he held her and helped her down from the heights in such a way that caused her to say with real gratitude, 'You make me feel as if I've come home.'

He cradled her to him. 'You make me feel the same. When will you marry me?'

'Whenever we can.'

He rubbed his jaw. 'I've got this damn christening tomorrow. I don't suppose I can get out of that.'

'Oh, no, you shouldn't! Anyway, we couldn't do it tomorrow, could we?'

He leant up on his elbow. 'No. I don't know how long it takes.' He tidied some damp wayward strands of her hair and pulled a silk coverlet over them. 'Will you come to the christening with me?'

'Carlos, I'll be working at it,' she reminded him.

'No,' he replied firmly. 'Get Gail and her mother and anyone else you can raise—Bill and Lucy—you've done it before. I need you with me, otherwise my family might prompt me into…being rude or unkind to them.'

Mia giggled but she soon sobered. 'Your mother will

be livid. Perhaps an occasion like a christening isn't the right time to break the news to her.'

'My mother is not nearly as interfering as she was, Mia, but, whatever, there's no point in hiding it.'

Mia thought for a moment, then, 'No. Anyway, I think we have to break the news to Gail. She'll be wondering where on earth I've got to.'

He stretched and looked disinclined to move.

'She could even come looking for me,' Mia said gravely, 'and we didn't lock the door.'

Carlos swore beneath his breath, then rolled over and enveloped her in a bear hug. 'All right. I get the message. I don't suppose we could shower together?'

'Ah.' Mia looked mischievous. 'We sure can. Come and have a look. This is the bathroom to beat all bathrooms.'

'There you are, Mia!' Gail said as Mia walked into her office to find Gail behind the desk fielding the phone. 'I've been looking for you. There's—oh, no,' she added as Carlos walked in behind Mia. 'Not you again.'

Carlos looked briefly startled, then amused. 'Sorry, Gail. I didn't realise I was on your blacklist. Why am I?'

Mia cleared her throat and started to speak but Gail overrode her. 'Why are you? You come and you go, Mr O'Connor, and every time you go I'm left to pick up the pieces.'

'*Gail*!' Mia protested.

Gail swung towards her. 'It's true. You've been devastated every time it's happened and—'

'Gail—' it was Carlos who intervened and he took

Mia's hand '—there won't be any more of that. Mia's agreed to marry me, we're very much in love and we've smoothed out all our problems. But I'd just like to say I can't thank you enough for being such a good friend to Mia.'

Gail stood stock-still then she ran round the desk to embrace Mia and then Carlos

'Oh, I'm so happy,' she cried tearfully. 'I don't know if I'm coming or going. When? When's the wedding? Are you having it up here? You could leave it all to me, you know.'

Mia was also mopping up some tears as she said, 'We haven't made any plans yet but, Gail, you'll have to handle the christening tomorrow because I'm going as a guest.'

'With pleasure.' Gail struck a nonchalant pose. 'I could do it in my sleep.'

Mia and Carlos were still chuckling as they walked into the garden as the sun set but he stopped suddenly and put his arms around her.

'I feel terrible,' he said, looking down at her.

'Why?'

'For leaving you devastated up here. I'm not sure why you've forgiven me.'

She slipped her arms around his neck. 'What Gail doesn't realise is that I sent you away.' She stood on her toes and kissed him.

'Even if it devastated you?'

She nodded and laid her head on his shoulder. 'What about you?'

'Angry, incredulous, bloody-minded probably says it well, every time I drove down this blasted mountain. Sick to think it meant more to you than I did, this place. All in all, a mess.'

'Well—' Mia stirred '—since it seems we've both been to hell and back, let's go to heaven.'

He lifted his head, his grey eyes amused. 'I hope you don't mean that literally?'

'Depends! Let's go back to the honeymoon suite—'

'You're not worried about putting the cart before the horse?' he broke in gravely.

'Not in the least. I was thinking of cooking you dinner, you see—an inch-thick steak, chips that are crisp on the outside and fluffy inside—oh, some English mustard hot enough to make your eyes water, some salad, but only iceberg lettuce, of course, maybe some mushrooms. I just have to collect the ingredients from the house.'

'Now that,' he drawled, 'is an offer I can't refuse.'

'Good.' She dimpled. 'Then we can worry about putting the cart before the horse.'

He grinned down at her. 'I can see you're going to be a right handful, Miss Gardiner.'

'It's my aim,' she said pertly.

CHAPTER TEN

THE DAY JUANITA'S twins were christened was a day to remember. It was cool and showery, as predicted.

Mia drove to her cottage and collected her clothes.

As she was about to climb back into the car, Bill intercepted her with a particularly Bill James-like salutation. He was driving the property utility, laden with bags of fertiliser, and he drew up beside her and leant out of his window.

'Hi, Mia! Heard the news, by the way—you'll be much happier as a married woman, believe me.'

Mia drew a deep breath and cautioned herself not to lose her temper. 'Thank you, Bill. I…I will try to be.'

'And you give Carlos my best wishes. I guess he must know what he's getting into, although not many of us guys do!' And, laughing cheerfully, he drove on.

Mia contemplated kicking something but refrained.

She must have still been wearing the remnants of a militant expression when she arrived back at the honeymoon suite, however, because Carlos immediately said to her, 'What's wrong?'

'Nothing.' She put down her clothes. 'How do you know anything's wrong, anyway?

'You look—' he meditated '—as if you'd like to kick the cat.'

Mia grimaced, then had to laugh ruefully and she told him about Bill.

'Of course I wouldn't dare to agree with him,' he replied with utter false gravity.

Mia clicked her tongue. 'You men are all the same.' She paused and fiddled with her cosmetic purse before putting it down beside her clothes and starting to plait her fingers.

'Carlos, I'm nervous. I'm really nervous. I don't think I can do this.'

'Mia—' he linked his arms around her waist '—yes, you can. Anyway, they all know now.'

She put her hands on his chest, her eyes wide. 'Your mother? Did she have a fit?'

'No. She told me it was about time I settled down. Juanita said the same. Mind you—' he frowned faintly '—I got the feeling something else was going on. They both seemed preoccupied, if not to say tense, and that was before I broke our news.'

Mia relaxed a bit. 'I hope so. I mean…all I mean is I'd rather not be the headline news.'

He bent his head and kissed her. 'You were my headline news last night. You have a unique way of putting the cart before the horse.'

A tingle ran through Mia at the memory of their night. 'It was lovely, wasn't it?' she said softly.

This time he hugged her, then, with an obvious effort, put her away from him. 'Maybe we should get dressed,' he suggested. 'We have been known to—' there was a wicked little glint in his grey eyes '—get carried away when we should be on our way out.'

Mia laughed and stood on her toes and kissed him. 'I remember. I'm going.'

He groaned but didn't try to stop her.

Mia changed into a figure-hugging yellow dress and a smoky grey-blue jacket belted at the waist. She'd decided not to wear any kind of hat for this christening and saw no reason to change her mind now she was a guest so she left her hair wild and riotous, just as he liked it.

But she drew an unexpected breath at the sight of Carlos in a pinstriped charcoal suit, pale green shirt and darker green tie.

'You look seriously handsome,' she told him.

He came to stand right in front of her. 'Good enough to be a godfather?'

'Oh, definitely!'

'Well, you look gorgeous, Mia, darling.' He took her hand. 'Ready?'

She hesitated, then nodded. 'Ready,' she said quietly.

It stopped raining as the baptism proceeded.

There was even some sunlight bringing rays of colour into the church through the stained glass windows, violet and topaz, jade and ruby.

Arancha was arrayed in ivory shantung: an exqui-sitely tailored suit and a poppy-pink hat. She had ac-knowledged Mia with an almost non-existent kiss on the cheek but she'd said, 'Let's be friends, Mia, let's be friends.'

And Mia, who had searched her heart and known she could never altogether forgive Arancha, had con-trived to reply warmly, for Carlos's sake, 'Yes, let's.'

She'd then been introduced to Arancha's celebrity chef, who'd told her he could probably give her some pretty good tips on cuisine and all sorts of things to do with the catering business.

Mia had felt Carlos tense beside her so she'd smiled brilliantly and replied that she'd love to hear them.

Juanita wore violet linen and Damien wore a dark suit. They both looked a little shell-shocked for some reason and each carried a sleeping baby garbed in a sumptuous lacy gown.

It wasn't until the naming of the babies came about that most of the mysteries of the morning were ex-plained. The girl was baptised Alegria Arancha and the boy Benito Francis.

'Good Spanish names,' Arancha said quite audibly, 'and why not include the mother's mother?'

Mia heard Carlos suck in a breath but it wasn't until the baptism was over and they were in the car head-ing back to Bellbird that they were able to give way to their mirth.

'For crying out loud,' Carlos said. 'She must have

bulldozed away at both of them to get them to change their minds.'

'I thought you told me she didn't interfere anymore?' Mia had to dab carefully at her eyes so as not to smudge her mascara.

'I didn't think she did! Something about Charlotte or Barbara, Henry or Banjo must have really riled her.'

'Well, I thought Juanita could stand up to her.'

'I thought she could. I was wrong. Mind you, the fight over names between Juanita and Damien was beginning to assume epic proportions so it could even have been a stroke of genius.'

Mia put her hanky away but she was still chuckling.

'You were good with my mother and her chef,' Carlos said as he swung into Bellbird's drive.

'I intend to stay good with her.' Mia put a hand on his arm. 'I don't know why but I feel different all of a sudden.'

'Different?' He looked comically apprehensive for a moment. 'How so?'

Mia drew a deep breath. 'I don't feel like the housekeeper's daughter any more. I wonder why?'

'Could it be because you're about to become—and willingly—the padrone's wife?' he suggested.

But Mia shook her head although she acknowledged his rueful look with the glint of a smile. 'No, I think it's because suddenly you all seem so normal.'

'I would have thought we were all bordering on insanity,' he objected and pulled up in front of the house.

'Not really. You have your fights, your ups and downs, your loyalties, your crazy times, just like everyone else. Look—' she shook her head and her expression was wry '—I know it sounds ridiculous to you for me to say I hadn't seen you all like that before, but it's true. And it makes me feel different.'

He turned to her and put an arm along the back of her seat. 'Are you serious?'

'Uh-huh!'

'Well—' he paused '—I've had a thought. It's occurred to me that I've neglected them for a time. It's occurred to me I ought to undertake some fence-mending exercises, like somehow getting Damien to forgive my mother for insisting he call his son Benito. Ditto Juanita. And it looked to me as if Damien and Juanita are feeling just about as hostile towards each other as it's possible to be, wouldn't you agree?'

'Oh, I do! They didn't even look at each other.'

'Right. I must say, I don't know what I can do about the celebrity chef who's popped up in our midst but—do you remember the wedding you had here that was about to flop unless you were able to pull something out of the hat?'

Mia's eyes widened. 'Yes…'

'From memory, you actually exhorted me to make the kind of speech only I could make to liven things up or you'd scream blue murder?'

Mia's lips twitched. 'I do,' she said solemnly.

'Can you promise me, though, that if I do stop this christening from flopping and manage to turn it into a happy, even joyful occasion, you won't go back to feeling like the housekeeper's daughter?'

'I won't, I promise,' she said huskily. 'Please do it. I love you,' she told him, smiling through the tears in her eyes. 'I love you, Carlos O'Connor.'

* * * * *

A sneaky peek at next month…

MODERN™

INTERNATIONAL AFFAIRS, SEDUCTION & PASSION GUARANTEED

My wish list for next month's titles…

In stores from 19th July 2013:

❑ The Billionaire's Trophy — Lynne Graham

❑ A Royal Without Rules — Caitlin Crews

❑ Imprisoned by a Vow — Annie West

❑ Duty at What Cost? — Michelle Conder

❑ The Rings That Bind — Michelle Smart

In stores from 2nd August 2013:

❑ Prince of Secrets — Lucy Monroe

❑ A Deal with Di Capua — Cathy Williams

❑ Exquisite Acquisitions — Charlene Sands

❑ Faking It to Making It — Ally Blake

❑ First Time For Everything — Aimee Carson

Available at WHSmith, Tesco, Asda, Eason, Amazon and Apple

Special Offers

Every month we put together collections and longer reads written by your favourite authors.

Here are some of next month's highlights— and don't miss our fabulous discount online!

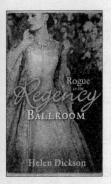

On sale 2nd August

On sale 2nd August

On sale 19th July

Save 20%
on all Special Releases

Find out more at
www.millsandboon.co.uk/specialreleases

*Visit us
Online*

Join the Mills & Boon Book Club

Subscribe to **Modern**™ today for 3, 6 or 12 months and you could **save over £40!**

We'll also treat you to these fabulous extras:

- FREE L'Occitane gift set worth £10
- FREE home delivery
- Rewards scheme, exclusive offers…and much more!

Subscribe now and save over £40
www.millsandboon.co.uk/subscribeme

The World of Mills & Boon®

There's a Mills & Boon® series that's perfect for you. We publish ten series and, with new titles every month, you never have to wait long for your favourite to come along.

Blaze®

Scorching hot, sexy reads
4 new stories every month

By Request

Relive the romance with the best of the best
9 new stories every month

Cherish™

Romance to melt the heart every time
12 new stories every month

Desire™

Passionate and dramatic love stories
8 new stories every month

- Rent. £20-00 ✓
- S/W. £ 5.00
  Shop. £20.00
  T.P. £ 5.00
  ──────────
       £50-00